For Sel[...]
a fello[...]

NO REPEAT OF
YESTERDAY

Best wishes

Peter

NO REPEAT OF YESTERDAY

PETER MORRIS

No Repeat of Yesterday

Published by The Conrad Press Ltd. in the United Kingdom 2023

Tel: +44(0)1227 472 874

www.theconradpress.com

info@theconradpress.com

ISBN 978-1-915494-57-3

Typesetting and Cover Design by: Charlotte Mouncey, www.bookstyle.co.uk

The Conrad Press logo was designed by Maria Priestley.

Printed and bound in Great Britain by Clays Ltd, Elcograf S.p.A

To May and Ron

1 WAR MEANS WORK

RAF Lakenheath, Suffolk, 12th April

0200 hours, pre-flight checks complete. Flight Lieutenant Nicole Dibaba taxied her unmarked F-95 to the threshold of Runway 24 and waited for clearance to fly north and wreak devastation on another undefended UK target. Whilst these unattributable nocturnal strikes could hardly be classified as conventional operations, the pilots of RAF 161 Squadron understood their value. Exceptional times called for exceptional measures.

Like every mission Dibaba had flown since the end of the Dark Age, Operation Landlord presented no technical challenges, no risk of opposition and no foreseeable threat to her safety. Once the bible-black F-95 had been relieved of its nine-tonne payload, the return flight to RAF Lakenheath, legally still an American base, would make even fewer demands of her skills. As ever, the National Broadcasting Corporation would continue to peddle the myth that the highly destructive raids were conducted by a still unidentified foreign enemy. Galvanised by the evidence of an ongoing external threat, a broken nation was taking major steps on the road to recovery.

Dibaba's comms crackled into life and she received the go-ahead from Flying Officer Olivia Gunatillaka, Lakenheath's Operations Manager. Keeping the nose of the aircraft straight, the pilot throttled up and the massive acceleration immediately forced her back into her seat. Within a matter of seconds her F-95 had left the ground. Dibaba retracted the landing gear, pulled up the flaps and by the end of the runway, the aircraft had accelerated to well over 200 knots. When the afterburners kicked in, Dibaba climbed, banked and initiated a well-practised routine of muscular contractions designed to maintain the supply of oxygen to her brain. The moment the aircraft levelled off, the g-forces eased and she allowed herself to relax.

As Dibaba monitored the instrument readings in her helmet display, a familiar voice competed for her attention.

'Good hunting, Freebird.'

Flight Lieutenant Mark Warszawski had taken off six minutes ahead of Dibaba and was cruising at 400 knots towards a target somewhere on the outskirts of Manchester.

'Radio silence,' insisted Gunatillaka.

'Because the entire world is listening, right?' said Dibaba. She had a minor talent for sarcasm, which some of the ground crew perceived as cocky. 'Good hunting, Stairway.'

If pressed, either pilot would have conceded that their missions had little, if anything, in common with hunting and could more accurately be likened to shooting fish in a barrel. 'Good hunting', however, had a better ring to it.

'Maintain operational silence,' said Gunatillaka, now growing impatient. 'No chit-chat. And no call signs. Use surnames. Call signs are American.'

Warszawski's riposte was immediate. 'I think, in legal terms our entire base is American, along with these F-95s. If Uncle Sam ever comes knocking, we're going to have an awful lot of explaining to do.'

The pilot muted his comms and Gunatillaka accepted his silence as some kind of moral victory. The Operations Manager had taken a major dislike to the pilots' adoption of call signs. One name per pilot, as she repeatedly pointed out, ensured clarity and obviated confusion. In spite of her frequent reminders, Gunatillaka also understood that 161 Squadron were unlikely to be cured of their unhelpful habit.

With Flight Lieutenant Dibaba's aircraft flying straight and level and the guidance system taking care of the next 150 nautical miles, the pilot was left alone with her thoughts. As was often the case, she found herself thinking about her parents, who had both succumbed to the fifth wave of Sleeper virus. From her mother, Dibaba had inherited her independence of mind and from her father her love of maths. Her athleticism and the powerful lungs could probably be ascribed to both. The alliance of East African and North European genes had bequeathed Dibaba brown eyes and cascading, ebony ringlets which she tied back when on active duty.

It was not lost on Flight Lieutenant Warszawski that his genial and sometimes feisty comrade was not only fun to hang out with but was undeniably easy on the eye. However, as Wing Commander Wakeman had made abundantly clear during their induction at Lakenheath, the Royal Air Force was not a dating agency. The pilots had a job to do and if they developed any kind of desire for romance, they were advised to invest in a copy of *Pride and Prejudice*.

Dibaba had first harboured ambitions of becoming a combat pilot at the age of fourteen. She had, however, experienced serious doubts about joining the RAF following a history lesson in which her class had watched footage of US aircraft napalming villages in Vietnam a century before. The teacher had also shared a startling sequence of black and white photographs showing a group of panic-stricken Vietnamese children fleeing from the attack. In particular, the agony and terror on the face of a naked and badly burned nine-year-old girl had affected Dibaba profoundly and left her frequently wondering if the pilot responsible for the bombing of the village had ever experienced any regret.

Dibaba's qualms were eventually allayed by the passing of the Defence of Britain Act, a controversial piece of legislation, which, in line with a United Nations resolution, precluded British military forces from foreign interventions and restricted them purely to the roles of deterrence and defence. The Act contained a clause, usually referred to as the Mortality Protocol, which specifically outlawed the targeting of non-combatants or the harming of civilians through foreseeable collateral damage. With this legislation on the Statute Book, Dibaba completed her studies at the University of Durham and signed up for twelve years in the RAF.

During both her initial officer training and her subsequent fast-jet conversion, Dibaba often stood out, though not always for the right reasons. Perhaps the most naturally gifted pilot her instructors had encountered in several years, she had also needed to learn uncomfortable lessons about respecting the chain of command and keeping her own counsel in situations where she might instinctively wish to raise an objection.

Warszawski activated his comms. 'Lakenheath Ground, this is Stairway. Job done. Now flying at nine tonnes less than take-off weight. Your redundant shopping mall is now an attractive investment opportunity.'

'Roger that, Warszawski,' said Gunatillaka. 'Return to station.'

'Thanks, Gunnie. Wilco.'

0218 hours. Dibaba had reached her approach co-ordinates. Cloud cover obscured the moon and with few light sources on the ground, the town of Sunderland betrayed little of itself. The pilot was not, however, flying blind. The display in her visor presented her not just with essential data regarding the status of her aircraft, but also provided a virtual image of the world around her. Overflying the mouth of the River Wear, she banked the F-95 hard and flipped open the cover to the mission drive on the instrument panel. Carefully, Dibaba removed the target key from the thigh pocket of her flight suit and slotted it into the back-lit receptor. A fail-safe against the loss of innocent life, the avionic key would now disclose the specific mission objective and supply the permission code to couple the guidance systems to the missiles beneath the aircraft's wings. Without it, there was no target, the ordnance would remain dormant and an attack would be impossible.

'Cheers, Gunnie,' she said, as the precise target data revealed itself in her display. 'Another knackered-out car plant. How much of this crap can there be left?'

'Dibaba, this is Lakenheath Ground. You know damn well that I don't select the targets.'

Sunderland, Dibaba was aware, had once been home to one of the most efficient automotive plants in the world. By the second half of the twenty-first century, however, the cycle of global banking crises, the waves of Sleeper virus and the widespread anarchy that followed in their wake had brought the city to its knees. Starved of investment and forgotten by

Westminster, Sunderland had managed to survive but not to thrive. The pilot painted herself a picture of what she was about to destroy. There would be an expanse of echoing structures, in all likelihood devoid of machinery. There would be leaking roofs, broken windows and the vague, lingering smell of industrial oil. The site would be deserted. There would not even be rats.

At this point in Operation Landlord, the population of Sunderland was alerted to the imminent raid by a signal transmitted from RAF Lakenheath. Unless they were not wearing their i-comm wrist device, since the first of January a legal requirement, the citizens were treated to an insistent vibration on their arm plus the keening of a World War Two air raid siren followed by an announcement delivered in a reassuring female voice.

'Your attention. Air-to-surface attack. Estimated four minutes. Please extinguish all lights. Stay in your homes. Remain calm.'

Dibaba began the final approach. Her visor depicted topography, structures and vehicles and confirmed the crucial absence of human heat signatures in and around the target. A moment later, twelve air-to-surface missiles pierced the night sky and accelerated mercilessly towards their objective. In the pilot's display each missile appeared as a pulsing, yellow dot, but she paid no more than cursory attention. She knew exactly what was coming.

'Lakenheath Ground. This is Dibaba. Cargo delivered.'

'Roger,' said Gunatillaka. 'Return to station.'

'Roger that, Gunnie. Wilco.'

Dibaba brought her F-95 round and with the twin turbofan

engines accelerating the aircraft to beyond the speed of sound, she registered nothing of the multiple explosions.

On the ground, the inhabitants of the districts closest to the target experienced a rapid succession of flashes, followed by a thunderous blast wave that shook their furniture and jangled their nerves. Having established that they and their loved ones were shaken but otherwise unharmed, few would return to their beds. Once the all-clear had sounded, adrenaline levels would subside and the fear would slowly give way to a collective sense of relief.

It had been a good night's work for Dibaba. There were no casualties and Sunderland now possessed another well-levelled, post-industrial site, ripe for redevelopment by any one of several government-backed corporations. Furthermore, the citizens of the city, unaware of the true nature of the attacks, had been reminded that their country was at war. With each successive raid, the patriots, the jobless and the laggards were increasingly ready to pull together and play their part in the reconstruction of their town and of their nation. Since the start of the conflict, the Prime Minister had used one particular catchphrase more than any other in his growing repertoire: War means work.

In accordance with the standing orders laid down by the Joint Forces Command, the prime-ministerial roadshow would sweep into Sunderland within days of the raid. Conveyed live by the National Broadcasting Corporation, the PM would condemn the craven enemy who intruded only in the depths of night. He would bolster morale, expressing his belief in the resilience of the nation and citing the hard-fought wars of the twentieth century. He would promise reconstruction, he would promise recovery and he would promise employment for all. There would be no surrender.

Dibaba activated her comms.

'Stairway, this is Freebird. You down yet? You know it's your turn to get the beers in.'

'Two minutes.'

'Operational silence,' said Gunatillaka once more, aware that she was probably wasting her time.

'Hey Gunnie,' said Dibaba. 'Drinks are on Stairway. See you both in the bar.'

'Roger,' said the Ops Manager. 'Approved.'

With Dibaba's F-95 safely over the North Sea, the Civil Defence units at Wearmouth played their own unwitting part in the elaborate charade. Receiving orders from RAF Lakenheath, the anti-aircraft units raked the now empty sky with lines of incandescent tracer fire, providing compelling content for the morning news.

Happy with her demolition job, Dibaba returned the target key to the pocket of her flight suit and instructed her i-comm to play 'Free Bird', a song by the long-dead rock band Lynyrd Skynyrd.

'Oh, for crying out loud,' said Gunatillaka, abandoning her protocols in exasperation. 'Every bloody time.'

'Come on, Gunnie. You love it really. And it's not like we have a whole lot to do for the next ten minutes.'

'Speak for yourself, Dibaba. Some of us have actual jobs to do down here. Anyway, report status on approach. Acknowledge.'

'Roger, Gunnie. Wilco.'

After several minutes in the guise of a slow, yearning ballad, the century-old track suddenly kicked through a rapid change of gears and transformed itself into an extended guitar blow-out that swooped and soared and felt like it never wanted to end. Whether Gunatillaka perceived 'Free Bird' as a timeless rock classic or a step on the road to tinnitus was immaterial to Dibaba. She cranked the guitars up loud.

Within half an hour of the track playing itself out, Dibaba would be ensconced in the Officers' Mess, sharing a beer with Warszawski and the other pilots whose safe return she routinely took for granted. Their night was by no means over.

2 FIRE AND STEEL

Sunderland, 14th April

Two days after the raid on the automotive plant, the Stadium of Light, once more the home of Sunderland Association Football Club, had the honour of hosting the prime-ministerial rally and the energy inside the ground was palpable. The pock-marked brickwork and boarded-up windows of the West Stand bore witness to the stadium's year-long role as the stronghold of the local kleptocracy during the extended period of civil strife known as the Dark Age. Thanks to the organisational capacity of the National Unity Party and the superior firepower of the Yorkshire Regiment, the incumbency of the more lightly armed criminal militia was a thing of the past. The stadium was once again in the hands of its rightful owners.

The nine-thousand-strong crowd, comfortably a fifth of the city's remaining population, had been accommodated exclusively in the East Stand and were buzzing with anticipation. Before them, a rectangular stage had been erected in the middle of the pitch and two lines of ramrod-straight marines flanked the route from the players' tunnel to the centre circle. It was sunny and a typically warm April afternoon. In spite of the substantial decline in the human population, global temperatures had not yet fallen and meteorologists continued to classify the British climate as Mediterranean. Many in the northern corner of the East Stand were already shielding their eyes from the dazzle of the low spring sun.

Around the stadium, video screens presented the crowd with a visual reminder of recent events. Shots of the massive explosions dissolved into close-ups of unflinching Civil Defence troops raking the sky with anti-aircraft fire. Panoramic sweeps of smoking ruins cross-faded to images of the Prime Minister listening to local residents as they pointed to the sky, detailed their escapes and expressed their delight at his presence. Around the East Stand, Union Jacks and banners with National Unity Party logos wafted lazily from side to side. At strategic points, NBC camera drones hovered in readiness for the Prime Minister's big entrance.

When Gilbert Lathum Henderton, in a Savile Row suit, classic white shirt and blue and silver club-style tie, emerged in spritely fashion from the players' tunnel, the eruption of noise could be heard some distance from the ground. Once on stage, Henderton stopped short of the lectern and basked in the applause. He was supremely easy in front of the cameras and the knowledge that his face, his voice and his words would be transmitted to every TV screen in the country filled him with unbridled satisfaction. A self-proclaimed alpha male, he not only liked to win, he liked to win big, win publicly and to be respected, admired and venerated for his victories.

The forty-year old leader of the nation was tall, slim and exuded physical fitness. He was one of the few people to have contracted, but not to have succumbed to, the Sleeper virus and was only too happy to publicise that fact whenever the opportunity arose. Like other survivors, he had seemingly emerged with a stronger immune system and a more vital physiology than before his illness.

Henderton had pale and slightly thin lips, a narrow nose and green eyes. He wore round-rimmed gunmetal glasses which appeared utilitarian and suggested a common touch, but cost more than most conscripts to the work brigades earned in a month. His once bushy, raven-black hair, so admired by family and friends in his youth, had been in retreat for years. On most mornings he minimised the contrast between what had gone and what remained with an electric trimmer set to 'shave'.

The Prime Minister surveyed the crowd, inhaled slowly and began.

'The people of these shores are engaged in a second Battle of Britain, a battle against a cruel and shadowy enemy, a foe unlike any opponent in the dark and regrettable history of warfare. Upon this battle depends the very survival of the British nation. Upon it depends our way of life and the survival of our civil institutions. Once again, we have fought off the fury of the enemy and deterred what was without doubt an assault of barbaric intent. And so I wish to thank you, to thank you all for the part you play in the defence of our historic freedoms and the reconstruction of this proud city.'

He paused knowingly and the crowd erupted once more into mass adulation, waving their flags and banners for all their worth. It took no more than a raised palm from the Prime Minister and the nine thousand voices were coaxed to silence. He could do no wrong.

Before the intervention of Henderton's NUP, Britain had been in such a chaotic state that the four horsemen of the apocalypse could scarcely have done a better job. When the fifth global banking crisis triggered widespread economic decline, even the most outwardly liberal governments were coerced into the harshest of austerity programmes. On the international stage, collaboration gave way to mistrust and mistrust was supplanted by isolationism. Populations turned inwards, the United Nations crumbled and the internet eventually fell dark.

When the final wave of Sleeper virus spread inexorably across the planet, the UK found itself ill-equipped for the existential challenge. The death toll in the first two months had been in the hundreds of thousands. A month later, it was in the millions. By the time the virus had run its course, more than eighty percent of the population of Great Britain had perished.

In the years of the Dark Age, thousands more lost their lives to starvation, to infection, or at the hands of people they might once have considered their neighbours. For too many, there had been no work. There had been only survival.

It was against the backdrop of social disintegration that Gilbert Lathum Henderton first made a name for himself. As the leader of the newly formed National Unity Party and the focus for the restoration of civil society in southeast England, he rapidly came to the attention of First Sea Lord, Admiral Teresa Patel, herself forging radical plans to reimpose order and reunite the country.

It was agreed between Admiral Patel and the NUP that the armed forces would continue to play the leading role in restoring order and shaping the future, but that it would be wise to avoid all semblance of military dictatorship. With the backing, and more importantly the sanction, of the Armed Forces, Henderton was appointed Prime Minister and became the political face of the new status quo.

Inevitably, there were setbacks. Army units were forced to engage in heavy fighting with local militias and groups of armed escapees from His Majesty's Prisons. The loss of life was considerable, especially in the more densely-populated areas.

In the maelstrom of civil unrest, the Admiralty's concept of ghost air raids by an unidentifiable foreign aggressor had been inspired and the nocturnal bombardments rapidly provided a fractured nation with the desire to unite against a common enemy. The threat of invasion fostered a renewed appreciation of strong leadership and a more widespread readiness to embrace the rule of law. Thanks to the covert raids conducted nightly by RAF 161 Squadron, the overwhelming majority of the UK's nine million citizens were coming to understand that they had significantly more to contend with than each other.

The PM invited the crowd to settle once more.

'The world outside these shores remains bathed in shadow. A curtain of darkness has descended upon the world we once knew. Behind that curtain lies what remains of our former friends, partners and allies. We do not know, indeed we can not know, which country, if indeed it be a country, has turned its might upon us. But I tell you this. This nation stands strong. This nation will not stumble or falter. This nation will triumph, regardless of the odds. We shall never surrender.'

Henderton waited. He knew the line would resonate as well today as it had done for its author in 1940 and the explosion of approval was as loud as it was predictable. If key elements of the Prime Minister's speech were cannibalised from Churchill, the pauses were all his own. Gradually, individual voices in the crowd combined to form a rhythmic chant, in which each syllable of his name was given equal emphasis.

'Hen-der-ton! Hen-der-ton! Hen-der-ton!'

'You know what,' said Lieutenant Commander York to the

colleague at her side. 'You have to say, he's good.'

'Of all the talents bestowed upon men,' replied Lieutenant Batista, 'none is so precious as the gift of oratory.'

York flashed him a quizzical look.

'Winston Churchill, October 1938.'

'Very witty, Lieutenant. Very witty. Although I have to say, slightly nerdy that you can give me the year and the month.'

The Royal Navy dress uniforms of Lieutenant Commander Leila York and Lieutenant Cameron Batista were identical, save for the fact that York was wearing a skirt and had one more row of gold braid on the sleeve of her jacket. York and Batista operated as liaison officers and had been assigned the kind of specialist role that did not feature in recruitment campaigns and purposefully defied easy description. Their duties ranged from inane public relations on the one hand to covert operations on the other and their work with the Prime Minister involved elements of both. Their brief from the Admiralty was, in the first instance, to manage the Prime Minister's security and to afford him all necessary assistance, as long as he remained on message and adhered to the policies determined for him by the Joint Forces Command. Should Henderton stray from official policy, however, the liaison officers were instructed to steer him quickly and unequivocally back on track. York and Batista were, in effect, the Prime Minister's overseers.

Lieutenant Commander York was thirty-two years old, had ice-blue eyes and shoulder-length, blonde hair tied back in a neat pony tail. She had a sharp mind, an instinct for tactics and a talent for motivating those around her. These qualities had served her greatly as captain of the GB Olympic hockey team and continued to do so as a Lieutenant Commander in the Royal Navy.

Lieutenant Batista was a year younger and a good fifteen centimetres taller than York. He had brown eyes, a Mediterranean complexion and neat, black hair with wisps of grey already revealing themselves at his temples. A talented footballer from an early age, he had signed for Brighton and Hove Albion on his eleventh birthday, but was heartbroken when they released him within a year. His metatarsals, the club had informed him, were 'made of glass'.

The gentle mockery of the Prime Minister was a measure of the trust that had developed between the two officers. They were unquestionably an effective team. However, whilst York always welcomed constructive suggestions from Batista, the chain of command was never in doubt. She was the Lieutenant Commander for a reason.

As the Prime Minister continued his bravura performance, the two Royal Navy officers positioned themselves to the side of the stage and monitored his every word.

'In the early hours of yesterday morning we dished out to the enemy the fire and steel that they have so often meted out to us. Now we all know that this war will not end today. This is not the end. Indeed, it is not even the beginning of the end. But it is perhaps the end of the beginning.'

He paused to allow this emotive line to register and to soak up the now inevitable eruption of applause.

'I think I may have heard that one somewhere before,' said Lieutenant Commander York.

'He didn't quite get it word for word,' said Batista. 'Close, but no cigar.'

The wry reference to Churchill's smoking habits was met with an approving smile by his commanding officer.

Once more, Henderton settled the crowd.

'Though this war may yet endure, the Dark Age is past. In its wake there are more opportunities for work, more opportunities for life. And I want to assure you that, as I speak, the work brigades are prepared and ready to provide employment in this historic city. There will be sweat and indeed there will be toil, but no citizen will be turned away. No-one will be left behind. Because war - means - work.'

As the crowd once more bellowed its appreciation, the cameras zoomed in on the rapt expressions of individual men and women, proud of the co-ordinated fightback against the enemy, inspired to join the National Unity Party, or enthralled at the prospect of a job.

Henderton wound himself up for his final flourish.

'I walk shoulder to shoulder with every man, woman and child of this great nation. We have before us an ordeal of the most burdensome kind. But I tell you this. In time, perhaps sooner than we may have dared to imagine, there will be peace, an enduring and unshakeable peace, but first there will be victory. There will be victory in spite of fear, victory in spite of sacrifice, victory plucked from the cold, dead hand of our defeated enemy.'

Through the forest of flags in the East Stand, a camera zeroed in on the face of a woman, perhaps the same age as Henderton, as she bayed her approval. The tears that moistened her cheeks were more than a simple response to the rhetoric. Thanks to the man on stage before her, she no longer paid protection money to a militia, she no longer wore a stab vest on a summer's day and she no longer traded sexual favours to buy food for her surviving daughter.

Lieutenant Commander York nodded to the technician at the mixing desk and the first bars of 'Jerusalem' drifted from the public address system. Henderton turned, waved and left the stage as sharply as he had entered no more than fifteen minutes before.

York and Batista escorted him past the lines of Royal Marines, through the players' tunnel and down to the secure car park beneath the stadium. Even there, they could hear the continuing clamour from his appreciative fans.

Waiting to convey the PM to the next destination were three olive-green Gurkha armoured patrol vehicles. A rhinoceros of a machine, the Gurkha was designed with enough armour plating and anti-ballistic glass to defy the most robust automatic rifle fire. In spite of its eight-tonne weight, the APV could accelerate to speeds in excess of eighty miles per hour and had the capacity, in extremis, to act as a rolling panic room. The first of the waiting vehicles already accommodated six heavily armed police paramilitaries; the second would welcome the Prime Minister, his stylists and his two liaison officers; the third was a spare to be used in the event of a mechanical failure to either of the others.

Escorted by armed motorcycle outriders, and joined overhead by a Comanche attack helicopter, the three Gurkhas drove the nineteen miles north to Newcastle International Airport where the PM would spend the night aboard his personal RAF transport plane. Tomorrow, he would reprise the whole performance at the Newcastle United stadium and the day after, the roadshow would be in Manchester. After that, the Prime

Minister would be bolstering morale and rallying the unemployed in some other recently bombed locality. His liaison officers had yet to inform him where.

Much as Henderton delighted in the adulation he received at these events, he was nonetheless tiring of the relentless merry-go-round of public performances dictated by the Joint Forces Command. He had not created the NUP to be a conduit for the instructions of others and he was beginning to feel the role of Prime Minister, for all its comforts, was becoming little more than an immutable travelling circus act. Whatever the deal he had made with Admiral Patel, Henderton had known from an early age that his vocation was not for subservience. It was for control.

3 ONE OF US NOW

Liverpool, 14th April

In a leafy corner of South Liverpool, the four inhabitants of seventeen Menlove Close were watching the NBC news bulletin from Sunderland as they slouched on sofas they hadn't paid for, in a house they had no legal right to occupy. In common with perhaps five million other people, Aston Daniels, Thomas Dunbar, Freya Daniels and Martina MacDermott were to all intents and purposes squatters. Their appropriation of this attractive, six-bedroom executive house did not, however, constitute an issue. The four occupants of the property could lead their lives certain in the knowledge that no lawyer would ever serve them with an eviction notice and no bailiff would ever hammer on their door.

By the time the Sleeper virus had reduced the UK population by twenty percent, house prices were already in free fall and as the death rate continued to grow, so did the stock of available dwellings. Once the population had collapsed to something in the region of nine million, supply had swamped demand to such an extent that the concept of buying and selling houses became redundant and a lack of funds ceased to be an impediment to climbing the property ladder. Survivors readily availed themselves of the opportunity to move into new properties unhindered by the involvement of estate agents, banks or lawyers. Relocation became a case of selecting a suitable house, ideally one with solar panels and running water, checking that the property was unoccupied, and moving in.

'You know what, we're gonna win this bloody war,' said Aston as he watched the Prime Minister close his speech to a tumult of flag-waving and applause.

Aston Daniels, the brown-haired, blue-eyed son of a moderately famous painter, was in his late forties, still marginally overweight and had draped himself on the sofa like a discarded towel.

'I just find it so bloody frustrating that we don't know who the enemy is,' said Thomas, who also appeared to be comfortably over forty. 'I mean, do they not know, or are they simply not telling us? Is it the Russians, for Heaven's sake? Or the Chinese? Or some tinpot dictator with an air force? Who the hell is it? I honestly can't believe they have no idea.'

Aston stroked his partner's forearm. Thomas responded to this intimate touch and relaxed a little.

'It's the Yanks,' said Freya, Aston's twenty-four-year-old daughter, who was mischievously throwing pebbles into the water to see if she could make waves.

'Yeah, right,' said Aston sarcastically.

'Well, they're the ones with all the stealth bombers,' she added in impish defence of her contention.

'I would describe that hypothesis as improbable, to say the least,' said Thomas, also taken in. 'The Americans were our allies.'

Martina pitched in. 'If you want my opinion, it's not the Americans, but it's not Europe either. Europe's gone. You know, like the rest of the world. So, God knows who it is. But I'm with Thomas on this. I want to know if Henderton knows.'

Appreciative of Martina's support, Thomas raised his eyebrows at Aston, as if to say 'See. I'm not the only one.'

Whilst Thomas, Freya and Martina had always been ready to cast a critical eye over the NBC's broadcast content, Aston had persisted in his faith like a young boy who did not want to believe his best friend's revelations about Santa's true identity. He saw absolutely no reason to doubt the Government's protestation that it had so far been unable to identify the source of the air raids. There had, after all, been no contact of any kind with the outside world for the best part of a decade.

Aston and Thomas had been together for almost four years, having met about eighteen months after the death of Aston's wife. Over much of his lifetime, Aston had been torn between his attraction to other men and his loyalty to the woman he had married. He had genuinely loved Marcella as a life partner and as a co-parent, but he was never attracted to her in the way that she had believed. A dedicated and caring nurse, Marcella had not survived the final wave of Sleeper virus. Aston still missed her and had told Thomas so much about her that his partner almost felt that he missed her too.

Aston was a talented musician. An excellent drummer but also a competent keyboardist and bassist, he had previously earned a reasonable living from performing, teaching and session work.

Thomas had grown up and attended school in London and had spent his entire adult life in academia, culminating in a successful tenure as Professor of Symbology and Semiotics at the now defunct University of Liverpool. His mother was certain that he had inherited his restlessly enquiring mind from her grandfather who, in the 1960s, had relocated to Britain from Barbados on completion of his doctorate in linguistics.

Although the couple shared a love of music, a passion for football and a common interest in all things culinary, it was the work brigade that had brought them together. After their day's labours, neither had mustered the energy to change and they still sported the ill-matched collections of dusty, black clothing that qualified as uniforms. They belonged to the Liverpool South work brigade and were currently deployed to the wastewater treatment works. Whilst both would return to their previous careers in a heartbeat if the choice were ever to present itself, they nevertheless soldiered in each day and derived a modicum of satisfaction from the knowledge that their work was as vital as it was unpleasant.

As happened on most nights, the NBC was providing the pair with an element of distraction at the end of another arduous day.

'I miss 3D,' said Aston, as he focussed on the close-up images of Henderton's enthralled supporters.

'2D's better,' said Thomas. 'The picture's sharper.'

'Can't *you* fix the 3D?' Freya asked Martina.

'Yeah. If you can source me a couple of original laser units,' said Martina, knowing full well that this was nigh on impossible.

Martina MacDermott was perhaps slightly older than Freya, but was somewhat shorter. She had black hair, blue eyes and a fair complexion and could thank her Irish grandmothers for her looks. The electronics expert was the newcomer to the household. In the first instance, she had struck a deal with Aston that she would enjoy free board and lodging whilst she fixed their failing solar panels, built a wind turbine in the back garden and converted their two Phaedron electric vehicles into a back-up power supply. As it turned out, Martina was generous, liked a joke and was fun to have around. An instinctive problem solver, she had restored the power within two weeks and become one of the family within four.

'We may not share a surname,' Thomas had said to her, 'but you are one of us now. Family, my young friend, is more than ever a constantly evolving term.'

Although irrepressible in many respects, Martina was reluctant to betray too many details of her previous existence, even to Freya. She grew up in Formby. Her parents and her boyfriend all died at the hands of a militia whilst Martina was living in Manchester. Her only surviving brother was in the RAF, but she had no idea what he did except that it didn't involve flying planes.

Freya Daniels had inherited her father's looks and his innate musicality, but she possessed her mother's more slender physique and unshakeable optimism, which Aston considered to be no bad thing. Whilst still a student at the Liverpool Institute of Performing Arts, she had fronted a raucous band which had played the student bars and had acquired a sizeable following on MuTube. Whenever Freya made it home before Aston and Thomas, she inevitably greeted them with a fresh pot of rosemary tea, some toast and jam and a smile that warmed the soul.

Freya and Martina were easy in each other's company, understanding of each other's hopes and fears, and had grown to regard each other as sisters. Still slouched on a sofa, Freya was wearing a scruffy blue hoodie and a pair of combat pants frayed at the pockets and the ankles. Martina was dressed in a washed-out T-shirt and a pair of belted-in work trousers that featured more pockets than she would ever need.

The extent to which their clothes might have been described as fashionable or otherwise was moot at best. The clothing industry, in as far as it existed, was focussed on the production of uniforms, both military and civil, and of Utility-brand underwear and socks. Tailored apparel was available in selected outlets, but was largely unaffordable. However, with the population hovering around the nine million mark, there was no shortage of second-hand clothes. Although Freya and Martina cared in principle about what they wore, they generally made do with shabby chic plundered from unoccupied houses.

The NBC broadcast ended with a still of Henderton's confident, smiling face and was followed by *The Meat-Free Show*, a vintage selection of celebrity recipes trawled from the archives. Throughout the broadcast, the news ticker continued to scroll from right to left.

'RAF interceptors repulse intruders over North East. Damage to former vehicle factory. No civilian casualties. PM applauds city's fortitude.'

Aston and Thomas retired to the kitchen, where they engaged in a typically lively debate about how to cook the four pieces of unidentified smoked fish that Freya had acquired for the price of a packet of amoxicillin.

Aston's daughter was officially registered as an antiques dealer. As far as the authorities were concerned, Freya Daniels traded predominantly in old Blu-ray discs, CDs, rare vinyl albums and the outdated equipment without which these items were merely useless bits of plastic. Off-book, the former performing arts student dealt in rare and expensive commodities such as pain-killers and antibiotics plus hard to source foodstuffs such as cheese, meat and fish.

Since moving in to Menlove Close, Martina had built up a thriving business restoring solar panels and repurposing electric vehicles for use as a supplementary power supply. Although both she and Freya liked to accept payment for their activities in high-value goods, they were careful to conduct a plausible number of transactions using Credits, taxable electronic currency transferred via i-comm. The young traders liked being accredited taxpayers, because accredited taxpayers generated income for the Government and, as a result, were exempt from conscription to the work brigades.

Whilst Freya organised some of her high-end pharmaceuticals into order of expiry date, Martina took herself to their spacious double garage in order to investigate a nagging issue with the back-up electricity supply. When she returned, having re-set the connections between the battery in one of the EVs and the domestic power circuits, a substantial fish and vegetable stew was cooking on the hob.

Lounging once more around the TV after their heartwarming meal, the four members of the household were suddenly disturbed by the ascending, reedy tones of the air raid siren keening from their i-comms.

'Shit,' said Aston. 'The bastards are coming in daylight now.'

The alert was, however, markedly different from the standard air raid warning. In the first instance, the siren was not replaced by the usual calm and reassuring female announcer, but persisted in its inescapable demand for attention. More significantly, the message, which crawled across i-comm displays and had insinuated itself into the NBC's news ticker, did not confirm an imminent threat to life and property, but read 'The strong do what they will and the weak suffer what they must. Thucydides.'

'What the fuck does that mean?' said Aston.

'It means the NBC has been hacked again,' said Thomas. 'It's not a raid.'

'Yeah, I worked that much out for myself.'

After maybe thirty seconds, the National Broadcasting Corporation managed to wrest control of its output from the interlopers, mute the siren and replace the words of the ancient Greek philosopher with a more familiar message. 'A strong nation must spurn the kiss of anarchy. Tomorrow is within our grasp. There can be no repeat of yesterday. Gilbert Lathum Henderton.'

'Fucking anarchists,' said Aston, almost spitting with contempt. 'Whose side are they even on? Imagine if all these fucking know-it-all anarchists were running the country. Where would we be then? Still drinking out of puddles and shitting in the garden. That's where.'

Thomas wondered momentarily whether to define the word 'anarchist' for his irate partner, but thought better of it.

'Imagine if we got to choose who runs the country,' said Martina. She knew this was waving a red rag at a bull, but she couldn't resist.

'Oh, we'll have a choice. When the time is right. Fucking anarchists. Lock 'em all up, I say. Throw away the key.'

'The thing is, though,' said Martina, 'I've never voted. Not ever. I was fourteen the last time there was an election. One day, and ideally sometime before I'm sixty, I want someone to offer me a choice.'

'Well I'm with the electrician on this one,' said Thomas. 'Your vote is your voice. It's a reminder that you matter and that you have the right to be heard.'

His partner was having none of it.

'Yeah, well. Voting's all well and good, but these anarchists haven't got a fucking clue. If it wasn't for the NUP, we wouldn't have flushing toilets and water from the tap, we wouldn't have a job, we wouldn't even be having this stupid fucking conversation.'

No longer able to contain his anger, Aston got up sharply and retreated to the small dining room at the front of the house to pound out his frustrations on his beloved Yamaha drum kit. Thomas withdrew to the kitchen.

In the dining room, Aston switched on a small Marshall practice amp and wired it to his antique iPod. After a predictable but inevitably doomed attempt to give voice commands to obsolete technology, he remembered that he needed to deploy his index finger and scrolled to 'Wipe Out' by a band called The Surfaris. The track was a twanging, guitar-driven instrumental with breathless, pulsating drum breaks and for two minutes thirty-nine seconds, Aston displaced his frustrations, matching the solos on the original track beat for hammering beat. He repeated this process four more times and when eventually he stopped, Thomas appeared at the door.

'Feeling better?' he asked.

'Like anarchists could run the country,' said Aston, his anger largely exorcised. He smiled, implicitly conceding that his tantrums were as ridiculous are they were overpowering.

Thomas tilted his head slightly to the side and conjured up an expression of sympathetic concern, as a parent might for a child who had finally stopped crying.

'You're a brilliant drummer, you know,' said Martina, when Aston returned to the lounge.

'And you are a brilliant wind-up merchant,' said Aston, shooting her a smile, 'but I forgive you. You're a good kid. Your heart's in the right place.'

'As is yours,' she said, returning the smile. 'And I forgive you too.'

Aston pinched his lips and nodded appreciatively. Martina had a real soft spot for him, in spite of his almost boundless propensity for taking the government-sponsored news at face value. The real problem, she was sure, was not Aston's faith in the message but the unimpeachable status of the messenger. For his part, Aston's genuine affection for Martina easily trumped his irritation at her impatient idealism. Their reconciliation was as effortless as it was inevitable and the pair moved on from their difference of opinion without the slightest hint of recrimination.

At some point in the future, Martina would decide that the time was right to sit her adopted family down and reveal to them that she was one of the selfsame 'fucking anarchists' who regularly disrupted the nation's airwaves with their spiky quotes. It would not, however, be anytime soon.

4 LAST ON THE GROUND

Oxfordshire, 14th April

At 0115 hours a crescent moon hung low in the sky. Operation Poseidon had proceeded exactly as planned and the extensive site of the forgotten vacuum cleaner factory on the western edge of Malmesbury was now a smoking wasteland. The F-95's scanners had revealed no hint of human presence either on, or near, the desolate Nu-Vac site and Flight Lieutenant Dibaba was returning to Lakenheath secure in the knowledge that the Mortality Protocol had been respected and that the inhabitants of the quiet market town had suffered little more than a bad night's sleep. She was the only member of 161 Squadron still in the air and was rounding off the operation by cranking up the volume on the relentless dual guitar coda to 'Free Bird'.

Flying Officer Gunatillaka was monitoring Dibaba's approach on the 3D virtual map in the centre of the Ops Room whilst intermittently checking flight data on the screens incorporated into her work station. She muted Dibaba's comms.

'Dibaba, this is Lakenheath Ground. Just to advise you, you currently have a thirty-knot tailwind, so I've flipped the runway. Go around. Approach from the northeast, fly heading two-four-zero. Verify.'

'Two-four-zero. Wilco.'

'As soon as you're down, I'll be in the bar. The gins are on me tonight. Acknowledge.'

'Roger that, Gunnie. Approved.'

At Lakenheath the pilot took the F-95 Lightning past the southern tip of the base and banked round in a long arc. Within fifty seconds she had turned though 180 degrees and had pointed the aircraft's nose into the wind. Dibaba levelled off and continued her descent.

'Final approach,' said Dibaba.

'Roger. You're looking good.'

By the time Dibaba was 500 feet from the ground, the landing gear was down and locked. Calmly, she lined up the runway lights ahead of her and brought the Lightning in. With her wings level and using the rudder to keep the nose where she wanted it, she touched down at about 150 knots with no more than a hint of bounce. Immediately, Dibaba deployed the twin parachutes from the rear of the plane, felt the braking force push her forward into her straps, and eased off the throttle. The aircraft ran itself almost completely out of momentum well before the end of the 3000-metre runway.

Dibaba taxied to the hardstand, ran the engines down and climbed from the cockpit of her F-95. An avionics technician promptly replaced her and began conducting the regular post-flight checks. Beneath the aircraft three technicians examined the intakes, wings and fuselage for any suggestion of damage. As 161 Squadron's operations were entirely unopposed, there was rarely anything that required attention, but nothing could be taken for granted. The turbofans and the flight instrument functions could be compromised by something as simple as a bird strike.

Two minutes after climbing from the F-95, Dibaba entered the Main Briefing Room, her helmet under her arm. With nothing to report other than the successful completion of another mission, she gave the thumbs up to Wing Commander Wakeman, the Head of Station, who acknowledged her return with no more than a cursory wave. He had discovered a perplexing statistic concerning cybersecurity at the base and the all too predictable outcome of Operation Poseidon had been relegated from his thoughts.

In the locker room Dibaba placed her helmet carefully on the bench and took off her flight suit. From her locker, she pulled on her blue-grey combat pants and T-shirt and grabbed the matching hoodie with the 161 Squadron emblem on the front and the word 'Freebird' written in marker pen on the back. From the outset, she had written her unapproved call sign in its amalgamated form. As a single word, it felt more like a name.

With the hoodie draped over her shoulders, Dibaba took herself to the Tech Room to surrender her target key and hand over her helmet and anti-g suit to Chief Technician MacDermott for inspection and, if needed, for tuning or repair.

Like the rest of 161 Squadron, Dibaba was still buzzing from the pre-flight stimulants they were required to take and she needed to unwind. When she arrived in the Officers' Mess, the rest of the aircrew, with the exception of Flight Lieutenants Itoje and Becker, were already well-ensconced in the musty, beer-stained armchairs.

'Where are Highway and Rosanna?' Dibaba asked, referring to the absent pilots by their call signs.

'Probably on an untested bunk in the dormitory by Locker Room C,' said Warszawski with a knowing look.

'Yeah, right,' said Dibaba. 'Like there are any of those left.'

The Officers' Mess had not been refurbished since the

American contractors carried out renovations throughout the base back in the early 2050s. The yellowish cream paint on the walls was fading and beginning to peel in places. Here and there, the textured white ceiling tiles sported brownish lap marks which testified to occasional water ingress. A vague smell of damp emanated from the wall in the storage room behind the bar.

In the bar itself, the upholstered furniture was well past its best and smelled like camping gear that had been left too long in a shed. Above the counter, it was still possible to make out the handiwork of a US pilot who, over the course of several meticulous hours, had once painted what at first glance appeared to be an entry from a dictionary:

ejection / ɪˈdʒek.ʃən / *noun* - giving the plane back to the taxpayers

At some point, the graffiti had been overpainted with cream emulsion, but the message had long since percolated through the repair. On the wall by the windows, a 2D TV screen silently relayed *The All Night News Show*. The speakers had stopped working long ago.

At the bar, drinks were served not by a sympathetic bartender with an ear for a troubled soul, but by a dented chrome dispenser, skilfully configured by MacDermott to debit Credits from the pilots' i-comm accounts. The machine offered an apparent choice of three drinks: beer, bourbon and the non-alcoholic summer-fruit cocktail. Only the beer option provided some inkling of the product that would be dispensed and even then, it was an industrial approximation of traditional British ale. For a glass of Utility gin, the pilots had to select bourbon. Whatever the season, the summer-fruit cocktail was resolutely shunned.

Having dispensed the first round of drinks to the medically over-stimulated pilots, Flying Officer Gunatillaka was now installed on a cracked leather armchair and, as good as her word, had a spare tumbler of Utility gin on the coffee table in front of her.

Dibaba joined her and smiled in acknowledgement of Gunatillaka's generosity. 'Cheers, Gunnie.'

'My pleasure, Flight Lieutenant.'

As usual, Warszawski gravitated to wherever Dibaba was sitting.

'Hey, Freebird,' said Flight Lieutenant Merton. 'Last on the ground. Must be your round.'

'That's not a thing,' said Dibaba.

'Well, it is now.'

'Then I guess that explains why you're always first back. Anyway, the drinks are on Gunnie tonight.'

She caught Gunatillaka's eye and raised her glass in appreciation. As much as the Ops Manager did not like the whole call sign thing, she was even less impressed with the nickname 'Gunnie'. She had, however, made a conscious decision not to correct the pilots now that she was off duty. Gunatillaka understood that the price of admission to tonight's show was simply to embrace their generous irreverence. It was the anniversary of her husband's death and she did not want to spend a single hour of it alone.

'I'm totally going to put on *Classic Rock Classics*,' announced Flight Lieutenant Bosko. 'Anyone want to bet on how long Highway and Rosanna will make the beast with two backs?'

As the comrades hazarded deprecatingly short guesses, Bosko walked across to the Squadron's impressive library of twentieth-century vinyl albums. In addition to the fifteen operational F-95s, 161 Squadron had also acquired from the USAF a vintage record collection and the means with which to enjoy it. The three hundred or so LP records and the powerful hi-fi system, along with the musty smell, had been waiting in the Officers' Mess the day the RAF moved in.

Bosko rooted left and right through the dishevelled collection of LP covers and eventually located *Classic Rock Classics*. Ten of the double album's twenty-three tracks had provided the inspiration for the squadron's unofficial call signs and were often played at volume after a mission. Bosko placed the record on the spinning turntable and dropped the stylus into the groove at the beginning of a song called 'The Joker'. The vinyl crackled briefly and she began to dance, swishing her almost straight black hair from side to side and beaming like a child on a swing. Much as she loved an audience, she didn't need one. When the track finally faded out, Bosko bowed histrionically and grabbed another beer.

The pilots promptly returned to their sweepstake, now suggesting ETAs for Becker and Itoje which they felt were most likely to win the bet rather than simply besmirch the prowess of two Squadron members who were currently working off the mission stimulants in their own particular way. The mockery would come later. And no doubt in abundance.

From his office in the Command Block, Wing Commander Wakeman could hear nothing of the jocularity in the Mess. Operation Poseidon had proceeded without incident or complication and the last F-95 had been back on the ground for almost an hour. By now the Station Commander would normally have congratulated himself on a job well done and would have retired to the relative comfort of his quarters. The information transfer summary on the screen in front of him, however, precluded any consideration of sleep. RAF Lakenheath, it had emerged, was transmitting marginally more data than was being generated by official communications. Given the absolute need for 161 Squadron's operations to remain blanketed in secrecy, the implications of a potential data breach were far-reaching and potentially catastrophic.

In the first instance the anomaly should have been registered by Chief Technician MacDermott, the officer with overarching responsibility for cybersecurity and electronic warfare counter-measures. The fact that MacDermott had not drawn the discrepancy to the Wing Commander's attention was, to say the least, puzzling. If there were perfectly innocent explanations either for the data leak itself or for MacDermott's failure to report it, the Wing Commander could not for the life of him imagine what they might be.

5 A LITTLE LOCAL DIFFICULTY

Newcastle, 15th April

The grey A-600 transport aircraft was waiting on the runway at Newcastle International Airport, its eight-bladed turboprops ticking over quietly and the ramp at the rear of the aircraft illuminated and lowered. The crew were standing by to receive the Prime Minister, his retinue of guards, stylists and liaison officers plus the armoured patrol vehicles which had ferried them from the latest morale-boosting rally in another requisitioned stadium.

It was growing dark and guide lights already marked out the shape and length of the runway. Although rain was expected and the horizon was becoming indistinct, patches of darkening blue could still be discerned between the slow-moving clouds. As the fading sun sank closer to the horizon, the rainclouds were imbued with a pinkish wash.

Admiring the shifting beauty of the approaching sunset, the pilot and co-pilot rehearsed a favourite joke.

'Red sky at night?'

'The fuel dump's alight.'

The convoy from the Newcastle United football stadium, headlamps piercing the gathering gloom, pulled onto the runway and approached the A-600. The three Gurkha armoured patrol vehicles aligned themselves with the ramp and the eight motor-cycle outriders tucked in neatly behind. With the overpowering roar of the Comanche's motors drowning out almost all sound below, the helicopter descended slowly and landed some eighty metres from the gargantuan aircraft. At the top of the cargo ramp, three of the transport's crew stood ready to guide the vehicles on board. They would have to exercise a little patience. Until the Comanche's twin turbo-shaft engines ran down and the rotors were close to still, the loadmasters would not hear each other speak.

Finally, the helicopter fell silent and the crew set about their work. They were supremely well-drilled and in a matter of fifteen minutes the Gurkha APVs and the motor bikes were not only lined up along the lower deck but were securely chained to the steel floor. As soon as the ramp was raised, the crew radioed through to the pilot that their cargo was loaded and stable and that they were good to go. Although the A-600 could comfortably accommodate the Comanche as well as the vehicles, the attack helicopter would be flying as an escort.

The Prime Minister, Lieutenant Commander York and Lieutenant Batista had settled into the VIP lounge on the upper deck immediately behind the cockpit. In the more prosaic seating area to the rear of the upper deck, the loadmasters were sharing out flasks of willow bark tea with the crews of the armoured patrol vehicles, the Prime Minister's stylists, his armed security guards and the police outriders.

The four turboprop engines slung under the wings of the A-600 began to drag its 95 tonne weight along the runway. The aircraft moved slowly at first, then gathered momentum. Within a thousand metres it no longer needed the runway lights for guidance. The behemoth was in the air.

In the prime-ministerial suite, York and Batista turned down

Henderton's offer of a cognac from his generously stocked drinks cabinet and the PM called through to the aircrew for some refreshments for his guests. The co-pilot of the A-600, emerged from the cockpit and conjured up two flasks of tea and some mugs from the locker by the connecting door.

The VIP section of the A-600 had been designed to accommodate the Prime Minister and a small contingent of staff in relative comfort. The PM enjoyed the benefit of a personal cabin with a double bed and dedicated bathroom facilities. He also had an office with a desk, a computer and mood lighting.

Located between the office and the cockpit, the lounge was expensively carpeted and boasted two pairs of grey leather armchairs, separated by an Art Deco Revival coffee table. On the wall dividing the lounge from the cockpit, a sizeable TV screen treated the Prime Minister to glowing accounts of his rallies, visits and achievements. By the escape door, a grey container harboured six standard-issue life vests plus a large, orange survival dinghy and the warning 'Do not inflate inside aircraft'.

Henderton carefully swirled the cognac in his glass, warming it with his cupped hand so that he could savour its aroma before tasting it.

'French,' he said to Lieutenant Commander York. 'The genuine article. There can't be much of this stuff left.'

'It's a good job I'm drinking the tea then,' she said.

'I thought the rally went rather well,' said Henderton, skilfully understating the situation in order to draw a compliment from his minders.

Batista obliged him. 'A major triumph, Prime Minister. The nation is in safe hands.'

York took a swig from her mug. 'Manchester tomorrow. More of the same, I think.'

Henderton sipped his cognac, before looking directly at her. 'So, Lieutenant Commander York, when will this pretence of a war end? When do we finally wrap up the phoney raids and declare victory?'

York and Batista did not need to make eye contact to know what the other was thinking. The Prime Minister had overstepped the mark. Strategic decisions were the gift of the Joint Forces Command and were not to be queried by their political appointee. York decided not to validate his brazenness with a direct answer.

'Prime Minister, I would say that every citizen with a new job, a ration book and Credits at the end of the working day is a victory. Every recommissioned sewage works or repurposed industrial site is a victory. Every new factory bottling beer, canning fish, or producing toothpaste and tampons is a victory.'

Henderton tapped the armrest of his chair impatiently. He would not be fobbed off.

'Beer and fish and toothpaste are all well and good. No question. Absolutely. Growing economy, crime down, esprit de corps et cetera et cetera. My point is, when do we declare victory in its truest sense? Incontrovertible, unequivocal victory?'

Increasingly disenchanted with his subservient position, the Prime Minister was beginning to strain at his political leash. Henderton was more than anxious to secure his place in history and to bask indefinitely in the adulation of the nation. He wanted to see his statue in Parliament Square and his portrait in the National Gallery. He wanted to have streets and parks and babies named after him.

'Prime Minister, I am sure that you will appreciate,' said York, still opting for diplomacy, 'that the First Sea Lord does not share her strategic plans with mere liaison officers. Our role is restricted to purely operational matters.'

Either Henderton had failed to see the parallel between York's situation and his own, or he was choosing to ignore it. She presumed the latter. He would not let the matter rest.

'Surely the Admiralty's plan is not for an unending state of war?'

'I would say that's unlikely,' said York dispassionately.

'Oh, for Heaven's sake,' retorted Henderton, now beginning to give vent to his frustration, 'this sanitised RAF pantomime will not convince the hoi polloi forever. Everybody knows that the best firework displays build to a crescendo and end with the biggest bang of the night. If we're to have a war, it should at least be an honest war. There should be blood and tears as well as sweat and toil. There should be pain and there should be grief. And in due course, there should be deliverance. There should be overwhelming victory and national celebration.'

He poured himself another cognac.

York still refused to be drawn. 'As I said, the First Sea Lord does not share her strategic plans with mere liaison officers. Now if you'll forgive me, I'm going to check in with the tower at Manchester.'

The Lieutenant Commander left her half-finished mug of ersatz tea and disappeared into the cockpit. Henderton caught Batista's eye and leaned forward.

'I like a woman in a uniform,' he said quietly. 'The last time I saw eyes that blue, they were on a husky.'

The Prime Minister had assumed that now the two men were alone together, York was fair game. Batista was only too aware

47

of Henderton's reputation for philandering, but this was not a topic of conversation the Lieutenant had been expecting and he was momentarily taken aback.

'Do you think she does it doggie style?' continued Henderton.

Batista spoke calmly and directly. 'Prime Minister, as my immediate superior, Lieutenant Commander York enjoys not just my confidence but my respect. I would also add, Prime Minister, that Lieutenant Commander York and I are comrades in arms and as such, we have each other's backs at all times and in all circumstances. Sir.'

'Indeed,' said Henderton. He took a sip of his cognac and an uncomfortable silence ensued.

When York returned, Henderton was engaged with 'pressing paperwork' and Batista was listening to an audiobook. The Lieutenant Commander seized the opportunity to close her eyes and doze.

On the approach to Manchester, the pilot's voice interrupted their silence with an announcement over the comms.

'Prime Minister, we appear to have a situation on the ground. The runway lights are down. I'll circle and await clarification from the tower.'

The engines grew louder and the nose of the A-600 rolled and lifted as the pilot banked and attempted to gain height. The night was impenetrable. Through the windows of the VIP section both the sky and the ground were pitch black and it was impossible to gain any sense of where the horizon lay or what was happening below.

'I'll check it out,' said York. She got up smartly and opened the door into the cockpit once more.

The aircraft continued to climb, then banked to the left.

'Are there parachutes?' asked Henderton, perhaps a little too nonchalantly.

'Only paratroops carry parachutes,' said Batista. 'And they bring their own. So, no. No parachutes.'

'Right,' said Henderton, clasping his hands together, interlocking his fingers and repeatedly squeezing the back of one hand with the fingertips of the other. 'Right.'

York reappeared from the cockpit, sat back down and strapped herself in.

'Prime Minister, as far as we can ascertain from the control tower, it's a turf war involving two rival outfits. As you are aware, there are still some locations where the authority of the NUP…,' she pursed her lips and subtly wobbled her head from side to side as she searched for the correct term, 'fluctuates.'

Lieutenant Commander York was alluding to the remnants of the local militias that had once dominated broad swathes of the country. They were now few in number and more focussed on profit than politics, but still possessed military weapons acquired years ago from abandoned army bases or taken more recently from their defeated rivals.

The snafu on the ground featured two militias, the Traffordistas and the Whyos, who had needed a quiet place to do business and had chosen the unfrequented space between the bays of the redundant and unlit Terminals 1 and 3. Each militia had arrived with an ageing but functional articulated lorry loaded with valuable contraband such as brand-new Utility socks, medication officially ear-marked for hospital use, vintage designer clothes or legacy whisky.

At some point during the torch-lit negotiation, something had been said on one side, offence had been taken on the other and the mood had immediately soured. In the ensuing stand-off, one of the Whyos, more used to brandishing his assault rifle than firing it, had inadvertently squeezed the trigger and loosed off a single round hitting the leader of the Traffordistas in the stomach and bringing her down flat on her back. Within a second, all hell had broken loose. Both groups, though well-armed, were strangers to combat training and had run willy nilly for cover, directing their assault weapons randomly behind them and emptying the magazines as they went.

Above the firefight, the A-600 banked hard again, affording Henderton, York and Batista a view towards the ground. Small flashes of light punctuated the darkness, but appeared to offer little cause for concern to a transport aircraft displaying no identification lights and flying at an altitude of two thousand feet.

The pilot had bad news.

'We understand from the tower that the local Civil Defence unit is down and its AA guns may be in the hands of irregulars. Manchester is therefore a no-go for this evening. I will make contact with Brize Norton and will advise in due course. Please remain strapped in. It might get a little bumpy.'

Henderton was clearly nervous. Whilst his war leader persona comfortably extended to posing for the NBC from inside an ops room or an armoured command vehicle, he had absolutely no desire to place himself in the line of fire. As Prime Minister, he considered himself far too valuable to be lost to a tracer round fired by criminal thugs with a hijacked toy.

On the roof of the airport car park, one of the Traffordistas climbed into the turret of the captured anti-aircraft system and took his seat, eager to teach the Whyos a lesson but totally unaware that the weapons would not fire downwards. He jerked the joystick hard to the left to swing the cannon in the direction of the sputtering exchanges of fire outside Terminal 3. Simultaneously trying to decrease the weapon's elevation, he pushed the stick forward, but unwittingly applied pressure to the trigger, releasing a stream of 35mm tracer fire into the night sky. The right-hand gun suffered a hang fire, which caused the system to malfunction and engage automatic mode. The turret then rotated continuously and uncontrollably through 360 degrees and would continue to fire wildly into the night until it had exhausted its supply of ammunition.

Still staring out of the window, the Prime Minister was startled by the glowing stream of tracer fire which passed uncomfortably close to the A-600, perhaps within a hundred metres. He uttered his default expletive, then listened. There was no message from the pilot and no unfamiliar sounds that might indicate damage. Henderton swallowed the last of his cognac and began audibly grinding his teeth.

'The anti-aircraft systems the Civil Defence use don't have modern guidance systems,' Lieutenant Commander York reassured him. 'They're legacy weapons. All sound and fury. I think we're good.'

'And I'd be surprised if the guys down there can see each other, let alone us,' said Batista. 'They're literally shots in the dark.'

'The Comanche's hit,' reported the pilot. 'Uncontrolled descent.'

Beneath the A-600, the attack helicopter, now missing its tail rotor and trailing flame, was spinning on its axis and rapidly losing height. The pilot was struggling to recover control of the Comanche, but his chances were slim and he knew it.

Unable to emerge from the spin or gain height, the helicopter slammed into the roof of Terminal 3, penetrated through two floors and caused an almighty explosion of fuel and ordnance which reduced much of the building to rubble. No more than a hundred metres away, the warring parties recoiled from the ear-battering blast, interrupted their exchange of gunfire for perhaps five or six seconds, then returned to their obdurate feud.

No-one aboard the A-600 observed the crash, but the co-pilot noted the loss of the Comanche's identification signal from his radar and reported this to Henderton, York and Batista. Perhaps a minute later, the pilot's voice crackled through from the cockpit.

'Prime Minister, I have diverted us to Brize Norton. There are no known issues en route and they have adequate accommodation.'

York, Batista and the aircrew all had quarters at RAF Brize Norton. The Prime Minister would be found a reasonably comfortable room in the accommodation block, but in all likelihood would spend the night in his private suite on the plane. In the interests of the PM's security, the police officers would, as they often did, bed down on the deck of the A-600.

'We can fly back to Manchester tomorrow,' said York. 'Once this little local difficulty has been eradicated.'

'And exactly how will we do that?' asked Henderton, clearly still somewhat rattled. 'Eradicate the difficulty, I mean.'

'Well, I assume the Admiralty will dispatch a force of marines strong enough to pacify the situation,' said York. 'If the militias are no longer at the airport, they will be tracked down and dealt with, by force of arms if necessary. One way or another this situation will no longer be "a situation".'

'And the Mortality Protocol?' said Henderton. 'Doesn't the Mortality Protocol preclude the use of armed force against civilians?'

'Prime Minister,' replied Batista, 'the Mortality Protocol is designed to protect innocent civilians from being targeted by, or suffering harm as a result of, military action. It clearly governs the execution of the RAF raids, but it is not there to prevent armed insurrectionists, irregular forces or criminal gangs from having their illegal activities curtailed.'

'An interesting distinction,' said Henderton, 'though not one that everyone might appreciate.'

A radical idea for the escalation of the currently bloodless war into a more authentic and compelling experience had already taken root in the Prime Minister's mind and he was beginning to ponder the obstructions that lay in his path. The Mortality Protocol was one of them.

6 SINGLE-PERSON PLAY

RAF Lakenheath, 20th April

0235 hours. In the solitude of the Tech Room, Chief Technician MacDermott finished checking the anti-g flight suits, the helmets and the oxygen masks and stowed them away ready for the next operation. His shift finally at an end, he wondered whether he should join Flight Lieutenant Dibaba's birthday celebrations in the Officers' Mess. MacDermott had, however, worked twelve hours straight, he was genuinely tired and he knew he wasn't good in a crowd. It was an easy call. He would wrap up his day as he wrapped up every day. He would play *Space Invaders*.

In the corner of his workroom, an antique arcade console was on permanent stand-by, ready to help the Chief Technician dissipate frustration or clear his head whenever he needed. The games cabinet, replete with retro-futuristic artwork, a screen no bigger than the head-down display in an F-95, and hopelessly tinny speakers, was something else the USAF had left behind in the Officers' Mess. Liberated from the bar by its current owner, it was unlikely ever to return.

The sides of the arcade cabinet sported scenes from an imagined B movie. Alien flying saucers descended from the night sky, zapping murderous green rays at towering skyscrapers, at the citizens in the streets below and at the USAF fighter jets trying to defend them. Several vivid explosions and a multicoloured mushroom cloud provided a backdrop to the scene of wanton violation. In the foreground, a frightened bird took flight and a bespectacled citizen in a pale blue jumper ran for his life. Located in the centre of the front panel at trouser-pocket height, an aluminium slot awaited the single dollar coin which would allow the game to begin. Although the two sets of joysticks and illuminated buttons on the console suggested the game could be enjoyed by competing players, MacDermott only ever played alone.

The two-metre-tall machine was heavy, but sat on castors for ease of movement. The mobility was essential, as every time he wished to play the game, MacDermott had to retrieve his one and only dollar coin from the sealed cashbox accessible from the rear of the cabinet. Having confirmed that he did not have company and that the internal workings of the console would remain obscured from the security camera, the Chief Technician rolled the arcade game away from the wall, opened the locking hatch with an unfolded paper clip and rooted around for the American dollar amongst the small collection of obsolete smartphones that he had secreted inside the cashbox. To ensure that the scratched and battered phones were never on public display, MacDermott had hot-wired their chargers to the game's internal circuitry. Back on his feet, the Chief Technician pushed the console against the wall, inserted the dollar coin and depressed the *single-person play* button. Within five minutes, the planet had been saved from the clunky, two-dimensional alien invasion, at least until the following day. With victory secured, MacDermott pulled the console away from the wall for a second time and, hidden from the CCTV camera by the considerable bulk of the cabinet, booted up one of his vintage smartphones. He selected a messaging app, typed 'Hey, sis. U gd?' in antiquated youth-speak and tapped the *send* symbol. The message transmitted, he concealed the handset once more inside the cashbox, ensured that the security plate locked as he snapped it shut, and replaced the cabinet against the wall.

MacDermott could, in principle, have maintained regular contact with his sister via i-comm, but all standard communications to and from RAF Lakenheath were monitored. Given the idealistic but completely unlawful nature of the activities Martina was involved in, she had absolutely no desire to attract the attention of the authorities. Whilst MacDermott understood his sister's longing for democracy, he did not wholeheartedly approve of her methods. Nevertheless, he harboured no doubts about the fate that would befall her, if she were to fall into the hands of Modsec, the Ministry of Defence security apparatus. The organisation, which styled itself as the 'Sword and Shield of the NUP', had a well-founded reputation for obdurate, no-holds-barred mission fulfilment and the Chief Technician was as keen as his sister for their clandestine exchanges to remain undetected.

7 OFFICIAL, SECRETS AND ACT

Liverpool, 23rd April

Unsurprisingly, the small group of activists who were responsible for the disruptions to the NBC's transmissions did not advertise their whereabouts. It was a quarter past nine on a warm, muggy evening and the houses which lined the quiet cul-de-sac in South Liverpool were silent and unoccupied, except for one. During the hours of daylight, any prospective squatters who might have wandered into Troutbeck Park Gardens would in all probability have been deterred by the broken windows, the cracked or missing roof tiles and the extensive spread of brambles and buddleia. Almost at the end of the close, where the detached family homes encircled a small and overgrown traffic island, a fastidiously blacked-out house attracted no more attention than its long-abandoned neighbours.

Number twenty-three Troutbeck Park Gardens was home to two couples who had been drawn together by circumstance, but lived together out of choice. Talira Shah and Ricky Yera on the one hand, and Kireina Perry and Kevin Dylan on the other, were deserters from various work brigades who now devoted their time to unrelenting and highly illegal political activism. Assisted by MacDermott's sister, Martina, they were the originators of the crawler messages that regularly invaded i-comms and TV screens across the nation. Their transmissions, which they referred to as 'stingers', were a growing cause of irritation to the Prime Minister and an intense focus of investigation for Modsec.

The four activists were installed in the darkened and poorly ventilated living room at the front of the house. Spread across three desks, two fifty-inch flat screen TVs, four interconnected laptops and a repurposed games console all generated heat. Kevin was steadily filling one of the screens with lines of multi-coloured code.

From the lounge, power cables ran into the hallway, through a roughly drilled hole in the wall to the garage and connected to a stack of lithium-ion power cells stripped from four Phaedron EVs. Were Freya to have walked in, she would have immediately recognised the handiwork as Martina's. To mitigate the heat in the lounge, the four occupants of the house had commissioned the young electronics expert to source an air conditioning unit from somewhere and she was currently out on the case.

Thumbing through a tatty copy of the *Oxford Dictionary of Quotations*, Kireina pitched ideas for their next stinger at Ricky and Talira.

'OK. Here's a possibility. What do you think of this? "Freedom only for supporters of the government, only for the members of one party, however numerous they may be, is no freedom at all. Rosa Luxemburg." I like that. We should definitely do that one.'

'Wasn't she a communist?' said Ricky.

'It doesn't say,' Kireina replied. 'She doesn't sound like a communist. But who cares what she was? It's a brilliant quote.'

'She was definitely a communist,' said Talira, wincing slightly from the irritation caused by a broken molar scraping against the side of her tongue.

Kireina scanned the page again. 'OK. Not a fan of Rosa Luxemburg. How about "Nations do not die from invasion; they die from internal rottenness." I'll tell who you said it, after you tell me what you think.'

'Was it Rosa Luxemburg?' asked Talira, reluctant to be caught out.

'Nah,' said Kireina. 'Abraham Lincoln.'

'It's a possibility,' said Talira.

'Yep,' said Ricky. 'Definitely.'

Kireina placed a hand on Kevin's shoulder, gently distracting him from the coding. 'So, Mr Hackface. Abraham Lincoln or Rosa Luxemburg? What do you think?'

'I think, you need to hash it out with Karla Marks and Friedrich Spencer. You three are the ideas people. Leave me to the breaking and entering.'

Before the Dark Age, Kevin had been a highly sought-after cybersecurity expert, commissioned by government departments and multinational corporations to conduct full penetration tests and expose vulnerabilities in their electronic information systems. Although his client organisations invested heavily in threat management systems, he understood that the weakest point in their defences was, almost invariably, the human interface. Armed with no more than a sharp suit, unshakeable self-confidence and a fake ID, Kevin had repeatedly demonstrated the ability to present himself as an executive from the upper echelons of the target organisation, have someone escort him to an available office and, once left to conduct his important business in peace, hack into their networks from within. When the covert visitor subsequently supplied his clients with a detailed report listing their areas of insecurity, he was careful never to advise them how their organisation had been penetrated in the first place.

Although the World Wide Web was a thing of the past, governmental bodies, including the state-sponsored National Broadcasting Corporation, had devised, or successfully preserved, discrete internal networks which enabled essential systems to function securely. These walled gardens facilitated internal data exchange, but were not connected to one another and could not be accessed from outside. It was Kevin who had used his specific skill set to infiltrate the NBC studios in Salford, upload hackware enabling the insertion of rogue content into the newsfeed, and return home with four *Dr Who* souvenir mugs in an old BBC presentation box.

Throughout the spring, the erstwhile cybersecurity consultant had been working on software which would ultimately enable the hackers to insert video as well as text into the NBC's news output. Once the coding was complete, he would make a return visit to Salford Quays and upload the vastly more powerful malware required to supplant the NBC's output with extraneous footage. To facilitate the transmission of the more advanced and data-heavy video content, the activists had also set themselves the not inconsiderable task of procuring a functioning outside broadcast dish.

Talira, Kireina and Ricky had gone round in circles arguing about potential quotes for their next stinger. Aggravated by the broken tooth, Talira's tongue was bleeding, her teeth were red, and the debate had been placed on hold. She was sitting on a dining chair in the hallway and was looking less than calm at the prospect of what was about to happen.

With the fingertips of his right hand on Talira's forehead, Ricky pushed her head gently backwards and asked her to open her mouth.

'Come on,' he cajoled. 'We can do this. I'll be careful. I promise.'

Talira breathed out decisively, opened her mouth slightly wider and tried to relax. From the white salad bowl Kireina was holding, Ricky produced a nail file, recently sterilised in the flame of one of their few remaining matches.

'Try to keep your head still,' he said calmly.

Ricky then held Talira's mouth open with his right hand and proceeded with his left to file away at the broken filling on the edge of her molar.

'Try to relax. If it hurts, I'll stop.'

'Get a room,' shouted Kevin from the lounge.

Talira and Ricky had met whilst studying for a degree in Philosophy, Politics and Economics at the University of Liverpool. They each had brown eyes and olive complexions, although Talira's hair, whilst not exactly black, was markedly darker than Ricky's. Talira could trace her heritage, at least in part, to a group of displaced Syrians who had settled in Britain some fifty years previously. Although the couple were beyond their earlier, more tactile phase, they remained relaxed in each other's company and had eyes for no-one else.

Directly from university, Talira had landed a post-graduate job in Salford Quays as a researcher and fact checker for BBC News. From the outset, Talira's line manager, determined to test her ability 'to weigh up arguments, respond thoughtfully to objections, and to remain calm in a fast-paced working environment', had not shied away from making demands. His new appointee, he soon realised, was a talent and after little more than two years at Media City, Talira's immediate superiors began to intimate that there might soon be an opening for her higher up.

When the first reports of a new and unusually virulent virus arrived on her desk, Talira went to considerable lengths to ensure that the BBC's news team received copy that was authoritative but consistent with scientific fact and in no way couched in sensationalism. Less than a year after preparing that first briefing, there was no opening higher up, no line manager and no BBC.

After graduation from Liverpool, Ricky made a name for himself as the Press Officer for the now-proscribed Green Party. When the virus that Talira had initially described to him as 'a potential cause for concern' claimed the lives of unprecedented numbers of people in every country on Earth, communications servers around the globe faltered and so did Ricky's career.

Later, as the National Unity Party began to drag the country forcibly out of the Dark Age, Talira and Ricky presented themselves to the newly resurrected and soon to be rebranded BBC in the expectation that their services would be welcomed. However, the issue of Ricky's former advocacy of the Green Party was raised almost immediately and they both gave the wrong answer to the question regarding the likelihood of their joining the NUP. Their applications were rejected and they were advised that their details had been passed to the Liverpool Riverside work brigade. Their time in the brigade had been punitive and the pair were inordinately glad to have taken their leave of it.

Ricky wiped the nail file on an old towel and Kireina passed a glass of water to Talira, who removed herself to the kitchen, rinsed her mouth and spat a soup of bloodied water and small filings of dental resin into the sink. The reluctant patient explored her boyfriend's handiwork with her tongue.

'You know what, Ricardo?' she said, a look of delighted relief on her face. 'That's brilliant. It really doesn't feel sharp now. Not at all.'

'Anyone else?' asked Ricky.

'Pass,' shouted Kevin.

'I'll take a rain check,' said Kireina.

In her teenage years, Ricky's impromptu dental assistant had been a prolific graffiti artist, adorning abandoned buildings with vivid, witty and engaging images satirising social hypocrisies or the attitudes of the over-mighty. After completing her Art and Design Foundation Diploma in Norwich, Kireina was accepted onto a degree course at the Royal College of Art.

This energetic young woman from an ambitious Anglo-Japanese family had acquired a criminal record before completing her first year at the RCA. Displaying the self-confident demeanour of someone who was apparently doing exactly what she had been commissioned to do, Kireina turned up one sunny December morning at the Tate Modern, charmed the security guards into helping her with her stepladder, dust sheets and spray cans, and inveigled them into keeping onlookers at a respectful distance whilst she worked. By the end of the day, she had adorned the wall of the Turbine Hall with a six-metre-wide image, a faithful reproduction of an eighteenth-century pen-and-ink plan of a slave ship, replete with almost three hundred manacled Africans crammed pitilessly into the hold. Above the ship she sprayed the caption 'More sugar, anyone?'.

The case became something of a cause célèbre and though Kireina's artwork ultimately remained in place, so did her conviction for criminal damage. In a world where spray cans had long been unavailable, the implantation of thought-provoking quotations into the NBC's sycophantic news stream provided the artist with an alternative way to cock a snook at the rich and the powerful.

Kevin and Kireina were indisputably kindred spirits. A little over three months before their arrival in Liverpool, Kevin had been conscripted into the East Thames work brigade. After forty-nine consecutive days manually backfilling the flood embankments in Westminster with rubble and earth, he had demonstrated the temerity to ask when the brigade would qualify for a day off. His enquiry simply provoked the commander into declaring that in view of Kevin's impertinence, he would in future be working ten, rather than the customary eight, hours a day.

The following morning, the disgruntled conscript cut his hair short, shaved off his unkempt beard and turned up to the brigade's headquarters in one of his more expensive professional suits. He presented himself as Investigator Revelstoke, a senior Modsec officer conducting random checks on work brigade registers in the hunt for persons of interest. Exuding an untroubled air of authority, he demanded to speak immediately to the unit's commander, requisitioned his office and swiftly hacked into the brigade's internal network. By the time a PA arrived with some ersatz coffee and a couple of biscuits for their high-powered visitor, Kevin had already expunged all trace of himself from the register of workers and had tweaked the finance algorithms so that he would continue to be paid each day, but at triple the usual rate.

No longer on the books of the East Thames brigade, Kevin planned, if it amounted to a plan, to walk to Liverpool in the hope of locating the house where his grandparents had lived and, if possible, moving in.

Aware that the halls of residence of the former universities were frequently used to house the work brigades responsible for the rehabilitation of minor offenders, he made his way from one college town to another. Having located a brigade residence, the deserter would change into his old work gear and, as the brigaders returned at the end of a shift, he would simply walk in and enjoy a half-decent hot meal, before hunting down an empty room for the night. It was in the refectory of the former student residence directly opposite Coventry Cathedral, that he met Kireina Perry for the first time.

Kireina had engaged him in conversation as he was quietly consuming his free bowl of potato-and-something stew. The pair exchanged pleasantries, traded deprecating but witty comments about the slop they were eating, and took an almost immediate liking to one another. Before long, they began to swap stories, tentatively at first, then in increasing detail and with growing confidence that each could trust the other. Kevin remembered clearly the notorious case of *the Tate Modern and the con-artist* and was charmed by the tale retold by its protagonist. Kireina was impressed not only by Kevin's professional audacity but by his apparent immunity to getting caught. She invited him to her room, where they spent the night together, partly enjoying each other's bodies and partly hatching a plan.

By the following lunchtime, all electronic records of Kireina's past and her membership of the Coventry Central work brigade were gone, although she too would receive a substantial pay-rise and continue to be credited at the end of each day. Having spent another night in Kireina's room together, the pair spirited themselves away the following morning whilst the brigade commander was still tucking into his full English breakfast. By the evening, Kevin and Kireina had walked as far as the outskirts of Birmingham and were asking directions to the university.

Eight days later, they arrived at the house in South Liverpool that Kevin believed to be his grandparents' former home. Looking for an entry point at the back, they were suddenly confronted by Talira and Ricky, clearly wary of intruders and still dressed in their work brigade black after a gruelling day shifting railway sleepers. When Talira pointed out the availability of unoccupied houses the entire length of the street, Kevin took stock of their dusty, black clothing and asked how they were enjoying life in the brigade. He swiftly followed his knowing enquiry with the offer of a tried and tested exit strategy, if they were at all interested.

Within forty-eight hours of accepting Kevin's proposal, Talira and Ricky had been ghosted out of the Liverpool Riverside work brigade; Kevin and Kireina had a room at the back of the house and the four deserters were talking about how they could make best use of their talents now that they had all retired from a life of grime.

Talira was still rinsing the blood and the larger chunks of filling from the kitchen sink when the four hackers heard the sound of an air raid siren howling from their i-comms.

'Not one of ours,' shouted Ricky from the ops room.

The standard air raid warning was accompanied as ever by the familiar, reassuring voice.

'Your attention. Air-to-surface attack. Estimated four minutes. Please extinguish all lights. Stay in your homes. Remain calm.'

Talira, Ricky and Kevin squatted on the floor in the kitchen, well away from the windows. Kireina walked to the hall, cut the power to all circuits in the house and groped her way back from the fuse box. There was nothing to be done other than to wait. The sound of the back door being pushed open caught them all by surprise.

'Put down any weapons and exit the building one at a time with your hands on your head,' said the indistinct figure in the doorway.

Both the voice and the attitude were immediately recognisable. It was Martina and she was wearing antique night-vision goggles. Not that the others could see them.

'Hilarious,' said Kireina.

'Just doing my bit for morale,' said Martina. 'The NUP would be delighted.'

'Any luck getting an air conditioning unit?' asked Ricky.

'Nope. At least, not one with a working compressor. But I did get these night-vision goggles. I was made up with them at first, but they're a bit crap, to be honest. Although, if any of you guys want to play rock-paper-scissors in the dark, I could definitely referee.'

Before anyone had time to respond, the kitchen was momentarily illuminated by the incandescent flash from the exploding missiles. The five activists knew what was to follow and immediately covered their ears with their hands. Perhaps three seconds elapsed before the thunderous blast caused them all to flinch and the windows to vibrate.

'Everyone OK?' asked Talira, once the noise subsided.

No-one was hurt.

Kevin calculated that they were less than a mile from the site of the attack. They speculated as to the possible target, but could settle on no obvious candidate.

'It'll be on the news,' said Kireina. 'Along with the daily worship of Saint Gilbert and the NUP.'

'That was too close,' said Ricky, clearly rattled. 'How the hell can the Government have no idea where these raids are coming from?'

'They must know,' said Talira. 'There was a time when the media would have been camped at the end of Downing Street, repeatedly yelling that very question every time the PM poked his arrogant, little nose out of that big, black front door.'

'Hey, Martina. Your brother's in the RAF,' said Kevin. 'He ought to know where the raids are coming from.'

'He may well do, for all I know,' said Martina, 'but there's no question I can ask him that doesn't feature the words "official", "secrets" and "act" somewhere in the answer. I don't even know where he's stationed.'

'OK,' said Kevin. 'If we really want to know where the bombers are coming from, I reckon we have two options. Either we hack our way into somewhere where the information is stored, or we find some way of tracking the aircraft that overfly British airspace.'

'Which is the easiest option?' asked Kireina.

'Honestly? Neither.'

8 APPLE FROM THE BARREL

RAF Lakenheath, 24th April

The US Air Force first deployed to RAF Lakenheath during the Second World War and over the years had fashioned it into a home from home for its service personnel. Wandering around the deserted streets and buildings of the southwestern corner of the base, a visitor could be forgiven for feeling that they were exploring the desolate film set for a long-completed movie located in small-town Connecticut.

At no point had there been any negotiation about the status of Lakenheath and in absolute legal terms, the station remained an American air base, but the USAF was an absentee tenant at best. When the repeated waves of Sleeper virus had been threatening to make the outbreak the most virulent pandemic in history, the US Government had taken the precipitous decision to repatriate all of its foreign-based forces and to do so as rapidly as possible. The immediate withdrawal of the 5,500 US military personnel and the 2,400 American civilians from Lakenheath had been as chaotic as it was hasty. Such was the disorder towards the end of the operation, that the helicopter evacuations from the US embassy in Saigon a century earlier had been made to look like tourist joyrides. Whilst the two massive Super Galaxy transport aircraft, flying round the clock for over a week, managed to repatriate all the US citizens on the base, billions of dollars' worth of military hardware had simply been abandoned where it stood.

Initially, RAF Regiment troops had maintained security at Lakenheath on behalf of its tenants, but after several years without a single communication from beyond the Atlantic, the Joint Forces Command came to the conclusion that the USAF was gone for good. The base was reclaimed and the fifteen American F-95 Lightning fighter-bombers, an assortment of trucks and eighteen redundant refuelling drones became, in effect, the property of the RAF.

161 Squadron, having no great need for the schools, retail outlets and family accommodation in the residential quarter of the base, occupied almost exclusively the collection of operational buildings that were located close to the hangars and runways. Many of the Squadron's personnel, however, regularly undertook the twenty-minute walk across the site to work out in the Upper East Side Fitness Center or play football in the High School sports hall.

The medical bay run by Dr Anja Kaminski was housed in the former USAF hospital and was the only official 161 Squadron facility based in the residential quarter. The doctor had walked the best part of a mile to Block A, only to be told by Wing Commander Wakeman that the purpose of their meeting was to assist him with a matter of security.

The doctor furrowed her brow.

'Wing Commander Wakeman, keen as I am to be of service, I have to confess that I'm at a loss to understand why you need the station's Senior Medical Officer to assist you with this.'

'The simple answer, Dr Kaminski, is that, as much as anything, we are meeting today in our capacities as Party members. I need someone in whom I can place my absolute trust.'

'Understood, sir. You have my attention.'

'We have a problem,' said Wakeman. 'A system-generated security report has indicated a data leak. On the surface, it's an insignificant amount, less than a kilobyte a month. But that said, a kilobyte is more than enough to transmit a command signal, or a codeword or who knows what.'

'And what does our Cyberspace Countermeasures Officer make of the report?'

'Well, here's the thing. Chief Technician MacDermott has so far failed to mention it to me.'

'Perhaps he's on the case.'

Wakeman tilted his head slightly and pursed his lips. 'Perhaps.'

'Sir, if you have concerns, why not just call in Modsec? They are all members of the NUP. "Sword and Shield of the Party" and all that.'

'Indeed they are, but I can't very well bring in Modsec without drawing this, shall we say, "situation" to the attention of my commanding officers and that would inevitably involve me having a torch shone up my arse whilst I explain how this… how this discrepancy has happened on my watch.'

Twice in one sentence, the Wing Commander had side-stepped the use of the word 'lapse'. His unease, however, could not be masked by the euphemisms.

'I see,' said Kaminski sympathetically.

'Yes, far better, I think, to remove the rotten apple from the barrel and present Air Command with the solution rather than the problem.'

'OK. With you so far. Do you have any suspects?'

'At this stage, only Party members enjoy my trust.'

'And how many people on station are Party members?'

71

'There are only two members of the Party on station, Dr Kaminski. I'm looking at one of them and you're looking at the other. It should, of course, go without saying, that the identity of NUP members within the RAF should not be made known to those outside the Party.'

'So what do you want me to do, sir?'

Wakeman activated the large monitor on the wall of his office. 'I need you to cast an eye over some recent security footage and tell me if any behaviours strike you as, well, unusual.'

'OK,' she said cautiously, 'but unless you have footage of someone who looks like they might be using an unsanctioned device, I don't see how I can be of use. I'm a doctor, not a criminologist.'

'Indeed, but as the station's Senior Medical Officer, you are responsible for maintaining the mental as well as the physical wellbeing of all personnel, are you not? You do mind as well as body.'

Although one of the thousands inspired to join the NUP by Henderton's iconic 'Green Shoots of National Recovery' speech, the doctor's Party membership had thus far made no serious demands on her time. Whilst the Senior Medical Officer understood that the surveillance of colleagues, to whom she owed a fundamental duty of care, could be construed as a betrayal of their trust, she rationalised that there was conceivably a traitor on station who potentially threatened the lives of everyone. She therefore had a duty to help find the treachery and cut it out like a cancer.

The Wing Commander called up the Operation Poseidon recordings and they began, perhaps unsurprisingly, with Camera 1 in Hangar 1. Wakeman scrolled through various on-screen thumbnails, pausing at scenes that piqued his curiosity before allowing the silent footage to play for a few seconds. At 0258 hours, three aircraft technicians inspected an F-95 Lightning; at 0329, a technician refitted an orange and white braking parachute to the aircraft; at 0420, a different technician checked the tyre pressure on the landing wheels; at 0434, the same technician refuelled the same F-95.

'All very mundane,' muttered Wakeman.

Kaminski agreed.

Keen to move on, the Station Commander selected Camera 17, which covered the bar in the Officers' Mess. The CCTV footage presented the two NUP members with a silent clip show of what had already gone down in 161 Squadron folklore as 'Gunnie's Post-Poseidon Piss-Up'. They saw Gunatillaka dispensing drinks to all and sundry, Flight Lieutenant Xu raising her glass and blowing a kiss at the camera, the pilots engaged in animated debate, Itoje and Becker arriving at the bar to general applause.

'What about the antics in the Mess? Anything strike you as out of the ordinary?' said Wakeman.

'You've got a group of pilots jazzed up on mission-meds and kicking back by drinking too much. To be honest, it would be out of the ordinary if they were doing anything else.'

Wing Commander Wakeman called up footage from the Tech Room. The security clips showed the Chief Technician carefully checking the integrity of flight suits and helmets, before squatting on the floor with his head and torso obscured by the games cabinet.

'What's he doing?' said Kaminski.

'Well as far as I can make out, our Chief Technician was

retrieving the coin he needed to activate the games console.'

They watched MacDermott engage in a frenetic game of *Space Invaders*.

'Does it not strike you as odd, Dr Kaminski, that MacDermott was playing some antique computer game whilst everyone else was having fun in the Mess?'

Kaminski pinched her lips before replying. 'Not everyone deals with stress in the same way,'

'Granted. The question is, what does he have to be stressed about?'

'The fact that his only real friend is a games console, perhaps? I'd hazard a guess that MacDermott does not have a treacherous bone in his body.'

The Medical Officer consulted her i-comm, sucked her teeth and apologised that she had several pressing appointments to keep. Wakeman thanked Dr Kaminski for her help, reminded her that their conversation had been strictly confidential and commissioned a Land Rover to transport her back to the med bay.

Although the security footage had revealed little of value, the Wing Commander had another card up his sleeve. It did, however, involve an element of calculated risk. He decided to give the matter some thought before taking actions that might just as easily alert the unidentified spook to the investigation as produce meaningful evidence of his or her disloyalty.

9 THE SOURCE OF THE ANOMALY

RAF Lakenheath, 26th April

Two days had elapsed since the Wing Commander's meeting with Dr Kaminski. In Wakeman's office, the air-conditioning system was struggling to cope with both the ambient temperature and the heat generated by the flickering server, the rack of networking equipment and the communications module mounted on the wall. The AC unit dripped as though it had a summer cold. Wakeman was still wrestling with the issue of the data leak and the fact that Chief Technician MacDermott, the officer responsible for cybersecurity and electronic warfare counter-measures, had not reported it to him.

MacDermott's failure to draw attention to the breach presented the Station Commander with a conundrum. Either the Chief Technician had failed to spot the system-generated alert, which seemed unlikely in the extreme, or he was aware of it and had chosen not to raise the matter. Neither scenario reflected well on MacDermott's professionalism or furnished Wakeman with the reassurance that would set his mind at rest.

The idea that the introverted *Space Invaders* addict might have the slightest motivation to compromise their security, or could be covering for someone who did, struck the Station Commander as close to preposterous although, in the absence of evidence to the contrary, MacDermott was as much a suspect as anyone else. Perhaps Dr Kaminski had been right. Perhaps this was a case for an MOD security team.

After considerable deliberation, Wakeman took a decision. He would rather confront MacDermott than bring in Modsec and potentially be forced to acknowledge the situation as some sort of personal failure. He made his way to the Tech Room, trying to formulate a game plan as he went.

When the Wing Commander abruptly interrupted MacDermott's programming of a target key and asked him to confirm that they were alone, the Chief Technician felt his senses immediately sharpen.

'We have a security issue,' said Wakeman, manifestly unhappy, 'and you, as our Cyberspace Countermeasures Officer, are going to solve it.'

'Sir?' said MacDermott, trying to sound puzzled, but feeling like the ground was about to disappear beneath his feet.

Wakeman placed an A4 sheet of paper onto MacDermott's cluttered desk.

'That is a copy of an automated report you recently received from our security systems. More data is being transmitted from our mast than our communications systems are generating. We have what appears to be a leak.'

The Chief Technician had been labouring under the impression that he was the only recipient of the automated security reports and was horrified to realise that the Station Commander had taken an interest in the minutiae of internal data flows. Outwardly, MacDermott still appeared calm, almost statuesque, but his adrenal glands were already pumping huge doses of stress hormones into his bloodstream. He remained silent for no more than a couple of seconds, but it was long enough to irk Wakeman. The Wing Commander wanted a speedier response than he was getting and adopted a tone which conveyed both frustration and indignation.

'How the hell has this happened on your watch?'

This was the first question that Wakeman was expecting to face, should he be forced to call in Modsec.

'Sir?'

'You're in charge of cybersecurity, for Heaven's sake. What the hell is going on?'

MacDermott's quiet demeanour concealed a mind suddenly racing as it hunted for an explanation that would placate the Station Commander.

'Sir, I monitor our data flows twice daily and I'm well aware of the report. I've already looked into it and it's, well, it's...' MacDermott paused momentarily. 'It's not a huge anomaly, sir. Less than a kilobyte in a single month. That's easily within tolerance. It's a discrepancy of...' MacDermott paused a second time, his eyes now drifting upwards as he calculated, 'less than 0.000001 percent. To my mind, probably no real cause for concern.'

Expressed in terms of the station's overall data flow, the discrepancy was indeed miniscule. Wing Commander Wakeman was, however, having none of it and would not be fobbed off with 'probably' any more than Modsec would be. His tone now bordered on the aggressive.

'Probably? For heaven's sake, just listen to yourself, MacDermott. A kilobyte is enough to transmit a command signal to an IED or a security code to an enemy. Is my Cyberspace Countermeasures Officer telling me he is "probably" sure that none of these things can happen?'

'No, sir. What I meant-'

'No!' snapped Wakeman. 'I hold you personally responsible for this situation.' The Wing Commander was again anticipating the dressing down he would receive if he did not resolve this issue and resolve it quickly. 'Perhaps you should put as much effort into your actual job as you put into that crappy little games machine.'

'Sir.'

Wakeman could see that the Chief Technician was feeling intimidated. That was good, he thought. It would concentrate MacDermott's mind on the urgency of the task in hand.

'Your working assumption from now on,' said the Wing Commander, 'is that we have a traitor somewhere on station. You will find the source of the anomaly and identify that traitor. And you will not under any circumstances what-so-ever discuss this matter with anyone. Not with anyone. Am I making myself clear, Chief Technician MacDermott?'

'Understood, sir. Perfectly clear.' MacDermott's next question was risky. 'Do you have any suspects, sir?'

'Everyone is a suspect, MacDermott. Speak to nobody else. Do your job. Full penetration tests on all our systems, security scans on everyone's communications. Leave no stone unturned. You will report to me the moment you have a result, or within seven days at the very latest. Have I made myself clear, Chief Technician?'

'Sir.'

'Thank you. End of conversation.'

The Wing Commander turned on his heels and walked out of the room, leaving MacDermott with his thoughts and feelings in a tangle of impossible choices. In his confusion, he took himself into a stock room, closed the door and yelled as he kicked violently at a wooden crate. The instinctive attempt at catharsis provided a momentary release, but made no lasting dent in the sense of impending calamity. Perhaps inevitably, the Chief Technician was drawn to the games console, but a dollar's worth of interplanetary warfare offered neither solace nor solution. As he played, a queasiness took hold in the pit of his stomach and his mind continued to race, although not in any useful direction.

10 RELEVANT TO
OUR NEEDS

Almost four weeks after the turbulent flight from Newcastle to Manchester, the Prime Minister was ensconced in his customary seat in the Cabinet Room of 10 Downing Street and was impatiently waiting for Stella Paterson, the director from NBC News, to give him the go-ahead to call the meeting to order.

With the burgeoning economy constantly vaunted by the NBC and his approval ratings higher than ever, Gilbert Henderton felt increasingly that his subservient relationship with the Joint Forces Command was no longer fit for purpose. He had never been easy with the idea of being monitored by two Royal Navy liaison officers, but the PM's forbearance had festered to such an extent that he now considered their attendance at Cabinet meetings to be nothing short of an affront.

Present this afternoon were the Prime Minister, the twelve members of the cabinet, the two Royal Navy liaison officers, the seven-strong NBC film crew and Dame Abigail Hartmann, Director of Ministry of Defence Security.

As ever, the Prime Minister was sitting at the mid-point of the slightly ovoid table, which allowed him to be seen to maximum effect by his Cabinet and to appear inclusive to the attendant cameras. The NUP leader was illuminated from above by two ornate, gold-plated chandeliers and on two sides by soft natural light diffused through diaphanous white curtains and bullet-proof glass. The NBC lighting technician had set up two softbox lamps to remove any unflattering shadows from the face of the Prime Minister and from those ministers positioned to his immediate left and right. Lieutenant Commander York and Lieutenant Batista were to remain out of shot throughout. In spite of the humid weather which had fallen over London like a net, the well-maintained air-conditioning ensured that the NUP Government could work in relative comfort.

The National Unity Party had begun life as a willing alliance of dyed-in-the-wool patriots, radical idealists and energetic humanitarians and was the only political organisation sanctioned by the Joint Forces Command. Faced with an existential crisis and a leader disposed to seek compliance rather than consensus, the coalition of strange bedfellows had lasted little more than six weeks. Now purged of impurities, the party consisted exclusively of Henderton-loyalists and the Prime Minister was rarely inconvenienced by debate.

The lighting director made a number of last-minute adjustments and gave the nod to Stella Paterson, the NBC director. Lieutenant Batista reminded Paterson politely that the meeting was going to address a number of sensitive issues and that approval would have to be secured from Joint Command before broadcasting any content relating to item two on the agenda.

'Rest assured,' said Paterson. 'I am nothing, if not professional. OK, I think we are good to go. Is everybody set? OK. Three, two, one…'

'Right, then,' began Henderton with characteristic

self-confidence. 'Welcome to our weekly operational review. I would like to remind you that this is a working meeting, not an unfiltered talking shop, and that we have all committed to starting with a positive assumption. I will therefore not dwell on any individual matter once I sense we are all in agreement. Right then, let's make a start. The order of business for today is: one, the distribution of reconstruction contracts; two, the eradication of unauthorised intrusions to NBC broadcasts; and three, the acceleration of national reconstruction.'

'Cut,' shouted Paterson. 'Sorry, Prime Minister. No need to bang your fist on the table to emphasise every point. It plays havoc with the audio and it can come across as a bit... well... overemphatic.'

'Right,' said Henderton, quietly peeved. 'Right. Got it.'

Ever the perfectionist, Paterson required three more takes of the welcome and the summary of business before she was happy.

'Right then. Point one,' continued Henderton.

'Cut,' said Paterson. 'Sorry, Prime Minister. Too many "Right, thens". You don't want to be known as "Right-then-Henderton".'

'For sure,' said the PM, awkwardly searching for something new.

Prompted by Paterson, the Prime Minister began afresh. The item regarding the distribution of Government contracts proceeded apace and amounted to little more than Henderton announcing the names of recently bombed towns, followed by the names of corporations that supported the NUP. The close-ups of attentive faces, acquiescent nods and hands patting the table in approval would be used more than once in the final edit.

'Thank you,' said Henderton, keen to move on. 'Item two on

the agenda. We are continuing to experience covert and, I have to say, phenomenally irritating intrusions into the broadcast output of the NBC, perpetrated, as far as we know, by person or persons unknown.'

'Cut,' said the director. 'It's "by *a* person or persons unknown". Not "by person or persons unknown". One more time.'

'Really?' said Henderton waspishly. 'You stopped me for that?'

Stella Paterson normally responded to expressions of frustration on the part of the Prime Minister with politely delivered reprimands such as 'Prime Minister, my role is simply to present His Majesty's Government in the best possible light. I am sure we are all in agreement on that.' She was, nevertheless, running low on patience.

'Forgive me, Prime Minister. But I directed two seasons of *Sex Island* and three seasons of *Celebrity House on Fire*. I think I know what people like.'

At this point, Lieutenant Commander York decided that it would be prudent to intervene.

'I'm wondering, Stella, given that time is of the essence, and some of us have places to be, if it would be possible to complete this part of the meeting without more retakes. You're unlikely to receive authorisation for the sensitive content in any case.'

'I think that might be a good idea,' said Henderton.

'Fine,' said a clearly disgruntled Paterson. 'Let's just take sixty seconds to breathe deeply and regain our composure.'

The Prime Minister decided that Stella Paterson might be better employed elsewhere in the NBC and with the gold-nibbed pen that once belonged to his father, calmly wrote her name on his agenda directly beneath Any Other Business.

After the brief interlude, Paterson counted them all back in and recording resumed.

'Right then,' said Henderton with manifest impunity. 'Unauthorised disruption to the NBC. We are continuing to experience intrusions into the NBC broadcasts, perpetrated, as far as we know, by person or persons unknown. Whilst the content of their quirky messages is little more than adolescent graffiti on a toilet wall, it is, as I'm sure you appreciate, the fact that they can pull off these juvenile stunts in the first place that constitutes the problem. And it is, I am sure we would agree, a problem that must be resolved as a matter of urgency. In short, we can no longer tolerate the intolerable.'

The Prime Minister chose the moment to pause, allowing his team to collectively mutter expressions of support or applaud by rapping the palm of one hand on the table top. Although the clapping was slightly too loud for the audio recording, Paterson consoled herself that the all-round expressions of approval could be edited into the coverage of Item One and would at least provide a counterpoint to the otherwise uninterrupted footage of the Prime Minister simply holding court.

'At this point,' said Henderton, 'I would like to hand over to Dame Abigail Hartmann, Director of Ministry of Defence Security.'

Hartmann expressed her thanks for the opportunity to update the Cabinet and began.

'As the Prime Minister so clearly states,' she said, catching Henderton's eye, 'the situation with the NBC must not continue.'

Henderton nodded sagely in agreement.

'Whilst the Cyberwarfare Unit at Modsec has the capability to disable these intrusions, usually within sixty seconds of broadcast, we do not yet understand how the hackers are penetrating the NBC's threat management system in the first place, so the exclusion of their signals remains a work in progress. It has so far proved impossible to discern any kind of pattern to the intrusions, so it is also difficult to predict when they will occur. Of course, once we apprehend the individuals responsible, we cut the head off the snake. Modsec, therefore, is engaged in a nationwide Priority One investigation and is working hand in hand with all civilian and military police forces to profile, identify and detain the criminals behind the disruptions.'

'Time scale?' asked Henderton.

'As I said, the investigation has a priority of one, so I would say it is potentially a matter of days.' She sounded confident of this, but in all honesty, she hadn't the faintest idea.

'Thank you, Dame Abigail. The UK Government is grateful, as ever, to Modsec for its input on all matters of security.'

The cabinet banged their hands on the table in a less restrained round of applause and Paterson began to look agitated once more. The table-rapping was interrupted, not by the NBC director this time, but by the sudden wailing of sirens emanating from the i-comms of everyone in the room. Given that all air raids were conducted at night, the alarm could only be the work of the criminals whose arrest the Modsec Director had so confidently predicted. The irony was lost on no-one. Hartmann, both embarrassed at the particularly unfortunate nature of the disruption and eager to tear a strip off her second-in-command, left the room abruptly and without a word. The alarm stopped and the uninvited statement scrolled across i-comm displays and the LED touchscreen immediately behind the Secretary of State for Transport.

'We have an obligation to fight for the world as it should be. Michelle Obama.'

Paterson was on the brink of interrupting the take, when she caught Lieutenant Commander York's eye and noted the cautionary expression on her face.

'Well, that's something I can actually agree with,' declared Henderton, trying to make light of the disruption. 'We'll cut that out later, I'm sure.'

Both York and Paterson nodded, although one more comfortably than the other.

The Prime Minister proceeded smartly to the final point on the agenda, impatient to get his teeth into the question of accelerating the pace of national reconstruction. The seemingly innocuous agenda item had been approved two weeks previously by the Joint Forces Command and had aroused absolutely no cause for concern at the time. When York had briefed Batista during the morning's journey from Brize Norton to London, she had been expecting no more than a mundane proposal from Henderton for the RAF to target a few more semi-derelict factories, perhaps in regions where the NUP felt it had not yet established itself to the extent that it might have wished.

The PM led with the assertion that the Party's readiness to execute radical policies had largely saved the country from anarchy and idleness, but that the nation now needed something more if the NUP was to galvanise the support of the doubters, the malingerers and the lost. This was met with the standard non-verbal expressions of approval around the table and restrained but audible words of encouragement on the part of Richard Moon, the Secretary of State for Justice.

The Cabinet members were anticipating, as were York and Batista, that Henderton would do no more than suggest that 161 Squadron should fly more missions and deliver more opportunities for redevelopment. When he proposed that the RAF should step up not just the number but the ferocity of their operations, a couple of backsides began to shuffle on their seats. Behind the cameras, York and Batista exchanged a look of considerable concern. The bull, it seemed, was entering the china shop.

'What do you mean by *ferocity*?' asked Moon, patently on edge.

'I think we all understand the word ferocity,' retorted Henderton. 'Not just more missions, but more firepower, more jeopardy, more crash, bang, wallop.'

'Yes, yes. But to what end?' asked Denis Oakfield, Secretary of State for Employment. 'How will ferocity accelerate reconstruction?'

'My thoughts entirely,' added Lieutenant Commander York. Officially designated as an observer, York was not, in theory, supposed to contribute to discussions unless invited by the Chair.

'Think of our history,' said Henderton, becoming increasingly animated and returning to his habit of knocking the table with his knuckles to emphasise key words. 'Think of the Blitz. Hitler, that over-mighty, brain-dead corporal, thought the Blitz would demoralise this country. He thought the workers would flee, lay down their tools and flee the city. But did that happen? Did the workers flee? The harder the Luftwaffe bombed, the harder the British worked. And it was we, not Hitler, who were the victors. I tell you, in the Imperial War Museum, you can read the diaries and letters of ordinary Londoners in which they are exhilarated by the bombing. Exhilarated. That's what we want. We want a modern Blitz.'

Health Minister Caitlin Bonner felt compelled to speak. 'Prime Minister, let's not forget that thousands died in the Blitz. Surely you're not suggesting-'

'Yes, indeed,' he snapped. 'Death is a fact of war. Thousands did, indeed, die. But did that dent our morale? Not for one second. It steeled our resolve. It made us what we are. And victory was all the sweeter for it. What I'm saying is that we now have to question whether the Mortality Protocol is any longer relevant to our needs.'

Henderton had completely overstepped the mark.

'Cut,' said York. 'This item is not on the agenda.'

'Well, I've just put it on the agenda,' said the Prime Minister, clearly unhappy to be interrupted.

York remained calm. 'I think everyone present is fully aware that all agenda items have to be cleared in advance by Joint Command. This topic has not been sanctioned for discussion.'

'Well, perhaps that is a situation that will not pertain for much longer. Perhaps you might like to remind the Joint Forces Command that, according to the constitution of this country, Parliament is sovereign.'

'I might. However, if I were to do so, the Joint Forces Command might draw the Prime Minister's attention to the fact that Parliament has been prorogued since this government acceded to power.'

'The prerogative of the Prime Minister,' said Henderton, dismissively.

The prorogation of Parliament was, in principle, the prerogative of the King, but York had no desire to debate the constitution. Neither Joint Command nor the NUP were on safe ground trying to cite constitutional precedent for their actions in recent years. She opted to remind Henderton of the realities.

'The Joint Forces Command might also point out, Prime Minister, that the NUP would not be in the elevated position it currently enjoys, were it not for the political and military support of His Majesty's Armed Forces. This meeting is closed.'

'What? Closed-closed? Finito?' asked Paterson.

'Finito,' said York categorically. 'No more meeting. No more recording.'

'And another thing,' said Henderton, directing his inimical glare directly at York. 'If the Joint Command can't do what I'm asking, I have plenty of friends who can.'

'I think we need to bring this session to a close, Prime Minister,' said Lieutenant Commander York, refusing to be drawn.

York and Batista gathered their things and left with no more than a cursory valediction. When the muscular, olive-green Gurkha armoured patrol vehicle pulled up outside the front door of 10 Downing Street, the pair climbed in through the rear hatch and briskly strapped themselves in.

'Brize Norton, ma'am?' asked the driver.

'No,' said Lieutenant Commander York. 'Change of plan. Joint Forces Command, Northwood Headquarters. And don't hang about.'

'Ma'am.'

'Radio ahead,' said Lieutenant Batista. 'Let them know we're coming.'

The Gurkha APV turned left out of Downing Street, proceeded north along Whitehall and exited the Westminster Security Zone. The armed Modsec officer at the door of Number Ten promptly reported the departure of York and Batista to a colleague in the Cabinet Room, who swiftly gave the nod to the Prime Minister. Henderton, having regained a degree of composure, called the cabinet to order.

'Ladies and Gentlemen, we shall reconvene in the Montgomery Room in the MOD in one hour. How many of you have not yet had the pleasure of using the tunnel?'

The Prime Minister allowed the room to clear, then sat back and considered the obstacles that still lay in his path. A more definitive conflict was looming than his spat with the liaison officers and Henderton was proud that his aptitude for pugnacity had done nothing but serve him well throughout his life. He had not become Captain of the First XI, divorced his wife, or streamlined the NUP without bellicosity and he had not the slightest intention of ducking a challenge now. Just as it was instinct, rather than considered belief, that fed his burgeoning desire for a more spectacular and visceral rendition of the war, every fibre in his being was now telling him to eliminate those who stood in his way.

11 PARTY BUSINESS

London, 26th April

In the slightly dank tunnel linking 10 Downing Street and the Ministry of Defence, Denis Oakfield and Richard Moon encountered Dame Abigail Hartmann, hurrying in the opposite direction.

'You want the Montgomery Room,' she said sharply as she approached. 'Just ask Security to point you in the right direction. You can't miss it.'

'You were right about York,' said the PM to Hartmann, the moment she re-entered the Cabinet Room. 'She vetoed the discussion and closed the meeting.'

'Did she, indeed? Well, there's more than one way to skin a cat. I think Joint Forces Command are, if I may venture an opinion, living on borrowed time.'

'Indeed,' said Henderton. 'The JFC can either get with the program, as our American friends used to say, or face the consequences. The time has come, I think, to be bloody, bold and resolute.'

'Have you spoken to your man at Lakenheath?'

'Next on my to-do list.'

Henderton activated his i-comm and from his contacts selected the highest-ranking NUP member in the RAF, namely Wing Commander Wakeman. Within seconds, the somewhat puzzled features of the PM's former school friend appeared on the large 2D display on the wall of the Cabinet Room. Wakeman was in his office.

'Jonnie,' began Henderton in an upbeat manner. 'Do you have company?'

'No, Prime Minister.'

'Good. Listen. We need to talk. Party business.'

'Understood. How can I be of service?'

'Well, Jonnie, before I get into detail, I would like to ensure that you understand the need for absolute loyalty within the Party if we are to secure the future of our nation. Can I count on your loyalty, Wing Commander Wakeman?'

There was a momentary hesitation before Wakeman replied.

'Of course, Prime Minister.'

Hartmann furrowed her brow. She wondered whether Wakeman had simply been surprised to have his fidelity called into question or had been bolstering himself to say what he knew he must.

'Excellent,' said Henderton.

'Is there anything else?' asked Wakeman, certain that there had to be.

'Listen. 161 Squadron has done a first-rate job so far. All down to you, Jonnie. All down to you. Now, with regard to the future, you will continue to receive orders regarding operations and targeting from RAF Command, but there will be additional missions communicated to you directly by the MOD. These missions may require, shall we say, modifications to existing protocols if the orders are to be executed in full. Will that present a problem?'

'Sir, the execution of orders is fundamental to the efficient functioning of any military force. I have executed every order

I have ever been given, going right back to our time together in the Combined Cadet Force. Similarly, I demand nothing less than the same response from those under my command. So, no, sir, it will not present a problem.'

'Excellent. Good to talk, Jonnie. Good to talk. Thank you. That will be all.'

The Prime Minister ended the call abruptly and redirected his attention to Hartmann.

'He's good. I think we can proceed,' said Henderton assuredly.

'But we want to be certain,' cautioned Hartmann. 'So far, Wing Commander Wakeman has found it unproblematic to serve two masters whilst they share a common purpose. We have yet to see where his true affiliations lie.'

'He is completely dedicated to the cause, I believe. Anyway, we were pals at Harrow. I think I have his loyalty.'

'Perhaps. But in my experience, loyalties can waver. To be absolutely certain of his commitment, we should put his testicles in a vice, and keep them there.'

12 CLEMENCY AND COSY CHATS

Seven harrowing days had passed since Wing Commander Wakeman set Chief Technician MacDermott the task of identifying the data anomaly which was the product of his fundamentally harmless but nonetheless illicit communications with his sister. Whilst trying to behave as though he had not gone almost an entire night without sleep, MacDermott had spent part of the day tuning anti-g suits and checking the results with the Squadron. His regular duties fulfilled, he steeled himself to face the meeting with Wing Commander Wakeman. Although the Chief Technician's collection of antique communication devices in no way constituted any kind of genuine security risk, he had no intention of blurting out the truth and throwing himself on Wakeman's mercy. The Wing Commander had not built his reputation on clemency and cosy chats.

MacDermott's attempts to figure out how he could placate the Station Commander without incriminating himself were undermined by the unremitting and nauseous feeling in the pit of his stomach. As he made his way along the corridor towards Wakeman's office, he caught himself wondering how the condemned felt as they walked to the gallows. Suddenly shocked at the power of his spiralling imagination to overwhelm his capacity for rational thought, the Chief instructed himself to snap out of the mawkish self-pity. He needed to focus on the problem in hand.

As MacDermott stood outside the door to the office occupied by Wakeman's PA, he was only completely sure of one thing: he was going to lie to his commanding officer. What remained to be seen was which lie he was going to tell.

Wing Commander Wakeman granted the Chief Technician permission to enter his office and asked him to close the door. He did not invite him to sit.

'Well?' said Wakeman.

It had been exactly a week and he was trusting that MacDermott would have devoted his extensive cybersecurity skills so effectively to the task of identifying the source of the leak that an arrest could now be made, loose ends could be tidied up and Wakeman could report his success to Air Command.

'Well, sir,' began MacDermott, attempting the faintest of smiles. 'Before we can know for sure that the anomaly we found does indeed amount to a communications breach, we have to eliminate from our enquiries all extraneous factors that may conceivably account for the alert.'

'So you have not identified the perpetrator.'

MacDermott could feel the faintest of tremors in his left eyelid.

'No, sir. At least, not yet. But as I said, sir, we have to rule out-'

'Yes, I heard you the first time. I instructed you to identify the perpetrator and time is very much of the essence. This is a matter of the utmost urgency. I'm telling you, this is very much on you, MacDermott, if you fail to come through on this. Delays in apprehending the subversive will be laid very much at your door. For crying out loud, you should have informed me of this anomaly the moment you received the report.'

Having once seen his father bellow furiously at their terrier for devouring an entire birthday cake when the true culprits had been MacDermott and his sister, the Chief Technician knew only too well how easily the cowed body language of a frightened dog could be interpreted by its owner as a sign of guilt. In the face of Wakeman's remonstrations, MacDermott made a conscious effort to appear relaxed but not unconcerned and knew he must somehow steer the conversation away from his failure to divulge the system-generated alert. The Chief Technician gambled and treated the Wing Commander to one of his own management mantras.

'To be honest, sir, I realised the data discrepancy was a bit, well, odd, even though it was, in absolute terms, very small. I apologise if my actions were presumptuous but, if truth be told, I was hoping to investigate the matter on my own account and to present you with a solution rather than a problem.'

The line struck a chord with Wakeman who intended to adopt exactly the same approach if ever he had to explain the leak to his own commanding officers. The Wing Commander paused. Was he being played? Was MacDermott that smart? Or that bold? Wakeman's tone softened slightly.

'So, what's taking so long?'

'Well, sir, as you know, we send signals in the form of microwaves. So, we have to be able to discount other sources of microwaves as the source of the discrepancy.'

'And they might be what?'

'Well. One possible source might be, for example, a signal from an i-comm in a passing car. Another might be the diffused edge of a distant radar signal, reflected back off one of our hangars and retransmitted by our mast. It might be a defective microwave oven in a kitchen, although I think that's a bit of a long shot, or it could even be the cosmic microwave background.'

'Let's just come back to the passing car idea. OK. That's not beyond the bounds of possibility, is it? Fair enough. Look into that. Check all perimeter security footage at the exact time of the anomalies. See if you can rule your passing car theory either in or out.'

'It's more of a hypothesis than a theory.'

'Is there a difference? No, don't answer that. I don't want to know. So, MacDermott. Check the perimeter footage and report to me. You never know.'

'Sir.'

'But in the meantime, do not let these theories distract you from the task I have set you. Run your checks. Drill down into our systems. Do not confide in anyone. Fix the problem, MacDermott. Fix the problem.'

As MacDermott left the Wing Commander's office, the nausea in the pit of his stomach was still there, but already felt more bearable. He knew that he had dodged a bullet, at least for the time being. He would sleep tonight. Eventually.

13 MINIMUM FUEL

RAF Lakenheath, 2nd May

At 0020 hours, Flying Officer Gunatillaka was tracking the progress of Flight Lieutenant Warszawski, the only member of 161 Squadron in the air. Xu and Finnan were in the Aircrew Ready Room on Quick Reaction Alert and everyone else had the night off. Warszawski had cleared the target area to the north of Cardiff and was already playing 'Stairway to Heaven' at a healthy volume.

The station ID illuminated on Warszawski's head-up display as the Ops Manager muted the song. It was frustrating, but he knew she was only doing her job.

Gunatillaka was a paragon of brevity. '161-whiskey-alpha, this is Lakenheath Ground. Report status.'

'Hey, Gunnie. Surprised you kicked off with "whiskey" there. I thought you were more of a gin kinda girl.'

Gunatillaka knew that she had virtually no chance of getting a straight answer out of Warszawski first time round and took his response in her stride.

'Hilarious, Warszawski. Report status.'

'Roger, Gunnie. Flying zero-eight-zero. Altitude one-five thousand. Operation Saddle Tank executed to plan. No complications.'

It was a surprisingly germane response. Presumably he was keen to get back to the music.

'Roger, Warszawski. Return to station.'

'Roger. Wilco. And just to be clear, by "executed to plan" I mean target acquired, missiles launched, target demolished, zero mortality. Wham bam, thank you, ma'am. So dear lady, please unmute my audio feed. Out.'

Seated in his immaculate office, Wing Commander Wakeman paid scant attention to the conversation between Gunatillaka and Warszawski as he monitored the entirely unremarkable progress of the mission on multiple data screens.

In the Technical Operations and Surveillance Room of The Blade, the fifty-six storey tower in Battersea Park which was the operational home of Modsec, Major Security Officer Legend was streaming the same data displays from the Ops Room at Lakenheath and was watching the progress of Operation Saddle Tank with more than cursory interest. She had been tasked with ratcheting up the ferocity of the Civil Defence units' responses to the night-time intrusions.

A short distance from the twin anti-aircraft cannon atop the roof of the multi-storey car park in Cirencester, two Civil Defence gunners were hunched over the monitors inside the trailer of their recently acquired Pipistrel tracking and guidance system. Mounted on the roof of the trailer, the radar would provide precise data regarding the location, altitude and bearing of any aircraft within fifteen miles. Furthermore, the Pipistrel's fire control system could in principle be used to lock-on to a target and enable the twin AA cannon to fire their tracer rounds automatically, and with clinical precision, across the calculated flightpath of the intruder. Locking-on, however, was massively risky as it also betrayed the location of the radar to the enemy and invited the immediate launch of a guided air-to-surface missile. The Cirencester Civil Defence unit was therefore under strict orders to track but not to lock-on.

Oblivious to the rattle of the diesel generator outside the trailer, the gunners waited in restless silence for their order to engage. They were both palpably on edge, intent on doing some real damage to the enemy but nervous about using the new equipment for the first time. Since the start of the war, the conscripts of the Cirencester Civil Defence had been given precisely two opportunities to fire their anti-aircraft cannon and in both cases they had done little more than aim randomly into the unfathomable black of the nocturnal sky. Never before had they been furnished with intel regarding the imminent overflight of an enemy aircraft and never before had they been able to make use of radar.

In the Tech Room at Lakenheath, MacDermott, tired but not yet ready to sleep, was rummaging in the cashbox inside the arcade games cabinet for the dollar he needed to be able to play *Space Invaders*. The coin located, he turned his attention to one of the antique smartphones he had squirrelled away inside the machine. He booted it up and checked his in-box. He had a new message from his sister.

'I'm gd tks. HB2U. xxx'.

The Chief Technician immediately shut down the phone and replaced the handset in the cashbox. The less time he spent on it the better. He took care to fully close the security plate and pushed the cabinet back against the wall. MacDermott then stood at the machine, inserted his dollar and repelled yet another alien assault. The extraterrestrial threat averted, the Chief Technician walked slowly to his quarters and went directly to bed. For the first time in a week, sleep claimed him within minutes.

Half of 161 Squadron's aircrew were hanging out in the Officers' Mess, waiting for Warszawski to return from his mission and stand them all a beer. Dibaba was strumming the chords to 'All Right Now' on the white Gibson SG Special, discovered by Flight Lieutenant Merton in a cupboard in Block D. Bosko was singing the lyrics with characteristic gusto whilst deploying a pair of kitchen scissors to trim the fringe of Callaghan's wavy brown hair. From an aesthetic point of view, the procedure would not end well. Merton, in spite of the guitar and the singing, had fallen asleep in an armchair, an unfinished bowl of Utility cornflakes abandoned on the coffee table to his left. Lounging on the sofa, Lopez was gently stroking the head of the black Labrador he had found sniffing around the bins the previous afternoon. Itoje and Becker had sloped off to bed, although not with each other on this occasion. On the permanently silent TV screen on the wall, the NBC was showing a selection of 161 Squadron's most recent demolition jobs followed by clips of the Prime Minister enthusiastically shaking the hands of grateful recruits to the ever-expanding work brigades.

In the Aircrew Ready Room, Flight Lieutenants Xu and Finnan were killing time until Warszawski's return, which would only be a matter of minutes, twenty at most.

Still at her desk in Modsec Central Office, Major Security Officer Legend noted that the F-95 was now within range of the radar in Cirencester and transmitted a single order to the commander of the Civil Defence unit, who in turn relayed it to the anti-aircraft battery on the roof of the Waterloo Car Park.

'Engage.'

Pushing the F-95 to Mach 1, Warszawski did not register the spray of tracer fire and the flashing fuel gauge was the first he knew that something was amiss. A single round from the 35mm anti-aircraft cannon had hit the underside of the Lightning's left wing. The shell had failed to penetrate the aircraft's graphene-composite skin but the energy of the impact had been transferred to a sensor, causing it to malfunction and to instruct the aircraft to begin dumping fuel. Warszawski repeatedly tried, and repeatedly failed, to close the valves jettisoning the cocktail of hydrocarbons from the tanks. The head-up display informed him that he had a range of 246 nautical miles and RAF Lakenheath was currently 144 nautical miles, but he was only too aware that the surplus could rapidly become a deficit, depending on the rate of fuel loss. As the gauge continued to flash, Warszawski throttled back the F-95 and switched his transponder code to 7700, indicating 'Emergency'. If his comms went down, Lakenheath would have only that as an indication of his status.

No sooner had Gunatillaka seen the squawk code, than she heard Warszawski's voice once more, this time devoid of its usual levity. The pilot was calm, but focussed, and there was an unfamiliar urgency in his tone.

'Mayday. Mayday. Mayday. Lakenheath Ground. This is 161-whiskey-alpha. Loss of fuel. Fuel remaining currently fifteen minutes. Assume minimum fuel on approach. Altitude one-five thousand. Heading zero-eight-zero.'

'Roger,' said Gunatillaka. 'Maintain altitude and heading. Acknowledge.'

'Maintain altitude one-five thousand and heading zero-eight-zero. Wilco.'

For the first time since she rejoined the RAF, Gunatillaka triggered a Quick Reaction Alert alarm. Once the signal regularly used to scramble fast jets from Lossiemouth or Coningsby to intercept Russian aircraft probing the margins of UK airspace, the QRA alarm had only one current function: to get someone into the sky as quickly as possible in order to give visual feedback to the pilot of the stricken aircraft and to the Operations Manager on station.

In the bar, the QRA alarm sounded from every pilot's i-comm causing the dog to howl in response. Needing no elucidation as to the significance of the signal, Warszawski's comrades dropped everything and rushed the two hundred metres to the Ops Room. Left alone, the dog finished off the remains of Merton's cornflakes.

Within eleven minutes of hearing the alarm, Flight Lieutenant Xu had scrambled, had created an almighty sonic boom over Newmarket, and was flying alongside Warszawski. From the ground, the F-95s were effectively invisible, but from the side, Xu could make out her comrade in the subdued light of his cockpit. She could see nothing else and that was a good thing; the Lightning was not emitting flame. She reported this to Warszawski and Gunatillaka, and the two pilots then exchanged a thumbs-up. Less than sixty seconds later the pair were joined by Finnan who took up position to the other side of Warszawski's F-95 and confirmed Xu's initial assessment.

The plan was now automatic. They would escort Warszawski

back to Lakenheath, closely monitoring his damaged aircraft for any changes; they would pull away as he made his final approach; and they would join him later in the bar.

'Minimum fuel,' said Warszawski, still almost two minutes from the base. It was going to be close.

'Roger, Warszawski. Approach heading zero-six-zero. Descend to one thousand. Acknowledge.'

'Descend to one thousand. Wilco.'

Warszawski lowered his landing gear. As he descended and lined up the F-95 with the runway, Xu and Finnan confirmed the landing lights on the aircraft's undercarriage were illuminated and the gear was down, then peeled away on either side and climbed to two thousand feet. Their job was done.

'See you later, guys,' said Warszawski. 'Beers are on me.'

'Roger, Stairway. Approved,' said Xu.

At four hundred feet, the cockpit of Warszawski's Lightning was suddenly plunged into total darkness and the controls ceased to respond. The F-95 began to bank and roll and Warszawski had only one possible course of action. He leaned forward, reached down and pulled the two levers positioned on either side of his seat. Instantly, explosive charges blasted the aircraft canopy clear as rocket boosters launched the entire seat, with Warszawski pressed into it, violently, and nowhere near vertically, out of the jet and into the inscrutable darkness.

Within moments, the pilot felt the seat fall away as the parachute deployed automatically, yanking him backwards and upwards. Instinctively, Warszawski glanced up to inspect the chute, then down to get a fix on the ground, but the darkness was impenetrable. He had ejected at a ridiculously low altitude and knew he should prepare for a hard landing. Ahead of him, an eruption of fire and thunder indicated where the jet had crashed, igniting what remained of the kerosene and naphtha in the fuel tanks. He was near enough to feel the shockwave from the blast and to see for a split second that he was way closer to the ground than he had imagined. Warszawski had no desire to break his legs and he did exactly what he'd been trained to do. He tucked his feet together, bent his knees, and prepared to roll at the moment of impact. As he raised his hand to pull the mask away from his face, his feet struck solid ground. Automatically, Warszawski collapsed with the momentum, dissipating the force of the heavy contact across the side of his body. He felt the sudden jolt as his helmet cracked against the dirt. Immediately, the wind caught his chute, dragging and bouncing him for several seconds through what felt like the damp earth of some kind of ploughed field. He was rolled onto his chest, friction from the ground ripped the oxygen mask from his helmet, and the line from the survival kit tangled tightly round his ankles. At last, the wind dropped and the disorientated pilot came to a stop. The billowing parachute deflated. The lines slackened and fell lazily to the ground.

Breathless, Warszawski rolled onto his side and unclipped the harness. He decided to allow himself a couple of seconds to catch his breath before untangling his legs, standing up and freeing himself from the chute. Perhaps fewer than thirty seconds had elapsed since he had pulled the ejection levers. Pain was pulsing in his right knee. He was breathing hard and was lying on his side in the dark, trying to push soil from his mouth with his tongue. When Warszawski turned his head, his consciousness seemed to swirl behind in a delayed rush. Would he even be able to stand? As his breathing became more

shallow and his eyelids grew impossibly heavy, the pilot's senses
deserted him and the stars slowly faded to black.

14 TAKE THE WIN

RAF Lakenheath, 2nd May

The Search and Rescue team wasted no time in tracking Warszawski's location beacon and found him in a twenty-acre potato field about a mile and a half to the southwest of the base. Following initial treatment to stabilise his right knee and suture the laceration to the skin, he spent a sedated night in the med bay at Lakenheath under the watchful eye of Dr Kaminski.

By eleven in the morning, the sedatives were beginning to wear off and the pilot was gradually linking his situation to the fragmented memories of his ejection from the F-95. He was wearing only his blue-grey trunks and his RAF T-shirt with the word 'Stairway' scrawled above the squadron insignia. The young medic supporting Dr Kaminski had removed the pilot's i-comm and the silver cross and chain from around his neck, had relocated both items to the control room and had checked him thoroughly for piercings. Although Warszawski was conscious, he was still far from completely alert and continued to stare blankly at the ceiling tiles.

Corporal Forest Jagala, the medic, had black hair parted in the centre and tied back in a tight bun. She had green eyes, almost invisible eyebrows, strong cheekbones and an honest and engaging smile. Her working uniform consisted solely of bottle-green scrubs and a pair of white trainers. Jagala's task was simply to prep the patient for a complete body scan, but her curiosity had got the better of her.

'Why did you write "Stairway" on your shirt?' she asked.

In response, Warszawski slurred the opening lines from the Led Zeppelin song that had inspired his call sign. The medic picked out something about a lady who wanted to buy a stairway to Heaven and somehow had the power to realise her deepest desires with a single word.

'Is that poetry?' said Jagala. 'Did you write that? I like it. It's kinda cool.'

'Your stairway lies on the whispering wind,' mumbled the pilot.

A voice cut in on the comm from the control room. It was Kaminski. 'That's the medication talking.'

'Oh, cheers, ma'am,' said Jagala. 'For a minute there, I thought I'd pulled.'

Jagala placed her hand on the sedated pilot's shoulder and asked him to relax and remain still. The irony was lost on Warszawski, but not on Dr Kaminski, who flashed her a smile from the control room. As soon as the conveyer began to transport the pilot head first into the humming, diagnostic scanner, Jagala joined Dr Kaminski in the control room.

The station's Medical Officer was studying a multicoloured, multi-layered computer model of the supine airman. Each coloured layer in the avatar represented a different aspect of the patient's physiology, such as the respiratory, nervous or immune system, and could be studied discretely or in combination with any other 3D data-set. An AI was already creating both specific diagnoses and a holistic assessment and would rapidly proceed to prognostics. Using a joystick, Dr Kaminski was able to direct the avatar on the screen to sit up, walk, run, and importantly, climb into a virtual F-95 cockpit and be subjected to a simulation of the g-forces that the pilots typically experienced during flight. Throughout this second phase, the AI continued to analyse the patient's physiology and diagnose any issues. Whilst the scanner could provide nanometre-accurate metrics for every bone, muscle and organ in Warszawski's body, the resulting avatar was shorn of the pilot's tousled rust-brown hair, possessed generic facial features and betrayed not the slightest hint of personality.

'Done one of these before?' asked Kaminski.

'Scans?' said Jagala, slightly bewildered. 'Yeah, plenty.'

'No. I know you've done scans before. Have you done a scan on one of these pilots before? One of the survivors?'

'You mean V-Survivors?'

'Yeah.'

The term 'V-Survivor' referred to the several thousand Sleeper victims, mostly military personnel, whose lives had been saved through the administration of an untested, anti-retroviral drug. In the early days of the final and most deadly wave of sickness, a group of Cambridge Pharma PhD students armed with a powerful AI platform had taken no more than the first, tentative steps to hijack the Sleeper virus and re-engineer the virulent disease into a powerful defence against submicroscopic infection. The Genetically Modified Sleeper Virus therapy, or GMSV for short, had been designed to potentiate the human body's immune and repair responses, but at that juncture was no more than an untested prototype. Given that over 90 percent of Sleeper patients were dying within a fortnight of infection, there had been no shortage of volunteers for the first impromptu trials.

'It's an amazing therapy,' said Kaminski. 'The reconfigured virus not only removes the Sleeper cells, no pun intended, but remains in the system, triggering T-cells to search out and destroy pathogens, and stimulating stem cells to effect repairs to damaged bone, tissue or organs. AI-designed and never properly trialled. Honestly, it's astonishing.'

'Sounds like you're out of a job, ma'am.'

'Pretty much. Have you ever wondered how the Squadron can party so hard and never get hangovers?'

'Makes sense.'

'Look at the knee,' said Kaminski, drawing Jagala's attention back to the avatar in the display. 'His system is in overdrive.'

In the process of ejecting, Warszawski had fractured his right patella and torn the meniscus beneath the kneecap. To illustrate her point, Kaminski reduced the image of the avatar to the single blue data-layer representing GMSV. It was particularly intense at the site of the injuries.

'You can actually see the repair in process,' said Kaminski. 'The laceration to the skin on his knee is already gone. If we want, we can use the scanner's magnetic resonance to focus the activity even more on a particular area, but I've rarely needed to do that. The GMSV generally seems to do pretty well on its own.'

'Shit,' said Jagala. 'You really are out of a job, ma'am.'

'Fun fact,' said Kaminski. 'The GMSV makes their blood look slightly different. It creates a strangely translucent... Do I mean translucent? No, not translucent. It lends an almost iridescent quality to the red blood cells. It's like they bleed sci-fi blood.'

'Now that's seriously creepy, ma'am. I might be going off him.'

'Maybe I'm overstating. He's still human. Just with a bit extra.'

'I guess he'd be good on a Friday night, then.'

'Well, I have two things to say to that, Jagala. One, what our patient may or may not be like on a Friday night is not an appropriate topic for a professional conversation. And two, it's not my field of expertise in any case.'

Jagala adopted a different tack. 'And the effects are permanent? Can I get some?'

'Not necessarily permanent,' said Kaminski, 'The modified virus will mutate eventually. It's just a question of when and how. Best case scenario, they die of old age first. Worst case scenario, Wakeman loses his entire Squadron with no warning in the space of a fortnight.'

'Shit. Does he know that?'

'Warszawski or Wakeman?'

'Warszawski.'

'Absolutely not. None of the survivors have been alerted to the possibility of complications and to my mind, it's better it stays that way. Without GMSV, they'd all have died years ago. Let them take the win, I say.'

'And what about Wakeman?'

'It's not something the Wing Commander and I have ever discussed.'

'Uh-oh. Speak of the devil.'

Wing Commander Wakeman and a civilian guest had appeared at the observation window on the far side of the medical bay. From the animated gestures Wakeman was making, he seemed to be explaining something in considerable detail. Kaminski contacted him via i-comm.

'The door to the med bay is locked, sir. If you want to take a look at the scans with us, you'll need to go round, not through.'

Wakeman joined Kaminski and Jagala in the control room and introduced his guest as Stella Paterson from the NBC.

'Stella is here to script the report on Warszawski's dogfight with an enemy aircraft,' he explained.

'It's more storyboarding really,' said Paterson. 'I don't really do scripts.'

The distinction was as much lost on the two medics as it was on Wakeman. Dr Kaminski politely explained to the visitor how the scanner worked and demonstrated how the avatar could be put through various physical activities whilst the AI extrapolated bio-medical outcomes. Concocting a subtle blend of information and obfuscation, the station's Senior Medical Officer described the function of the avatar's blue data-layer merely as 'immune response monitoring'. The NBC guest was impressed.

'So what is the scanner telling you?' asked Paterson. 'Overall?'

'It's telling us that Flight Lieutenant Warszawski is going to make a full and speedy recovery,' said Kaminski.

'That's excellent news,' said Paterson. 'I love the avatar. Can you make it do a handstand?'

'I could,' said Kaminski, 'if there were a legitimate medical reason. But there isn't.'

'Show our guest anyway,' said Wakeman.

Later, as the Wing Commander escorted the enthralled Stella Paterson from the medical bay, Dr Kaminski wondered to what extent he was aware of the questions surrounding the longevity of V-Survivors and decided that she needed to have a private conversation with Wakeman at the earliest opportunity.

The Doctor's i-comm pinged. 'Another request for an update from Dibaba,' she said. 'That's the third since we brought him in.'

'Hell, ma'am,' said Jagala, with a glint in her eye. 'Looks like I've got competition.'

After a late lunch, Dr Kaminski trekked across the base to Block A and made her way directly to the Wing Commander's office. Expecting Kaminski's appearance to herald some revelation about the incriminating behaviour of a member of the ground crew or perhaps even one of the pilots, her enquiry about his understanding of the effects of GMSV initially disappointed him. Once the Medical Officer outlined the possibility of the eventual and potentially cataclysmic mutations to the virus-based therapy, the realisation that he could lose the entire Squadron came like a bolt from the blue.

'How quickly?' he asked. 'When might this happen?'

'Hard to say,' said Kaminski. 'Maybe next month. Maybe in a year. Maybe never. All viruses mutate. Sometimes significantly. Sometimes not. And it may not happen to all of them.'

'Do you have any contacts with the people that made the drug?'

'Cambridge Pharma? No. I'm not sure they even exist anymore.'

The flabbergasted Wing Commander thanked Kaminski for raising the matter, dismissed her and immediately contacted Air Command, who seemed to know even less than Wakeman about the long-term stability of GMSV. Less than an hour after getting absolutely nowhere with his enquiry, Wakeman decided to reach out to a contact with serious clout: his old school friend, Gilbert Lathum Henderton.

As a survivor of the virus and one of the last people to have been treated with GMSV, the Prime Minister read Wakeman's message not merely with surprise but with considerable alarm and called immediately for Priority One investigations to be conducted by both the Department of Health and the Ministry of Defence. In his reply to the Wing Commander, Henderton thanked him for drawing the matter directly to his attention and promised to get back to him just as soon as he knew more. After all, without 161 Squadron, the entire strategy for rebuilding the country would be compromised. There would be no war, and without war, there could be no deliverance. Yet, as important as the Prime Minister considered the final victory to be, he had been blindsided by the idea that he might conceivably not be around to celebrate it or to take the enormous credit he deserved.

15 THE GREATER PART OF VALOUR

Liverpool, 5th May

At close to two o'clock in the morning, Martina MacDermott was crouched, wrench in hand, on the roof of a rusting outside broadcast van in a scrapyard not far from the River Mersey. The unseasoned thief had been struggling to loosen the bolts securing the satellite dish to the roof of the vehicle and was beginning to tire. Suddenly, Martina froze and listened intently for any repetition of the dull metallic thud that had punctuated the silence of the yard. If discovered, she would struggle to come up with an explanation that would stand up to any form of official investigation.

Martina closed her mouth and tried to breathe steadily and quietly as she listened and waited. Slowly, she turned her head in the direction of what had sounded perhaps like a car door closing. She heard no footsteps, perceived no voices and registered no further unsettling sounds. Significantly, there were no signs of torchlight. Martina lifted her right hand to her temple, rotated the definition button of her night-vision visor to max and carefully scanned the yard. Though pitifully below the quality of military grade goggles, the visor was still good enough to enable her to pick out moving human forms amongst the heaps of static, rusting vehicles. She saw no-one.

Perhaps the noise had been nothing more than a feral cat or a prowling fox. Whatever the case, she was spooked.

Martina had spent forty minutes trying to slacken each of the six steel bolts that secured the satellite dish to the roof of the ageing van. Demonstrating an almost wilful inertia, the bolts simply refused to yield. The plan had only ever been to reconnoitre the scrapyard and, if the opportunity arose, to check out the dish and maybe loosen the retaining bolts to allow speedy removal at a later date. Tired and growing increasingly frustrated, the young trespasser decided that she had done as much as she could for one night and that, at least on this occasion, discretion was the greater part of valour. After waiting perhaps ten minutes without any further suggestion of company, she wrapped the wrench in an old T-shirt and placed it carefully into her rucksack. Taking care not to snag her jacket, Martina slid cautiously down the windscreen and the hood of the redundant vehicle. With her feet back on the oily ground, she crouched down, scanned the yard with her visor and listened for perhaps sixty seconds. Confident, but by no means certain, that she had not been observed, Martina opted for the darker of her two pre-established exit routes. With the visor still at maximum resolution, she slipped quietly to the perimeter fence, located the patch of wire that she had cut through an hour earlier and pushed the severed sections far enough apart to squeeze through. As her head emerged, she dragged the side of her neck along one of the lengths of rough-cut wire and felt both the sharpness of the scratch and the wetness of the blood that it had drawn.

The supply of electricity to the city's street lamps had long been disconnected. Nevertheless, Martina was keen to preserve the batteries in her night-vision googles and dialled the resolution down. Taking care not to rush, she retraced her steps to the Mersey, hugging the walls and the buildings and stopping regularly to scan behind her and listen for footsteps. At the river, she turned left and walked the mile or so along the unlit path beside the flood wall to the premises of a once-thriving Chinese restaurant. Her white Phaedron van was still the only vehicle in the car-park. She climbed in the back, closed the door quietly, lay down on the old floral-print sofa cushions and was soon soundly asleep.

By six thirty, the sun was up and Martina was already awake. She had not slept for as long as she would have liked, but it was the third day of the current heatwave and she was uncomfortably warm inside the poorly ventilated van. Somewhat to Martina's surprise, her i-comm pinged. It was a message from Freya who was clearly aware that she had been out all night.

'You OK? Or did you get lucky? x'

The reply was deliberately vague but reassuring.

It was already way too stuffy in the van and Martina needed fresh air and a bathroom break. She wound down the windows slightly on either side of the cabin, escaped the overheating Phaedron and walked towards the river. Ahead of her, gentle steps led up to the half-open main door of the defunct Quanjing restaurant and she wondered if the toilets were still serviceable. Peering through the door, there were no signs of recent activity. Although dilapidated, the place didn't smell too musty. Martina walked cautiously along the corridor towards a curved dining area which she could see enjoyed a panoramic view of the slow-moving river. To her left, a wooden door was painted with a large letter F. The toilets, it turned out, were not too shabby and, being devoid of carpet, smelled better than the rest of the building. Her search for a forgotten toilet roll, perhaps lurking in the corner of the cupboard beneath the sinks, revealed a large packet of tampons which she accepted with gratitude. There was no soap, but in one cubicle she found strips of torn up Chinese newspaper to wipe her backside with and, to her surprise, the toilet flushed. That was a result in anyone's book.

When Martina walked through the back door of the house in Troutbeck Park Gardens some twenty minutes later, Kireina was munching her way through a bowl of cereal and Kevin was sitting in what he now referred to as the 'Batcave-slash-Ops-Room' and was already busily formulating code. Talira and Ricky were still in bed.

Kireina greeted Martina with a cheerful 'Hey'.

The unsuccessful and sleep-deprived tech thief responded with an identical greeting and going straight to the sink to wash her hands, declared 'You will not believe the night I've just had.'

'Well, whatever your night was like, Martina,' shouted Kevin from the lounge, 'you might want to save the anecdotes for later. I think we've got visitors.'

Months ago, Martina had installed a small security camera onto the burglar alarm mounted on the wall of the first house in the street and had linked it to number twenty-three with four fifty-metre lengths of fibre-optic cable spanning every back garden between. The activists had seen police vehicles pass the end of the close often enough, but this was the first time one had pulled into the road and had stopped.

'Shit. I think I may have been followed,' said Martina.

Kevin got up, walked swiftly to the fuse box by the front door and cut the power to the house. The security camera would function on its back-up batteries for maybe an hour.

'Everyone to the bunker,' he said.

Kireina ran up the stairs and hammered on Talira and Ricky's bedroom door. It sounded quiet in there and she hoped they were not doing anything they couldn't stop in a hurry.

'Bunker,' shouted Kireina. 'We've got company.'

She hurried through to the bedroom at the back of the house. To the right was a large fitted wardrobe running almost the full length of the wall. Kireina slid the mirrored, central door to the right to reveal a row of coats on hangers. She pushed some of the clothing to one side and then slid the panel at the back of the wardrobe to the left to expose a painted, wooden door behind. With the door opened, she quickly passed through the wardrobe into the small en-suite bathroom it concealed and was swiftly followed by Martina. Moments later, Talira and Ricky arrived, both wearing ill-fitting pyjamas. Finally, Kevin squeezed through, carrying a shoebox full of old external hard drives. He dragged the front door of the wardrobe back into position, pulled the coats together, slid the back of the wardrobe into place and closed the bathroom door gently behind him.

'It may be nothing,' he whispered, 'but we need to keep it quiet.'

He left it at that. Nobody spoke.

The translucent glass window had not been blacked out, so the five hackers could all see each other easily enough. To avoid being observed from the garden, they squatted in a tight circle on the floor. After a few moments, Kevin slipped his arm around Kireina's waist and rested the palm of his hand on her side. With all four fingers, he gave an affectionate squeeze to her tightening stomach muscles, then stroked the edge of her ribcage reassuringly with the side of his thumb. Kireina relaxed slightly and rested her head on his shoulder. Responding to another squeeze from Kevin, the young artist smiled and gently took hold of his free hand. As the taut, unsettled silence persisted, Martina looked up at the window, replayed the events of the night and tried to deal with the nagging thought that in spite of all her precautions, she had somehow brought the wolf to the door.

The bunker was kitted out for a short stay. Five bottles of water stood ready in the shower tray. In the cupboard under the sink, two boxes of Utility digestives would be enough to stave off temporary hunger. There were also two flashlights with fully charged batteries. Unnecessary in the daylight and a total giveaway in the dark, the torches had seemed like a good idea at the time. If anyone needed to use the toilet, the others would have to close their eyes and put their fingers in their ears. Martina was glad she had used the facilities at the restaurant.

An hour passed without a word being exchanged and, more importantly, without hearing any sounds either outside or inside the house.

Kireina was the first to break the silence, but only at a whisper.

'What do you think?'

'Give it another hour,' said Talira, as quietly as she could.

'I'm not sure I can wait another hour,' said Ricky with an obvious grimace. 'I'm going to need to take a dump at some point soon.'

At this juncture, Martina noticed a dark perpendicular shape through the frosted glass of the shower door. She slid the door carefully to one side, to reveal an assault rifle.

'What the fuck is that?' she asked in as serious a whisper as she could muster. 'Fuck. We don't want to be caught with that.'

It had not exactly been the most stress-free twenty-four hours of Martina's young life.

'It's an AK-47,' said Kevin. 'It's at least a hundred years old. I don't think it works. And it's not even loaded. The magazine's completely empty.'

'For Christ's sake, just get rid of it.'

'She's got a point,' whispered Kireina.

An uneasy silence followed. When the conversation finally resumed, it was in the same muted tones as before.

'You've been bleeding,' said Kireina, both concerned for her friend and keen to move on from the AK-47 discussion. 'What the hell have you been doing?'

'Well, there's good news and bad news,' said Martina. 'The good news is that I found what looks like a serviceable satellite dish on an old outside broadcast van at the scrapyard. The bad news is that it'll probably take a pneumatic wrench to get the bolts off, which is out of the question, and the van's completely blocked in, so you can't drive it away.'

'Why don't we just ask if we can buy the dish?' asked Talira. 'Or the van?'

'Too risky,' said Ricky. 'What if they inform the boys in blue?'

The allusion to the police, reminded them of why they were hiding in their own private Narnia in the first place and they fell silent once more. But not for long.

'I could liberate an outside broadcast van when I pay my next visit to the NBC,' suggested Kevin.

'In principle, that's a great idea,' whispered Talira, 'except the NBC don't base their OB units in Salford. At least, they didn't when it was still the BBC. They were all stationed in Milton Keynes or somewhere.'

'Shame,' said Kevin.

There was a ping from Martina's pocket. She took out an antiquated smartphone and checked the message.

'Hey, Sis. Glad ur ok. Gonna b busy for a bit. x'

She replied with a 'thumbs up' emoji and returned the phone to her pocket.

'Brother,' she informed the others.

Ricky farted, and Talira slapped him angrily on the arm.

'I'm sorry, guys,' he said. 'I've really got to take a dump.'

It was quickly agreed that enough time had elapsed for it to be reasonably safe for the group to evacuate the bunker.

Allowing Ricky the privacy he so obviously needed, Kireina, Kevin, Martina and Talira slipped back through the wardrobe, into the bedroom and gingerly made their way downstairs. Kevin flicked on the main power switch and waited by the CCTV monitor. The police van had gone. When he reviewed the footage, he could see that the van had spent less than ten minutes parked at the end of the road whilst the two officers did no more than eat their breakfast. Reflecting on the time they had spent huddled together in the cloistered bathroom, he questioned whether the fitted wardrobe disguising the door to the bunker would have fooled the police officers. It would fool some, he decided, but perhaps not all. He got up from his desk and walked purposefully out of the lounge, intent on retrieving the AK-47 and burying it in the back garden of the house next door. At the top of the stairs, he changed his mind.

Ricky, he remembered, was still in the bathroom. Kevin would have to deal with the antique weapon some other time.

16 A QUESTION OF PROGRAMMING

RAF Lakenheath, 22nd May

Three weeks after Dr Kaminski's unexpected bombshell about the potential instability of the Genetically Modified Sleeper Virus and the questionable longevity of the V-Survivors, Wing Commander Wakeman was still waiting for responses to the issues he had raised with both RAF Air Command and the Prime Minister. He had so far received nothing of use from his own commanders and no further messages from the PM and he was growing more impatient by the day. Whilst he felt that it was not within his gift to pester the Prime Minister, he could nevertheless see a way forward. The solution to his potential problem lay in the eighteen mothballed MQ-25 refuelling drones currently biding their time in Hangars 11 to 20.

The abandoned USAF aircraft had been designed originally as autonomous strike bombers, but in the wake of the fourth global banking crisis, the original Pentagon order for 250 MQ-25s was cancelled by Congress and the existing test aircraft were repurposed as remotely piloted fuel tankers, intended to extend both the range and the shelf-life of carrier-based US Navy jets. Eventually, eighteen unwanted MQ-25s found their way to Lakenheath, ostensibly to provide in-flight refuelling for the F-95s, but they were to all intents and purposes unnecessary and had seen no operational use.

Although the unused drones in the hangars were officially designated as remotely piloted tankers, Wakeman understood their history and could see no serious obstacle to their reconfiguration as strike planes. By retro-engineering the redundant aircraft, he could, he believed, create a formidable shadow squadron, permanently on standby to fill any gaps if required. The only potential stumbling block to his plan was the fact that remotely piloted aircraft such as the MQ-25 still required pilots, no matter how remote. For the repurposed tankers to operate as he imagined, they would have be reconfigured as autonomous aerial vehicles, usually referred to as AAVs within the RAF, and for that, Wakeman needed to speak to his Chief Technician.

'The artificial intelligence for autonomous flight is pre-installed but deactivated,' said MacDermott, happy to be a focus of the Wing Commander's confidence and relieved not to be quizzed again about the data issue. Enjoying the moment, he was reluctant to burst Wakeman's bubble by reminding him of the catastrophe in northern England that had caused the United Nations to outlaw all military use of autonomous drones some ten years previously.

'Converting remotely piloted aircraft to autonomous mode,' continued MacDermott, 'is therefore, in principle, no more than a question of programming. Obviously, with aircraft that have been out of service for a number of years, they would need to be checked and overhauled by our technicians. But as I said, everything is, in theory, possible.'

'We have eighteen MQ-25s,' said Wakeman. 'Have your technicians identify the twelve most airworthy. Prepare the best three for test flights asap, but keep working on the other nine. If necessary, cannibalise the rest for parts.'

'Yes, sir.' At this point, MacDermott's conscience got the better of him. 'I'm sorry to have to point this out, sir, but I feel I would be failing in my duty if I did not mention the UN resolution on the military use of AAVs. Is that resolution still-'

'The UN resolution,' retorted Wakeman, 'proscribed the use of AAVs, not their construction, not their testing and not their maintenance, so you need have no worries on that score. In any case, the UN is no longer around to pass judgement.'

'We would have to ensure there could be no repetition of Halifax,' said MacDermott.

'Halifax? Halifax was a one-off. It was a tragic mistake, the product of human error. It could never happen again.'

It was entirely accurate to describe the destruction wreaked upon a small Yorkshire town as the product of human error, as it was a human being that had programmed the incorrect target data into the AAV's guidance system. Little over a week before he died, USAF Technical Sergeant Mike Pedroia, a father of three from Brooklyn Heights, had been assigned the responsibility for programming four F-88 Hellfire drones as part of a training exercise to destroy an unoccupied, non-productive oil platform in the North Sea. Believing, as most Sleeper victims did at that point, that his headache, sweats and aching back constituted nothing more than the start of a winter cold and determined to play his part in the exercise, Pedroia had ignored his symptoms and soldiered in to work. Although not patient zero on the base, he had not been far behind.

Sergeant Pedroia had programmed Hellfires many times before, but never with his head aching, his eyes bleary and his judgement in a sea fog. Having correctly entered the latitudinal co-ordinate for the Helvellyn B oil rig, he mistakenly typed a minus symbol when specifying the platform's longitude. Muddling degrees east and degrees west would have been no more than a minor error in a high school geography test, but Pedroia was not in the classroom. Instead of targeting 600,000 tonnes of scrap metal with only the heaving waves for company, the Technical Sergeant had prepared the Hellfires to attack the historic Yorkshire town of Halifax, and to do so on a December afternoon when the bustling Christmas market would be crowded with shoppers.

The incorrect co-ordinates entered by Pedroia were only the first part of the problem. Once the sergeant had at last comprehended that the drones were heading somewhere other than their intended target, he had of course done his level best to obviate the looming catastrophe. The Hellfires, however, were governed by an on-board AI which upon launch, left every operational decision in the hands of the autonomous aircraft. Designed to resist cyber-attacks attempting to confuse the Hellfires' guidance systems or install a kill switch, the AAVs' threat management systems wilfully fended off Sergeant Pedroia's increasingly desperate attempts to abort the flights. Of the estimated three and a half thousand people enjoying a glass of mulled wine, or buying hand-crafted Christmas gifts, almost a thousand lost their lives that afternoon and a thousand more were injured. Three days later, Pedroia died too. Within six weeks of the disaster the Hellfires had been repatriated to the USA. The honeyed stone Georgian buildings that surrounded the Halifax market square were still awaiting reconstruction.

MacDermott was not so easily convinced that there could never be another Halifax.

'Indeed sir, it was the product of a human error. No question. But whilst the odds of something like that-'

'Chief Technician MacDermott,' snapped Wakeman, 'you have your orders. Thank you. Dismissed.'

Still uneasy about repurposing the MQ-25s into autonomous combat machines, but happy that the question of the data leak now appeared to be on the back burner, MacDermott obeyed his orders and organised his technicians to work on the resurrection and conversion of the remotely piloted aircraft. Within forty-eight hours, the first team had already identified the most promising of the mothballed drones and had begun detailed checks on the structural integrity of every component. Once inspections were complete and any necessary repairs carried out, two teams of technicians would work on the avionics and the propulsion system respectively.

As well as overseeing the technical overhaul of the aircraft, the Chief Technician also made uncomfortably rapid progress with his own task of writing the coding needed to transform the remotely piloted fuel tankers into autonomous and implacable combat weapons. As he worked, he attempted to reassure himself that the more he acquainted himself with the MQ-25's operating system, the easier it would be to discover a vulnerability and to install a kill switch.

17 URGENT MATTERS
OF STATE

It was not long past daybreak on an uncommonly damp morning and Lieutenant Commander York was barely awake. The thunderstorms of the evening before had settled into a persistent drizzle from a pale grey sky. Above her, the gentle percussion of the rain on the metal roof muffled the occasional sound of activity from a nearby hangar and contributed to her reluctance to get out of bed. Cocooned beneath the lightweight duvet, she was warm and relaxed. Lieutenant Batista's arm was draped lazily across her stomach.

The ritual care with which York and Batista had removed each other's uniforms at the end of the evening and had hung them neatly in the small, steel wardrobe reflected both a degree of natural fastidiousness and the knowledge that they would be wearing the same clothes the following day. Once their uniforms had been hung out of sight, their discrepancy in rank became, at least until morning, an irrelevance. The random locations around the room of their discarded underwear offered no clue as to how slowly and how delicately they had removed the most intimate items of each other's clothing, but attested to the mischievous abandon with which they had been cast aside.

Batista's black Utility trunks dangled from the grey reading lamp on the corner of York's desk. Utility brand was the only type of underpants he possessed and, fortunately for him, York thought he looked good in them, or at least, in the ones he let her see. The trunks now hanging from the lamp were the newest pair Lieutenant Batista owned and suggested that when he had dressed the previous day, he had already had some inkling as to how the evening might unfold. A bundled pair of tights lay on the carpet about a metre away from York's laundry bag, the result of an attempted three-pointer by Batista. Also on the floor was one of the white T-shirt bras which York wore when she was in uniform. The black pants, which she later discovered at the bottom of the bed, were much less prosaic and suggested that she too had anticipated how their day might play out.

She was still dozing when her i-comm on the desk emitted the Classic Bell ringtone. It was Navy Command and she needed to take the call. York gently slid Batista's hand from her torso, pulled herself upright and, to create at least some vague feeling of being dressed for work, swaddled herself in the duvet. She muted the speaker on her i-comm and inserted an earbud. Batista, though aware of the activity, did not fully waken. When eventually he opened his eyes, York was engaged in what was clearly a conversation with a senior officer. She looked intently at the Lieutenant and placed the tip of her right index finger over her buttoned lips. He nodded and she pointed towards the door.

Batista knew the drill. He would collect his things and get dressed. When York had a moment, she would pull on a dressing gown or some fatigues and would casually look outside the room. If the corridor was empty, he would then leave and return to his own quarters. In due course, she would message him to say what time she was going for breakfast. He would arrive no sooner than ten minutes after the given time and request permission to join her. Within five minutes, she would leave and he would finish his cornflakes alone. After their carefully choreographed breakfast, the liaison officers would reconvene no more than two minutes before the arrival of the armoured patrol vehicle which was to take them to the Prime Minister's official country residence at Chequers Court. York would brief Batista in the Gurkha.

In the Technical Operations and Surveillance Room in Modsec Central Office in Battersea Park, Intelligence and Data Analyst Anita Chandra was huddled in front of a large monitor. The young Modsec operative was replaying and analysing the conversation relayed via the listening device secreted the previous day in York's room. On the monitor, the Lieutenant Commander's spoken words had been converted to text. Although the voice-to-text conversion software had an impressively high level of accuracy, Chandra still needed to correct a number of errors manually before she could present the transcript to her superiors. York and Batista's lovemaking had proved particularly challenging for the *Vox-It* app and the Modsec officer had resorted to overtyping many of the mistranslations of their intimate exchanges with the catch-all term 'indistinct sex talk'.

Chandra was one of perhaps twenty Modsec analysts in the Technical Ops room who had been conducting similar operations throughout the night. In the subdued lighting, the small red light on the side of her colleague's noise-cancelling headphones was beginning to seem unnecessarily bright. Her lower back was aching.

Chandra's immediate superior, Intelligence Officer Roybould, tapped her lightly on the shoulder.

'Anything of value?'

Given that the data analysts wore noise-cancelling head-phones, Chandra could not understand why Roybould persistently spoke to her whilst she was wearing the headset.

'Sorry?' she said, once the headphones were removed.

'Anything of value?'

'Well I can tell you two things,' she replied, taking the opportunity to arch her back and relieve the stiffness in her lumbar region. 'Firstly, our friends in navy blue go at it like bunnies. We have a transcript of that for what it's worth. But more importantly, York had a twenty-three-minute call with the Admiralty at 0620.'

'Did we intercept it?'

'It was encrypted, so no.'

'Predictable. Did you get the audio?'

'York was wearing an earbud so we just have her side.'

'Well that might give us something. OK. No worries. We may have better luck with the Gurkha.'

Outside the accommodation block at Brize Norton, it was once again pouring with rain. York and Batista stepped back as the eight tonne Gurkha APV pulled up. They greeted the driver, climbed in through the rear crew door and strapped themselves into the nearest seats. There were no other passengers and the pair sat facing each other.

Batista looked at York, widened his eyes and flashed her a smile.

'Did you sleep well, Lieutenant Commander?'

They were in uniform once more and that kind of knowing look was not part of the deal. She would not reciprocate.

'I always sleep well, thank you,' she replied in a pointedly aloof manner. 'Lieutenant Batista, I need to get you up to speed on the communication I received from the Admiralty earlier today.'

As far as York was concerned, their cloak and dagger relationship did not, and undoubtedly could not, exist beyond the confines of her quarters. Batista knew from the pronounced formality of her response that she was not happy.

'Ma'am,' said the Lieutenant.

He had crossed a line that they had agreed was there for a reason and it would not happen again. He was now completely back on duty.

York ran through the key points of her briefing from the Admiralty.

'In a nutshell,' she began, 'we're to cut the PM some slack over reconstruction, but tighten his leash with regard to the war. So, reconstruction first. The official line is that contracts are a civilian matter and he can have complete freedom of manoeuvre to share them with whoever he pleases: friends, NUP supporters, whatever. It doesn't matter.'

'And the war?'

'Yes. Now, with regard to his regular pronouncements about the future course of the war, Joint Command are more than a little hacked off that Henderton is continually going off-piste here, particularly with regard to the Mortality Protocol. They want us to rein him in.'

'Specifically?'

'Specifically, we have been instructed to tell him in no uncertain terms, that under no circumstances is he to promise imminent victory, glorious or otherwise. And he is not to alarm the population with talk of sacrifice or warnings of inevitable casualties. He will, however, promise that the Armed Forces will defend the citizens of this country at all costs, if necessary to the detriment of his economic targets. In effect, he will remind the nation of the Mortality Protocol and shackle himself to it.'

'Couldn't be clearer,' said Batista.

'Also, he is to stop plundering Churchill's classic speeches. The Admiralty will provide a scriptwriter.'

In the Surveillance Room at Modsec, Anita Chandra gestured to Roybould to come over to her station. The conversation was now appearing as text on her screen.

Roybould was a happy man. 'Couldn't be clearer,' he said, deliberately echoing Batista's words. 'Well done, Chandra. The Prime Minister and the Party will be most grateful. Time for you to get some sleep, I think. But before you go, encrypt the transcript and transmit it to the PM. Tag it "Urgent and Confidential". In the meantime, I'll speak to him directly. I suspect it will not be long before the Prime Minister knocks our tight-knit military junta off its over-promoted perch. Joint Command are going to be in for a surprise.'

The forty-mile journey took the best part of an hour, but York and Batista had done it before and even in the rain it was a pleasant enough excursion through a gently undulating rural landscape. Finally, the armoured patrol vehicle stopped before the imposing black gates at the entrance to the walled estate of Chequers Court, the elegant Elizabethan mansion which had been the official country residence of the Prime Ministers of Great Britain since 1917. It was still raining stair-rods and the inclement weather had slowed their journey a little, but they were nevertheless in good time for the meeting. Two Modsec guards dressed in black paramilitary uniforms and matching bullet-proof vests emerged from the mobile command unit in front of the red-brick gatehouse. They were armed with assault rifles and signalled to York and Batista to get out of the APV.

'Lieutenant Commander York and Lieutenant Batista, Royal Navy Liaison. We have a meeting with the PM at eleven,' said York, expecting little fuss from the guards.

The paramilitaries requested identification and, in a departure from usual practice, disappeared with the proffered ID cards into the command unit. York shrugged at Batista. To avoid waiting in the rain, the two liaison officers climbed back into the Gurkha.

'You know,' said York, 'during the Second World War, Churchill refused for almost three years to use Chequers as his country retreat because he thought the security was so bad.'

'That probably means he got them to build a concrete bunker about ten metres down,' replied Batista.

'Quite probably. He loved his bunkers.'

'He was bonkers about bunkers,' said Batista, smirking slightly at the alliteration. 'Completely Willy Wonka about bunkers. Completely bat-shit Tonka Toys about-'

'Quit while you're ahead, Lieutenant,' York advised him with a smile. They were good.

Eventually the two sentries re-emerged and two more armed guards appeared on the far side of the portal. York and Batista climbed out of the APV once more and were required to confirm that they were unarmed before submitting themselves to a body scan. This was also new. After returning the ID cards to their owners, the guards inspected both the inside and the underside of the Gurkha and then instructed the driver to proceed at no more than walking pace and to follow the two guards already waiting inside the grounds. In response to a signal from the mobile command unit, a Modsec security guard in a control room within the historic manor opened the towering gates remotely. As soon as the entrance to the estate was clear, the driver restarted the Gurkha and the vehicle crunched its way slowly up the gravel drive behind the two Modsec paramilitaries.

To their left, about fifty metres from the drive, York and Batista registered the brooding shape of a T-85 Marksman self-propelled anti-aircraft system. From its boxy, armour-plated turret, twin 35mm cannon pointed towards the heavens in defiant readiness. The bold imprints from its caterpillar tracks and the churned earth where it had been manoeuvred into position suggested that the anti-aircraft platform had not been there for long. York and Batista looked at each other quizzically. If the Joint Forces Command had taken a decision to upgrade security at Chequers, no-one had seen fit to brief the two liaison officers. It was more likely, York concluded, that the installation of the formidable weapons had been carried out without the knowledge of the JFC.

In the Surveillance Room at Modsec HQ, the analyst who at 0800 hours had replaced the flagging Anita Chandra listened to the surprised exchanges between York and Batista in the APV, whilst observing the progress of the vehicle from the cameras installed at the gatehouse, along the drive and on the roof of Chequers itself.

Still following the guards, the Gurkha turned left. Ahead of the armoured patrol vehicle stood a three-metre high brick wall and another set of tall, wrought-iron gates through which York and Batista could see the entrance to the fifteenth-century red-brick manor. Beyond the imposing portal, there were yet more black-uniformed paramilitaries. The two sets of guards acknowledged each other and the gates were opened electronically. In another break with precedent, the Gurkha APV was allowed no further, and York and Batista were instructed to leave the vehicle once more. They passed through the wrought iron gates which promptly closed behind them. Skirting the manicured, four-leaf clover lawn which acted as the centre of a gyratory system for those vehicles that were permitted though the gates, the two liaison officers made their way through the continuing rain to the main doors.

At the top of the steps, they were greeted curtly by an unfamiliar Modsec officer who ushered them to the oak-panelled Hawtrey Room and asked them to wait. The officer departed and two more guards joined York and Batista, carefully positioning themselves at the door to create the impression that they could intervene should the guests take it upon themselves to go anywhere without permission.

'We have a meeting with the Prime Minister scheduled for eleven,' said York.

'Yes, ma'am,' replied the taller of the two guards. He did not respond in any other way.

York decided to take a seat on the tan leather armchair in front of the polished Steinway grand piano. Batista opted for the sofa. From his position, his attention was drawn first to the numerous portraits that adorned the walls, then to an impressive stained-glass window which carried the inscription 'This house of peace and ancient memories was given to England as a thank-offering for her deliverance in the great war of 1914–1918 and as a place of rest and recreation for her prime ministers for ever.'

'It's certainly peaceful,' he thought, 'but is Henderton even here?'

At ten past eleven the Modsec officer who had initially received them re-entered the room. York and Batista stood up.

'We have a meeting with the PM,' said York, beginning to tire of hearing herself say it.

'The PM is attending to urgent matters of state. He knows you are waiting.'

The officer turned and left the room once more. After a further fifteen minutes, York's thoughts began to drift. She started to wonder how many famous and infamous backsides had graced her armchair with their illustrious presence. Suddenly, she realised that she was simply killing precious time. York stood up impatiently and the guards tensed slightly, ready to intervene if necessary. Noting their reaction, the Lieutenant Commander walked purposefully away from the door towards one of the windows. It was still raining, though perhaps less heavily, and the sky remained a uniform grey. She observed that the windows no longer had locks or catches and that the panes had been upgraded to aluminium oxynitride laminate glass and dressed with a matrix of zinc strips to mimic the original Elizabethan leaded lights. The anti-ballistic panes, she reflected, would comfortably stop bullets fired from handguns or assault rifles and could thwart 0.50 calibre armour-piercing rounds. York wondered exactly what the Prime Minister was expecting.

Now firmly ensconced on the sofa, Batista had, except for some brief moments of reverie, resisted the temptation to relive the events of the previous night. He was watching the guards closely and was working hard not to show it. Eventually the Modsec officer returned.

'The Prime Minister can fit you in now. You've got five minutes.'

18 REFUGE OF THE GUILTY

RAF Lakenheath, 10th June

On the bank of monitors covering an entire wall of his office, Wing Commander Wakeman, with his Chief Technician beside him, was watching the final preparations for the first test flight of the reinstated MQ-25. The USAF had maintained the aircraft to their usual exacting standards and the RAF technicians checking the propulsion system and the avionics had found little that required attention. For his part, MacDermott had followed his orders from Wakeman and had dutifully reconfigured the drone so that it no longer required remote pilot control and would complete any programmed mission autonomously. This was not, however, a situation which provided the Chief Technician with the slightest sense of satisfaction. In spite of his best efforts to detect a vulnerability in the aircraft's operating system, he had so far failed in his attempts to install some kind of fail-safe. As things stood, the MQ-25 would be incapable of deviating from its programmed objective. Wing Commander Wakeman, however, suffered no such qualms about the absence of a kill switch and he had ordered both himself and MacDermott a large mug of frothy, cappuccino-style root coffee, evidence that he was also feeling particularly buoyant about the likely outcome of the forthcoming test flight.

About a mile from Wakeman's office, ground crew completed final checks and adjustments beneath a leaden sky. It was as warm as ever but there was little in the way of sunshine and the thick cloud cover trapped both the heat and the humidity. The technicians working on the MQ-25 were sweating like ripening cheese.

No longer bearing any USAF insignia, the aircraft was completely grey and practically the same colour as the sky. The fuselage of the MQ-25, with its smooth, rounded contours and flattish profile reminded MacDermott of the body of a whale shark, albeit one with a snout so narrow it would be incapable of feeding itself. At the rear, twin outward-canted butterfly fins made up the aircraft's double tail. To the side, the gently swept wings at first sight looked improbably small for a plane with such a fuselage, but the Chief Technician had absolutely no doubts about its ability to get off the ground. For the test flight, streamlined fuel pods hung beneath the MQ-25's wings. The pylons, which allowed the unpiloted aircraft to connect to, and communicate with, its external fuel tanks, were standard NATO fitting and could as easily accommodate a more lethal payload on a future occasion.

From a safe distance, the ground crew conducted diagnostics during several engine run-ups, returning each time to the repurposed aircraft, opening up access flaps into its underbelly and making ever more finely tuned adjustments. As soon as MacDermott received confirmation that the overhauled AAV was good to go, he informed Wakeman, who personally transmitted the command signal for the aircraft to begin its mission. The MQ-25's operating system took control, the single Rolls-Royce turbofan engine fired itself up and the reconfigured drone completed its first autonomous taxi along the apron to the runway.

About five hundred metres from the hangar, the engine noise attracted the attention of Flight Lieutenants Dibaba and Warszawski who had been exercising the Squadron's stray Labrador on the unkempt fairways of Lakenheath's once thriving golf course. Both pilots had a soft spot for retrievers and the walks had become an almost daily ritual for the pair since Warszawski's release from the med bay some five weeks previously. They were now sitting on the remaining two patches of soft sand in an almost completely overgrown bunker and were debating whether life had evolved from light, as Dibaba maintained, or whether, as Warszawski contested, the term 'evolution' could only be applied to biological processes.

'If relationships can evolve, so can light,' said Dibaba. 'I rest my case.'

Warszawski shook his head resolutely. 'That's not science. It's semantics.'

The well-exercised and gently panting dog, who came with a collar, a plaintive look and an appetite, was curled up at their feet. He now had a functional leash fashioned from the severed cord and clip which not long ago had connected Warszawski to his survival kit following his ejection from the stricken F-95. Before them, a chewed and slobbery stick lay on a still visible patch of sand. At this point, Dibaba and Warszawski recognised the increasingly urgent tones of the turbofan engine running up in preparation for take-off, pressed pause on their discussion and looked intently in the direction of the aircraft. Their view was partly obscured by pines.

'Hey, Freebird,' he said, with a puzzled expression on his

face. 'What the hell do you think they're up to over there by Hangar 11?'

'Fuck knows.'

'Is that a drone?' asked Warszawski, knowing full well what it was, but surprised simply to be seeing one on the runway.

Dibaba fixed her gaze on the aircraft. 'It's one of the tankers, right? Why would we be testing a tanker?'

'Maybe Wakeman's planning a tanker display team,' said Warszawski in typically facetious manner. 'He'll have them all sprayed red by next week.'

Dibaba smiled. She liked hanging out with Stairway.

'Is it for us?' she said. 'Why would we need in-flight refuelling? Where would they want us to go?'

'Beats me,' said Warszawski, before turning his attention to the still panting, black Labrador. 'What do you think, Tiger?'

The dog responded to the attention by raising its head and cocking it to one side with a look which charmingly combined both curiosity and anticipation.

The sound of the turbofan grew louder and the MQ-25 accelerated effortlessly along the runway, took off without incident and climbed steeply, rapidly disappearing into the clouds and out of sight of the two curious pilots.

Above the cloud cover, the self-governing drone flew its pre-determined figure-of-eight test route, taking in Cambridge, Peterborough, Norwich and Cromer. In Wing Commander Wakeman's office, both he and MacDermott closely monitored the aircraft's flight functions and operations. It all looked perfect.

Happy with the performance of the MQ-25, Wakeman conducted one final test. He sent an abort code to the drone.

With its mission still incomplete, the aircraft simply ignored the command and refused to deviate from its programmed course. About twenty minutes later, the unpiloted aircraft descended through the canopy of clouds and brought itself in to land. There was a screech of tyres and a puff of smoke as the wheels touched the runway, but otherwise the landing was flawless. The drone taxied to the hangar, stopped at the exact point at which it had started its engines and powered down. Wing Commander Wakeman sat back in his chair and allowed himself a moment to bask in the enormity of his achievement.

'Congratulations, Chief Technician,' he said, patently delighted with the test. 'Job well done. Now prepare the other eleven.'

'Impressive,' said the visitor who had insinuated herself unannounced into Wakeman's office and had also been watching the landing of the MQ-25.

Caught unawares by the unexpected comment, Wakeman straightened sharply and stared over his shoulder.

'Who the hell are you?'

The visitor calmly produced her Modsec ID card from the inside pocket of her jacket.

'Major Security Officer Benjamin. Forgive the intrusion. May I sit down?'

The Modsec officer was slim but by no means tall. She had straight black hair and dark brown eyes. Benjamin was not in uniform, but was wearing a tidy, grey trouser suit and a yellow ochre blouse. Wing Commander Wakeman was certain that he had glimpsed the strap of a shoulder holster as she produced her ID.

Keen to get down to business, the Modsec officer looked

around for a spare chair, pulled one from a nearby desk and sat facing the still baffled Station Commander. It was as warm in the office as ever, but she kept her jacket on.

'How can I help you?' asked Wakeman.

He was unfamiliar with the chain of command within Modsec and could not work out from Major Security Officer Benjamin's title whether she outranked him. He decided, on reflection, that if she had the brass neck to ambush him in his own office, it would be sensible to assume that she did.

'Perhaps, MacDermott, you could leave Agent Benjamin and myself to-'

'MacDermott can stay,' said the Modsec officer, asserting her authority. 'That was an impressive landing, although perhaps a little hot. You'd expect a drone to be smoother, wouldn't you? Mind you, it's not exactly flying on factory settings, is it now? Perhaps a bit more fine-tuning, Chief Technician MacDermott.'

Wakeman was flummoxed. How the hell could the modifications to the MQ-25 have come to the attention of Modsec? He waited for Benjamin to get to the point. MacDermott simply followed suit.

'I expect you know why I'm here,' she said, and waited. The question was deliberately calculated to unsettle and Wakeman's bewilderment was plain to see.

'To be honest,' said Wakeman, still trying to regain his equilibrium, 'your visit is completely unexpected. What can I do for you?'

'Well,' said Benjamin. 'We at Modsec are more than a little concerned about the security leak at the base.'

She paused again.

Wakeman was in a flat spin. Already caught off guard by Benjamin's appearance in his office and her apparent knowledge of the MQ-25 programme, he asked himself how in God's name she could have latched onto this too.

'We are investigating it,' he said, failing to mask his unease. 'It's all in hand.'

'Spare me the fairy stories,' retorted Benjamin. 'The bottom line is, Wing Commander, that you have a data breach at the base, you've known about it for weeks, you've fumbled around in the dark trying to fix it and you still do not have the faintest idea who is responsible. In the meantime you have directed your cyberwarfare specialist to dedicate his precious time to creating a squadron of illegal AAVs with massive strike capability instead of addressing your ongoing security problem. Does that about sum matters up?'

Wakeman was completely stupefied. The shit had well and truly hit the fan, but he still hadn't got the faintest idea what Benjamin was doing in his office or where she was going with her revelations. Once again, the Station Commander did not respond. MacDermott, rooted to his chair, was rendered almost incapable of speech and could feel the blood pulsing in his neck.

'Ah, silence,' said Major Security Officer Benjamin with a satisfied grin. 'The last refuge of the guilty. It goes without saying that you've made an unholy mess of this data-'

'It was less than a kilobyte,' asserted Wakeman, perhaps more boldly than was wise.

His emphasis of the miniscule size of the data leak made no impression on Benjamin.

'I think you both need to listen, and to listen carefully,' said the Modsec officer. 'Take notes if you like. A security breach is a security breach, regardless of size. And this unholy cyber-crap-fest happened on your watch, Wing Commander Wakeman. On your watch. And you, Chief Technician MacDermott, you are responsible for data-security and yet you devote your time to building illegal AAVs rather than doing your real job. Looked at from any angle, this is a serious breach. Who knows what data is being divulged to God-knows-who? This station is compromised and the consequences for both of you will be severe and far-reaching.'

Having become accustomed to expressions of praise and approval throughout his successful career, the Wing Commander's situation was unprecedented. His mind was now spinning as he tried to understand what was happening and delineate his options. MacDermott did not have the slightest idea what to do and was simply hoping that Wakeman would make some kind of a stand.

'By midnight tonight,' continued Benjamin calmly, 'neither of you will any longer be members of the Royal Air Force. On my say-so, your service records will have been expunged and replaced with civil records littered with convictions for theft, fraud and deception. You will find yourselves en route to some godforsaken northern work brigade, where you will spend the next twenty pitiful years atoning for the string of nasty little crimes your records will show you have committed.'

Both Wakeman and MacDermott were utterly thunder-struck by the astonishingly rapid turn of events. Wakeman's instinct was to fight. He wondered where the nearest firearm was and whether Benjamin had brought back-up. As it stood, he and MacDermott outnumbered her.

'Of course, we might not need to go down this road at all,' said Benjamin, unveiling a smile that suggested an unexpected capacity for charm, 'if you felt you might be able to lend assistance to Modsec and to the Prime Minister.'

'Meaning what, specifically?' said Wakeman, wary of what he might hear.

'Meaning, that in the light of the unpleasant fate which might otherwise befall you, you may now feel predisposed to help the Prime Minister in redressing the balance of power in our broken country. Your autonomous toy, currently sitting on the pan outside Hangar 11 might, for example, have the tactical capacity to assist the Prime Minister in his constitutional ambitions.'

19 NOTHING TO CHANCE

Liverpool, 24th June

In the kitchen of seventeen Menlove Close, Freya and Martina were chatting over a bowl of cereal. It was eight o'clock on a sunny summer's morning and even in the shaded interior of the house it was already warm. Freya opened the kitchen windows, sat down opposite Martina and poured some expensively sourced milk onto her Utility cornflakes.

'Who is it?' asked Freya, with a glint in her eye.

'Who's what?' replied Martina, genuinely confused.

'The guy who's worth spending so much time away from home for.'

'There's no guy,' said Martina. 'It's just work.'

Freya raised an eyebrow.

'No, not that kind of work,' said Martina emphatically. 'I've got a tricky job on and I need parts that I can't always get easily. I sometimes have to hunt around for them. In unusual places. When most people are asleep.'

'Yeah, right,' said Freya. 'What's his name?'

'Nothing.'

'Dad and Thomas think so too. They're gonna ask you as soon as they get home.'

Thomas and Aston had been at work since six and it was the first day of a new duty. The pair were currently in the fetid darkness of a sewer, five metres below the streets of central Liverpool, tasked with doing their bit to clear a seventy-metre-long fatberg estimated to weigh perhaps thirty tonnes. The congealed masses of grease, oil, micro-plastics, faeces and other bodily fluids that were blocking several of Liverpool's sewers were a legacy of the once much larger population fed to a now unimaginable extent on sugary, fat-laden foods. Furthermore, the saponified cake blocking the sewer also contained concentrations of prescription medicines, muscle-building supplements and street drugs and was topped off with a cocktail of infectious bacteria. Unsurprisingly, it smelled vile.

Not only in Liverpool, but across the country, fatbergs threatened to flood homes and places of work with sewage and represented an ongoing threat to public health. Although Aston and Thomas did not volunteer for this duty, the pair both recognised the importance, as well as the urgency, of the work they were doing. That said, nothing could have prepared their nostrils for the overpowering stench that greeted them as they penetrated the sewer at the start of the morning's shift.

'They say you get used to it,' Thomas said to Aston the first time his partner gagged. He was lying. Even wearing protective clothing and half-face respirator masks, there was no escape. The repugnant aroma simply didn't relent.

Aston and Thomas had so far failed in their attempts to break up the blockage using an industrial hose with a high-pressure jet and now had to resort to the deafening brute force of pneumatic drills. The ambient temperature in the sewer was higher than above ground and the two workers were rapidly lathered in sweat beneath their protective gear. The determined and long-suffering pair had to labour for an hour before they were at last replaced by the relief team. As they climbed from the sewer at the end of the first of their four one-hour shifts and pulled off their respirators, they greeted their replacements as they would inevitably do at every changeover.

'It's a shit job,' said Thomas.

'But someone's got to do it,' quipped Aston. 'See you in an hour.'

Commander Duke, the brigade leader, knew this was probably one of the worst tasks she could give to her charges and was not unsympathetic to their situation. By way of recognition, she had promised the whole fatberg squad National Hero of Labour medals on completion of the job.

'Where can you spend the medals?' was Aston's first question.

Above ground, another team was loading the first dislodged lumps of the disgusting amalgam onto a truck. The blocks would be taken away to be cleansed of impurities and infection and processed into biodiesel which would then fuel hospital generators, military vehicles and ageing combine harvesters.

Before Martina left for work, Freya gave her a cardboard box containing thirty six boxes of paracetamol, twelve half-finished packs of antibiotics and a wholesale carton of one thousand condoms, all seriously out of date.

'So, what are you going to trade this lot for?' asked Freya.

'Trust me, Freya,' said Martina with a smile. 'It's gonna be good. You'll be made up, when you see what I get.'

'Are you sure the contraceptives are not for personal use?'

Freya smiled and her brown eyes twinkled at Martina again.

'Oh, Freya. Chance would be a fine thing.'

After leaving the house, Martina drove her van to the end of Troutbeck Park Gardens and picked up Kevin. This morning, the cybersecurity expert had showered, washed his hair and shaved more carefully than was usual. He had put on a freshly acquired and expensive-looking, dark-navy suit that fitted him particularly well and would help him exude an air of untroubled authority. His white shirt, starched with a little cornflower, looked crisp and professional and the understated pattern on his tie suggested that he was someone who had nothing to prove. With the exception of the counterfeit Rolex which Kevin had owned for years, the clothes had all been sourced from unoccupied houses in Troutbeck Park Gardens.

Within sixty minutes, Martina and Kevin were heading south along the Trafford Road in Salford and were looking for the Exchange Quay tram stop which was no more than a mile from Media City. Martina recognised the turn-off towards the stop, crossed the tram lines and pulled over perhaps a hundred metres further on.

Before making his way to the tram, Kevin took a minute to ensure that he had everything he needed. He confirmed that he had his Modsec ID in one of the internal pockets of his jacket and the NBC Cybersecurity badge from his previous visit in the other. He also checked that he had two rubber-tipped pencils and a small notebook ready to jot down a username or some other vital piece of information that he might glimpse over a hapless shoulder. Finally, he verified that the padded envelope inside his briefcase contained the external hard-drive harbouring the code that would massively enhance their access privileges within the NBC's broadcast systems. Once installed, the hackware would not only have the capacity to upload and broadcast extensive video content but also the resilience to fend off attempts to interfere with its functionality or block its output. Satisfied that he had left nothing to chance, he assured Martina he would be back by lunchtime and climbed out of the van.

Although the wait for the next tram felt inordinately long, the journey to the end of the line at Media City would take no more than ten minutes. Kevin's modus operandi would be the same as on his previous visit. He planned to use the Modsec ID to get past security and switch to the fake NBC badge once inside. On the tram, however, a better opportunity presented itself. Kevin picked out a smartly dressed woman with an NBC identity badge clipped to a lanyard around her neck. She looked at her watch three times during the first five minutes of the short journey and was clearly in a hurry. She would, he decided, be perfect. Confident that the crisply turned out professional was a senior figure who would be known to the security guards, Kevin calmly took out his own NBC badge and clipped it to the lapel of his jacket. He was careful to get off the tram slightly ahead of his mark and as soon as she was clear of the doors, he excused himself and asked her for directions to the NBC.

'That's the easiest question I'll be asked all day,' she said. 'It's the building right ahead of us.'

'I'll walk with you,' said Kevin.

They exchanged brief introductions over the hundred-yard walk across the plaza. He was David Jones from NBC Cybersecurity in London and he had a meeting with the head of enterprise technology. She was Olivia Hastings, the producer of *The Meat-Free Show*, and she was sorry she was walking so quickly, but she was running a little late.

On arrival at the main entrance, Olivia was immediately recognised by the security guard and was politely ushered through, along with her guest. Once inside, Olivia asked

Kevin where he needed to go. The putative cybersecurity officer thanked her warmly for her help, but said appreciatively that he'd taken enough of her time and would check in at reception. Olivia smiled, wished the visitor a good day and hurried to the lift. Once the doors had closed behind her, Kevin headed directly for the stairs. The two NBC staffers he passed on his way did not bat an eyelid.

On the third floor, the newsroom was a hive of activity. The output editor was engaged in excited conversation with a story producer; a package producer was offloading his frustrations onto a director; and a production assistant was locked in some kind of whispered dispute with the political editor. No-one paid the slightest bit of attention to the sharp-suited interloper who breezed through their animated workspace.

To the side of the production room, Kevin identified a well-appointed but unused office and quietly let himself in. Once inside, he closed the door, flipped on the lights and sat down at the less than tidy desk. Immediately, he powered up the computer and felt around underneath the desktop, quickly finding a sticky-note bearing a user ID. Kevin voiced the user name into the system and with the help of the automated brute-force tool on the drive in his briefcase, generated a viable biometric passkey in under sixty seconds. As the trespasser began the process of uploading the code he had so diligently worked on over recent weeks, there was a knock at the door.

He answered with an authoritative 'Yes. Come in.'

A younger woman, perhaps an assistant or an intern, with straw-coloured hair and a diffident smile, opened the door somewhat tentatively and was patently surprised to see an unfamiliar face.

'Oh, sorry,' she said. 'I was looking for Ellie.'

'Ellie's not here today,' said Kevin, still focussed on the screen. He looked up and made eye contact with his hesitant visitor. 'Actually, I was expecting Olivia Hastings. Have you seen her?'

'No, sorry,' said the young woman, not sure if she knew who Olivia Hastings was.

'No worries,' said Kevin, breezily. 'What was your name, again?'

'I didn't say. Sorry. I'm Ruby. Hi.'

'Could you get me a glass of water? Thanks, Ruby.'

By the time the tumbler of water arrived, Kevin had uploaded the meticulously prepared code that would enable him to insert extended video clips into the NBC's regular output. Within five minutes of putting the glass to his lips, he had also downloaded several potentially interesting files from a folder labelled 'Cabinet meetings - technical'. One file, entitled 'downingst2', particularly piqued his curiosity.

Kevin logged off, switched off the lights and left the office. He finished his glass of water in one of the breakout pods overlooking the central atrium and wondered if Talira had ever sat in the same place when she was working there. On his way back down to the lobby, he spotted Olivia Hastings and gave her an appreciative wave.

Once outside, Kevin waited for the next tram and was back with Martina within fifteen minutes.

'*Hola*,' he said as he opened the door of the van.

The broad smile and his arbitrary use of Spanish testified to the success of their operation.

The return journey should in principle have taken no more

than an hour, but a cordon of armoured patrol vehicles steered all traffic off the M62 and into the Burtonwood service area where the police were inspecting vehicles for militia contraband. Although Martina's accredited trader ID checked out immediately, it struck the police officer as somewhat odd that her passenger should be so well-dressed. The combination of Kevin's Modsec ID and his authoritative manner, however, were all it took to persuade the sergeant that he needed ask no further questions.

About thirty minutes after being shepherded back onto the motorway by the police, Martina pulled over outside a house on Menlove Avenue where apparently John Lennon had once lived.

'We did it,' said Martina, positively beaming. 'We did it.'

'We certainly did,' said Kevin, nodding with satisfaction. If he seemed less enthusiastic than Martina, it was simply because he had done this so many times before. As far as the cybersecurity expert was concerned, the outcome had never been in doubt.

Kevin waited for a lull in the traffic, before opening the van door.

'*Adios*, Martina. *Hasta mañana.*'

Reminding himself to take his time, the hacker walked the four hundred metres to the end of Troutbeck Park Gardens, looking for all the world like someone returning from a busy but not unbearable day at work.

'*Hola,*' said Kevin, as he breezed through the back door of the house. Upon hearing his voice, Kireina ran from the lounge, threw herself at her boyfriend and hugged him for all she was worth.

'I take it today went well,' said Ricky, smiling broadly.

'Better than well,' said Kevin. 'Absolutely fucking amazing.' Whilst today had, in many respects, been a regular day at the office for Kevin, the significance of what he had done was only now sinking in.

'Can I send?' shouted Talira from the lounge.

'Oh I think so,' said Kireina enthusiastically.

'I haven't put a delay on it,' shouted Talira.

Simultaneously, the alarm sounded from their i-comms and Talira's stinger crawled across the screen.

'The media's the most powerful entity on Earth. They have the power to make the innocent guilty and to make the guilty innocent. Malcolm X'

'Interesting choice, Talira,' said Kevin. 'Are you getting a bit radical in your old age?'

Martina did not drive home, but headed towards the river. Close to the city centre, slightly beyond the Quanjing restaurant, she pulled over outside a two-storey, redbrick Victorian dock building. The hoists on the roof and the massive, wooden sliding doors along the side wall attested to the structure's history as a riverside warehouse. The fading 'Royal Mail' sign on the tower suggested, however, that the building had enjoyed several roles in its long lifetime. The cavernous storehouse, so close to the once bustling docks, was both the home and the workplace of one of the most prolific antiques dealers in Liverpool, a man who referred to himself only as 'PJ'.

'Ah, MacDermott the Mystery Cat,' said PJ warmly. 'I was wondering how long it would take for you to reappear.'

'Hey, PJ,' said Martina. 'You got my stuff?'

'It's all on order,' he assured his visitor.

Martina had long been curious about the trader's moniker, but when she asked him why he called himself 'PJ', he deftly refused to be drawn. The manner of his response was practised yet somewhat wearied. She was clearly not the first to ask.

Martina showed the middle-aged and badger-haired trader the contents of the cardboard box that she had brought from Menlove Close: thirty six boxes of paracetamol, twelve partially full packs of antibiotics and a thousand condoms, exactly as agreed. Everything was well past its 'use before' date but that would not deter buyers. PJ would shift the lot within a week.

'How do I know they're all there?' asked PJ, referring to the condoms.

'They're all there, PJ, every single one. But I'm happy to sit and watch whilst you count them out.'

PJ raised his eyebrows, looked to the ceiling and then shook his head as though weighing up whether to trust her.

'And you'll replace that broken solar panel for me too?' he said.

'Yeah. No problem.'

'Then we have a deal. And remind me. What are you trying to cheat me out of for this?'

'It's all on the list I gave you.'

'Oh, yeah. The New Beatles. Come back in a week.'

In Troutbeck Park Gardens, the mood was buoyant. Kevin was delighted that he had picked the lock to the NBC's video transmission systems and intrigued by the production files that he had discovered. Kireina, although she knew Kevin's professional history, had nonetheless been on tenterhooks all day and would not let him out of her sight until morning. Talira and Ricky, who had also spent the day in a state of moderate anxiety, were both astonished and deeply impressed at how smoothly Kevin and Martina had pulled the whole thing off.

Following a celebratory meal of Ricky's Shepherdless Pie, a vegetarian dish yet to appear on *The Meat-Free Show*, Kevin ushered the others into the Batcave-slash-Ops-Room, opened the files he had stolen from the NBC and selected the one which had particularly aroused his curiosity.

'What do you make of this?' he asked.

The 'downingst2' document was watermarked 'Confidential' and appeared to be a briefing for the programme editor of NBC News on the agenda for a forthcoming Cabinet meeting. There were four items listed: One - Escalation of raids (Embargoed); Two - NBC funding formula; Three - Expansion of dental provision; Four - Synth-bio military personnel prognosis (Embargoed).

'Well, I think we're all good with item three,' said Talira with a wide-eyed smile.

'But what about point four,' said Ricky, clearly puzzled. 'Synth-bio military personnel? What the hell does that mean?'

'Search me,' said Kireina. 'Synth-bio? All sounds a bit sci-fi. Maybe it's code for something.'

No more than five hundred metres away, Martina arrived in Menlove Close still bubbling from the success of the trip to Salford Quays and her subsequent visit to PJ's. She hopped out of the van and headed down the sloping path. Suddenly, she saw that the front door was wide open, as was every single window in the house. Whilst it was a warm evening, it was no warmer than most, and this appeared to be a completely excessive response. Martina's mood instantly subsided. She walked in tentatively, her heartbeat rising.

'What's his name?' boomed Aston from the kitchen, when he spotted Martina creeping into the hallway. Martina almost jumped out of her skin.

'Hey!' shouted Martina, relieved and annoyed in equal measure. 'I was worried. Why the hell are all the windows open?'

'Honey, if you'd spent all day doing want we've just spent all day doing, you'd want the windows open too.'

'For the rest of time,' said the disembodied voice of Thomas, who from the sound of it was also somewhere in the kitchen. 'Listen. You know the saying that someone "hung around like a bad smell"? Well today, Martina, that smell hung around with us.'

Freya appeared and was exploding with curiosity about the fate of the high-value merchandise that she had supplied to Martina earlier.

'So then, spill the beans. What did you trade it all for? A present for your boyfriend?'

'Hell, Freya, not that again. But no. Not a present for my imaginary boyfriend.'

'So?'

'Well,' said Martina, the glint back in her eye. 'All I'm gonna say right now is, what good's a drummer without a band?'

20 BELOW RADAR

RAF Brize Norton, 25th June

The Prime Minister spent the night in his private quarters aboard the massive A-600 transport plane that regularly ferried him up and down the country. After breakfast, he would fly from Brize Norton to Leeds to address the first of a number of rallies that had not been instigated by the military leadership but by the NUP. Henderton understood only too clearly that his refusal to attend today's meeting of the Joint Forces Command in Northwood would unsettle his political overlords and raise questions about his dependability, possibly even about his loyalty. He was, however, supremely unconcerned. As the PM tucked in to the full English breakfast sent over from Canteen 2, he was confident, for a multitude of reasons, that today was going to be a very good day indeed.

He had the pilot order him a plate of toast with raspberry jam and farm butter plus a second cafetière of Premium-brand ersatz coffee which, considering it was made primarily from acorns, wasn't that bad at all. The Prime Minister took his time drinking the coffee and reviewing the text of the speech he would ostensibly be making to the crowd in Yorkshire. As far as Henderton was concerned, Joint Command's recent insistence that he avail himself of a scriptwriter was simply an affront too far and he had immediately and contemptuously binned those manuscripts provided for him in favour of his own more ambitious flights of rhetoric. Seeing absolutely no point in changing a winning formula, the Prime Minister had, to a substantial degree, found inspiration for his forthcoming address amongst the pages of his well-thumbed copy of *Churchill - Our Greatest Orator*.

The eleven thirty departure meant that York and Batista could enjoy a lie in. Judging by the distribution of each other's underwear around the room, they'd clearly had a good night. Batista's black underpants were on top of the wardrobe and would take some finding. York's bra had landed half on and half off the bookshelf. Her knickers would be no easier to locate than Batista's trunks. As ever, their uniforms hung neatly in the wardrobe, ready for duty.

Half-draped in a sheet, Batista rolled onto his front. Their torsos overlapped slightly as he kissed her softly on the lips and ran his finger from her right hip to her breast.

'He's got the hots for you, you know,' he said as he played affectionately with her nipple.

'Who?'

'Henderton.'

'What?' she said in disbelief. Was Batista teasing her?

'He said so. When we were on the plane. That time over Manchester when we were shot at by the militia.'

'Seriously? Seriously? Oh, God no. Yuck.' She paused. 'Are you jealous?'

'No. But also yes. Kind of.'

'Good. So you should be.'

They exchanged another kiss.

In the Technical Operations and Surveillance Room in Modsec HQ, their conversation was being recorded and would be pored over by an intelligence analyst.

'Do you think we might have been a bit noisy last night?' asked Batista, knowing they hadn't been, but wanting to let her know that it had been fun.

'The first time anyone hears us will also be the last time,' said York, adopting a slightly more serious tone. 'This stays below radar.'

Batista reflected for a moment. 'So. I have a question. What exactly is this? Where are we going with this?'

'What exactly is this? It is what it is.'

She was careful to be vague, unwilling to spoil something that seemed to work by encumbering it with definition.

'Let's take some leave,' said Batista. 'Together. It wouldn't have to be exactly the same dates. As long as they had a few days in common.'

'Leave? When does anyone ever get leave? Now I know you're completely out of your tree.'

York kissed him softly.

Their relationship had so far functioned on an entirely ad hoc basis. As such, Batista's suggestion of taking leave together constituted a radical step and was not a subject York wished to explore. She had certainly never fantasised about the two of them cooking a ratatouille together, kicking through the long grass on a country walk, or going for a drink in a newly discovered pub.

She delicately pointed out that they needed to start their day and the pair spent a couple of minutes hunting down their missing underwear. Items retrieved, Batista kissed York once more and left her room, respecting their usual protocols to avoid detection. They reconvened, apparently by chance, at breakfast.

Over porridge and an unidentifiable herbal tea, York briefed Batista about the Leeds trip. Joint Forces Command were beginning to lose patience with the Prime Minister, who was increasingly behaving as though he needed neither the support nor the sanction of the Armed Forces. He had declined to attend the quarterly Joint Forces Command meeting, which was not his prerogative, and the NUP was holding an unauthorised rally in Leeds, which was equally unacceptable. York and Batista were therefore to accompany the PM to Leeds and monitor him more closely than ever. As the rally was unsanctioned, no manuscript had been prepared for Henderton's address, so the liaison officers were to check anything of his own concoction, edit it as necessary, and ensure that he sang from the correct hymn sheet. They were to report absolutely anything remotely out of the ordinary to the Admiralty. Immediately.

21 NOT A DRILL

Northwood, London, 25th June

As Lieutenant Commander York, Lieutenant Batista and the Prime Minister readied themselves for take-off, the leading figures in the British Armed Forces were sitting down together in Briefing Room A of the Joint Forces Command complex on the outskirts of London. Although no more than fifteen miles from the Whitehall Security Zone, the leafy suburb of Northwood was a haven of relative calm. Chairing the meeting was Admiral Teresa Patel, First Sea Lord, Chief of Joint Operations and, to all practical intents and purposes, the most powerful person in Britain. Gathered around the table in their impressive service uniforms were fifteen of the most senior officers in the British Navy, Army and Air Force. Manifestly absent were the Prime Minister and Dame Abigail Hartmann, the Director of Modsec.

Admiral Patel caught the eye of her PA. 'Well, we know Henderton has sent his apologies, the toad. What about Hartmann?'

The PA shrugged.

Whilst the Joint Forces Command continued to waste its time waiting for the increasingly unlikely arrival of Henderton's spymaster, eighty miles away at RAF Lakenheath the signal to scramble caught Flight Lieutenants Merton and Bosko completely off guard. Although they were officially on standby and ready to respond to a Quick Reaction Alert, no operations were ever conducted during the hours of daylight and QRA duty was, in effect, no more than a nominal assignment, a chance to chew the fat with a comrade or catch up on some reading. Merton and Bosko exchanged puzzled glances.

'What the fuck?' said Bosko.

Merton requested confirmation from the Ops Room.

'Affirm. Alert State Scarlet. Scramble,' said Gunatillaka with absolute clarity.

Both pilots knew that Alert State Scarlet could mean one of only two things: either information had been received about an enemy attack on a specific target or an attack was expected within minutes. They also knew that both of these scenarios were completely impossible. As always, two F-95s stood poised for action on the Operational Readiness Platform and within two minutes of hearing the alarm, both Bosko and Merton were strapped into their seats and were running up their engines.

'Bosko, Merton, this is Lakenheath Ground. Abort QRA response,' said Gunatillaka unexpectedly. 'Acknowledge.'

'What the fuck, Gunnie?' said Bosko. 'Are you kidding me? Is this a drill?'

By way of an answer, Gunatillaka simply repeated her original message.

'Roger,' said Bosko, baffled and strangely frustrated. 'Wilco. Running down.'

'So, is this a drill?' asked Merton.

'Negative. This is not a drill,' said Gunatillaka.

It was at this point that the pilots saw the two MQ-25s, armed with Partisan missiles, taxiing onto the runway. Bosko uttered her usual expression of disbelief, but this time more slowly and with each word punctuated by a crisp, open-mouthed pause.

'What - the - fuck?'

In Briefing Room A of the Permanent Joint Headquarters complex, two chairs remained conspicuously empty.

'Both Henderton and Hartmann should be here,' complained Air Chief Marshal Dilger. 'I don't like it. Can we still rely on these two?'

'Our liaison officers are keeping tabs on Henderton,' said Admiral Patel. 'He's always been an egotistical arse, but I think maybe the time has come to ask ourselves whether his naked ambition is getting somewhat out of hand.'

'Indeed,' said the Air Chief Marshal.

The two autonomous aircraft overflying St Albans at 700 knots in broad daylight were glimpsed before they were heard. In the six minutes it had taken the MQ-25s to fly this far, the fleeting sight of the low-level strike planes and the thunderous roar that trailed them had terrified and excited in equal measure. For some, the aircraft had to be enemy bombers now bold enough to attack without the cover of darkness. For others, they were undoubtedly RAF interceptors racing to the defence of London.

'Perhaps the NUP itself is reaching its sell-by date,' suggested Patel. 'We are ultimately stewards of the commonwealth, not dictators. It's always been the stated goal of Joint Forces Command to restore democracy once the time is right.

Otherwise, what is our stewardship for? Do not misunderstand me. I'm not saying that we have necessarily reached that juncture, but perhaps it is time to start creating a roadmap to our desired destination.'

'And what about Henderton?' asked Air Chief Marshal Dilger. 'If he's outlived his usefulness, what do we do with him?'

They were the last words that Dilger would ever speak. The two Partisan missiles from the first MQ-25, approaching at over Mach 2, were not heard by anyone in the meeting. There was no warning of impending danger, no time to process what was happening, no chance to react. The entire Joint Forces Command was wiped out in the simultaneous explosions which destroyed not only Briefing Room A, but most of the block in which the meeting was being held. No more than two seconds later, the aircraft streaked overhead before banking into the long 180 degree turn which would redirect it back towards Lakenheath. The ruins of Block A were engulfed in flame and were belching plumes of swirling, oily smoke. By the time the second drone had repeated the performance of the first, nothing useable remained of blocks A, or B, or of the airy, modernist atrium which had once won an award for its architect. Over two hundred people had been killed. Most of them would never be identified.

On the A-600 flying north to Leeds, the Prime Minister was engrossed in a strawberry yoghurt. York was reading the draft of Henderton's speech and was occupied making notes in the margins or crossing out unacceptable sections. Batista was watching York, ready to offer advice if required, but she didn't ask and he didn't mind.

'Some of the content falls outside agreed parameters,' said York with diplomatic circumspection. 'I've adjusted the text where necessary, so that it respects protocols.'

'Whatever,' said Henderton without looking up from his yoghurt. The disdain was palpable. 'Render unto the Admiralty that which is the Admiralty's.'

The Prime Minister and the Navy liaison officers received the Alert State Scarlet message simultaneously.

'Hell,' exclaimed Henderton. 'Something very serious is going on.' He delivered his line convincingly enough, apparently ignorant of the details but electrified by the threat level. He might perhaps have been wiser to express unmitigated bafflement or confusion.

York and Batista were both astonished by the alert.

'I'll check it out,' said York as she disappeared into the cockpit.

'It's probably nothing,' said Batista.

The PM appeared to have relaxed. Within a minute, York reappeared, the grimmest of expressions on her face.

'It's definitely Alert State Scarlet,' she said. 'The situation is confused but there has been some sort of attack on Joint Headquarters. Multiple explosions. Significant loss of life. I've told the pilot to abort Leeds and return to Brize Norton. We need to get you to a place of safety, Prime Minister. The Comanche will escort us all the way.'

'Agreed,' said Henderton. 'The chopper can take me to Chequers as soon as we land.'

At Northwood, the billowing smoke polluted the air. The noise from the orange rescue helicopter overhead and the wailing sirens of dozens of approaching ambulances and fire engines did not reassure that help was at hand, but contributed to the overall sense of chaos. There had been no further explosions from what remained of Blocks A and B, but the scores of fire fighters in breathing apparatus, struggling to douse the flames or staunch the smoke, would make no headway for hours.

In Block C, police officers, medics and assorted personnel attended to the numerous casualties. Some had experienced lucky escapes and sat clutching minor injuries, disorientated but comforted by colleagues. Others lay motionless on the ground as paramedics did their utmost to revive them. The unluckiest amongst the injured had been abandoned in favour of those with better chances. Two police officers in high visibility jackets helped one of the civilian personnel negotiate an unsteady path through the carnage to the improvised triage station outside. The woman was dazed and did not speak. She was missing both shoes and the left leg of her trousers. The blood from her bared knee trickled almost lazily down her shin. A team of six green-uniformed paramedics arrived, laden down with rucksacks, holdalls and cases of medical equipment. As they walked, glass crunched uncomfortably underfoot. They were immediately directed to the collapsed corner of Block C, where fire fighters had already managed to extricate some of the survivors from the rubble.

In the Operations Room at Lakenheath, the arrival of Wing Commander Wakeman and Major Security Officer Benjamin subdued the commotion. They would no doubt explain to the assembled Squadron exactly what was going on. Benjamin, as had become usual, took the lead.

She was, she stated, not yet in full possession of the facts but would do her best. There had apparently been some kind of power struggle within the Armed Forces. A group, she understood, of senior officers within the Army or the Navy had detonated a number of bombs within the Joint Headquarters buildings in an attempt to eliminate Joint Forces Command and seize power. The rapid deployment of AAVs by Wing Commander Wakeman, to whom the nation owed an immense debt of gratitude, had liquidated the conspirators and thwarted the attempted coup. The situation at Northwood, she regretted, was not pretty. There had inevitably been considerable loss of life. The Partisan missile, as the pilots were aware, was not a subtle weapon. RAF Lakenheath was to remain at Alert State Orange until further notice. She would brief the Squadron again at 0800 hours, when she hoped to be able to say more.

MacDermott retreated to the Tech Room, retrieved his dollar and inserted it into the games console. He spent the next three hours feverishly repelling alien invaders and trying to displace thoughts of the day his younger brother had died at the Christmas market in Halifax.

After landing at Brize Norton, York escorted the PM to the Comanche helicopter which would fly him to the security of Chequers in fewer than twenty minutes. Although careful not to betray his feelings, he was inordinately happy. The day could not have gone better.

'Good luck, Prime Minister,' said York with a sincerity she would later regret.

In spite of the fact that his liaison officer had patently been assigned to keep the PM in check as much as render him assistance, the ice-blue eyes, the uniform and the implacable nature had always made her an attractive proposition. The knowledge that she would soon be disempowered served only to whet his appetite.

'Dangerous times, Lieutenant Commander York,' he said. 'Dangerous times. Although a good time to have friends in high places. Have you ever considered joining the Party?'

'I am, and will always be, a Royal Navy officer, sir,' replied York. 'With regard to parties, I'm more fancy dress than political.'

22 NO OTHER WORD FOR IT

Liverpool, 27th June

It was a sunny Thursday. Liberated from the work brigade for the day, Thomas and Aston were ensconced on the sofa with Freya. Ersatz tea in hand, they were watching the state funeral organised to commemorate the victims of the Northwood raid.

Three days had elapsed since the destruction of the Joint Command Headquarters and the Prime Minister had declared today to be a national day of mourning. Schools were closed, shops were closed, and work brigade commanders had instructed their charges to stay at home in order to watch the solemn events in London and to give thanks for their own deliverance. Martina, who was confident that PJ never closed his warehouse under any circumstances, had what she termed 'an errand to run' and would be back as soon as she could. In spite of the events in London, she was brimming with excitement and had made the others promise to be in when she returned.

In the lead-in to the funeral, Alexander Chant, the veteran NBC commentator, deployed his practised gravitas to remind the nation of the horrors of the recent assault on the Joint Forces Command Headquarters. Aware of the need to dispel rumours, he confirmed that the raid had been orchestrated by defeatists within the British Armed Forces who had betrayed their motherland and had thrown in their lot with the enemy.

As Aston became increasingly agitated at the idea that high-ranking military leaders could commit such reprehensible acts in order to save their own skins, Thomas's gnawing incredulity got the better of him. When he suggested that perhaps he and Aston should take the announcement with a pinch of salt, Aston suggested that perhaps his partner might like to stop patronising him. Following a surprisingly short sequence of increasingly gnarly exchanges, Aston stomped off to hammer out several energetic iterations of 'Wipe Out' on his drum kit before embarking on a series of extended and unrestrained solos.

'You shouldn't wind him up so much,' said Freya. 'You know what he's like.'

'Oh, we always make up,' replied Thomas. 'We never go to sleep on our anger. You can thank the drum kit for that.'

With the sun high in the sky, temperatures in London already exceeded thirty degrees. In his inimitable, measured tones, Alexander Chant informed the nation that after tolling the time at noon, Big Ben would remain silent for the remainder of the day in recognition of the sacrifice made by the 276 victims of the Northwood bombing.

In the street below the Gothic Revival tower which housed the Great Bell, the flag-draped coffins, ostensibly containing the mortal remains of the members of Joint Command, rested on six slate-grey gun carriages. A nineteen-gun salute resounded from nearby Saint James's Park, and the veteran commentator, perhaps overreaching himself in his desire to convey the sombre mood to the viewers, described the report of each gun as 'the sound of the departed, banging sonorously on the doors to the afterlife'. As the rumbling echoes of the final shot faded slowly to silence, a single drum started to beat and the cortège began its tour. The coffins were escorted by a company of Royal Marines marching at ceremonial pace, their rifles inverted in respect.

The Band of His Majesty's Royal Marines began a somnolent lament and the six gun carriages were each drawn through the streets of Westminster by an armoured patrol vehicle as black as any Victorian funeral horse. The many thousands of mourners, allowed for today into the Westminster Security Zone, watched in respectful silence or exchanged whispered observations about the cheerless cortège. In many places, Union Jacks and NUP banners waved languorously in the still summer air.

The procession crawled past the Cenotaph, past Downing Street and out of the Security Zone, before continuing its measured and doleful march beneath the welcome shade of the Plane trees lining the Mall. On the balcony of Buckingham Palace, the King, befogged by Alzheimer's but attended by his devoted and indefatigable staff, looked on and wept quietly, uncertain of whose funeral he was watching and distressed by his inability to remember. The cortège skirted Saint James's Park and passed Whitehall once more. After an hour, it ended its mournful journey at Saint Paul's Cathedral.

During the service of remembrance, which featured carefully selected texts from a variety of faiths, the Prime Minister evoked the iconic images of the cathedral dome standing undamaged amidst the fire and smoke of the Blitz, a symbol of unyielding British determination. He thanked God for deliverance, before focussing his thoughts on the victims.

'We lament the cold-blooded murder, and there can be no other word for it,' said Henderton looking directly at the camera, 'of some of the most dedicated, the most loyal and the most patriotic citizens this nation has had the privilege to know. Many thousands of words have been spoken in the days since the craven assault on Northwood, but none of those words were really adequate. Words never are in the face of senseless tragedy. Words cannot describe how the British people felt when it heard of the untimely demise of so many who defend and serve our nation. Not until the vacuum of disbelief was filled with the horror of comprehension did any of us truly realise how much we had lost. We shall remember them. And we shall dedicate our inevitable victory to their memory.'

Following the mass, the heavy caskets were returned to the gun carriages and slowly transported to a pier close to the Tower of London. The coffins, still dressed in their Union Jacks, were carried aboard the Royal Navy motor launch *Bellerophon* and the procession took to the river.

Above the Thames, ten MQ-25s roared overhead in a tight arrowhead formation. Two of the aircraft in the overflight, Alexander Chant informed the nation, had been responsible for driving off the enemy aircraft that had attacked Northwood.

'We're gonna win this bloody war,' said Aston who had reappeared, fresh from a shower, still dripping and dressed only in a towel. 'We're gonna win it. Did you see those planes? Fuck me. We've got to build more of those bad boys. But, hey. Thank God we have Gilbert Lathum Henderton to lead us through all this, eh? What is it he says? "There will be peace, but first there shall be victory. Victory in our time." Something like that.'

Aston and Thomas exchanged a conciliatory smile.

'Amen to peace,' said Thomas. 'And with any luck, as well

as peace there'll be brigade work that involves daylight and fresh air.'

'You've lost weight,' said Freya to her father.

'We've all lost weight,' replied Aston.

'Well, that's something I can definitely thank the Prime Minister for,' said Thomas.

Aston traipsed back upstairs to get dressed, and Thomas made space on the sofa, ready to clasp his partner's hand on his return. Freya and Thomas continued to watch as camera drones followed the progress of the launch past the Shard, beyond the Isle of Dogs and on towards the glinting steel towers of the first of the Thames tidal barriers. As the *Bellerophon* neared the enormous floodgates, the NBC cameras descended and tracked the boat from a stationary position about four metres above the lapping water. Seconds after the motor launch had passed between the mammoth central piers of the barrier, the three-thousand-tonne sluice gates began to rise slowly from beneath the Thames in a flourish conceived by Henderton himself to represent the finality of death. Gradually, the gates obscured the *Bellerophon* from view. The cameras held position and, in time, the Navy launch, the oaken caskets and the Union Jacks that adorned them were gone. The live coverage gave way to a drip-feed of highlights, underpinned by the reassuring strains of Elgar's 'Nimrod'.

At Gravesend, and well out of the sight of cameras, the coffins were to be removed from the deck of the launch, transported by military truck to Maidstone and incinerated beneath a pyre of oily, wooden railway sleepers.

Tiring of the clip show, Freya strummed quietly at the strings of the unplugged American Ultra Telecaster that Martina had presented to her the previous week. It had been a while since Freya played lead in her raucous band whilst studying at the Liverpool Institute of Performing Arts, but she had her father's natural facility with music and would no doubt soon feel that she was completely up to speed.

'It was a moving funeral,' said Freya.

'I thought the bit with the Thames Barrier gates was a tad corny,' observed Thomas.

'I liked it,' said Freya. 'The gateway to Heaven or Valhalla or something. It made me cry.'

'Ah, the NBC will be delighted,' said Thomas with a wry smile. 'Their work is done.'

Not long after the end of the broadcast, Martina returned from PJ's warehouse which, as expected, had remained open in spite of the national day of mourning. Excitedly, she ushered Freya, Thomas and the now fully dressed Aston out to the van, which she had reversed onto the redbrick drive at the front of the house.

'My Lords, Ladies and Gentlemen, I give you... ta-daaah.'

She opened the rear doors with a flourish, like some kind of music hall impresario revealing a headline act. Freya, Aston and Thomas could only gawp in amazement. It looked like Martina had burgled Abbey Road.

'Give me a hand,' she said.

Martina pointed to an identical pair of synthesisers. 'Neither of them work quite right, but I reckon I can make one decent keyboard out of the two of them.'

Excitedly, Freya and Thomas carried the keyboards into the house.

'Oh, I'm rocking out just thinking about this,' said Freya.

'We are so gonna have a blast. It's gonna be so much fun. We're gonna be a kick-ass band, alright. And that's kick-ass with a capital kick.'

Thomas, regretful that he did not get any further than Piano Grade Six whilst at school, fretted that he might be somewhat out of practice. Freya was certain, however, that his skills would be more than adequate for what she and Martina had in mind. When Aston opened the case containing a pristine Fender Precision Bass, his jaw fell slack in amazement.

'It works fine,' said Martina. 'Good as new.'

Martina disappeared once more and returned with a scratched white Maxxbook laptop sporting a small diagonal crack across one corner of its antique screen. With another gleeful flourish, she booted it up and showed them the suite of somewhat dated but nonetheless useable professional recording apps.

'Not only do we have more instruments than you can shake a stick at,' she said with a smile. 'We also have a studio. We just have to decide what to play.'

She handed Thomas a bag containing a pair of vocal microphones with cables, gave one of the two stands to Freya and passed the other to Aston. Two Marshall practice amps and more cables emerged, plus a twelve-string electric guitar and a wooden box rammed to the top with tambourines, maracas, cowbells and other assorted percussion instruments. As the other three excitedly set up the bass and the mics in Aston's drum room, Martina brought in a cardboard box containing three scruffy books of classic music: *Stevie Wonder - Anthology*; *Guitar Tab Gold - The Rolling Stones*; and *The Best of the Who - Full Lyrics and Chords*.

'I've heard of The Who,' said Thomas, picking the book from the box. 'They're a grammatical conundrum. Why do you think they gave themselves such a curious name?'

'Who knows?' said Martina. 'Maybe The If was already taken.'

'Hey, look at this,' said Thomas, suddenly upbeat. 'They have a song called "Won't Get Fooled Again". We should definitely play that one. Maybe we could get the Prime Minister on vocals.'

23 LINES OF COMMUNICATION

RAF Brize Norton, 27th June

The base at Brize Norton remained at Alert State Orange and was completely locked down. RAF Regiment troops had blockaded the gates and were patrolling the perimeter day and night. At all levels, brooding suspicion infected previously straightforward interactions and undermined trust in the occasional communications received from RAF Air Command in High Wycombe. Lieutenant Commander York and Lieutenant Batista had dedicated the better part of the last seventy-two hours to their frustrated attempts to contact Royal Navy Headquarters and garner reliable intelligence about the course and ramifications of recent events. In spite of the persistent i-comm reminders, they paid scant attention to the state funeral beyond listening to the Prime Minister's eulogy at Saint Paul's Cathedral.

When Batista knocked on the door to York's quarters and announced his return from the Command Block, she was couched at the desk beside her bed voicing contact names to her i-comm and repeatedly failing to establish lines of communication. Having received permission to enter, Batista confessed that he had failed to glean any useful information from uneasy conversations with both the Station Commander and the Ops Manager. The good news, if he could call it that, was that he had signed out two Glock 17 service pistols from the armoury. He sat down and gently placed the blue-grey holdall containing the weapons beside his chair whilst York returned to her efforts to contact Royal Navy Headquarters in Portsmouth. Realising that she did not need to be distracted, Batista lifted the black boxes containing the Glocks from the holdall and focussed his attention on removing the magazines and, as quietly as he could manage, safety-checking the two semi-automatic service pistols. Satisfied that they would work if needed and that the spare clips were full, he returned the weapons to their boxes and the boxes to the holdall.

By the end of another afternoon struggling to gain some meaningful insight into the events in Northwood and the palpable shift in the balance of power, York was no further forward. That the Joint Forces Command had been murdered was patently obvious, and working out who had the most to gain from their sudden elimination did not require a masters in criminology. Just how the prime suspect, who had brazenly used the word 'murder' in his address at Saint Paul's, might have mustered the support from within the Armed Forces to carry out such an audacious and startling coup remained completely unclear. In this regard, Lieutenant Commander York was anxious to establish how far the NUP and Modsec might have infiltrated the British military, and the RAF in particular. Right now, there was only one person that she knew with absolute certainty she could trust and he was sitting behind her, checking the pistols for a third time and waiting patiently for her instructions.

'Shit,' said York in exasperation. Yet again she had failed to connect to Navy Command in Portsmouth. 'Same bloody message every time. Same bloody, fake, irritating pre-recorded voice. "The Ministry of Defence is currently working to re-establish lines of communication." Yeah, right.'

'So, all comms are down except for Modsec. How the hell did they manage to organise the funeral?' said Batista.

'Search me.'

She allowed her head to drop, breathed out slowly and, with her elbow on the desk, rubbed her forehead with the thumb and index finger of her right hand. Batista returned the weapons boxes to the holdall, got up from the chair and did something he shouldn't. He crossed the room and began to massage her neck and shoulders. They were in uniform, he knew he was breaking their rules, and Batista was fully expecting to be rebuffed and in all probability reprimanded. To his surprise, York said nothing. He felt the tightness in her muscles and applied greater pressure with his thumbs. The Lieutenant Commander closed her eyes and began to relax her breathing. When he saw her shoulders begin to drop and her head tilt back slightly, he leaned forward and kissed her on the crown of her head. York turned, causing his hands to slip from her shoulders. She met his eyes and breathed a single word.

'Lips.'

It was an invitation, not a command. As York stood up, Batista embraced her, and they kissed with an eagerness bordering on urgency.

The Modsec Intelligence and Data Analyst listening in to their conversation had a clear idea of how the rest of the afternoon would play out. She got out of her chair, stretched, and seized the opportunity to take a bathroom break and fetch herself a pasty from the canteen.

24 QUITE THE REVERSE

It was eight o'clock in the morning. The temperature in Suffolk had already reached twenty five degrees and there was not a cloud in the sky. The arrival of the three black Modsec armoured patrol vehicles at the main gate of RAF Lakenheath was expected, but only by Benjamin and Wakeman. The Wing Commander had stationed himself in his office, ready for the inevitable query from the RAF Regiment guards on duty at the gate. Sitting in a Land Rover at the main entrance to the base, Major Security Officer Benjamin had at this point been waiting for over twenty minutes and had exhausted her limited reserve of patience. When the armoured patrol vehicles at last arrived, she presented her ID to the duty guards and instructed them to raise the barriers. As soon as the RAF soldiers received confirmation from their Station Commander, the red and white booms rose to vertical and Benjamin waved the angular Modsec APVs through.

Wing Commander Wakeman then issued a station-wide announcement via i-comm that the base was now at Alert State Orange. Using the exact form of words issued to him by Benjamin, he reassured all personnel on station that he had taken the decision, given current uncertainties, to provide additional security measures on site and had, after much nego-tiation, been able to secure the services of one of the newly formed Modsec units. There would be a meeting for pilots and operations personnel at 0900 hours in the Main Briefing Room. Other briefings would follow as required.

Flight Lieutenants Xu, Merton and Finnan had been woken by Wakeman's call and hauled themselves reluctantly out of bed. The remaining pilots were already having breakfast in the bar and bolted down as much of their Utility cornflakes as they could before making their way to the Main Briefing Room. Once the pilots were gone and the bowls were unattended, the Labrador had a field day.

When the aircraft technicians arrived at Hangar 11 to begin their shift converting the remaining MQ-25s to strike capability, they were surprised to find one of the black Gurkha APVs already stationed by the side doors. The eight Modsec personnel, some male, some female, but all dressed in charcoal paramilitary uniforms, had quit the Gurkha and had been idly waiting for their arrival. They formally introduced themselves, then asked one of the technicians to put the kettle on and make them a brew.

The driver of the second armoured patrol vehicle had parked by the security barriers at the main gate. Pleasantries with the RAF guards concluded, the squad had divided into four teams of two and had initiated patrols of the base which would apparently take all day.

The third group had left its vehicle close to the doors to Block A and, at Benjamin's behest, was now waiting in the Main Briefing Room, ready to be presented to the Squadron. Like the team now enjoying a mug of ersatz outside Hangar 11, the Modsec squad in the Main Briefing Room were dressed in black paramilitary uniforms. Their service pistols discretely holstered, they chatted amongst themselves as they awaited the arrival of Major Security Officer Benjamin and Wing Commander Wakeman.

Benjamin took the lead. She asked her squad to introduce themselves in turn by rank and surname, almost as though conducting an icebreaker at the start of a corporate team building event. At Wakeman's suggestion, the pilots and operations crew of 161 Squadron uneasily followed suit.

'I apologise for the lack of advance notice,' said Benjamin, 'but following the events at Northwood, I am certain the Squadron can appreciate that all security arrangements have to be cloaked in a measure of secrecy.'

The Wing Commander nodded.

'But allow me to reassure you,' she continued, almost benevolently. 'You need have absolutely no cause for concern at the arrival of my colleagues. Quite the reverse. The Modsec teams are here to provide much-needed security at a time of national crisis.'

'Excellent,' said Wakeman.

'There is, however, another matter I wish to broach with you,' said Benjamin in a markedly less reassuring tone, 'and it is not one that gives me any kind of pleasure. You will no doubt have been aware of my presence on station for some days. Today it is my duty to inform you that my primary purpose here is to investigate a security breach. We have reason to believe there may be a link between this station and the perpetrators of recent events in London.'

'That doesn't make sense,' said Dibaba.

'Your naivety astonishes me, Flight Lieutenant. But I am certain that neither of us would like sensitive information to fall into the hands of the enemy, would we?'

'There is no enemy,' retorted the pilot.

'Oh, there's always an enemy,' said Benjamin. 'Or have we learnt nothing from Northwood?'

'I think, Dibaba,' said Wakeman, 'the briefing should be seen as an opportunity to listen.'

'Sir.'

Benjamin moved on from the question of the security breach and proceeded to inform the Squadron that there would be significant changes to tactics in future operations. She did not go into detail and the statement elicited a degree of curiosity but no immediate concern. Her announcement, however, of the Government's decision to jettison the Mortality Protocol as no longer fit for purpose provoked audible inhalations of surprise, the nervous stiffening of posture, and the exchange of bewildered glances.

'There may be operations which involve an increased element of risk,' she continued. 'There may potentially be collateral damage and, in some instances, this may result in a regrettable loss of civilian life.'

Dibaba could not restrain herself. 'Is this serious? The Mortality Protocol?'

'The war is a reality show, Dibaba,' said Benjamin abruptly. 'And the reality show just got real. The time has come to cry "Havoc!" and let slip the gods of war.'

'Flight Lieutenant Dibaba,' said the exasperated Wakeman, 'you will remain silent for the remainder of this briefing, and that's an order.'

'Yes, sir,' she replied. 'Understood.'

With an edge of sarcasm directed at Dibaba, Benjamin

thanked the Squadron for listening, turned sharply on her heels and left the room.

With his Modsec overseer gone, Wakeman was left to elucidate a number of organisational matters. The three paramilitary teams would rotate duties between Hangar 11, external security patrols and Block A. All Modsec personnel would use Briefing Room G as a dedicated breakout room during their stay, and would be housed in Block J. They were not, under any circumstances, to be disturbed. The Wing Commander then announced, almost as though it were an afterthought, that Major Security Officer Benjamin would be interviewing all ground crew and each member of the aircrew individually and in due course. Wakeman dismissed the Squadron without inviting questions. He was clearly unhappy, predominantly with Dibaba. The more lip he heard from her, the better he liked his AAVs.

Following the dismissal of the Squadron from the unscheduled briefing, Itoje and Becker were due on Quick Reaction Alert and reported to the Aircrew Ready Room. Both harboured suspicions that any discussion might somehow be overheard, so they sat in unquiet silence and tried to read. Merton, Finnan and Xu had returned to their bunks, but sleep stubbornly eluded them. In the Mess, the collective mood was subdued. By now Bosko would normally have selected some guitar-driven classic from the rack of vinyl, but today she flicked aimlessly back and forth through the extensive collection of albums, lost in thought and too distracted to make a choice. Lopez, Bosko, Callaghan and Dibaba had retrieved their breakfast bowls, failing to notice that the dishes had been licked scrupulously clean by the Labrador, and were pouring out more Utility-brand cereal and milk. Like Itoje and Becker in the Aircrew Ready Room, they were nervous that somehow Modsec might be eavesdropping.

'OK,' said Warszawski. 'I'm going to say it. What the fuck is going on?'

'The loss of innocent life is what the fuck is going on,' said Dibaba.

'But surely they're not going to have us bombing civilian targets,' said Bosko, perhaps trying to convince herself as much as reassure the others.

'Then why abandon the Mortality Protocol?' said Dibaba. 'Why?'

That black and white image from her schooldays of the young Vietnamese child, her clothes burnt off by napalm, her face racked with pain and terror, fleeing from a home now lost in rolling, dark grey smoke would not leave Dibaba alone.

'Maybe there's a threat from abroad,' ventured Callaghan.

'There is no abroad,' said Lopez categorically.

They were out of ideas. Silence slowly descended as they made their second attempt at breakfast. The dog, struggling to be noticed, flopped its head onto Warszawski's thigh, expecting the neck muscles behind its ear to be rubbed immediately. The Labrador had to repeat the prompt several times before the pilot responded as desired.

Bosko, having initially given up on the albums in order to focus on her breakfast, leapt suddenly out of her armchair, possessed with an idea. She had decided that it was, after all, an excellent idea to play some classic rock at high volume, partly to lift everyone's spirits and partly to piss off anyone who might be listening in. She knew the ideal recording for the job and quickly prised Led Zeppelin's fourth album from the pile.

'How about this for a slice of turn-it-up-to-eleven?' she said as she dropped the needle onto the first track of side one and cranked up the volume.

Although Bosko's question received little more than nods of faint acknowledgement from her fellow pilots, the energy of the music gradually had the desired effect, appropriating their attention, causing feet to tap and fingers to drum on the armrests. By the start of the last song on the album the Squadron was at least distracted, if not exactly happy.

The final track was a reworking of an old blues number about the Great Mississippi Flood. The song began with a slow, commanding and portentous drum beat, joined after two bars by moaning harmonica, bluesy electric guitar and steady bass. As the singer wailed a repeated lament about the unrelenting rain that threatened to breach the levee on the Mississippi and unleash a flood that would destroy his home, the song built to a crescendo of anguished vocals, squalling guitar riffs and echoing harmonica, anchored throughout by that ominous, pounding beat. The groove was compelling, almost hypnotic, but Bosko was now wondering how much attention was being paid to the baleful lyrics. Probably not much, she decided. Who really ever thinks about the words to these things? After several brooding minutes, the music ground to a halt, leaving the song's protagonist displaced by forces beyond his control and facing an uncertain future.

'Maybe we should have played side one twice,' said Warszawski philosophically.

'Fuck it,' said Dibaba. 'I'm going to speak to Wakeman.'

Wakeman's PA claimed not to know where he was and

Gunatillaka could do no more than inform her that the Wing Commander had been in the Ops Room earlier, but she had no idea where he might have gone. Dibaba's concerted attempts to track Wakeman down turned out to be as futile as her comrades' efforts to dissuade her from confronting him.

When Dibaba returned to the bar, she found a note on her breakfast bowl. It had a single word scrawled on it in Warszawski's inimitable, spidery handwriting: football. She grabbed her kit from her room and jogged the mile or so to the old American High School. Arriving at the Sports Hall, she found Warszawski, Lopez, Bosko, Callaghan, Merton, Finnan and Xu venting their frustrations on a defenceless ball in a frantic game of five-a-side, albeit with only four players per side and a black Labrador making up the numbers for one of the teams. The dog had rapidly picked up the concept of chasing the football and pushing it around with its snout, but its understanding of the rules extended no further. Nevertheless, the Labrador was having the time of its canine life. This was more than could be said for the seven pilots who were almost insanely intent on dissipating their pent-up aggression by shooting early, shooting often and above all, shooting hard. Dibaba worked out which team the dog was theoretically playing for, got changed and displayed a commensurate lack of subtlety as she took her first cathartic shot on goal. By one in the afternoon, the pilots had been playing for almost an hour, the temperature outside was approaching thirty-two degrees and the teams were all too hot and too short of breath to continue.

As the flyers emerged from their cold showers and began the slow walk back to Block A, Major Security Officer Benjamin, now Station Commander in all but name, and

Wing Commander Wakeman were still locked in discussion in her office in Block J. The Prime Minister, Benjamin enthused, displayed a true understanding of human nature in his assertion that the increased sound and fury, the sense of threat and the experience of suffering would ultimately bolster popular morale, exactly as the Blitz had done over a century before. Although the Modsec officer was the driving force behind the changes to operational tactics and Wakeman was hardly in a position to take issue with anything she proposed, the Wing Commander was nonetheless a loyal member of the NUP and was only too ready to back the Prime Minister's plans. When he put it to Benjamin that his pilots might struggle to accept missions in which civilians would inevitably die, she reminded him in no uncertain terms that both he and his Squadron had only one real mission and that was to obey orders.

The two NUP members dedicated the remainder of their morning to planning a series of operations that would give the citizens of the UK the kind of tooth and claw experience of conflict that the Prime Minister so eagerly desired. Benjamin called up a map of Britain on her laptop and pointed out the Civil Defence anti-aircraft batteries that Modsec had now furnished with Pipistrel radar systems. The fifty-year-old equipment, she somewhat condescendingly explained to the Wing Commander, was obsolete, but would nevertheless look good on the *Six O'Clock News*. Wakeman was fully aware that the radar represented no major threat to 161 Squadron. The system was, he concurred, complete junk. In any case, the Civil Defence commanders would know that any attempt to lock on to an F-95 with their antiquated systems would simply betray their position and invite an immediate and deadly response from the air.

Nevertheless, Wakeman felt the need to point out that the safety of the pilots could never be completely guaranteed. The chances of a Civil Defence potshot bringing down an aircraft were low in the extreme, but, as Warszawski had recently discovered, they were not zero. Whilst the death of a highly trained pilot would be regrettable, the Wing Commander reassured Benjamin that it would not in any way diminish the Squadron's capacity to pursue the PM's objectives. In the event of pilot loss, Wakeman could, he was proud to say, fill any gaps from the shadow squadron of AAVs.

Benjamin nodded and suggested that the Prime Minister would, in any case, probably leap at the opportunity to invite some grieving relative to Westminster and, with the NBC on hand to capture the emotion of the encounter, activate his talent for empathy. He would no doubt find the perfect form of words to convey the gratitude of the entire nation and respectfully present the next of kin with a small black box containing a gleaming Distinguished Flying Cross, a medal which the deceased flyer would never have the chance to wear. Every cloud, Benjamin mused, had a silver lining.

25 THE SOUND OF TRUMPETS

RAF Lakenheath, 2nd July

In spite of the sudden arrival of the contingent of Modsec paramilitaries, the situation at RAF Lakenheath, at least on the surface, appeared relatively calm. Major Security Officer Benjamin had reassured the Squadron that the few traces of disloyalty within the RAF had been rooted out and consequently the Alert State at Lakenheath had been downgraded to White, indicating 'no specific threat' or 'situation stable'. Whilst the Modsec officer, and those who commanded her, might well have been feeling invulnerable, the terminology did not resonate with the members of 161 Squadron. As far as the pilots were concerned, the influence of Modsec was spreading like a fungus whose sparse and short-lived fruiting bodies belied the web of unseen filaments that connected and fed them.

On the base, the work to convert all twelve of the tanker drones to strike capability continued apace. Additional missile pylons had been located in the Consolidated Parts Store and were being fitted to the three MQ-25s currently in the Maintenance Hangar. The first of the four aircraft already fully equipped as fighter-bombers was waiting in the Corrosion Control Hangar, where that afternoon, it was to be sprayed black in readiness for nocturnal operations.

In the dim, blue light of the windowless Operations Room, Chief Technician MacDermott, inordinately troubled by recent events, was trying to allay his anxieties and create the impression, should Wakeman or Benjamin choose to observe, that he was devoting his undivided attention to the task in hand. Privately, he had not the slightest desire to fulfil his unwelcome and unconscionable duty, but he was in an inescapable bind and was struggling to see a way forward. In his two years at Lakenheath MacDermott had been as happy to program the weapons systems for 161 Squadron's missions as the pilots had been to use them. Today was different. If, during Benjamin's briefing the previous morning, he had allowed himself to hope that the principle of the Mortality Protocol would in essence be preserved and that the promised tactical changes would be inconsequential, he now knew better. The parameters for Operation Boltmaker, presented to him that morning by Wakeman, had made his blood run cold. The immediate proximity of the Linacre Specialist Care Centre to the target zone made substantial collateral damage an absolute certainty and would inevitably result in significant numbers of civilian casualties. The Mortality Protocol, which had previously spared the Squadron from crises of conscience, was not only 'no longer fit for purpose', as Benjamin had put it, it was lying face down in a ditch with a hunting knife between its shoulder blades.

The pilots had seen neither hide nor hair of their Wing Commander since the previous day's briefing, but they had all received an update via i-comm that new missions were currently being scheduled. They spent much of their morning again playing breathless, spleen-venting football in the American High School or vigorously working out in the Upper East Side Fitness Center.

In spite of their physical exertions, Flight Lieutenants Dibaba and Warszawski remained perturbed in equal measure by the murders at Northwood, the brazen hypocrisy of the state funeral, and Benjamin's apparently unchallenged dominion over Wing Commander Wakeman. After lunch, they decided to spring themselves from the agitated gloom that descended on the Mess and exercise the seemingly tireless Labrador that had taken such a shine to them.

The troubles that weighed upon the two pilots were naturally of no concern to the dog who, as ever, was straining at the leash and provided them with immediate distraction. Ideally they would let him chase an old tennis ball for thirty minutes, but releasing a young and excitable Labrador so close to the runway of an Air Force base was perhaps not the wisest thing to do. In any case, they didn't have a ball. They would, however, find an inexhaustible supply of sticks beneath the trees which flanked the fairway of Lakenheath's formerly immaculate golf course.

'This guy needs some time off the leash,' said Dibaba as the dog pulled even harder.

'I know the feeling,' said Warszawski.

'Yeah, copy that. I'll find him a stick.'

Beneath one of the several towering beech trees that flanked that section of the golf course, Dibaba located a short but weighty length of fallen branch and the Labrador could not contain his excitement. Warszawski let the young dog off the leash and Dibaba slung the muddy stick as far as she could. Within seconds the delighted Labrador had retrieved it and plonked it back at her feet, eager to chase until he could chase no more.

The sudden roar of turbofan engines distracted the pilots, but not the dog. The first of the MQ-25s, back from an initial test flight with a full complement of ordnance, passed to their right, executed an immaculate landing and taxied towards Hangar 11. The other two followed at perfectly regular intervals.

Dibaba and Warszawski continued their conversation, whilst repeatedly throwing the chewed and increasingly slobbery stick for their tireless canine friend.

'It beggars belief,' said Warszawski contemptuously. 'Two of our MQ-25s kill almost 300 people and then they literally parade them over London in honour of the dead. What the fuck is going on? And how the hell has Wakeman been dragged into this godawful fucking mess?'

'Wakeman's about as likely to question orders as those drones,' said Dibaba. 'What I'd really like to know is, who issues the orders in the first place?'

'Well, clearly not Joint Command. Modsec?'

'Maybe, but Benjamin didn't show her face on station until after Wakeman began converting the MQ-25s.'

'That doesn't mean that Modsec didn't give the original order.'

'True.'

'Are Air Command in on it? Surely not.'

'Fuck knows.'

'Shit,' said Warszawski. 'Wakeman converts the MQ-25s into combat-ready AAVs. Benjamin shows up out of nowhere. The Mortality Protocol is shelved. The drones destroy Northwood. Modsec takes over the base. And the Prime Minister's sitting in Downing Street with his arse in the cream. And it all happened right under our noses. Why the hell didn't we see what was going on?'

'Because we trust our commanders to do the right thing,' said Dibaba, 'and the Squadron couldn't function if we didn't.'

Warszawski shook his head. 'We should've seen it, though. We literally should've seen it coming.'

'Hell. Coulda, shoulda, woulda,' said Dibaba. 'You can't foresee what you can't imagine.'

'I guess.'

'My Dad used to say hindsight is the least merciful form of wisdom.'

'Which means what?'

'Which means, at least I think it means, it's important to know how we got here, but we should learn from it without obsessing about things you can't predict. Something like that. Don't get so preoccupied with analysing the past, that you don't see the future about to smack you in the face.'

'At school,' said Warszawski, 'I had a maths book that had the answers in the back. Why isn't life like that?'

The pair continued to exercise their almost inexhaustible dog whilst attempting to map out the possible course of future events. They rapidly agreed that they would refuse to comply if instructed to attack civilian targets and debated whether any of their fellow pilots might somehow be pressurised, perhaps by Benjamin, into executing iniquitous orders. Confident that their comrades would also refuse, they decided that the Squadron should ideally come to a collective decision to respect the Mortality Protocol come what may. Whether any such decision should be made known to Wakeman in advance was a thornier question. Uncomfortably, Warszawski and Dibaba found themselves beginning to think the unthinkable and wonder whether a time was approaching when they would have no alternative but to borrow a Land Rover and absent themselves permanently from the base.

Eventually, the young Labrador began to tire and lay down by a bunker, panting and chewing at what remained of its saliva-laced beechwood stick. Dibaba and Warszawski sat down on the sand and left the dog to get its breath back. Aware that they could never foresee the unimaginable, they continued in their efforts to imagine the foreseeable.

'I wish my Dad was here,' said Dibaba.

'Well you've got the dog,' said Warszawski. 'And me.'

Their eyes met and she smiled.

'That's good enough.'

By early evening, Dibaba, Warszawski and their canine friend had joined Flight Lieutenants Callaghan, Bosko, Lopez and Xu in the bar once more. The pilots were draped in customary fashion across the armchairs and were now displacing their concerns by listening to *Classic Rock Classics* and taking bets on Itoje and Becker's whereabouts. Perhaps infected with a minor dose of paranoia, Lopez and Callaghan checked as best they could for listening devices and satisfied themselves that their conversations were not being overheard.

One issue that the Squadron could not lay at Benjamin's door was the unfortunately imminent exhaustion of their supply of alcoholic drinks. Whilst the pilots did not believe they were drinking any more than was usual, the reserve of under-strength beer had already run out and the dispenser was beginning to gurgle as it conjured up the last of the gin. They were clearly deluding themselves.

A message announced itself with a tinny ping on Dibaba's i-comm. Was she the first to be called for interview by Major Security Officer Benjamin? She checked the message whilst the others waited for her explanation.

'It's from MacDermott,' she reassured them. 'There's an issue with my helmet. He wants me to check it out this evening.'

'This evening?' said Callaghan perkily. 'Sounds like a date. You know he's got a major crush on you.'

'There are no majors in the RAF,' quipped Dibaba.

'Oh, witty. So witty,' said Callaghan, the sarcasm belying his genuine amusement. It was the first time he'd cracked a smile since Wakeman's briefing.

Bosko put Led Zeppelin's fourth album on again, promised to play the first side on repeat and strapped on her air guitar. The format of the evening was now fixed.

At eight thirty, Callaghan reminded Dibaba of her assignation with the Chief Technician. It was clearly not a date, yet Warszawski was strangely uncomfortable at the idea of Dibaba's meeting with MacDermott being described as such.

It was not always easy to spot MacDermott in the muted light of the Tech Room. The logical first point of call was his work station, but if the Chief Technician was not to be found huddled over his computers, the games console was the next best bet.

MacDermott's private haunt created a ramshackle impression. There were several desks, some of which appeared, judging at least by the dust, never to have been used. Shelves were laden with books, folders, journals, boxes and manuals. Unmarked, translucent plastic crates occupied almost every available space. One crate appeared to be full of cables. Another looked like it contained hard drives or perhaps redundant modems. A third was brimming with unidentifiable electronic components of varying shapes and sizes. There was a repair station, littered with tools, and a tool station which held only those implements that

MacDermott rarely used.

Dibaba wondered at first how the Chief kept track of everything, but closer observation revealed an abundance of order. The anti-g flight suits on the rack were arranged alphabetically by pilot name. All hung facing to the left, the pilot's name badge on the shoulder clearly visible. The helmets, all permanently on charge, followed the same pattern. The seven sets of coloured folders on the shelves were organised according to the sequence of colours within the visible light spectrum. Within each set, there were also seven folders, each adorned with a different coloured label, once again sequenced from red to violet. Next to the folders, well-thumbed biographies of Voltaire, Thomas Hobbes, Thomas Jefferson, Goethe and Mary Wollstonecraft progressed from the narrowest to the widest. At this point, Dibaba began to divine patterns almost everywhere.

Try as she might, she could not see MacDermott. When she messaged him, he emerged from a side room she had assumed to be a cupboard.

'Sorry,' he said. 'You got my message, then'

'I did indeed. Something about my helmet?'

'Well, your visor display, really. It has a small fault. Well, not so much a fault, as a deficiency with the input filters. Are you with me so far?'

Dibaba tilted her head slightly and scrunched her nose. 'Not completely.'

'OK. Have you ever had the NBC news ticker scroll across your visor display?'

'NBC news? No. Can't say that I have. I'd have told you. Is that a thing? And why would it happen anyway?'

'It's really an issue with the input filters. Didn't I say that?

Anyhow, it's not a big deal, but there's an outside chance it could conceivably happen. Anything that scrolls across your i-comm might also scroll across your visor display.'

'But you can fix it, right?'

'I can. In fact, I'm working on it, but it's not straightforward. It might be sorted before your next mission, but chances are it won't. Just don't go apeshit with me if it happens.'

'OK. Got it. Thanks for that. Is that it? Are we done?'

'Unless you want to play *Space Invaders*.'

Dibaba had not the slightest desire to play *Space Invaders*. She wanted to go back to the bar and she wanted to talk through some serious shit with Warszawski.

'Tempting as that is, Chief,' she said, 'it's been a crazy couple of days. I'll take a rain check, if that's OK.'

MacDermott ignored Dibaba's cue to bring the conversation to a close.

'The thing about *Space Invaders*,' said the Chief Technician, 'is that they are not bound by the Mortality Protocol, so they kill in large numbers and to the sound of trumpets.'

'To the sound of what now?'

'To the sound of trumpets.'

'Jeez, MacDermott. What are you smoking in that cupboard?'

'It's Voltaire. "It is forbidden to kill, therefore all murderers are punished, unless they kill in large numbers and to the sound of trumpets." Voltaire would have approved of the Mortality Protocol.'

'Then I approve of Voltaire,' she said. 'Are you OK, though? I know it's been a weird couple of days.'

Neither of them were remotely at ease, and both of them knew it.

'I'm fine. As long as we don't start killing in large numbers and to the sound of trumpets.'

'Amen to that,' she said. 'But you're sure you're OK?'

'I'm fine,' he lied. 'Honestly.'

Dibaba thanked MacDermott and headed back to the bar, struggling to process what had just happened. Might the Chief have somehow been off his face on tranqs or had he been genuinely trying to tell her something? Either way, he hadn't made a whole lot of sense. She resolved to message Dr Kaminski and ask her to keep an eye on him.

Contrary to Dibaba's initial suspicions, MacDermott had not been self-medicating, but was so befuddled by indecision that the difference was not easy to see. Her feeling that he might somehow have been trying to communicate something important was, however, bang on the money. Obtuse as MacDermott had been, he had genuinely been attempting to plant a seed in her mind and incorporate her into a convoluted plot to save the lives of possibly hundreds of innocent civilians.

MacDermott was far from sure that the subterfuge he had devised was perfect, but he bolstered himself with the thought that we are all guilty of the good we did not do and that an imperfect plan was infinitely better than no plan at all. Once Dibaba was well out of the way, MacDermott pulled the games console from the wall, retrieved one of his burner phones from the cashbox and sent a message to Martina.

'Hey, sis. Can u do me a favor?'

From the outset, the Chief Technician and his sister had deliberately used outdated textspeak and Americanised spellings in their communications in an attempt to create some plausible deniability, should their exchanges ever come to the notice of prying eyes. MacDermott had also hacked the operating system of his phones so that the correct time and date appeared on the homepage, in the calendar and on the clock, but all the messages appeared to have been sent nine years, seven months, five days, three hours and one minute before their actual despatch. Were the devices ever to be discovered, his exchanges with Martina would appear to date from the time when Lakenheath had been the exclusive preserve of the US Air Force. Whilst these precautions had initially provided MacDermott with a sense of security, he was now fundamentally unconvinced that someone like Benjamin would be deceived for long.

Acutely aware that it was risky to continue using his smartphones, but seeing no viable alternative, the Chief dug out a small bottle of methylated spirits from one of his crates and a tatty rag from another. With his head practically inside the machine, he set about sanitising the surfaces of his antique phones. Before he had finished attempting to remove all traces of his DNA from the first device, a reply pinged in from Martina.

'Name it. Gotta go out tho so not 2nite. xxx'

He fired off a classic 'thumbs up' emoji and returned to the meths and the rag.

Back in the Mess, Dibaba wandered into the bar, still baffled by her exchange with MacDermott.

'Stairway?' she asked as she scanned the room.

'Bad news,' said Bosko. 'We've hit rock bottom. We're out of liquid entertainment. Stairway and Watchtower are on a humanitarian mission to break in to the X-Change superstore over in the mall.'

The Labrador, who had responded with immediate and predictable excitement to Dibaba's arrival, was now sitting by the glass exit door, repeatedly looking out towards the runway and then straight back at Dibaba. The slightly cocked head and supplicating eyes pulled at her heartstrings and she simply could not refuse. She would speak to Warszawski later.

By the time Dibaba and the dog reached the golf course, it was already dark. The sky was devoid of clouds and the canopy of stars offered her a reminder of the immensity of the universe and the ridiculous temptation for sentient beings to locate themselves at its centre.

She sat down in one of the bunkers close to the first hole. Although it was partially overgrown with weeds, the sand was still in evidence and it made for a malleable and reasonably comfortable seat. Based on the feeling of the sand beneath her backside and the view of the stars above, she felt she could almost be sitting in the dunes on the North Norfolk coast, far away from the baffling events of the day. Dibaba lay back and gazed upwards once more. The Labrador lay down too, rolled onto its side and leaned its warm back against her hip. Dibaba liked that.

'Did you know,' she said to the dog, 'there are billions of stars in every galaxy and billions of galaxies in the universe. And the stuff they're beaming out, the stuff we can see, we imperfect humans call that "light". It's what we evolved from, if you think far enough back in time. If you see a light flash across the sky, that's a shooting star, although they're not actually stars at all. Just bits of rock. They might be small like a grain of sand or as big as, I dunno, a Land Rover. And you see those seven stars there? They really are stars. They're called "the Plough". They have pubs named after them. If you need to find your way at night, you can use those seven stars to locate the North Star. Or a pub. And seven? Seven is a prime number. Prime numbers are cool. They're by far the best numbers. Did you know that? Yeah, of course you did. Do dogs have favourite numbers? Or maybe just Labradors?'

Calmed by the tone of Dibaba's voice as she expressed her meandering thoughts, the dog had already fallen asleep. The pilot listened to the slow rise and fall of the Labrador's breathing, rested on her back and waited for the next meteor to dart across her field of vision. She still wanted to talk to Warszawski, but it was a warm night and she was comfortable and it was cosy with the dog against her side. Before long, Dibaba too had succumbed to oblivious sleep.

26 THROUGH THE RAIN

RAF Lakenheath, 3rd July

It was daylight. Dibaba was uncertain whether it was the dog's enthusiastic licking of her ear or the slow patter of lukewarm rain on her cheeks and eyelids that had woken her. She knew she was not in her room, but it took her a second to allay her bewilderment and work out that she had spent the night in the bunker of an overgrown golf course. Given the events of the previous day, she had slept remarkably soundly. Her i-comm, however, revealed that there was a briefing for the Squadron at 0800 hours and she was therefore already twenty minutes late. Feeling strangely uncomfortable about being watched by the dog and aware that Modsec paramilitaries were exploring the site, she thought better of peeing in the bushes and set off back towards Block A. The summer rain increased in intensity and Dibaba was soon soaked to the skin.

'It's all right for you,' she said to the Labrador. 'If you really loved me, you'd offer me your coat.'

They continued in the direction of the main buildings beyond the runway. The dog was impervious to the elements and happy to be heading towards a known source of food. The pilot was drenched, bedraggled and increasingly eager to use the bathroom.

Presently Dibaba made out the shape of an RAF Land Rover skirting the runway and heading towards her.

'I think it would be fair to say you're not Wakeman's favourite person right now,' said Warszawski as Dibaba and the dog climbed in. 'Jeez, Freebird. You look like shit.'

'Tell me something I don't already know.'

'He thinks you've gone AWOL. I saw that Bonzo was gone, so I told Wakeman you took the dog for a walk before breakfast and hadn't returned. That didn't exactly put his mind at rest.'

The Labrador chose this moment to shake itself dry, showering the two human occupants of the vehicle and most of the cabin with rainwater. Unable to see clearly, Warszawski was forced to stop the Land Rover in order to wipe the inside of the windscreen with a rag, which he fumbled from the netting pocket beneath the side window.

'How did you know where I'd be?' Dibaba asked.

'Where else do we go with the dog? Anyway, as I said before, you look like shit. There's a blanket behind your seat.'

Dibaba reached around behind her, grabbed the tatty grey blanket from the back and began rubbing herself down. It wouldn't exactly get her dry but it would make enough of a difference for her to feel less dishevelled. As she reached for the RAF greatcoat Warszawski had also slung in the back, the crates of Whoopty Whoop wheat beer and boxes of Tennessee bourbon whiskey, liberated from the X-Change superstore the night before, commanded her attention for no more than a second.

'We need to talk,' she said.

'You know what, Freebird. Usually when a woman says that to me, it's followed by "Can we pretend it never happened?", but I'm guessing you have something else on your mind.'

Still rubbing herself down, Dibaba launched into an extended and impassioned rant about the Defence of Britain

Act and the Mortality Protocol, about the duty of the RAF to defend and not to endanger the citizens of the UK, and about the inferences that should, or should not, be drawn from Benjamin's talk of changes to their operational tactics. 'As you so eloquently put it the other day, Stairway, what the fuck is going on?'

On the approach to the admin buildings, Warszawski stopped the vehicle a second time and made out that he wanted to wipe the interior windows once more. What he really wanted was to give Dibaba the chance to vent as much of her outrage as possible before she encountered Wing Commander Wakeman.

'Maybe we're reading too much into this,' he said, more in hope than conviction. 'Maybe they're just creating a bit of political latitude in case of some cock-up. You know, like Halifax.'

'Then why tell us the war just got real?'

'Good point. I guess we'll find out soon enough. Anyway, how was your confab with the Chief Technician?'

'Shit,' she said, shaking her head. 'Don't get me started on MacDermott.'

Being infinitely more concerned that the Squadron, and perhaps the entire Royal Air Force, might be taking unlawful and unethical orders from Modsec, Dibaba had already relegated the uncomfortable conversation with MacDermott to some secluded backwater of her consciousness.

'MacDermott,' she continued, 'is in a really strange place right now. He's always been a bit, you know, well a bit kind of ill at ease, but I think he might be losing his grip on reality.'

She then treated Warszawski to a blow by blow account of her bewildering fifteen minutes with the Chief Technician.

'*Space invaders* and mass murder to the sound of trumpets?' said Warszawski in disbelief. 'Really?'

'Really.'

'What is that guy smoking?'

'That's exactly what I said.'

'Maybe you should mention it to the Doc.'

'Already done it. But you might just as easily want to mention me to the Doc.'

Warszawski restarted the engine of the Land Rover.

'Briefing was just more of the same,' he said. 'I'll tell Wakeman you twisted your ankle.'

Neither sound was close, but the crack of a pistol shot and the clatter of a semi-automatic weapon instantly hijacked their attention. Determined to locate the source of the gunfire, Warszawski and Dibaba scanned the middle distance intently but could make out only a pair of aircraft technicians peering through the rain in the direction of the golf course. To get a better fix on the source of any further shots, the two pilots wound down the windows of their vehicle, allowing the rain to pour in on Dibaba's side. Now joined in their scrutiny by the Labrador, Warszawski reported via the Land Rover's radio that they had heard what sounded unmistakably like an exchange of gunfire.

The message was acknowledged by Gunatillaka who requested his location and instructed him to maintain his position and to report any developments. Dibaba, Warszawski and the dog watched and waited for a number of minutes, but there were no further gunshots. The aircraft technicians quickly took the decision to return to the hangar and no doubt reported the incident too.

Eventually, Gunatillaka made contact again. She informed Warszawski that Modsec had the situation under control and that he was to stand down. In front of the vehicle, two flirting wood pigeons flapped noisily past, causing the dog to bark excitedly and Gunatillaka to put two and two together.

'I assume you've located the pilot that goes with that dog,' she said. 'I'll put the kettle on.'

27 FIRST LOYALTY

Liverpool, 3rd July

Two hundred miles away, the rain was, if anything, heavier. The frequent downpours had ushered in a phase of noticeably lower night-time temperatures and in the bedroom overlooking the bramble-infested rear of twenty-three Troutbeck Park Gardens, Kevin and Kireina were sleeping soundly. Their bodies nestled closely together, their snores on occasion almost in tandem, the pair were blissfully unaware of the breakfast of pancakes and blackberry jam that had been prepared for them by Talira.

In spite of the more benign temperatures, Talira had not slept well. She was anxious to convene a house meeting and express her concerns that they might be about to invite more attention upon themselves than was wise. For now, Ricky was bearing the brunt of her disquiet about the hacked NBC file containing the agenda for a forthcoming Cabinet meeting. In spite of the ear-bending, her partner was in a buoyant mood. Not only did his home-made blackberry jam go well with Talira's Canadian-style pancakes, their debate evoked fond memories of gradually but inexorably falling in love with her as they regularly argued about philosophy at university.

'I don't know how you can be so sure about this,' said Talira as she spooned a dollop of jam onto another pancake. 'Modsec will be all over this like a rash the moment someone twigs that the stinger is somehow linked to the content of classified documents.'

'I'm good with it,' replied Ricky, his enunciation hampered by the winning combination of pancake and jam. 'The others are all good with it too.'

'But this is a step change. It's a big deal, a big effing deal. This is not just sloganeering.'

'Oh, come on. I would hardly categorise quoting Nelson Mandela and Michelle Obama as sloganeering. Don't we want people to think for themselves?'

'Yes, of course we do,' said Talira, helping herself to more jam. 'But this is gutter journalism. "Synth-bio soldiers shock horror!" It's dressing rumour up as fact. It's sensationalism, Ricky. It's tantamount to saying "Killer robots poised to enslave UK". It's not what we were trained to do.'

'To be fair, none of this is what we were trained to do,' said Ricky, betraying not the slightest hint of doubt in his voice.

'It's one thing to want people to think for themselves,' she said. 'It's quite another to tell them what to think. If that's what we're about to do, we're no better than the NUP.'

Hardly had Talira finished the sentence before she was ambushed by her emotions. Overcome, she put her head in her hands and fell silent. Ricky immediately got up, moved round the table to her and encouraged her gently to her feet. She had tears in her eyes.

'Come here,' he said, pulling her into an embrace and stroking her hair. He kissed her affectionately on the forehead. 'What was it Professor Underberg used to say?' At this point in their conversation, Ricky attempted a Swedish accent. 'Journalism's first loyalty is to citizens. It must serve as an independent monitor of power.'

Talira smiled.

'You are not going to win me over with a crap impression of my favourite professor.'

'That's as may be,' said Ricky, reverting to his less mellifluous natural voice, 'but at the very least, we want people to know that they're not being told the full story. If they understand that, they might start asking questions.'

He kissed her again on the forehead. Talira looked up, kissed him on the lips and smiled appreciatively. The kiss was pleasantly laced with blackberry jam. Reassured that their differences were purely academic, Talira relaxed a little and the pair soon returned to the pancakes.

'Professor Underberg also used to say that the essence of ethical journalism is a discipline of verification,' said Talira. 'If we don't even know what "synth-bio" means, how can we report on it?'

'It's precisely because we don't know what it means, that we must report on it,' insisted Ricky. He once more adopted his clumsy approximation of Professor Underberg's vocal mannerisms. 'A journalist must be allowed to exercise their personal conscience.'

'The poor man will be turning in his grave,' said Talira. 'You're getting worse each time.'

'Oh, I don't know. I think he'd be flattered that we can still quote him word for word.'

'And what about Modsec?'

'Ah, Modsec, schmodsec,' said Ricky. 'The stingers can't be traced.'

'According to Kevin.'

'And Kevin should know. It's what he does.'

Talira ran her tongue around her mouth, gathering

recalcitrant bramble seeds from between her teeth and reflecting on where to draw the line between daring and recklessness.

'You know what, Ricardo. That impression of Underberg was dire. Utterly and completely dire.'

As her emotions lightened, Talira was edging towards a decision. Outside, the rain continued much as before. At this juncture, the couple had devoured substantially more than half of the jam and most of the pancakes. Kireina and Kevin would never know.

28 THE BEST INTERESTS OF THE SQUADRON

RAF Lakenheath, 3rd July

Dibaba left the Labrador with Warszawski and spent the morning sorting herself out after her impromptu night under the stars. First, she extended her apologies to Wakeman's PA, but offered only the vaguest explanation for her absence from briefing. The pilot's bedraggled appearance and wet clothes were enough, however, to suggest the veracity of Warszawski's dog-walking cover story without forcing her to engage in an outright lie. Dibaba then showered, dug out some dry clothing and threw her damp fatigues into the nearest washing machine. Shortly before twelve, she headed to the Mess for a long overdue breakfast.

'You could at least put on a limp of some sort,' said Warszawski as she made her way towards the kitchen. Immediately, the dog ran to her, its head low and its tail whipping Bosko's legs as it passed.

'Did you find out about the shots we heard?' asked Dibaba.

'It's under investigation,' said Warszawski. 'By Modsec.'

Before Dibaba could ask him anything else, the air raid alarm sounded and a stinger message, looking to all intents and purposes like a genuine news crawl, ticked across the screen of their i-comms.

'PM considers deployment of synth-bio troops. Fierce debate in cabinet. Decision imminent.'

Dibaba grabbed some cereal and joined Warszawski. She ate quickly, but before she was more than halfway through the cornflakes, the mellow, female voice that usually accompanied official air raid alarms called politely for the nation's attention. She reassured the citizenry that all was well, but that some i-comms might be experiencing technical difficulties in some regions. Updates would be despatched and would install automatically. She thanked everyone for their attention and wished them a successful day.

'Well, today is now officially Wacko Wednesday,' said Warszawski. 'Was that somehow news that we're not supposed to see or another "Thought for the Day" from the hacktivist quote-mongers?'

'Hmm, I wonder,' said Dibaba, her eyes wide and her mouth betraying half a smile.

'Synth-bio troops, though? What the hell does that mean? Is it like cyborgs? Can we do that?'

'Yeah, they're designed by talking unicorns and built by elves. Look, Stairway, forget that.' Dibaba put her cornflakes to one side and leaned in so as not to be overheard. 'That was definitely gunfire this morning. We both heard it. And now Modsec are all over it? Shit, I don't like this. I really don't like this.'

Warszawski inclined himself towards Dibaba and adopted a similarly conspiratorial tone. 'Gunnie said someone was taken to the med bay, but she's not sure who.'

'Could it be Wakeman? Is that why we're not getting any information?'

'Gunnie's your best bet if you want hard information, but like I said, she don't know a whole lot.'

'Shit. Wacko Wednesday it is.'

'Military cyborgs would be amazing though. Don't you think? Literally amazing. If they replaced us with cyborgs, we'd be free. You and Doggie the dog could sleep out every night.'

Dibaba flashed Warszawski a smile. 'You know what, Stairway, I think someone might have watched too much sci-fi during his misspent youth.'

'Nothing wrong with that. If you think about it, even Shakespeare wrote sci-fi.'

The apparent intimacy of their conversation had attracted the attention of the others in the bar. The pair were too tempting a target and Merton was the first to take a shot.

'You've got say, they make a cute couple. They've got a dog. They go for walks in the rain. I think I might even sense another two-backed-beast sweepstake in the offing.'

He smirked, and elicited smiles from Bosko, Callaghan, Xu, and Becker.

Callaghan then pitched in. 'I need to warn you though, Freebird, as a friend and a comrade. If you two are going for a stroll down Beastie Lane, you really need to be aware that Stairway habitually launches before he reaches the target area, if you know what I mean.'

'We're talking about sex here, right?' said Dibaba, parrying the taunts.

'You bet your Sweet Child O' Mine we are,' said Callaghan, beaming with satisfaction.

'Well, if it's sex we're talking about,' said Dibaba, 'I'm only too happy to inform you that Flight Lieutenant Warszawski is excellent in the sack.'

The silence confirmed that the brassy response was not what the others were expecting.

'This guy never, and I mean never, launches early and he always hits the target. One hundred percent. And if ever there's a sweepstake, guys, seriously, I'd advise you all to go long.'

The smiles persisted but no-one mustered a comeback. Dibaba looked directly at Callaghan.

'Yeah, Flight Lieutenant Warszawski here is a go-all-night, Olympic standard, sexual athlete. At least, that's what your sister told me, the last time I saw her.'

There was uproar and Callaghan immediately became the new butt of the Squadron's mirth.

'Smooth,' said Warszawski. 'Which sister was it?'

'The one who works in the Cock and Bull Arms in Bullshit Street. Right, I'm going to see if I can talk to Gunnie. You're welcome, by the way.'

No-one apart from Warszawski noticed Dibaba leaving. Gunatillaka, it turned out, knew no more than she had already revealed to Warszawski and was equally concerned about the stultifying lack of information. The remainder of the day passed without any further incident, but furnished neither elucidation nor reassurance.

At 2100 hours, the operations team and all aircrew were summoned by Wakeman to a meeting in the Main Briefing Room. He began his address to the assembled group with an air of gravitas which the Squadron were unused to hearing. As the Wing Commander spoke, his words were captured by his i-comm and reverberated around every building and hangar on station. Wakeman regretted that there had been an accident following a misunderstanding between a Modsec patrol and some of the RAF Regiment troops who also bore responsibility for security at the base. The misunderstanding had resulted in injury to Flight Lieutenant Jaffrey who, following emergency treatment in the med bay, had been transferred to a hospital in London. Wakeman emphasised that the Modsec colleagues were present on station at his invitation and that all instructions from Modsec personnel should be understood as being issued at his request and in the best interests of the Squadron. Without permitting questions, the Station Commander terminated his address and left the room. Whilst neither Benjamin nor any of her paramilitaries were present at the briefing, the burgeoning authority of Modsec could be heard in every word that Wakeman uttered.

29 STEALING IS NOT THE HARD PART

Liverpool, 4th July

In the kitchen of the house in Troutbeck Park Gardens, Martina buttoned her smartphone into one of the pockets of her work pants and returned to the fraught discussion with Kevin and Kireina.

The electronics expert did not need reminding that she had already tried and failed to loosen the bolts anchoring the satellite dish to the rusting outside broadcast van in the dockside scrapyard. She knew the bolts were seized and she knew the dish was heavy and unwieldy. Nevertheless, it was too tempting a target. She was adamant that it could be liberated and she wanted to do it tonight, ideally with Kireina and Kevin along for support. She was, however, growing increasingly impatient with their apparent negativity. They, on the other hand, were equally frustrated with Martina's seemingly unshakable determination to land herself in prison.

'Just listen to yourself for a second,' said Kevin. 'You've already tried once and got absolutely nowhere. Whether you want to use a pipe wrench, an impact driver or whatever, there is no technique that doesn't involve making some sort of noise or falling off the roof. Honestly, Martina, as far as I can see, there's no scenario that doesn't involve the risk of injury, or arrest, or possibly both.'

'And Salford didn't involve risk?' said Martina, now feeling patronised.

'Well, yes, to an extent. You could argue it wasn't a hundred percent risk-free, but the point about Salford is, I knew exactly what I was doing. I'm good at that stuff. It used to be my job before all of this.'

'Believe me,' said Kireina. 'Prison is no walk in the park. Been there. Done that.'

'But what the hell was the point of what we did in Salford if we can't actually broadcast anything? We need a dish. And I know exactly where we can get one. Honestly you two, we can do it. We can absolutely do this.'

They were at an impasse.

'We could go back to the idea of stealing a van from the NBC,' said Kireina, looking to broker a peace. 'That would be even better than a dish. Plus, we would know it was working.'

'But we've been through that,' said Martina. 'The NBC vans could be anywhere. They come to Liverpool sometimes, if there's been a raid or whatever, but who knows how long until the next one? And how do we steal a van right from under their effing noses anyway?'

'The stealing is not the hard part,' said Kevin, an idea now forming in his mind. 'The question is, what will attract the NBC to Liverpool?'

'Couldn't you just hack into their schedules and send them here?' asked Kireina.

Martina immediately spotted the flaw in her friend's suggestion.

'Wouldn't they just turn round and go back home as soon as they worked out they'd been sent here for no reason?'

'They would need a genuine reason to be in Liverpool,' said Kevin. 'And I think I might know someone who's good at attracting the attention of the media.'

In response, Kireina shot him a knowing smile. 'I think I can guess who you have in mind.'

Martina had not the slightest idea what they were talking about, but she was, without a doubt, intrigued.

'Hear me out,' said Kevin, now confident that he had a solution that would preclude both the hospitalisation and the imprisonment of their headstrong and impetuous friend. He reminded Martina of the massive media attention provoked by the uninvited appearance of Kireina's graffiti art in the Tate Modern and proposed that the right image in the right location would be guaranteed to attract the NBC to Liverpool like wasps to a beer glass.

Martina quickly agreed that Kevin's proposal was inspired, played to their collective strengths, and avoided unnecessary risk.

Kireina promptly took herself for a solitary walk around Calderstones Park, mulled over several possibilities and returned maybe two hours later with an idea that was ingenious in its simplicity. Without further ado the three drove the five miles from Troutbeck Park Gardens to Liverpool John Lennon Airport, where, from the comfort of one of the front seats of Martina's van, Kireina studied the iconic self-portrait of the airport's namesake and sketched a number of designs in various combinations of colours.

Over root coffee and oat biscuits the following morning, both the detailed plan and the final choice of artwork were agreed by all five activists and Martina volunteered to procure the necessary paint and brushes. There was only one real place to go if she wanted the exact colours that Kireina had specified:

PJ's warehouse on Sefton Street.

'Ah, the Mystery Cat returns,' said PJ with a smile as soon as he saw Martina. She introduced Talira and Ricky as 'business partners' and he greeted them with customary warmth. PJ genuinely liked Martina and was hoping that she would be offering him more stocks of pharmaceutical or contraceptive products, regardless of age. Not only was the mark-up substantial but the fact that he might have these items in stock drew in a healthy number of customers who inevitably succumbed to impulse buys.

The interior of the ground floor had bare redbrick walls and tall, boarded-up windows, largely obscured to a height of three metres by shelving made from assorted lengths of scaffolding poles and planks. Two lines of monumental cast-iron pillars, straddled by riveted girders, ran the entire length of the building and supported the considerable weight of the floor above. The impression of solidity and permanence was immense. Between the columns, larger items rested on the cool stone floor. Thanks to Martina's work on the solar panels, the warehouse was sufficiently well lit for clients to be able to read PJ's hand-painted signs and navigate their way amongst the stock without stubbing their toes or bruising their foreheads.

Having traded for over five years, PJ had amassed an imposing and organised collection of items which most people could no longer acquire by plundering abandoned shops and houses. His clumsily painted signs drew the visitor's attention to sections such as 'Rechargeables and PARTS', 'Padlocks with keys', 'Home entertainment', 'DIY - tools, unused materials etc', 'Cleaning products - sealed', 'Prescription glasses', 'Personal Hygiene UNUSED', 'Underwear NEW and RARE', and 'Vintage Magazines'. Talira and Ricky had never seen such an array of antiques in a single location, but were clear about their priorities and resisted the temptation to browse.

The couple could only watch in admiration as Martina negotiated with the hard-boiled trader in his own domain. Repeatedly, Martina sent PJ shuffling around for better options as she rejected cans of paint that felt underweight, colours that were not as claimed, and brushes that she considered to be sub-standard. Finally, Martina offered PJ half the quantity of analgesics he was demanding and, after several protestations of impossibility on both sides, they finally settled at seventy-five percent. It was three o'clock in the afternoon and the three hackers had sourced everything Kireina needed.

Martina's approach to dealing with PJ was always to leave him with the erroneous feeling that he had dominated the bargaining process and that he had got her to pay more than she intended. In spite of the impression Martina created that she had already found everything she needed, there was another significant item that she was after. Having paid the smiling PJ with a shoebox of painkillers, her attention lingered pointedly on the obsolete and dusty payment card reader to the side of the counter. She knew exactly what PJ would do next.

'Take that if you want it,' he said. 'I don't think it even works.'

'And what about these?' said Martina, pointing to a plastic crate of assorted Blu-ray discs.

'Yeah, alright,' said PJ. 'Those too.'

PJ did not normally give anything away for free, but he knew that the gifts would encourage Martina to think of him next time she wanted to offload some prescription meds. Martina knew that Aston and Thomas would be delighted with the Blu-rays and that anything they'd already watched could be traded on by Freya.

Happy with their acquisitions, Martina, Ricky and Talira then drove the seven miles north to the gates of Seaforth Dock. Whilst Martina once more played the role of the insouciant getaway driver, Talira and Ricky prised the vehicle registration plates from abandoned, windowless trucks still lined up at the gates as though at any moment they might be ushered in to collect their cargo.

From there, and at Kireina's recommendation, they drove the two miles further north to Crosby to visit the Antony Gormley installation, originally designated *Another Place* by the artist but always known locally as 'The Iron Men'. Having parked, they walked between the dunes to the beach and wondered at the lines of identical, life-sized and corroded human figures all staring out to sea. Though many of the original iron statues had been lost to the waves, the survivors were still an impressive and thought-provoking sight. Those farthest from the dunes already stood waist-deep in the advancing tide, their inscrutable gaze fixed permanently on the horizon, perhaps in silent reflection, perhaps in timeless anticipation.

'Kireina told me there were a hundred to start with,' said Ricky. 'There can't be more than fifty now.'

'Fifty's not bad,' said Talira. 'They survived better than we did.'

'Why are they here?' said Martina, almost entranced by the lines of identical, rusting figures.

'I guess, to make you ask questions,' said Talira.

The following morning, Martina taxied Kevin and Kireina

to Otterspool promenade and dropped them at the tram stop about half a mile from Auto-Drive Trucks. The riverside firm had once been a traditional rental business, but was now no more than a Government vehicle pound. Kevin and Kireina, dressed all in black, rode the single stop on the tram, walked confidently into the office of the former hire company and presented ID cards showing Kevin to be a senior commander of the Liverpool Central work brigade and Kireina to be his security officer. Credentials established and pleasantries exchanged, Kevin simply requisitioned two white eight-tonne trucks in working order for an indefinite period. He regretted that he was not at liberty to divulge details, but knowingly assured the office manager that the trucks would be engaged in vital Government work. She would, he confided, be helping the NUP and indeed the entire country take another meaningful step on the road to normality.

Although the slightly flustered assistant on the desk had not previously dealt with a vehicle requisition, Kevin guided him through the admin, giving him what appeared to be official paperwork and providing him with a reference number to quote and a card featuring the authentic contact details of NUP Central Office in Whitehall.

An hour later, Kevin and Kireina fitted the two trucks with the registration plates acquired from Seaforth Dock and parked them on a busy light-industrial estate, no more than half a mile from John Lennon airport. They did nothing else for three days other than to visit the vehicles each morning and ascertain that they had not been tracked and reclaimed. Satisfied that the trucks were now theirs, they meticulously cleaned any surfaces they had touched.

During this time, Martina carefully modified the antique card reader she had acquired so casually from PJ so that it would capture signals from a much greater distance and could thus be used to intercept and clone the security code from an electronic vehicle key.

Satisfied that the reader worked exactly as she wanted, she addressed herself to an entirely different matter, namely the unusual favour her brother had requested, and sent him a confirmatory message.

'All done, bro. xxx'

30 QUIET PURPOSE

Liverpool, 7th July

Towards the end of the evening, the group of activists polished off one of Kireina's more successful vegetable stews and devoted the best part of two hours to reviewing in detail their plan to separate the NBC from one of its outside broadcast vans. Having satisfied themselves that the planned operation was viable and that every aspect of the enterprise had been considered, Talira and Ricky took themselves to bed. Martina walked home, leaving her van in Troutbeck Park Gardens.

Kireina opened up Martina's van, loaded the various pots of paint acquired from PJ and covered them in a duvet. Kevin fetched the brushes, plus a stepladder, the two torches from the shower and Martina's night-vision visor. Kevin would drive and Kireina would attempt to work using the goggles. Having warmed the paint and kept it insulated throughout the evening, it would hopefully show up as slightly hotter than the surface she planned to modify and allow her to track her brushstrokes more easily. She would use the torches only to check colour and only if she absolutely needed to. It had now been three years since Kireina last created anything on this scale, but she was more than ready to get going.

They arrived at their chosen spot at the airport shortly before midnight, worked with quiet purpose and were back home by one thirty. Kireina was buzzing and decided that she wanted to make love to her brilliant and audacious boyfriend, ideally immediately and right there in the kitchen. Kevin, who did not wish their housemates to discover them butt naked on the kitchen floor, opted to lift Kireina up and carry her to the bedroom. Although intending the exact opposite, the pair made so much noise that they disturbed Talira and Ricky before they had even made it to the top of the stairs.

'When did we move in with a couple of rowdy, oversexed teenagers?' mumbled Ricky drowsily.

'Dunno,' whispered Taira. 'But I think we can assume they're happy with their night's work.'

31 ALLOTTED SPACE

Liverpool, 8th July

When airport personnel arrived for work on Monday morning, they did not all see it at first. The four-metre high image of John Lennon's face, reproduced from a sparse, rapidly drawn self-portrait, had been skilfully adapted so that it was now shorn of its shaggy locks and bore the unmistakeable features of the Prime Minister. The slogan 'above us only sky' now read 'our victory is nigh'.

Based on Talira's experience at the BBC, news of the commotion at John Lennon Airport would have reached Salford before the NBC news producer had sat down to chair the planning meeting for the day. He or she would undoubtedly want a story producer, a reporter and film crew despatched to Liverpool and would commission an outside broadcast van. Depending on the location of the nearest available vehicle, it could arrive at any time that day. In all probability, the story producer and presenter would be likely to turn up first, potentially before lunch.

When Steven Hastings, a politics correspondent for the NBC and Karen Nilsson, his producer and stalwart friend, arrived at the normally unstaffed security cabins at the entrance to the airport site, they were halted by Kevin who was sporting a high-visibility jacket and was carrying a clipboard.

'Welcome to Liverpool John Lennon Airport,' said Kevin.

'Could I trouble you for your names?'

'Karen Nilsson, Steven Hastings, NBC.'

'Excellent, we've been expecting you. Drive round to the Hilton, round that way, on your left, and go into their car park. My colleague will direct you to your allotted space.'

'Thank you,' said Nilsson cheerily.

'Oh,' said Kevin, almost as an afterthought, 'I have an outside broadcast van listed too. Is that not coming?'

'It's on its way,' replied Nilsson. 'But it's coming from Birmingham, so probably won't be here before two at the earliest.'

As the white Phaedron sports utility vehicle with the NBC livery drove into the car park of the Hilton and approached the main entrance, Karen Nilsson received a wave from Ricky, who was wearing an identical jacket to Kevin's. He ushered them to a numbered space close to the main doors.

'Bizarre,' said Hastings. 'Completely bizarre. The entire car park is empty, but we have to be guided to a specific space.'

'If he wasn't doing that, he'd probably be in a work brigade,' said Nilsson sympathetically.

Still, they were close to the main entrance and the pair thought no more of it. When they emerged from the car, Ricky helpfully pointed out the small crowd currently admiring Kireina's artwork at the entrance to the terminal. He also gave them an insider tip: the café in the hotel was quiet, had functioning air conditioning and would definitely be more comfortable than hanging around in the car. Grateful for the pointer, they opted immediately for the Strawberry Fields Café in the Hilton, where they would map out their plan of attack and await the arrival of the outside broadcast crew. They chose a window seat with a view of the almost entirely vacant car park. Ricky spotted them at the window and combined his beaming smile with another friendly wave. They reciprocated, albeit in a more diffident manner.

Shortly before a quarter to two, the NBC outside broadcast van, complete with transmission dish on the roof, was directed by the cheerful attendant in the high-vis jacket to a numbered space in direct line of sight of the windows of the hotel café, but a good seventy-five metres further back than Karen Nilsson's SUV.

Ricky approached the van and gestured to the driver to lower the window.

'You're closer here to the graffiti thing,' he explained. 'You won't have to lug your kit so far. Your colleagues are already having lunch in the hotel.' He pointed towards the café. 'That's them.'

Hastings and Nilsson, who had received regular updates from Birmingham on the progress of the outside broadcast team, could not help but notice their arrival. The crew of four vacated the van and checked with the smiling attendant that the entrance to the Hilton was via the door that they could see in front of them. He responded with a cheery affirmative and as the NBC driver locked the van with his radio key, Ricky activated the modified card reader in his left-hand pocket and cloned the vehicle's security code.

Before the crew had reached the lobby of the hotel, Martina, arrived in the first of the two stolen Auto-Drive trucks. To obviate any deposit of fingerprints inside the cabin, she had pulled on a pair of close-fitting driving gloves. Directed officiously by Ricky, she parked the truck on the hotel side of the outside broadcast vehicle, completely obscuring it from the view of its crew.

Immediately, Ricky walked round to the NBC van and, now out of sight of the café, unlocked the doors with the antique card reader, removed his fluorescent jacket and climbed in.

No more than ten seconds later, Talira, sporting red and black cycling gloves, arrived in the second truck and parked it alongside the first. She jumped out, walked round to the passenger door of the outside broadcast van and climbed in next to Ricky who duly started the motor. Ricky then waved to Martina who was still waiting behind the wheel of the first stolen truck. The pieces were all in place.

As soon as Martina began to edge slowly away, Ricky followed suit, shadowing the Auto-Drive truck exactly and carefully ensuring throughout the manoeuvre that he could neither see, nor be seen from, the windows of the Hilton café. From the hotel, the abandoned Auto-Drive vehicle perfectly concealed the absence of the hijacked van.

Once the outside broadcast van and the truck shielding it from view were beyond any possible line of sight from the hotel, Ricky simply overtook the Auto-Drive truck and drove on ahead. His route back to Troutbeck Park Gardens was somewhat circuitous, but had been carefully chosen to avoid the few traffic cameras that he knew were still operational.

Martina stopped at the exit to the airport to pick up Kevin, who had covered his hands with a pair of black ski gloves. They took the rental truck further than they needed, abandoned it in Penny Lane, and walked back to rejoin the others in Troutbeck Park Gardens. As soon as they arrived, the five hackers threw themselves into a round of celebratory hugs and ebullient congratulation before reminding themselves that they still needed to hide the stolen vehicle.

Once the wing mirrors had been removed, there was enough room to drive the vehicle gingerly up the overgrown front drive, along the side of the house and then accelerate it off the paving and into the back garden, flattening brambles and buddleia in the process. Ricky and Talira dragged the rotting wooden side gates back into position before returning to the front of the house to confirm that the OB van could not be seen from the road.

With the aid of the aluminium ladder, Kireina climbed onto the roof of the NBC van and covered it with a length of old brown carpet from the house next door. With the carpet strapped in place, she cut branches of buddleia and sycamore from the garden behind and did the best she could to make the vehicle undetectable from the air. In due course the hackers would source some netting and set about camouflaging the van more effectively, but for now, Kireina's handiwork would have to do. Later, they intended to push the battered Phaedron EV from the house opposite onto their own drive, masking the damage they had caused to the saplings and wildflowers.

Finally back inside the house, the five activists indulged in a round of unfettered celebration, reliving key moments of the heist, admiring each other's calmness, or weeping with laughter at their sheer brass neck. The exuberant hijackers congratulated themselves in equal measure on their teamwork and their shared determination. They had come a long way within the space of a fortnight. Not only had they created wide-ranging access privileges deep within the NBC's internal systems, they had acquired a modern outside broadcast van with fully functional production and transmission capabilities. All they needed now was to create the kind of broadcast content that would do justice to their efforts and prod the slumbering giant of democracy.

32 HELL IN A HANDCART

Portsmouth, 9th July

The public arrest of the Second Sea Lord, Sir Harry de la Tour and the subsequent detention of the Deputy Chief of Naval Staff, Dame Aliyah Armstrong were documented for the nation by the NBC crew that arrived on the heels of the paramilitary snatch squads.

As the putative traitors were escorted from the Henry Leach building at Navy Command in Portsmouth, the hovering drones captured their discomfiture from every possible angle. The NBC story producer was particularly keen to secure shots of their distraught faces, the insignia on their arms, and the restraints that pinned their overlapped wrists uncomfortably behind their backs.

The NBC did not, however, cover the dawn raids on the homes of Anthony Grover, the Assistant Chief of Naval Staff, and Luna Mason, the Finance Director. No cameras preserved for posterity the image of Grover's son weeping uncontrollably as his father was frog-marched in bare feet and pyjamas to an armoured patrol vehicle or the sight of Mason's wife being beaten to the ground with the butt of an assault rifle as she tried to intervene.

In Canteen 2 at RAF Brize Norton, two Modsec paramilitaries, part of the unit now providing additional security at the base, were intently focussed on the broadcast of the arrests as they chomped their way through their breakfast. Five tables to their left, both York and Batista were suddenly feeling particularly aware of their navy-blue dress uniforms. Keen to avoid undue attention, York flirted with the idea of purloining some RAF fatigues, or better still, some of the black paramilitary kit that Modsec favoured. The RAF fatigues, she concluded, might be the easier option. On the TV screen, the camera zoomed in on the handcuffs restraining the Deputy Chief of Naval Staff as she was escorted to a Modsec patrol vehicle.

'They have the power to make the innocent guilty and to make the guilty innocent,' said Batista in as muted a tone as he could muster.

'Quoting the anarchists now?' said York 'That may not be the wisest idea in present company.'

Batista furrowed his brow. 'What the hell is going on?'

'I think I know regime change when I see it,' said York, trying not to let her tone betray her disquiet.

'Any word from Command?'

'None. All communications automatically connect to the MOD. Some overbearing staffer at the Ministry was clearly anticipating my call. According to Whitehall, our role is now, and I quote, "to support the PM in whichever way he requires. No intel to Navy Command. No reports. No comments on his draft speeches. Wipe his arse if he asks." I missed out the word before "arse". Two syllables.'

York checked that the two paramilitaries were still engrossed in the NBC report.

'Modsec are literally everywhere,' she said. 'Well not literally, but it's starting to feel like it.'

'It's like dealing with the bloody Masons,' said Batista.

'Except you can't tell who's in the Masons. But I know what you mean.'

Batista could not shake off the feeling that the pair stuck out like sore thumbs in their Royal Navy uniforms. He knew it was a bad idea and was expecting nothing other than an instant rebuttal, but again dangled the idea of taking some leave together.

'And the Oscar for "Most Impractical Idea of the Year" goes to Lieutenant Batista,' said York with a gentle shake of the head.

It was a rejection, but not as total as he might have expected.

'I'm not saying it wouldn't be nice,' she continued, opening her eyes a little wider. 'In fact it could be very nice.'

He knew what was coming and supplied the inevitable connective for her.

'But?'

'But everything. Henderton. Northwood. This,' she said, cocking her head in the direction of the TV screen. 'The country could be going to hell in a handcart and we have to figure out what to do. Right now, I can no more contemplate leave than desertion. Let's face it. This job was never nine to five. We're married to the Navy. Assuming there still is a Navy.'

As the sensational images of the handcuffed traitors were shared with the nation, the Prime Minister himself was soaking up the broadcast, brandy in hand, from the comfort of his private suite on the RAF A-600 transport which had spent the night on the runway at Brize Norton. As ever, the PM was to be accompanied on the flight by his long-standing Royal Navy liaison officers. However, with Henderton's hands now firmly on the instruments of power, York and Batista would from now on be required to function as smartly dressed flunkies and would be expected to do so in such a way that it acknowledged their subservient position. There would be no more snitching to Navy Command, no more advice, and no more restraint. There would certainly be no refusals.

Once the Prime Minister's growing retinue of stylists, attendants and Modsec security officers had followed the armoured patrol vehicles and the motor-cycle outriders aboard the A-600, the RAF would transport them to Southampton airport, leaving them with no more than a twenty-mile journey by road to Navy Command HQ in Portsmouth. From the office of Admiral Teresa Patel, the recently deceased First Sea Lord, Henderton was to address the nation at this time of existential crisis and reassure the citizens of the UK once more that he would turn the tide of war and defeat the tyrannical foe.

The speech, which was to be broadcast live on the NBC *Six O'Clock News*, would be followed by the usual archive footage of the Prime Minister waving to adoring crowds or shaking the hands of cheerful brigade workers. The transmission would conclude with live coverage of the remaining Royal Navy commodores, their left hand planted on a bible, swearing an oath of allegiance to Gilbert Henderton, Prime Minister, Lord Protector, and Commander-in-Chief of British Armed Forces.

33 DOING JUST FINE ON HIS OWN

Liverpool, 9th July

Enjoying their regular, sewer-free Saturday away from the South Liverpool work brigade, Aston and Thomas were watching the live news report from Portsmouth in astonishment. Aston was incensed that the Navy had tried to orchestrate a military coup. Thomas, on the other hand, never ceased to be amazed at how readily his partner absorbed the narrative constructed for him by the news managers at the NBC. The multiple and ardent expressions of support for the Prime Minister, presented in an extended flurry of soundbites, left Aston in no doubt that he shared the views of the rest of the country, if not of the perpetually analytical man he lived with.

The broadcast over, Aston spent much of the afternoon teaching his doubting Thomas how to adapt his exemplary classical keyboard skills to the task of playing funk and it was not all plain sailing. They made as much progress as they could with Stevie Wonder's 'Superstition', but eventually, and perhaps predictably, became frustrated with one another.

'You're not getting it,' said an exasperated Aston. 'To play funk you've got to rip up the Grade Six rulebook and get down to the feel. It's about letting go and getting locked into the groove.'

This did not make a whole lot of sense to Thomas. He did not understand why he could not simply play the notes, chords and arpeggios exactly as printed on the sheet music and Aston did not understand why he would want to. Having no intention of letting their frustrations fuel another spat, they decided to put 'Superstition' on ice and leave it for another day.

By late afternoon, Aston and Thomas were nestled on the sofa in anticipation of the State of the Nation address that the Prime Minister was scheduled to make. They had been joined by Freya and Martina, both back from a busy day doing whatever it is they did at work. The presence of the two sisters helped further soften the mood.

'My fellow citizens,' began Henderton earnestly. 'So far, we have fought the loathsome apparatus of enemy intrusion. We have ridden out the storm of war and have defended millions from conflict and conflagration, from subjugation and starvation.'

'That's a lot of big words,' said Aston.

Thomas was only too happy to agree.

'Meet the new boss,' sang Freya. 'Same as the old boss.'

'What are you on about now?' Aston asked his daughter. 'That doesn't make any sense.'

'It's from a song,' said Freya. 'By The Who.'

Aston shrugged, looking none the wiser.

'You know. The one that Thomas likes the sound of,' she said. 'Oh, for Heaven's sake, Dad, it's on your iPod. You should give it a listen. Honestly, you'll love it. It's brilliant. And the drum parts are amazing. We should definitely give it a go.'

'As long as it's not funk,' said Thomas. 'Funk has defeated me.'

'It's not funk,' replied Freya. 'Though there's nothing wrong with a bit of funk. Nothing wrong with a groove.'

'She sounds more like you every day,' said Thomas to his partner.

'Nothing wrong with a groove,' said Aston.

On the TV screen before them, the Prime Minister was exuding an unusually pronounced air of resolve.

'However, the enemy, with all its firepower and military strength, will descend upon us with renewed potency, as it did so cruelly in the cold-blooded attack upon Northwood. There will be destruction, perhaps as never before, but we shall prevail. I am completely confident that we shall prove ourselves once again able to defend our island home, to turn the insatiable tide of war, and to defeat the unspeakable menace of tyranny.'

'If you deepened his voice and gave him a Sleeper throat, he'd sound like the creepy guy with the shiny black helmet in those *Star Wars* movies,' said Martina.

'That is the resolve of His Majesty's Government,' intoned the Prime Minister. 'That is the will of the National Unity Party and of the nation. The National Unity Party and the British people will defend to the death their native soil, rooting out disloyalty and exposing treachery wheresoever it may lie. We shall not yield and we shall not fall. We shall continue to the end. We shall fight with growing force and increasing ferocity. We shall never, I say never, capitulate, but I tell you this. Our vainglorious and foolish enemy will soon cringe upon his knees and beg for terms, as he licks the bitter wounds of ignominious defeat.'

The determined expression on the Prime Minister's face cross-faded to an image of the Union Jack fluttering proudly against a summer sky. Almost inevitably, the image was underpinned by the strains of 'Rule Britannia'.

Thomas was distracted from the broadcast by the vibration of his i-comm. It was, he assumed, a message from their work brigade commander reminding Aston and Thomas that they had an early shift the following day. Aston's i-comm, however, remained dormant. An invitation from the Prime Minister was the last thing Thomas was expecting to see.

'With the British nation at last on the brink of victory,' it read, 'the Prime Minister cordially invites interested citizens to register their interest to attend a Congress of All The Talents. This event represents an exciting opportunity to help lay the political, economic and social foundations of post-war Britain. The conference will welcome a broad range of contributions from citizens with an established pre-war background in political thought, journalism, broadcasting and influencing. Attendance will be free and all travel and accommodation expenses will be covered. Date and location to be advised. Say "talents" to register.'

'Members of work brigades need not apply,' thought Thomas. In any case, the invitation bore the hallmarks of those endless phishing scams that had been prevalent when there was still a functional internet. Convinced it was an attempt to defraud him of his personal data or access his i-comm Credits, Thomas simply deleted the message.

'They must think I was born yesterday,' he said.

'What was it?' said Aston.

'Hacker stuff, I think. Supposedly an invitation to a conference in London to discuss the future of the UK. Apparently, the Prime Minister needs me to help him run the country.'

'I think he's doing just fine on his own,' said Aston, before taking a healthy swig from his mug of ersatz tea.

34 INCONVENIENT TRUTH

Portsmouth, 9th July

Neither York nor Batista had any particular talent for simply killing time. In the atrium of the Henry Leach Building, some three floors below the First Sea Lord's office, they were following the PM's instructions simply to await his eventual reappearance and were consequently at something of a loose end. There was no conversation they could have that would not be overheard and they settled into silently reading old and perfunctory messages on their i-comms or deleting outdated entries from their contact lists.

The Prime Minister's morale-boosting speech to the nation evidently complete, he swept suddenly into the lobby and instructed the two liaison officers to look sharp and to follow him to the APV. York and Batista boarded the Gurkha armoured patrol vehicle once more and travelled with Henderton to Southampton Airport, escorted as usual by police outriders front and back and a Comanche attack helicopter above. During the forty-minute journey, the most powerful man in Britain had little of consequence to say to his liaison officers, but left York with the uneasy feeling that his attention was focussed almost exclusively on her legs.

In his private suite aboard the A-600, Henderton poured himself a glass of Cognac, located his customary armchair and swirled the brandy in the glass, gently warming it with the palm of his hand. The liaison officers sat opposite, with Batista in his usual place to York's left. The Prime Minister, now feeling the master of his own destiny, was only too eager to demonstrate his comprehensive and unassailable authority to his former Royal Navy minders. He slowly looked Lieutenant Commander York up and down, then switched his attention to Batista.

'You. Lieutenant,' he said with manifest disdain. 'We're out of sparkling water. Get me six one-litre bottles of water. Spa water, I mean, not that carbonated crap. And we're leaving in twenty minutes. If you're not back, I'm not waiting. You can make your own way back to Brize Norton.'

'Very good, Prime Minister,' said Batista, caught off guard by the PM's particularly supercilious tone. He was not sure where he would find six bottles of fancy water at such short notice, but he would do his best. Henderton watched the Lieutenant leave, took a sip from his glass, then turned his attention once more to York.

'Today went well,' he said, clearly not needing affirmation. 'I have to say, I feel for you, Lieutenant Commander York. The news that elements within Navy Command were orchestrating a coup must have come as a terrible surprise.'

Henderton knew full well that York was no fool and completely understood what had been happening in the past fortnight, but he wanted her to embrace the narrative.

'It is never easy to be presented with an inconvenient truth,' she said.

Leaving his glass, the Prime Minister got up, took three seemingly casual steps across the cabin, and placed himself in the seat vacated by Batista.

'Strange times, Lieutenant Commander York, strange times. You are in a difficult position. Yes, an extremely difficult position. Although I have to admit, I always welcomed your presence on our trips up and down the country.'

'Thank you, sir,' she said somewhat diffidently. Why was he sitting there? This did not feel at all comfortable.

'I know you were required to fulfil a brief that extended beyond simply ensuring my security, but those days are over. Permanently. That said, Lieutenant Commander, bygones, I think, can be bygones. I could, without the slightest inconvenience, find a new role for you. As part of my personal team.'

'I'm not really Modsec material,' said York. 'Neither is Lieutenant Batista.'

'I was only referring to you,' said Henderton. As he reached the final word of the sentence, he patted her on the knee and his hand lingered. 'Every Napoleon needs a Josephine. Every Anthony needs a Cleopatra.'

'And every tinpot general has his hand up history's skirt,' snapped York, as she swatted his hand from her leg and removed herself to the far side of the cabin.

Henderton was silenced but unperturbed.

'Not available,' she scowled. 'If you're after a bit of tail, get yourself a husky.' The look on her face was beyond angry.

'An ungrateful cow should not look a gift horse in the mouth,' said the Prime Minister dryly.

The speed and ferocity with which York picked up Henderton's half-finished glass of Cognac and flung it at his face caught the Prime Minister completely unawares. He flinched only at the last moment and the glass, which might otherwise have caught him in the eye or on the forehead, glanced off his crown and shattered against the cabin wall.

'I'll go and find some fizzy water,' announced York with manifest contempt. She exited the suite directly, strode the length of the hold and walked straight down the ramp at the rear of the aircraft. The loadmasters sensibly got out of her way.

The Modsec duty officer, attracted by the sound of breaking glass and the sharp exit of Lieutenant Commander York, entered the prime ministerial suite to enquire if everything was OK.

'You can stand down, Watson,' said the Prime Minister. 'Just a little local difficulty.'

'Let me help you with that,' said the Modsec officer, noticing small fragments of glass on the PM's shoulder. 'I'll get a brush. Prime Minister, do we have an issue with the liaison officers?'

'To be honest,' replied Henderton. 'I've had just about enough of our friends in navy blue. They've had their noses up my arse for far too long. Do not allow them back on the plane.'

'I'll alert the guards, sir. Access will be denied.'

'Good,' said Henderton. 'But don't hurt the pretty one.'

Watson raised an eyebrow.

'Yes, the woman, for God's sake. Lieutenant Commander York.'

'Just thought it best to be clear,' said Watson. 'No surgeon wants to amputate the wrong leg.'

'Indeed.'

'And after we refuse them access?'

'Get rid of them.'

'Again, Prime Minister, just to be clear. In what sense to you mean "get rid of them"?'

'Not in the Thomas Becket sense.'

'I'm sorry, sir. I'm not really up to speed with the Thomas Becket situation. Could you refresh my memory?'

'Right. Clearly not someone you know. The point is, he's dead. Thomas Becket, that is. No need for that. Find something useful for them to do at the MOD, something that doesn't involve them ever having to cross my path again. Is that clear enough for you not to amputate the wrong leg?'

'Yes, Prime Minister.'

'Good. See to it. Now, I believe you said something about getting a brush.'

Watson located a small dustpan and brush in the kitchen, reappeared promptly and carefully swept the shards of glass from the shoulder of the Prime Minister's suit, from the armchair and from the carpet.

35 ONLY OBEYING ORDERS

Oxford, 11th July

In the lounge on the ground floor of the Linacre Specialist Care Centre, Johanna, Maggie, Safdar, Catrina and Colleen, a group referred to fondly by some of the nurses as the 'non-dairy nonagenarians' sat wheelchair-bound in a rough circle. They knew that they were in some sort of hospital and they knew they had all seen the other patients before, but recalling each other's names or why they were even there was a daily struggle which few of them won.

Anne Koumetio, a dementia nurse in a smart, blue uniform, equipped with a multicoloured beachball and infinite patience was co-ordinating a game of catch. Some of the residents could throw the ball to others in the group and celebrate the achievement each time with a smile. Others had crystal clear memories of playing catch as a child, but were puzzled that their frail bodies could no longer manage the ball. In the corner of the room an elderly woman, who was not part of the game, delivered a relentless torrent of expletives and personal insults. In due course, a second nurse appeared and subtly repositioned Rhona, a former social worker, so that she could no longer see those particular residents who, for reasons she no longer remembered, she loathed and repeatedly threatened to assault.

When eventually the nonagenarians tired of their game, Nurse Koumetio handed out large-print versions of the lyrics to 'Hey, Jude'. As she sang the first verse, they all realised that they knew the song and began to join in. The nurse removed her guitar from its battered black case, reminded the residents that the words were on the sheet of paper and led them through the ballad, in which, unusually, it was they who were offering sympathy and encouragement. Whilst it was unlikely that any of the group reflected on this change of perspective, their faces nonetheless lit up as they sang a familiar tune. When they reached the coda, Nurse Koumetio allowed the extended chant to continue for as long as the singers wanted it to.

Many in the Dementia Wing had so few family members who had survived both Sleeper and the Dark Age that visits were few and far between. Some had no real sense of the passage of the days, the weeks and the months. Some wondered if their deceased husbands and wives knew that they were in hospital. Some were looking forward to the day when their parents or grandparents would visit.

Johanna Henderton had changed noticeably in recent months. She now struggled to hold herself upright in her wheelchair for much more than an hour and consequently spent increasing amounts of time in bed. The ninety-year-old had phases where she was reluctant to eat, drink, or swallow the tablets that treated her blood pressure and persistent urine infections. It was many years since the Prime Minister last spent time with his grandmother. Nonetheless, she spotted him regularly on the TV in the lounge and always knew that she had seen him somewhere before.

When a day much like any other day at Linacre had eventually drawn to a close and darkness enveloped the Specialist Care Centre, some of the residents slept soundly, in all probability with the help of medication. Others woke repeatedly throughout the night and cried out in their confusion for help.

0215 hours. Flight Lieutenant Dibaba's F-95 was still several minutes from the outskirts of Oxford. As with all of 161 Squadron's missions, Operation Boltmaker required the pilot to fly to the co-ordinates given in briefing, insert the target key into the mission drive to reveal the precise objective and, having verified that the target betrayed no human heat signatures, obliterate it. Whilst the F-95's avionics constituted a powerful AI in their own right, the targeting system was incomplete by design. Unless a pilot physically removed the target key from a flight suit pocket and introduced the necessary coding into the system, no objective was established and the air-to-surface missiles remained dormant on their pylons. The pilot was there to obviate the kind of implacable mission fulfilment that had cost so many people their lives in Halifax.

The ten minute flight from RAF Lakenheath allowed Dibaba a brief window for reflection. She wondered for how long Oxford would continue to be thought of as the 'City of Dreaming Spires', given the demise of its world-famous colleges. She also found her thoughts drawn to her relationship with Warszawski. Were the two of them somehow getting too cosy? Living in each other's pockets? Certainly, the whole 'cute couple' thing that so amused the rest of the Squadron was beginning to wear a bit thin. Maybe she and Warszawski needed to spend a bit less time together. Perhaps she should talk to him about their relationship the next time they exercised the Labrador. Or was that just something that cute couples did? She experienced no epiphanies and quickly the pilot returned to thinking about the task in hand.

Dibaba was immensely curious about the identity of her target. She ruled out the expansive automotive plant at Cowley, which was fully engaged in the replication of components for a wide variety of foreign-built military vehicles, agricultural machinery and trams. However, the closure of the university and the demise of its bio-science and digital industries had bequeathed to the city an extensive and now completely desolate science park slightly to the north of the rambling complex of colleges. That had to be it.

As Dibaba reached the co-ordinates assigned to her in the briefing for Operation Boltmaker, she overflew the river Thames which fleetingly reflected the moonlight of a cloudless night. She brought the F-95 round and flipped open the cover to the mission drive. Carefully, she removed the target key from the pocket of her flight suit and slid it into the port.

The anomaly in Dibaba's visor display was immediately obvious. The target had been acquired, but had not been clearly identified.

'Hey Gunnie,' she said. 'My display has some kind of glitch. I have no target ID. Just the acronyms "OSP" and "ACD" which I've never seen before. Acknowledge.'

'Dibaba, this is Lakenheath Ground. My read-out is the same,' replied Gunatillaka. 'No idea what the acronyms stand for. Stand by.'

'Roger. Wilco.'

Moments later, the pilot was blindsided by something that she had never expected to see on a mission. A cluster of heat signatures lit up a peripheral section of her display.

'Zoom,' said Dibaba. 'Signatures above thirty-six degrees.'

The scanners locked on to the site on the edge of the

unidentified target zone, expanded the image on the head-down display and revealed what must have been hundreds of glowing yellow shapes.

Dibaba's pulse accelerated and her thoughts went into overdrive. This couldn't be right. Those people were so close to the target area that they would be caught in the blast.

Whilst the Linacre Specialist Care Centre had not been selected as a target in itself, an empty street was all that separated it from the semi-derelict Life and Mind Building on the edge of the redundant Oxford Science Park. The Osiris missiles, programmed to obliterate the abandoned research and development facilities, would spare neither the hospital nor its three hundred residents and staff. Major Security Officer Benjamin, who now exercised executive control of target selection, had simply designated the contiguous residential site as 'ACD' or 'Acceptable Collateral Damage'.

'Zoom,' said Dibaba again. The scanner zeroed in once more on the hot section of the display and intensified the image further. Dibaba could clearly identify a number of sleeping figures, perhaps in a hostel or possibly a work brigade barracks. She could also make out a human figure as it approached one of the supine forms and leaned over it. Between the glowing human shapes, various machines also emitted powerful heat signatures and Dibaba suddenly realised exactly what she was looking at.

'Gunnie, it's some sort of hospital. I don't know what's going on, but as far as I can see, there's a hospital within the blast radius. The missiles will take it out completely. I'm going to scrub the mission. Acknowledge.'

'161-Delta-India. Negative. Do not abort. The target zone

contains legitimate targets. Do not abort. Acknowledge.'

The voice belonged to Wing Commander Wakeman.

'It looks like there's some kind of hospital, sir.'

'It is not your job to tell me what it looks like, Dibaba. Those heat signatures come from a militia stronghold. Fulfil the mission. Launch your missiles. Expedite.'

In the lounge of twenty-three Troutbeck Park Gardens in South Liverpool, Martina was sitting somewhat impatiently at Kevin's computer station. Sleepy and unaware of exactly why her brother had asked such an unusual favour of her, she was increasingly wondering if she was going to be sitting there all night. Suddenly, her smartphone pinged, she received the go-ahead from MacDermott and immediately activated *send* on the display unit in front of her. Within a second, a message crawled across every TV screen and i-comm in the country, across the monitors in the Ops Room at Lakenheath and across Dibaba's visor display.

'RAF saves Oxford hospital from destruction by enemy aircraft. Hundreds of lives saved. PM trumpets courage of British pilots.'

If confirmation were needed, there it was.

'Launch your missiles, Dibaba,' Wakeman ordered.

'Negative,' said Dibaba. 'Unable.'

She pulled the target key and replaced it in the pocket of her anti-g suit. Dibaba could not know for sure how many glowing human forms she had seen in her display but it must have been in the hundreds. The anger at what she had been set up to do transcended anything she had experienced since the death of her parents. There was no way Wakeman could have been unaware of the hospital and no way he could have thought that it would escape unscathed. Absolutely no fucking way. The destruction of the hospital had clearly been factored into the mission. And here it was. Here was the ugly truth that had skulked behind Benjamin's perfunctory comments about the Mortality Protocol. Yet this was hardly 'potential collateral damage'. This was pre-meditated, cold-blooded murder.

Nine minutes later Dibaba was lining the F-95 up with the landing lights at Lakenheath. The image of the young, napalm-scorched girl from the Vietnam War had stubbornly refused to leave her thoughts. Not for one second had she considered listening to 'Free Bird'.

'Throttle back,' said Gunatillaka. 'You're coming in hot.'

'Thanks, Gunnie. Wilco.' She refocussed on the landing.

'Also, Wing Commander Wakeman would like you to report to his office once you're down,' said Gunatillaka.

'No surprise there,' said Dibaba, patently seething.

Once back on terra firma, Dibaba stormed through the Main Briefing Room, through the locker room and straight to the Tech Room. Her look of thunder was mitigated only by a brief nod of acknowledgement to MacDermott as she pushed her helmet and mask into his hands. Still wearing her flight suit, she proceeded directly to the Wing Commander's office, marched in and flung the target key onto his desk. She was surprised not to see Benjamin at his shoulder.

'What the fuck is going on, Wakeman?'

'Stand to attention, Dibaba. And it's Wing Commander Wakeman.'

'I nearly just killed every patient, nurse and doctor in a fucking hospital.'

Wakeman banged the heel of his hand on the desk. 'What you did, Dibaba, was fail to carry out your legitimate orders. This a war, Dibaba, a war. And you are a soldier. Soldiers obey orders.'

'*Ach, ja.* I voss only obeying orders,' she retorted in a mock German accent. 'How did that go down at Nuremberg?'

If Wakeman was angry, Dibaba was apoplectic. The Wing Commander was, however, still sufficiently in control of his faculties to understand that things would only get uglier if he persisted with his dressing down. A shout-off would not cure her of her insubordination and he bit hard on his anger. He informed Dibaba that she was grounded until further notice. She would surrender her i-comm, she would confine herself to quarters and she would be seen by Dr Kaminski for a psychological assessment.

'And is the psycho the one who commits the murder or the one who stops it?' she said, before bouncing her i-comm onto Wakeman's desk and barging out.

In the locker room, Dibaba kicked off her boots, cantankerously firing them in entirely different directions. She ripped at the zip fastener on her flight suit, shrugged the suit down over her shoulders and yanked her arms out of the sleeves. As she tried to kick the trousers off her legs, she succeeded only in tangling them frustratingly round her ankles. Having grappled her legs from the flight suit's almost wilful grasp, she picked it up from the floor and slung it forcefully at the lockers opposite. The suit slapped against the grey metal doors and crumpled to the ground, its resistance finally over. Dibaba remained planted on the slatted bench for several minutes, breathing hard, grinding her teeth and staring at the lockers in front of her.

Somehow stung out of the brooding, she stood up abruptly, went to her locker and hurriedly put on her combats and hoodie. She relocated her discarded boots, retrieved the mangled anti-g suit and carried it, still inside out, to MacDermott in the Tech Room.

The Chief Technician had followed the progress of Operation Boltmaker intently and was both relieved and delighted that Dibaba had aborted the mission. He could see from her intense stare and twitchy demeanour, however, that she was completely steamed up. Her suit also appeared to have been on the receiving end of a severe beating.

'Problems?' he asked.

'You could say that.'

'Want to tell me?'

'Not particularly.'

Dibaba was being uncharacteristically curt and she knew it. In spite of MacDermott's bizarre references to Voltaire, it was now patently clear to the pilot that the Chief Technician had been contriving, in his convoluted way, to alert her to the fault lines in Operation Boltmaker. He had done his complicated best to deflect her from attacking a working hospital and killing its residents. She knew that he deserved her gratitude, but she was a battleground of emotion and her goodwill towards a well-intentioned colleague had been bludgeoned aside by anger. Right now she had nothing but seething contempt for Wakeman and Benjamin, the architects of a mission which had sidestepped the Mortality Protocol and could so easily have left her with innocent blood on her hands.

'You did the right thing,' said MacDermott, as he straightened out the flight suit and hung it on the rack. 'Voltaire would have approved.'

'Well maybe next time, Voltaire could use the words "target" and "hospital" at some point and not leave me guessing what the fuck he's on about,' said Dibaba, still venting her spleen in completely the wrong direction.

The Chief Technician did not respond. Dibaba knew full well that MacDermott should not have been the butt of her misplaced anger, but it was not an emotion that was easily checked by reason. She took a deep breath, tried to regain some modicum of composure, and started again.

'I'm sorry, Chief,' she said, now making a conscious effort to slow down and consider her words. 'Ignore that. I'm still pretty wound up. Listen. Thanks. Thanks for what you did. You did the right thing. Definitely. You took a risk, I know. But next time, and shit, let's hope there isn't a next time, next time, just give it to me straight. Spell it all out in words of one syllable instead of confusing me with Voltaire and effing trumpets.'

'I thought we might be overheard,' he explained. 'It was a stressful day. I was trying to be subtle.'

Dibaba was forced to smile.

'Subtle. Yes. Well. Full marks for subtlety. But, you know what. If you'd just told me about the hospital in the first place, it wouldn't have gone to the wire. I'd have carelessly dropped the target key in the Aircrew Ready Room before take-off. Then on approach, I'd have discovered that the key was missing and I could have scrubbed the mission without Wakeman being any the wiser.'

Dibaba allowed MacDermott a moment to reflect on this.

'Plus,' she said, 'I might have walked away with no more than a typical Wakeman bollocking for my obvious stupidity.

As it stands, I am now one hundred percent grounded pending a psychological evaluation.'

'Shit. I'm sorry about that, Flight Lieutenant. That's... Well, it's not what I intended. I suppose it wasn't..., I suppose it wasn't a great plan.'

'I know,' said Dibaba sympathetically. 'They say no battle plan survives contact with the enemy. Yours didn't survive contact with a friend.'

Neither of them spoke for a couple of seconds.

'Some of the others are in the bar,' said MacDermott, anticipating what she would want to do next.

'I'm confined to quarters,' said Dibaba. 'So, no bar. No bar. Not until Kaminski says I'm sane.'

When Dibaba arrived at her room, a Modsec paramilitary was standing at her door.

'Goodnight, ma'am,' he said politely as she let herself in.

Dibaba did not reply. The soldier would stand there all night.

Sitting quietly in the half-light of the office on the ground floor of the Linacre Specialist Care Centre, Duty Nurse Natasha Morphy was taking a break during a rare phase of the night that found all of the residents simultaneously sleeping. The nurse was savouring a hard-earned mug of ersatz and a couple of digestive biscuits. Enjoying the rare moments of peace, she thought about the crawler message on her i-comm and wondered which hospital had been targeted. As she dunked the first digestive in her coffee, it occurred to her, that she might possibly have registered the sound of an aircraft as she was stroking Johanna Henderton's hand and encouraging her to go back to sleep.

36 A FIRST TIME FOR EVERYTHING

Liverpool, 12th July

It was shortly before five thirty and it was already light. There was a slack tide on the Mersey and not a breath of wind in the morning air. Across the road from PJ's warehouse in Sefton Street, three police armoured patrol vehicles pulled in and waited. Some two hundred metres from the target of the raid, two larger police vans with side windows no bigger than document wallets stood by, ready to be called on when needed. Sefton Street itself had been cordoned off at either end, but the officers stationed on the roadblocks had little to do other than to observe. No vehicles required redirection and no onlookers, eager for a glimpse of some hapless miscreant being dragged to a van, had to be turned away. The streets were deserted.

At five thirty precisely, Detective Inspector Smith communicated the order to go. Immediately, six armed officers exited each of the APVs via the rear doors, only too happy to get out of the poorly ventilated vehicles and into the fresher morning air. Quickly, and without any verbal communication between them, four police officers stationed themselves outside the two pairs of monumental wooden gates overlooking the street. Four others covered the gates to the side. They were dressed in black tactical uniforms which, save for the word 'police' clearly visible in large white capitals across the torso and back, were identical to those worn by Modsec.

The remaining ten officers gathered at the main doors. At the signal from Sergeant Wood, an officer swung a steel battering ram forcefully at the lock. A second bludgeoned the base of the door where he assumed a bolt secured it to the ground. Usually two or three swings of an Enforcer battering ram, generally referred to by police officers as 'the big red key', were enough to force entry to domestic premises, but the doors to the warehouse were solid oak and throughout their history had been fitted with bolts and locks strong enough to deter intrusion. The repeated impacts were insufficient to break the doors open and after twenty seconds, each officer needed to be relieved by a colleague. It made not the slightest difference.

Eventually one of the first floor windows immediately above the police officers was opened tentatively and a bleary-eyed and baffled PJ asked the Detective Inspector what exactly was going on.

'I have a warrant to search these premises,' said DI Smith.

He glanced at Sergeant Wood, who passed him the necessary documentation. The Detective Inspector waved it at PJ and asked him to unlock the doors. Confident that the few remaining cartons of painkillers he bought from Martina would not easily be found, and keen to present an impression of innocence, PJ acquiesced. He closed the window and descended the stairs, but struggled to open the doors. Unfortunately for DI Smith and his team, the force exerted by the police battering rams had been more than enough to jam the modern security lock at the centre of the door and cause the floor bolts to seize in their barrels. After several minutes of frustrated effort, PJ traipsed back up the stairs to inform the police officer that, regrettably, the door mechanisms were stuck fast. The Detective

Inspector, certain that PJ was simply stalling whilst accomplices assiduously destroyed evidence, threatened to have his officers break in through the windows. With a somewhat obsequious expression of regret, PJ informed DI Smith that in order to protect his valuable stock from the attentions of criminals, the lower floor windows were both barred and boarded over on the inside. Furthermore, the huge wooden doors to the side were bolted into the ground below and into the vaulted brick ceiling above. They were also braced laterally by a number of scaffolding poles and to complicate matters further, they were completely blocked by shelves which were also constructed from scaffolding poles and were fully laden with stock, some of it exceptionally heavy. The police had, it appeared, imprisoned PJ in his own warehouse. The trader offered to try the lock once more and disappeared back downstairs.

'Well, sir. I think we can safely say he won't be doing a runner,' said Police Constable Thompson. 'Should we take the Enforcers back to the APV?'

'I never thought I'd have this much trouble getting into a whorehouse,' said Sergeant Wood.

'What?' said the DI, a completely quizzical look on his face. 'It's not a whorehouse. It's PJ's warehouse.'

'Well, it says "whorehouse" on the warrant.'

The DI demanded the document from Sergeant Wood and there it was in black and white: 'PJ's whorehouse, Sefton Street, Liverpool L3 4XX'. A competent officer and a stickler for correct procedure, DI Smith was dumbfounded by the error.

Two days previously, he had meticulously dictated both the application to search the warehouse and the draft warrant for signature by a magistrate. He had detailed the suspected link of PJ's warehouse to the supply of illicit medication and had specified the power under which the warrant was to be issued, the material sought, the date of the proposed search and the exact address of the premises. He had followed procedure to the letter. What DI Smith had failed to do, however, was to foresee that his dictation software, set to Standard British English, might translate his pronunciation of 'warehouse' as 'where house' and that the autocorrect app would see this as an attempt at spelling 'whorehouse'.

'Shit,' said Smith. 'The effing warrant's not legal. We'll have to stand down.'

'Only if PJ notices,' said Sergeant Wood.

The Detective Inspector mulled over his options and decided to call for a fire tender to enable access to the warehouse via the window above the main doors. As he waited for its arrival, DI Smith agonised over the time that PJ would have to flush any illegal medication down the toilet and shred, or even burn, the cartons. When the Detective Inspector finally climbed the ladder and wafted the warrant in front of PJ, the trader asked to examine it and spotted the error almost immediately. As confident as PJ was that the police would find it nigh on impossible to locate his stash of meds, he saw absolutely no reason why he should afford them the opportunity. He drew attention to the anomaly in the warrant and regretted that, whilst he was keen to assist the police in any way he could, they too were expected to respect the rule of law. He politely suggested that the police officers might wish to return the following day with a warrant to search a warehouse rather than a brothel.

'By which time you will have destroyed every last scrap of evidence,' said DI Smith.

'Except I won't actually need to,' said PJ with an affected air of indignation, 'because I've got nothing but legally purchased stock on the premises. And you are, Detective Inspector, like I said, completely welcome to search the building. Once you've got a correctly worded warrant.'

DI Smith knew that, in purely legal terms, PJ was holding all the aces. There would be no point applying for another warrant and no point searching the warehouse. The element of surprise would be gone.

'Listen, PJ,' said DI Smith, keen to glean some quantum of success from the monumental cock-up. 'We like you. This is where we get our pencils and paper clips and all kinds of crap the police needs to get through the day. It's not you we're after, PJ. Not you at all. It's the big guys, the suppliers, the dealers. So, if you felt able, in a spirit of, let's say, public service, to give me some kind of meaningful information, a key name of a supplier for example, or an address, then all of this unwanted attention could magically go away. Otherwise, my friend, it is my duty have to inform you that we will be back in two days with a new and legally watertight warrant to search your warehouse big time. And who knows? Maybe we'll need to remove every single saleable item for forensic examination. Maybe the next person who wants to shop at PJ's will find the shelves completely bare, except of course, for those items that accidentally and regrettably got broken during the carefully executed but very legal search.'

PJ reflected for a moment. He knew where his interests lay.

'There is this one person who comes here, a woman. She sometimes offers to pay, off-book like, with a box of out of date meds. Obviously, and I want to make this dead clear, I refuse all such offers.'

'Obviously.'

PJ had only one supplier. However, much as he liked Martina, he would sacrifice her in a heartbeat to protect himself and preserve his stock. When DI Smith finally descended from the ladder, he had the name of a young woman in her twenties. She had black hair and drove a white van.

'What about the doors?' yelled PJ. 'I'm trapped.'

'I'll send for a locksmith,' shouted DI Smith. 'You'll have to pay for it yourself. Legally.'

Whilst Thomas and Aston were starting their afternoon shift in the sewers and PJ was haggling with the locksmith, Martina and Freya were experiencing the unremitting joy of thrashing out some raucous guitar music in the back room of seventeen Menlove Close. They were rehearsing 'Won't Get Fooled Again', an eight minute assault on the ears originally recorded the best part of a century previously by The Who. Both women were enthralled by the anger, the iconoclasm and the energy of the music, so patently missing from the AI-generated fluff of their youth. The bristling lyrics, which both defied tyranny and portended the uncertainty of revolution, provided an invigorating escape from the NBC's moth-eaten songs of blind faith and chauvinism.

Gifted with a soulful singing voice, Martina readily nailed the emotion in the song's lyrics without trying to mimic the singer on the classic recording. From the guitar tablature, Freya could see that she could get through ninety-five percent of the eight-minute monster with A, G and D, but rapidly discovered that playing those chords with the taut aggression of the original would require practice.

'Don't strum it,' said Martina. 'Imagine you're trying to make the guitar say "Yaggerdang!" Don't be kind to it.'

Whilst Martina had a good ear, she had no formal musical training and could put it no other way. This was, however, exactly the advice that Freya needed. Immediately, her attack sounded more like the original and she began to feel that she was driving the song with both authority and economy. After running through 'Won't Get Fooled Again' four more times, with each iteration patently better than the last, Martina suggested they fire up the battered Maxxbook and try out its recording software.

Aston and Thomas, hot, sweaty and exhausted from their daily battle with central Liverpool's subterranean fatberg, walked uncomfortably through the front door. The build-up of hydrogen sulphide in the bowels of the city centre was causing them pains in their legs, intermittent headaches and despite the safety goggles, some redness around the eyes. The recent asphyxiation of two long-serving colleagues meant that the remaining workers were required, for the time being at least, to complete longer shifts. Since their daily efforts to remove the smell of the sewers from their hair had become an exercise in futility, Aston and Thomas now shaved their heads at the end of the working day. If it was at all possible, they smelled even worse than usual and were desperate for a shower.

Without getting too close, Freya distracted them briefly with the promise of rosemary tea, toast and blackberry jam, to be served as soon as they were clean. She also informed them that after the toast and jam, the two sewer rats would be practis- ing 'Won't Get Fooled Again' over the vocal and guitar tracks recorded that afternoon by the two women of the house. Whilst Aston and Thomas rehearsed the drum and keyboard parts, she and Martina would cook, and when they had all eaten together, they were going to watch a movie from Martina's box of Blu-ray discs. Neither of the two work brigaders had any real desire to do anything tonight other than fall asleep watching *The Meat-Free Show*, but buoyed by Freya's bright-eyed enthusiasm and bribed by the tea and toast, Aston and Thomas quietly acquiesced.

Whilst Freya and Martina attempted to concoct something presentable from the glut of spinach, carrots, courgettes and onions they had collected from the plot in the garden, the showered and noticeably less aromatic Aston and Thomas resisted the draw of the cookery show and located themselves in their front-room studio. They listened first to the original version of 'Won't Get Fooled Again' and then to the recording made earlier by the two women. Before the first play-through of the girls' guitar and vocal track was finished, Aston felt compelled to play along, installed himself behind his drums and gamely set about emulating the combination of backbeat and clattering fills on the 1971 classic. Thomas joined in on the keyboard, but when they got to the end of the song, he complained that the repeating keyboard sequence made him feel like one of those anonymous figures in the M.C. Escher prints who climb an infinitely ascending yet paradoxically quadrangular staircase, constantly moving, yet simultaneously going nowhere. Aston had never heard of M.C. Escher and had no idea what his partner was talking about.

'I just feel like I'm playing the same thing over and over again,' said Thomas.

'The keyboard is what anchors everything else to the rhythm,' shouted Freya from the kitchen. 'The drums and guitar have to follow the keyboard.'

'OK. A bit like a continuo,' said Thomas. 'I think I can get my head round that. There's a first time for everything, I suppose.'

'You know what I'm going to call our band?' said Aston. 'The Fatberg Four.'

'From the top?' said Thomas.

Aston and Thomas played over the Who's original track once more. As the anti-authoritarian thrust of the song became apparent to Thomas, he wondered how many times Aston would have to hear the words 'new revolution' rhyme with 'new constitution' before he decried the song as the work of anarchists. The anticipated outburst did not, however, materialise. Perhaps Aston was too tired to care. Perhaps he was too focussed on the drumming. Or perhaps the act of drumming itself made him immune to anger. As the long-deceased singer belted out 'Meet the new boss / same as the old boss' and the song came crashing to its close, Aston reflected on that puzzling final couplet.

'I don't really get what they're singing about,' he said, 'but if we did get a new boss, maybe we wouldn't smell like shit all the time.'

Freya tasted the low-tomato ratatouille she had concocted, realised that it lacked flavour, but decided against adding any more of their precious stock of black pepper. She went to the garden, cut some more rosemary and bunged that in instead. In the living room, Martina rooted through the box of Blu-rays she had acquired from PJ, searching for some kind of inconsequential comedy to round off the day. One case did not contain the movie advertised on the jacket but some Maxxbook-compatible software. She would look at that later.

The meal, though not up to the standards set by the two men in the family, was tasty, satisfying and somehow redolent of summer. After eating, the Fatberg Four ignored the need to wash up and settled down to watch Martina's chosen movie. Intriguingly entitled *Ghostbusters*, it was set in London back in the 2030s. Thomas thought it might have been a remake. Scene by scene, Freya and Martina found themselves gradually distracted from the plot by the fascinating exterior shots of the capital. Articulated buses, black taxi cabs and private EVs gridlocked the streets. Hurrying Londoners and visitors from around the world competed for space on the litter-strewn pavements. The underground trains were jammed with passengers. Along the embankments of the river, the flood walls were conspicuous by their absence. Camera-wielding tourists packed Trafalgar Square, Covent Garden Market and the observation platforms of the Shard. The traffic lights changed automatically from green to amber to red, the animated advertising hoardings cajoled and enticed and the London Eye rotated effortlessly on its axis. Everything seemed to work.

'You forget how many people there were,' said Freya. 'I know this is a movie, and it's years ago, but was Liverpool like that too?'

'I think so,' said Martina tentatively, trying to picture the half-forgotten world of her early teens.

Unfortunately, the only two people in the room who could answer Freya's question with any kind of authority were already soundly asleep on the sofa.

The following evening, the four rehearsed 'Won't Get Fooled Again' as a band. Thomas discerned that Aston was mouthing the lyrics 'Then I'll get on my knees and pray / We don't get fooled again' each time Martina sang them, and he was curious as to whether his partner had found some significance in the words or was just blithely singing along. Following the group rehearsal, they set about recording each track separately and then captured video footage of the band playing over their own impressive take of the iconoclastic song.

Martina's friends in Troutbeck Park Gardens were baffled when she asked them if they'd heard of the Fatberg Four, were intrigued when they saw her fronting the band, and were genuinely impressed when they heard her perform.

'The girl can sing,' said Kevin. 'A star is born.'

'Maybe that should be our first broadcast,' suggested Talira.

'Hell, no! Not with our faces all over it,' said Martina in horror.

'Well, no, obviously not,' agreed Talira. 'I was thinking, maybe we could put screenshots of Henderton over the backing track.'

'I've got a better idea,' said Kireina. She turned to Martina. 'Do you know if there's any animation software on that laptop?'

Martina scrunched her nose as she shrugged. 'Dunno. You'd have to look.'

'Still no luck getting us an air con unit?' asked Kevin.

'No. No luck on that front, Kev. Not yet, anyway. But I did wonder if you might all be interested in this. You know how we were wondering about where the raids are coming from? Well, take a look at this.'

From the cargo pocket of her work pants, Martina produced a case for the movie *Miami Girls*.

'Seen it,' said Kevin, unsure what the movie could possibly have to do with the air raids.

Martina removed the shiny disc from the case and handed it to Kevin, who held it directly under one of the kitchen lights to get a better look. Written in indelible marker on the otherwise blank surface of the disc were the words *Flight Tracker 360*.

'It came with that random box of Blu-rays that PJ chucked in as a freebie,' said Martina. 'The guy sees himself as a hard-core wheeler dealer, but in all honesty, he's a bit of a pushover.'

It was an opinion shared by Detective Inspector Smith, who at that moment was sitting in his somewhat compact but admirably tidy office in the Central Police Station. Over a mug of ersatz coffee and a cheese sandwich, the DI mulled over the threads of information supplied to him by PJ. Although the details of the trader's pharmaceutical supplier were sketchy, the suspect would no doubt be in their system somewhere.

37 NOBODY WALKED THE STREETS

Liverpool, 14th July

After the unusually early start on the morning of the drugs raid, neither DI Smith nor Sergeant Wood turned up for work much before nine thirty for the following two days. Whilst the thwarted search of PJ's warehouse could in some senses have been seen as a failure, DI Smith had at least extracted some potentially useful intelligence regarding a habitual supplier of illicit pharmaceuticals.

Although little progress had been made the previous day, painstaking research conducted throughout the morning by Sergeant Wood connected the scraps of information provided by PJ to a registered trader and electronics expert living in Formby, a quiet seaside town some ten miles to the north of Liverpool.

Unwilling to be frustrated a second time, DI Smith devoted considerable care to the production of a legally watertight warrant, secured the signature of a magistrate and checked every last spelling and punctuation mark on the document. By late afternoon he and Sergeant Wood were pulling up outside the address that Martina MacDermott had supplied for her Ministry of Employment registration.

As Sergeant Wood pushed the gate aside, she rapidly observed that the sprawling redbrick property looked unoccupied and judging by the broken windows, the rampant Virginia creeper and the endearing red squirrels, had been so for some considerable period of time. Nevertheless, DI Smith adhered strictly to procedure by knocking on the slightly open front door and announcing that they were police officers in possession of a warrant to search the premises. Receiving no reply, it took a degree of effort to shoulder the door further ajar, but they were in. Their first impressions were not encouraging. Much of the furniture was gone, but the flaking Peace and Love graffiti, the psychedelic Jimi Hendrix mural and the ubiquitous statuettes of Hindu deities suggested that the house might at some point have functioned as a hippy commune. A search of every remaining drawer and cupboard in every dusty room revealed neither pharmaceuticals nor anything that could possibly be linked to Martina MacDermott.

The process of going door to door and trying to find nosy neighbours to interview, rapidly revealed itself as an unmitigated waste of time. Nearby properties were also abandoned and overgrown and in the immediate neighbourhood nobody walked the streets.

No further forward in their investigation, the police officers returned to their vehicle and drove back to the station. Although the search of the empty house with a once much sought-after postcode had been disappointing, they could at least rule the address out of their enquiries. Ever the dogged detective, DI Smith did not give up, but took the decision simply to organise a stakeout of PJ's warehouse. Two detective sergeants would spend every waking hour of the next fortnight waiting for the reappearance of the dark-haired woman with the white electric van whilst a snatch squad would remain on standby at the station, ready to drive the short distance to Sefton Street at a moment's notice.

38 A REAL ASSET

RAF Brize Norton, 14th July

The spurious enemy raid on Northwood had removed at a stroke the most significant obstacle impeding the Prime Minister's path to uncontested power. In the weeks that followed, Modsec worked assiduously to consolidate Henderton's position. The most senior officers in the Admiralty now languished in a high-security correctional facility on the Isle of Man, uncertain of their eventual fate. Closer to home, the subservience, if not the loyalty, of officers immediately below the rank of Admiral had been secured through a combination of death threats, blackmail and squalid incentives, reinforced wherever necessary by exemplary demonstrations of violence.

In accordance with the directions of the Prime Minister, Intelligence Officer Watson had dismissed the two Royal Navy liaison officers from the PM's service and had assigned them insignificant roles in separate parts of the country. Lieutenant Commander York was due to relocate to RAF Lakenheath, where she was to support Modsec in an ongoing investigation. Batista was to be involved in an unspecified duty with the MOD in Whitehall.

It was mid-afternoon and there was a familiar knock at York's door.

'Please excuse the interruption, Lieutenant Commander York. I just wanted to formally say goodbye before I left.'

Batista was carrying a rucksack over one shoulder and was dragging a navy-blue, wheeled holdall behind him. York did not invite him into her room as she had a fair idea how that would pan out.

The Lieutenant Commander stepped outside and closed the door quietly behind her. 'Can I offer you a really rather inadequate cup of coffee in the canteen?'

'Indeed, ma'am. Lead the way.'

He followed, rolling the holdall behind him.

The pair had seen each other on a daily basis for almost two years and had been pursuing their furtive off-duty relationship for much of that time. Batista felt the urge to tell her how much he was going to miss her, but he knew this would sound completely misplaced with them both in uniform. Furthermore, he could not predict how she might react to such a declaration, no matter how guarded.

York was struggling to process her thoughts about their imminent separation and was equally at a loss to communicate how she was feeling. In spite of the increasing frequency of their nights together and the fact that Batista inhabited her dreams when she slept alone, York was still reluctant to define her emotions and was unwilling to say anything to Batista that might invite him to express more than she was ready to hear. Throughout their relationship, it had been York who had steadfastly upheld the integrity of their professional lives and dissuaded Batista from the slightest inappropriate remark or facial expression whilst they were in uniform. She had successfully shielded their relationship from prying eyes and had congratulated herself on her ability to do so.

In the canteen, they drank their ersatz coffee within earshot of RAF personnel and Modsec paramilitaries.

'Well, I wish you all the best, Lieutenant Batista,' said York. It's been truly excellent working with you. We made a first-rate team, I think. No doubt orders will cause our paths to cross at some point in the future. It would be a pleasure to work with you again.'

'Thank you, ma'am. It's been a pleasure working with you too.' He looked at his i-comm and stood up. 'I'm afraid I have to go now.'

His statement was untrue, but the charade had already become excruciating. York also got to her feet.

'Ma'am.'

'Lieutenant.'

Batista turned and dragged his holdall to the door. York sat down again and looked at her coffee, surreptitiously tracking his exit out of the corner of her eye. Batista knew better than to turn and smile.

Although York had always been the one with her finger on the on-off switch, today was altogether different. Whilst she had hardly been looking forward to their approaching separation, she had not expected the constrained formality of Batista's valediction to provoke such strong emotions or trigger such a sense of impending loss.

Thirty minutes later, Lieutenant Batista dumped his bags into the Gurkha, climbed in and began the seventy-mile journey to the Ministry of Defence in Whitehall where he was to report to a Modsec officer whose name, apparently, was Legend. Although he was the only passenger, his driver seemed unusually reluctant to engage in any form of conversation. After a few minutes of staring at the indisputably pleasant Oxfordshire countryside, Batista's i-comm pinged. He was heartened to see that it was a message from York.

The Lieutenant Commander had toyed with the idea of borrowing Shakespeare's 'Parting is such sweet sorrow', but had ultimately reined herself in. Having reminded herself that her insistence on professionalism had thus far protected both their relationship and their careers, and having factored in the current maelstrom of uncertainty, it hardly seemed the time to risk blowing their cover. All things considered, York had opted in the end to maintain decorum and had dictated a short but heartfelt valediction.

'Take care.'

Batista would know, she felt certain, that there were no circumstances under which she would message any other colleague in such an informal manner and she hoped that he would read between the lines. Hoping for a more overt expression of her feelings, all Batista could see between the lines was empty space.

In the low light of the Surveillance Room at Modsec Central Office in Battersea Park, Major Security Officer Legend tapped Data Analyst Anita Chandra on the shoulder. Chandra dutifully removed her headphones.

'What have you got?' enquired Legend.

Chandra scrolled through her on-screen notes. 'Well, we had the usual bedtime Olympics, some indistinct whispering, and several hours of intermittent snoring. Batista's habitual sneaking out at the crack of dawn was followed by the inevitable chance encounter over breakfast. Then they spent the morning apart. Largely she's been wasting her time in the Ops Room trying to make contact with senior figures at Navy Command. No idea what Batista's been up to. They met up again shortly before Batista left and York invited him to the canteen, but we have no intel on that conversation. So, that's pretty much it. I'll forward you the transcript of everything that was said in her room. It's mostly farmyard grunting and the occasional use of the affirmative, followed by whispering, a period of silence, then the snoring, again not unlike something you might hear on a farm.'

Although curious as to how the software might have captured their non-verbal expressions of passion, Legend nevertheless declined Chandra's offer of a transcript. She sensed an opportunity and wanted to get her surveillance officer up to speed.

'Romeo and Juliet know a little bit too much about the PM and the NUP for my liking,' she began. 'If I had things my way, we'd simply eliminate the pair of them, but as the Prime Minister has specified redeployment rather than liquidation, let's see if we can turn the situation to our advantage.'

Chandra removed her fingers from the keyboard and rotated on her chair to face her supervisor. She was intrigued.

'York and Batista may be tight whilst they're screwing each other senseless,' said Legend, 'but it doesn't mean we can't get one of them to turn on the other, or better still, on what's left of the Admiralty.'

'A tame Navy liaison officer would be a real asset,' said Chandra. Having spent the past six months on dimly lit night shifts, she was hoping that Legend's plan might involve some operational experience, ideally in the fresh air and during the hours of daylight. 'So what do you want me to do?'

'Find me something, Chandra. Continue to monitor

their i-comms. Link in, if you can, to the security cameras at Lakenheath and see if you can organise a team to install surveillance in York's room. Batista will be housed in a plush high-security apartment in Admiralty House, so you understand, I presume, what that implies.'

'Presumably once used for high-ranking foreign guests, so full surveillance already installed.'

'You catch on quick. In my experience, if you want to bend someone to your will, you just need a recording of them betraying some dirty little secret or a video of them stark bollock naked with a hooker. So, find something to create a pernicious and unremitting threat to their cosy little lives. See if you can set up a honeytrap for Batista. Be the honeytrap if you like. If you can't get any mileage out of him, he can always disappear.'

'I thought the PM didn't want them liquidated?'

'The order really only applies to York,' said Legend, quietly exasperated with the restriction.

Chandra looked quizzical.

'Ah, you know the PM and the ladies,' said Legend almost philosophically.

'Although,' countered Chandra, 'what the PM doesn't know, can't really hurt him.'

39 MAKE THEM SQUIRM

London, 14th July

As the rays of the evening sun slanted through the foliage of the London Planes, Batista's taciturn driver proceeded along the Mall and stopped at Checkpoint Alpha, the control point at the entrance to the Westminster Security Zone. Having received clearance to proceed, he drove a short distance along Whitehall before turning into Horse Guards Avenue and bringing the armoured patrol vehicle to a halt outside the entrance to the Main Building of the MOD. Batista grabbed his bags, thanked the tight-lipped driver and climbed out via the rear hatch. He slung the small rucksack over his shoulder and took in the sight of the monumental stone figures of *Earth* and *Water* which reclined on towering plinths and flanked the main entrance to the imposing building. Yet again, Batista looked at the disappointingly terse i-comm message from York and following her lead, dictated an equally concise response. He then clattered the wheels of his holdall up the steps and presented himself to the Modsec guards on the doors. They were clearly expecting him.

In the lobby of the MOD, the scan of Batista's luggage immediately triggered an alarm. When the holdall was subsequently searched by hand, the guard produced a Glock 17 semi-automatic service pistol, a shoulder holster and five clips of ammunition.

'I'm afraid, sir,' said the young paramilitary, 'that visitors are not permitted to bring weapons into the MOD. I am obliged to retain both the pistol and the ammunition for safekeeping. You may keep the holster.'

Perhaps less than a minute after Batista had surrendered his weapon, Major Security Officer Legend arrived at reception, apologised to the Lieutenant for the strict security, but expressed her confidence in his understanding, particularly in the light of recent events. She presented him with a security pass and led him straight back out of the building. Once again the wheels on his holdall clattered on the concrete steps, the sound reverberating from the Portland Stone plinths to left and right. They walked a short distance along Horse Guards Avenue, passed the guards at the entrance to Whitehall Gardens and arrived at Admiralty House. There, Legend showed Batista how to open the external doors with his pass and took him up the broad, scarlet-carpeted stairs to his accommodation.

The spacious Georgian apartment comprised two large bedrooms, each with an en-suite bathroom plus a study, a well-equipped kitchen and a sizeable lounge. Beneath the TV screen, a selection of Blu-ray discs of classic British movies promised him perhaps some modicum of distraction during what would inevitably be a solitary evening. The walnut bookcase was laden with works of British literature from Chaucer to Woolf and the drinks cabinet was stocked with various bottles of well-matured single-malt Scotch whisky. It all struck Batista as massively beyond his needs.

'The best we could do at short notice,' said Legend with self-assured irony. 'You'll report to me in the MOD Main Building at 0800 tomorrow. You'll be working with the Modsec team investigating the irritating, anarchist toe rags who impose their sad little quotes on the NBC's newsfeed. Whilst at work, your flat will be cleaned and restocked with food or whatever you require. Just leave a note in the kitchen if there's anything you need.'

From her work station in the Surveillance Room in Modsec Central Office, Anita Chandra watched her supervisor show Batista around the apartment. It would definitely be good to get away from her desk and the organisation of a successful honeytrap operation could do her career no harm whatsoever.

Lieutenant Commander York stood alone on the runway at RAF Brize Norton, glad that it would be a short flight to the former USAF base at Lakenheath. The A-600 had its full complement of crew, but York was manifestly the only passenger waiting to board. She knew the transport could not have been laid on for her personal benefit and assumed that the colossal plane would be collecting a much larger and more valuable cargo from her destination. The first of the load managers ushered her on board and directed her towards the hundred and twenty seats set aside for troop transport. The Lieutenant Commander chose a position furthest from the ramp and buckled herself in. As she waited for the running up of the four turboprop engines to announce the imminent take-off of the A-600, York wrestled with the temptation to keep looking at her i-comm. When finally she felt the aircraft accelerate along the runway, the ping from her device was drowned out by the roar of the engines, but she felt the vibration against her wrist. The message was from Batista.

'Thanks, ma'am. You too.'

Whilst his message was a perfectly reasonable response to her own prosaic valediction, she nevertheless felt disappointed that he hadn't said more. Neither of them were particularly good at this.

As the flight progressed, her thoughts switched from what she had left behind to what might lie ahead. RAF Lakenheath, she was certain, was the home of the squadron that had carried out the devastating raid on Northwood. Had they done so willingly? If so, how had their co-operation been secured? The significant Modsec presence on the base no doubt went some way to answering those questions, but she might well be walking into a snake pit and would need to be wary. She was glad she had the Glock.

After a typically effortless landing, the mammoth aircraft came finally to a stop and the engines began to run down. York glanced once more at her i-comm, but there were no further messages. As soon as the Lieutenant Commander received the go-ahead from the loadmaster, she hauled her bag down the ramp of the A-600, turned, and squinted into the low evening sun. There appeared to be no sign of the Land Rover that she had been told would collect her. Before long, York picked out the throaty rumble of three Gurkha APVs, an M942 multi-purpose truck and two brawny Oshkosh MTVR cargo trucks approaching in convoy. They were clearly not coming on her account.

With little else to do, she watched the drivers arrange the vehicles in a neat line ready for loading, before cutting their engines and standing by. The black Gurkhas were presumably Modsec vehicles, but the olive-green trucks all sported US Army markings and were loaded with large wooden crates.

Black-uniformed paramilitaries slowly removed themselves and their kitbags from the APVs and, at the behest of the load-masters, boarded the aircraft. The drivers remained with their vehicles, awaiting instructions to crawl up the ramp and into the belly of the transporter. Although York could muster no insight into the relocation of the troops and the vehicles, she at least understood how the A-600 had been available to ferry a single Royal Navy officer and her modest personal belongings the relatively short distance from Brize Norton to Lakenheath.

Having spent forty minutes alternately watching the vehicles being loaded aboard the aircraft and musing at the growing redness of the sun as it sank towards the horizon, York spotted the approaching Land Rover. Major Security Officer Benjamin pulled up on the turf some twenty metres from where York was standing and flashed her headlights. The Modsec officer was not in a good mood and would not be getting out of the vehicle.

Lieutenant Commander York opened the Land Rover's passenger door and introduced herself.

'Get in,' said the Modsec Officer disdainfully. 'Throw your bags in the back. I'm Major Security Officer Benjamin. You will be working for me.'

Whilst York had not imagined a military band and a guard of honour to celebrate her arrival, her reception by Benjamin was more peremptory than anything she might have anticipated.

As soon as York was inside the vehicle, the Modsec officer lifted her foot off the brake, pushed it down hard on the accel-erator and the Land Rover lurched forward.

'Right, Lieutenant Commander York. Let's not beat about the bush. The last thing I need right now is some Navy reject on work experience. Unless you can replicate the work of twenty-four Modsec paramilitaries, you're not a whole lot of use to me. So listen carefully. I'm going to give you a straight-forward but time-consuming task and I don't expect to hear from you again until you're done. With me so far?'

'Yes, ma'am,' said York, peering out of the window but unable to perceive much in the advancing gloom.

'Following a possible data breach on this incompetently run excuse for an RAF base, I need you to conduct interviews with every member of personnel on station. Best case scenario, it's either an anomaly or someone is using an unregistered i-comm to say "Hi" to their grandmother. Worst case scenario, someone is transmitting sensitive data to a third party, though exactly who that third party would be, is, quite frankly, beyond me. Nonetheless, the Station Commander and the Cyber-Security Officer are both pooing their sweaty, blue-grey pants that I'll find something that shows their security set-up to be the slack-fest it probably is. And if that helps keep them both honest, then so much the better.'

'What is the size of the data breach?' asked York. As unhappy as she was to play factotum to an ill-tempered battle-axe, the only way she could see of getting back to Brize Norton was to suck it up, keep things professional, and get the job done.

'Small,' said Benjamin, no longer interested in the detail. 'Very small. Kilobytes. Quite frankly this investigation is a boil on my backside. It is not, by any means, the only thing I have on my plate and to be honest, I have bigger fish to fry. So, Lieutenant Commander York, interview them all one by one and make them squirm. Let's see if someone suddenly does a runner. Record all interviews verbatim, but provide me with a succinct summary via i-comm, not in person, at 1800 hours each day.'

'Where would you suggest I start?'

'Really?' said Benjamin sharply, now irritated by the enquiries. 'You're asking me that? Will you want your arse wiping too? OK. I'll give you a heads-up. Don't bother with Flight Lieutenant Dibaba. I'll be dealing with her personally following a bout of insubordination. The woman's a heart-on-your-sleeve, mouthy cow with a stubborn faith in the ideas of the past, but she's definitely not cut out for espionage. The first characteristic of a good spy, as you well know, is not to draw attention to yourself.'

'Indeed, ma'am.'

Benjamin pulled up abruptly at the Command Block. 'Get out,' she ordered. 'Ask Flying Officer Gunatillaka to sort you out a private work station somewhere and a room in the Main Accommodation Block. Any problems, just mention my name. I will present you to the Squadron at morning briefing. After that, I don't want to see your face until you've completed your assignment. If, in the meantime however, I need for any reason to ask you to jump, the only question I expect to hear from you is "How high?". Have I made myself clear?'

'Yes, ma'am.'

'And one final thing, Lieutenant Commander York. Do not upset me. Not as long as you want to see your backstairs Mediterranean boyfriend again.'

40 REMNANT THREADS

RAF Lakenheath, 14th July

As disgruntled as Benjamin was at the suddenness of the MOD instruction to withdraw her troops in order to provide enhanced security for the Prime Minister, she could not contest the logic of the decision. For months, Henderton had nurtured a burning desire to relocate from his somewhat prosaic town-house in Downing Street to a home more in keeping with the ornate style and undeniable splendour of presidential residences such as the Elysée Palace or the White House. Eventually his gaze had fallen upon the Italianate grandeur of the Foreign and Commonwealth Office building standing unused and largely empty, a mere stone's throw from Number Ten. Two hours after asking himself why he hadn't thought of it before, Henderton had redesignated the Grade 1 Listed building as the official residence of the Prime Minister of Great Britain.

The recently christened 'Whitehall Palace' was, however, presenting Modsec with ongoing security and logistics issues. Although located within the Westminster Security Zone, the Prime Minister's opulent new residence was, at the rear, uncomfortably close to the publicly accessible Saint James's Park. To guarantee the leader of the nation the same level of security that he enjoyed at Chequers, considerable numbers of armed personnel were suddenly required. Many of the relocated para-militaries would be somewhat disgruntled to discover that their first duties involved removing desks, cabinets and redundant office equipment from the Prime Minister's designated apartments in the Palace and lugging bedroom furniture and fitness machines from his suite of rooms across the road in Number Ten.

The departure of Benjamin's own unit left her not merely with fewer eyes and ears around the station, but in a potentially vulnerable position, particularly considering the incident that had led ultimately to the death of Flight Lieutenant Jaffrey. The fact that she had been sent an unwanted Navy liaison officer to replace twenty-four armed paramilitaries did nothing to lighten her mood. Without devoting too much time to her decision, she resolved that she would need to commandeer a detachment of Wakeman's RAF Regiment troops to replace her own departed personnel. Only then would she start to feel that she was once more running the base from a position of demonstrable strength.

The decision taken, she contacted Wakeman via i-comm. When his wrist device announced the incoming call, the Wing Commander was poring over the data-rich screens in his office, immensely satisfied that the last of the identified MQ-25 tanker drones had been successfully converted to strike capability.

'Wakeman, this is Benjamin. Stop what you're doing and listen.'

'Yes, ma'am. What can I do for you?'

'You will no doubt be aware that I have returned my Modsec troops back to the MOD for urgent duties. I therefore need twenty-four replacement troops from the ranks of the RAF Regiment plus a number of Land Rovers to replace the APVs. But listen. I don't want anyone who was involved in the Jaffrey incident or in fact anyone even remotely connected to those involved. You will make it crystal clear to the troops you select that they are no longer members of the RAF Regiment, that they have been reassigned to Modsec and that they are answerable only to me. And leave them in no doubt that you are completely in agreement and that this represents a significant promotion. And find them some black uniforms, or at the very least some black berets or something, so we know who's who. Relocate my troops to Block J and have them ready for inspection by 0800 tomorrow. Have I made myself understood?'

'Yes, ma'am,' replied Wakeman, uncertain how he was to sort the matter out in so little time.

A hint of a breeze began to mitigate the oppressive heat that had built up in the Command Block at RAF Lakenheath. Wakeman gave himself an hour to complete the selection process for Benjamin and, after pondering various possible approaches and deciding that none were suitable, he ranked everyone in the RAF Regiment in ascending order of age and picked the twelve youngest males and the twelve youngest females. He transmitted the list to his PA, who called them to a briefing in Block J to be held at 2300 hours.

Despite the rampant speculation amongst the young troops as to the purpose of the unexpected and unusually late briefing, none of them had come anywhere close to predicting the announcement that Wing Commander Wakeman ultimately made. The Station Commander congratulated them on their transfer and promotion to Modsec, asked two lance corporals to remain behind, and dismissed the rest to get their things and relocate immediately to Block J.

Wakeman informed the two NCOs that, pending the arrival

of official black Modsec uniforms, they would be required to improvise. If no suitable uniforms could be found, they would have to wear black berets to differentiate them from regular RAF troops. He ordered them to take a Land Rover and check out Hangar 21 where there were still hundreds of crates of unused US supplies, presumably including items of uniform. They might, if they were lucky, be able to locate a stock of black Special Forces fatigues. Failing that, the berets worn by USAF Tactical Air Control units would do the trick in the first instance. If the lance corporals found nothing in Hangar 21, the Wing Commander suggested, they might also try breaking in to the X-Change superstore in the shopping mall on the western side of the site. Wakeman was adamant that the Modsec stand-ins should have clearly identifiable uniforms ready for their 0800 briefing, even if the lance corporals had to spend all night on the task.

One look at the ranks of numbered wooden storage boxes in Hangar 21, stacked to a height of five metres on heavyweight, industrial shelving, told the two NCOs that all night might be nowhere near long enough to access, break open, and rummage through all of the crates. Not unreasonably preferring to get at least some sleep before their morning briefing, they opted for a raid on the old X-Change superstore and equipped themselves with assault rifles to facilitate entry. When they arrived, they found to their surprise that they could simply slide the doors open. Two hours later, they returned to block J with a selection of kitchen knives and a box of twenty-five black, low-profile baseball caps each sporting the Stars and Stripes on the front.

By the morning, the twenty-four co-opted Modsec soldiers had successfully removed the American flags with the aid of the serrated blade on the kitchen knives. In all but a handful of instances, the outline of the original badge could still be discerned as a rectangle of short remnant threads. On the rear of the caps, the words 'Ralph Lauren' in small white capitals arched over the semicircular window above the adjustable leather strap. With luck, neither Wakeman nor Benjamin would notice.

41 OUT OF HARM'S WAY

RAF Lakenheath, 15th July

Flying Officer Gunatillaka was surprised to see that she was not the first person in the bar that morning. The Royal Navy Lieutenant Commander, whose accommodation she had organised the previous night, had located herself in an armchair near the window and was quietly eating her breakfast. The Mess, Gunatillaka noted, was different. The abandoned beer glasses, tea mugs and cereal bowls had been cleared, washed and stacked neatly on the bar; the armchairs had been aligned into a geometric arrangement; the table tops had been wiped.

The liaison officer, apparently, liked things tidy and that met with Gunatillaka's approval. The Operations Manager was nevertheless puzzled by York. Modsec seemed to favour the unexpected arrival, the psychological ambush, the hammer-blow statement of control. York had walked in the previous night with all the swagger of a bedraggled rescue dog.

The Lieutenant Commander looked like she had not had a whole lot of sleep, she checked her i-comm more often than was healthy, and she had, as far as Gunatillaka could tell, been up since dawn trying to create some measure of order from chaos. York did not create the impression of someone who was here by choice. It could, of course, be an act.

'May I join you, ma'am?' asked Gunatillaka, breakfast in hand.

'Feel free,' said York, disturbed from her reverie. 'Not the tidiest bunch, are they?'

'Oh, some are better than others,' said Gunatillaka philosophically. 'The funny thing is, they can land an F-95 on a dotted line in the dead of night, but they can't put a spoon in a cutlery tray in broad daylight.'

'Maybe that's because they don't have an Ops Manager guiding them in.'

'Sounds about right, ma'am.'

York looked again at her i-comm.

'The briefing's not until 0800,' said Gunatillaka, fully aware that York was not checking the time. 'There's no rush.'

Gunatillaka weighed up the possibilities. York might be impatient for news of a hospitalised parent, a reply from a wavering lover, or an order to return to Brize Norton. If York was a Modsec stooge, she was a particularly edgy Modsec stooge, either a lousy actor or a brilliant one. Had she perhaps been sent out of harm's way or sent where she could do no harm? The Ops Manager decided to go with her gut feeling about the Lieutenant Commander and give her the benefit of the doubt. Having made that call, Gunatillaka risked a question which, if she had misjudged York, could have deleterious consequences.

'Forgive the intrusion, ma'am, but I'm just wondering how a Royal Navy liaison officer comes to be having breakfast on an RAF base, before reporting to a Modsec officer who, on paper at least, she outranks?'

York was completely taken aback. This was a ballsy question and absolutely not the kind of matter the Operations Manager should be prying into. Had Benjamin put her up to this? Or was Gunatillaka signalling that she knew York was in a bind?

'I'm really not at liberty to answer questions of that nature,' said York with practised circumspection, 'any more than you are to ask them, I suspect.' The Lieutenant Commander caught Gunatillaka's eye, raised her eyebrows and betrayed the faintest flicker of a smile. For an uncomfortable moment, neither of them spoke.

'Perhaps we should leave that there,' said York. The suggestion came across more like advice to a trusted friend than a warning to an adversary. 'In any case,' she added, 'it's a long story.'

'Well, if your brief is to get the Squadron to keep this place tidy, you're on a hiding to nothing,' said Gunatillaka. 'They call it "the Mess" for a reason.'

Gunatillaka agreed to meet York outside the Main Briefing Room at 0755 and to give her a running who's who of the arrivals. The Squadron were inevitably wary of the Navy liaison officer who, Benjamin announced, would from now on be conducting the interviews regarding security at the base. Lieutenant Commander York, however, cut a markedly different figure to the increasingly supercilious Benjamin and somehow seemed already to have been given the Gunatillaka seal of approval. York privately noted that Flight Lieutenant Dibaba, the pilot who had recently refused to follow orders, was not on Quick Reaction Alert, but was also not present.

After the briefing, Gunatillaka ushered York to a work station in an unused room still adorned with a portrait of the most recent, and most recently deceased, US President. In the privacy of the office, the Operations Manager readily helped the Lieutenant Commander construct an interview schedule for every member of personnel on the base. Realising that she would have over 150 interviews to complete, York decided that each conversation would be no longer than five minutes and would have only three significant questions, to which she fully expected everyone to answer in the negative. When Gunatillaka dared to refer to the task as 'Operation Wild Goose Chase', York did not bat an eyelid.

42 MISSION COMPLETION

RAF Lakenheath, 15th July

After a week in the company of the same four walls, Dibaba was more than keen to leave her quarters, even if only to be subjected to a psychological evaluation by Dr Kaminski. Throughout her detention, she had enjoyed no contact with anyone other than the tight-lipped Modsec paramilitaries who had brought her food and guarded her door. Although she had, for the most part, slept well during her confinement to quarters, she had on occasions registered the sound of the converted MQ-25s taking off or landing during the night.

That morning she had been surprised to have her breakfast delivered by a young RAF lance corporal in combat fatigues and a black baseball cap. Later, as she followed the guard to her psych eval, she spotted the white Ralph Lauren trademark and struggled to suppress her amusement. Presumably the soldier behind her was sporting the same branding on the back of her own headgear.

'Nice caps, guys,' said Dibaba with a smirk as they left the accommodation block and began the twenty minute walk to the med bay. 'Does the Regiment have a new sponsor?'

'Something like that, ma'am,' said the fresh-faced guard walking behind her.

Dibaba's escorts left her in the med bay and took up position outside the doors. The pilot was immediately unsettled by the steely presence of Major Security Officer Benjamin. This was not going to be the one-to-one psych eval that Dibaba had anticipated.

Although the med bay had no external windows, it was always well-illuminated and seemed to be the only room on station with adequate air conditioning and ventilation.

Dr Kaminski and Dibaba exchanged pleasantries, but Benjamin remained inscrutably silent. The station's Senior Medical Officer began by reminding Dibaba that the purpose of the evaluation was to assess whether she was psychologically fit to conduct missions and that she did not pose a danger either to herself or to her colleagues.

'But unarmed civilians are fair game,' added Dibaba pointedly.

Benjamin did not react, but maintained her gimlet-eyed silence and continued to listen intently. Although Dr Kaminski was an admirer of strong leadership and was keen for the NUP to put the country back on its feet, she was not one of those party devotees who had traded their conscience for the membership card. She harboured clear ethical concerns about what the Modsec officer had ordered her to do, but consoled herself that if she persuaded Dibaba to see the error of her ways, it would keep the headstrong pilot from the firing squad. Benjamin herself had not the slightest qualms about executing recalcitrants, but was acutely aware that Operation Ironstone, the large-scale mission the Prime Minister had ordered against an array of high-profile targets, would require every aircraft the Squadron could muster. She would therefore prefer, at least for one more mission, to cure Dibaba of her insubordination and return her to active duty.

Uneasy with the Modsec officer's icy presence, Dr Kaminski pressed on regardless. She asked Dibaba to sit in the dentistry chair and reclined the seat slightly. On the counter to the side, a number of monitors, their displays all reading zero, stood ready to measure the pilot's physiological responses. Kaminski patted Dibaba on the shoulder, reassured the pilot that she was not about to have a molar extracted and asked her to make herself as comfortable as possible. Dibaba breathed in slowly, then released her breath perhaps a little too forcefully to suggest that she was feeling relaxed. Dr Kaminski proceeded to attach sensors to the pilot's temple, to her left arm and to her solar plexus.

'Nothing to worry about,' said Kaminski sympathetically. 'They're just so I can monitor your heart rate and blood pressure.' In spite of the Doctor's attempts at reassurance, the initial readings confirmed that her subject was feeling less than serene. 'That's a normal response,' said Kaminski to Benjamin. 'White coat syndrome. We'll wait till it settles.'

'That won't be necessary,' said the Modsec officer curtly. 'Please proceed.'

Kaminski complied.

'Flight Lieutenant Dibaba,' began the Doctor, 'you are, by all accounts, an excellent pilot. You have an enviable record of successful missions and no history of indiscipline. Yet, out of the blue, you fail to comply with your orders to complete a routine mission. There is, and I have no doubt you are expecting this, only one question I can possibly want to ask you. And that is, of course, why?'

Dibaba simply cited the Defence of Britain Act. All orders, she reminded Kaminski, were subject to the Mortality Protocol.

Anything that did not comply with the Mortality Protocol was not a legitimate order.

In spite of Benjamin's concession to allow Kaminski to conduct her own psych eval, the Modsec officer was unused to relinquishing control and now felt compelled to intervene.

'The Mortality Protocol,' she scoffed. 'And what if we told you that the Linacre Hospital was the source of a new strain of Sleeper virus that could wipe out everyone in the entire country within a year.'

'And is it?' said Dibaba, certain that this was as much a bluff as Wakeman's contention that the hospital was a militia stronghold. They should at least have taken the trouble to get their stories straight.

Benjamin wondered aloud whether Dr Kaminski would perhaps like to elucidate. It was the prompt for the Doctor to embark upon the fabrication that the Major Security Officer had scripted for her. Kaminski duly revealed to Dibaba that a new and highly virulent strain of the Sleeper virus had indeed been identified. The information the Doctor was divulging was of course highly classified and it was for that reason that there had been no mention of the virus in the briefing for Operation Boltmaker. Government virologists had established that the Linacre Specialist Care Centre in Oxford was, in fact, ground zero. It was unequivocally in everyone's interest to stop a potential pandemic dead in its tracks and Operation Boltmaker had been intended to eradicate the infection at source. Dibaba had, through her ill-informed decision-making, perhaps now compromised the health of an entire city. Dr Kaminski regretted that, as a result, many more pockets of infection might have to be targeted and larger numbers would inevitably lose their lives.

'You honestly expect me to believe this bullshit?' said Dibaba. 'If that had been the case, the target would have been the hospital itself. But in any case, since when do we execute the sick?' She could feel the blood warming her cheeks.

'Dr Kaminski, I feel the Flight Lieutenant is so sharp, she may one day cut herself,' said Benjamin, before turning her attention once more to Dibaba. 'It was not so long ago that the sick were executing the healthy,' she asserted. 'The needs of the many, Flight Lieutenant Dibaba, outweigh the needs of the few.'

Dibaba knew she had heard that saying before, but struggled to recall where. On the monitor, both her heart rate and her blood pressure continued to rise.

'And do the needs of the many outweigh the rights of the few?' retorted Dibaba. 'Isn't there a United Nations Declaration of Human Rights? Don't the sick have a right to be cared for?'

'The United Nations?' sneered Benjamin. 'Don't give me that guff. The future will be written not by the United Nations but by our united nation. Singular. We are the authors of our own destiny.'

'Or the *Bumper Book of Bollocks*,' said Dibaba peevishly.

It was clear that the Flight Lieutenant's mindset was not to be easily remodelled. Benjamin smiled. It was time for a change of tack.

'They say that it doesn't take a sledgehammer to crack a nut,' she began, 'but in my experience, a sledgehammer will do the job just as well. So, let me spell it out for you, Flight Lieutenant Dibaba. Your refusal to obey orders constitutes treason and no government tolerates treason. You are an officer in the Royal Air Force and your loyalty must be absolute and must be seen to be absolute. You will henceforward carry out all instructions in full and you will do so to the best of your considerable ability. If, for any reason whatsoever, you choose not to obey orders, you know the penalty for treason is death. Your demise would, of course, be regrettable, particularly when you consider how long it takes, and how much it costs, to train a half-decent pilot. I personally, however, would not mourn your loss for an instant. Have I made myself clear, Flight Lieutenant?'

'Perfectly,' said Dibaba, steadfastly avoiding eye contact with Benjamin and trying to betray not the slightest flicker of emotion.

'In which case, it only remains for Dr Kaminski to remove the sensors and pass you fit to fly, whilst I tell our friends outside that you are free to go. You will keep the nature and content of our conversation completely confidential. Thanks for your input, Flight Lieutenant. It was good to chat.'

Once Dibaba had gone, Benjamin advised Dr Kaminski never to play poker as she was a lousy liar. Kaminski imagined that Benjamin was not much of a doctor.

Dibaba now wanted to do three things: get her i-comm back, get a beer, and spend some time offloading to Warszawski. When she arrived at the Command Block hoping to reclaim her i-comm from Wing Commander Wakeman, her entry was respectfully barred by RAF Regiment soldiers with black assault rifles and matching baseball caps.

She opted to go to the bar. She could certainly get a beer and, if Warszawski was not there, she would in all probability encounter one of her fellow pilots who could contact him via their own i-comm. She steeled herself for the inevitable banter which seemed to erupt whenever they were spotted within touching distance of each other.

The sound of 'The Joker' being played at high volume announced to Dibaba that she would for sure encounter Flight Lieutenant Bosko, in all likelihood engaged in a round of histrionic lip-syncing for the entertainment of all. The Labrador was beside itself with excitement when Dibaba walked in. Bosko was, as Dibaba had expected, dancing like no-one was watching and Itoje and Xu were watching like they'd never seen her dance before. Bosko turned down the music, walked briskly across to Dibaba and hugged her. Eager to be part of the fuss, the Labrador jumped up at the pair of them.

'Did Stairway post bail?' asked Bosko. The banter had started early.

'Let out for good behaviour,' said Dibaba.

'So what happened on Boltmaker?' asked Itoje.

They already knew from Gunatillaka that Dibaba had refused to complete her mission, that a hospital of some sort had been precariously close to the target area, and that the pilot had railed abusively at Wakeman on return. They also knew that Dibaba had been grounded and kept incommunicado in her quarters pending the outcome of a psych eval with Kaminski, but they wanted the full story and they wanted to hear it from its protagonist.

'Just an electronic hang fire,' she lied, 'probably a problem with the key. The missiles failed to launch. Benjamin's been all over me like measles.'

The pilots rapidly read between the lines. Either Benjamin had somehow secured Dibaba's silence, and anyone who knew the pilot would consider that unlikely, or Dibaba was trying to protect them from becoming accessories to her act of insubordination.

'Bummer,' said Itoje.

'What's with the black baseball caps?' asked Dibaba.

'Ah, no way,' said Xu frustratedly. 'That was my original choice.'

Dibaba was confused. Flight Lieutenant Xu explained that during their comrade's absence, the Squadron had run a sweepstake regarding the first question that she would ask on her return. There had been three votes for 'Did you miss me?' and six for 'Is the dog with Stairway?'

'Talking of Stairway,' said Dibaba. 'Can one of you reprobates tell me where he is? I still don't have my i-comm.'

'I think he's with Blondie,' said Xu with a smirk. 'You'd better watch out, Freebird. You've got competition.'

Dibaba had no idea who 'Blondie' was, and was not in the mood for the banter.

'Stairway can date who he likes,' she said, batting away the jest. 'He's a free agent.'

'It's his security interview,' said Bosko, feeling the need to reassure Dibaba in spite of her protestation of disinterest. 'It's hardly a date.'

'Well, can somebody message him that I'm looking for him? And holy shit. What's been going on in here? Who tidied up?'

'Must have been Gunnie,' said Bosko.

When Xu messaged Warszawski that his work-wife was out of prison and was gasping for a beer, Dibaba simply rolled her eyes and shook her head.

'A huge plate of denial with a side of misdirection,' thought Bosko. 'What is her problem? She could do a lot worse than Stairway.' In fact, Bosko wouldn't have shied away from taking a shot at Stairway herself, if she thought for one moment that he might have eyes for anyone else. Keen to move on from that thought, Bosko returned to *Classic Rock Classics*, cranked up the volume on a track entitled 'Can't Get Enough' and returned to her vivacious and unrestrained lip-syncing.

Warszawski appeared some ten minutes later to a further round of cheap jibes about his friendship with Dibaba. It did not take the Labrador long to spot the pair once more in each other's company and work out that a lengthy walk and some serious stick retrieval might be on the cards.

Several hours later, when most of the Squadron were asleep, an MQ-25 accelerated along Runway 24 and took to the air. Operation Pedigree, which was being managed exclusively by Wing Commander Wakeman, was an exact re-run of Boltmaker but with one exception: the unreliable human component had been removed. Within an hour, the Oxford University Science Area, and the neighbouring Linacre Specialist Care Centre to its side, had been completely flattened. Wakeman was thoroughly satisfied with the operation and determined to use the AAVs in future as his preferred means of mission completion.

43 STORY TO TELL

RAF Lakenheath, 16th July

0100 hours. Although the Squadron had been given the night off, Gunatillaka could not sleep and wondered if there might be someone still hanging around in the bar. The Mess turned out to be empty, but as the Ops Manager returned to her quarters, she spotted light leaching from beneath Lieutenant Commander York's door. Certain there was more to the Royal Navy officer than met the eye, Gunatillaka knocked tentatively. After a few seconds, the Lieutenant Commander appeared. She was still in uniform.

'Fancy a drink, ma'am?' said Gunatillaka, brandishing an almost untouched half-bottle of Utility. 'You're not the only one with a story to tell.'

As the pair talked and intermittently refilled each other's glasses with gin, each played sympathetic barkeep to the other. Gunatillaka began by treating York to a couple of inconsequential but unquestionably funny 161 Squadron anecdotes, before detailing the more sinister sequence of events that led to Dibaba's grounding and then spilling the beans about the repurposed MQ25s. York reciprocated with a few eye-openers of her own concerning the behaviours and ambitions of the Right Honourable Gilbert Lathum Henderton and expressed her growing fears for the future.

In time, Gunatillaka drifted onto the subject of relationships, and York's heart went out to her as she recounted the loss of her beloved family to the indiscriminate cruelty of the Sleeper virus. Gunatillaka revealed that she was on her second period of service with the RAF. Having initially fulfilled a six-year contract with integrity, she had subsequently trained to be a teacher. It was on holiday with a colleague in Florida that she first met Ash, her future husband and the father of her two children. During an almost unbearably hot afternoon, she encountered this passionate wildlife photographer hunched in a canoe on the Wekiva river, unobtrusively capturing images of a young alligator nurturing her brood of hatchlings in the shade of an overhanging bank. It was a scene that still occupied Gunatillaka's thoughts at least once a day.

When her soul mate and their beautiful twin girls were taken by the virus, Gunatillaka suffered, as many people did, a form of survivor syndrome. She often experienced garish flashbacks to her husband's removal to the Intensive Care Unit or to the day she said goodbye to her beloved children.

Her job as a primary school teacher, along with many aspects of daily life, lost meaning and became impossible. Feelings of guilt for having had the dumb luck to be the one surviving member of their beautiful family fuelled long phases of daytime irritability and night-time insomnia. To escape the reminders of their life together, she decided, almost on a whim, to leave her job in Gloucestershire and head east.

Eventually Gunatillaka pitched up in the quiet Suffolk village of Great Finborough. There she found an outwardly picturesque thatched cottage, abandoned after repeated flooding from the nearby stream and still reeking of the deposits left after the septic tank had backed up during each inundation.

In the years of lawlessness, she somehow scratched a living as a peripatetic primary school teacher and did her best to clean the place up and turn it into a home. Occasionally, she made a little additional money selling some of the thousands of old vinyl albums that she found lining the extensive shelving in the room at the end of the cottage.

When civil society began to reconstitute itself and the RAF was calling out for former crew to re-enlist, Gunatillaka leapt at the chance of a familiar structure and regular pay. It did not take the Medical Officers at Lakenheath long to realise that she was suffering from Post-Traumatic Stress Disorder. After sixteen weeks of trauma-focused cognitive behavioural therapy, she took the first steps towards fashioning some sense of perspective and began at last to sleep for more than four hours a night. The RAF had offered her an old life that was also a new life and she never went back to Gloucestershire.

Almost inevitably, Gunatillaka asked the displaced Lieutenant Commander if she had a significant other in her own life. York emptied her glass. The wistful look on her face and the slow intake of breath were tantamount to an affirmative, but hinted at complication. As York gradually recounted her tale, Gunatillaka took a shine to the solitary Navy Officer who, it turned out, had the cojones to confront the Prime Minister but not her own commitment issues. The Ops Manager determined that she would have a private word with York's interviewees and tip them the wink that the Lieutenant Commander was not here out of choice, that she knew her task had little point to it and that she was simply working her ticket back to Brize Norton.

The two officers raised a glass to hope. The shots downed, York proceeded to talk in surprising detail about several aspects of her relationship with Batista, but repeatedly left Gunatillaka to infer the depth of her feelings for the Lieutenant.

'Why don't you just tell him?' the Operations Manager finally asked.

It was not an easy question to answer, but having listened intently to Gunatillaka's account of the loss of her husband and children and her description of the emptiness that followed, York agreed it would be better to say something rather than nothing. In spite of the gin and the sympathy, she was none-theless nervous of making an unbridled declaration.

'Just decide how you feel and say it,' said Gunatillaka, as she got to her feet. 'You're a long time dead.'

She decided that she would leave York with that thought and bid her goodnight. The Lieutenant Commander smiled and thanked her for reaching out.

At three in the morning, York messaged Batista, nailing a line from *A Midsummer Night's Dream* that she had once learned at school.

'The course of true love never did run smooth.'

Shortly before six, she received a reply.

'Love sought, is good; but given unsought, is better.'

The genie had squeezed its way out of the bottle. York smiled and lay back on her pillow, relieved and delighted in equal measure. She looked forward to speaking to Gunatillaka at breakfast.

44 FINGERTIPS ONTO
THE SCREEN

Liverpool, 16th July

Unaware that PJ's warehouse had been staked out for several days by two increasingly bored detective sergeants, Martina returned in search of camouflage netting for the outside broadcast van plus an overdrive pedal for an electric guitar. Emerging empty-handed from the store after a difficult conversation with an unusually tight-lipped and edgy PJ, she found herself confronted by the two police officers who reassured her that they were simply conducting random checks.

They proceeded to ask her a series of mundane questions which seemed to have little purpose beyond testing her familiarity with the data on her identity card. Certain that the officers would not catch her out and that she would soon be allowed to go about her business, Martina remained relaxed and happily responded to their enquiries. Without warning, a white van not unlike her own pulled up sharply by the entrance to the warehouse and disgorged its uniformed snatch squad. Martina was bundled unceremoniously into the unmarked vehicle, placed under arrest, and taken directly to the Central Police Station.

To DI Smith's frustration, the search of Martina's clothing and of her van produced neither pharmaceuticals, nor indeed anything of an illegal nature and the officers were unable to find any incriminating content on her i-comm. Her assertion that she had no fixed abode and sometimes slept in her van or lived periodically in abandoned houses was well within the bounds of possibility, but left the Detective Inspector in absolutely no doubt that Martina was simply concealing the whereabouts of her stocks. It did not require someone of DI Smith's experience to realise that the outmoded smartphone found in Martina's possession could be significant and might well contain useful intelligence. With luck, he would perhaps discover extensive lists of criminal contacts or details of transactions and payments received. The young woman's insistence that she had found the antique handset on the floor of a house she had recently slept in, but had no idea how to operate it, was also plausible, but did not withstand Sergeant Wood's suggestion that DI Smith should try pressing their prisoner's fingertips onto the screen. The handset recognised Martina's bio-data and sprang immediately to life.

To the Detective Inspector's dismay, there was not a scrap of tangible evidence to be found on the phone. The only accessible data the handset seemed to contain was a sporadic conversation between the prisoner and someone she referred to as 'bro'. To a casual observer the dialogue might have come across as no more than the kind of inconsequential chat that any two siblings might easily indulge in, but DI Smith took nothing for granted and wondered if the messages had perhaps been written in some sort of private code. One entry in particular, containing an unusually precise news headline about the RAF defending an Oxford hospital, stood out from the more usual interplay of gentle repartee and inquiries about health. However, if the conversations were in some form of code, neither the Detective

Inspector, nor anyone else at the Station, had the faintest idea how to decipher it.

It was Sergeant Wood who contacted the NBC to enquire about the puzzling headline and discovered that it corresponded exactly to the wording of a recent hoax news crawl. She rapidly came to the conclusion that their detainee might be connected to the hacker ring that Modsec was hunting and brought her suspicions to the attention of her boss. Impressed, DI Smith made an immediate call to the Ministry of Defence and spent a frustrating twenty minutes listening to synth-pop or being reassured by a saccharine voice that his call was important. By the time he was eventually connected to Major Security Officer Legend, he had allowed his thoughts to drift and his initial attempt to explain the reason for his call was far from succinct.

Once the Modsec officer had encouraged DI Smith to spare her the unnecessary details and get to the point, it took Legend mere seconds to realise the potentially enormous value of this new intelligence. She thanked DI Smith for his diligence, instructed him not to release the prisoner under any circumstances and arranged for a Modsec armoured patrol vehicle to travel to Liverpool the following morning.

45 A GODDESS INDEED

London, 16th July

The Prime Minister spent the earlier part of the morning at the devastated Northwood Headquarters of the former Joint Forces Command. He was filmed solemnly laying a wreath before reciting from memory a few lines from Laurence Binyon's enduring poem 'For the Fallen'. The cameras also captured the PM subsequently dressed in pristine, orange overalls, appreciating the efforts of the work brigaders who were assiduously clearing blocks of concrete and lengths of twisted metal and were still digging out blackened body parts from the rubble.

The roadshow then relocated to Saint Benedict's Primary School for Henderton's second engagement of the day. The Prime Minister travelled in his customary Gurkha armoured patrol vehicle with police motorcycle outriders in front and behind. The once ever-present Royal Navy liaison officers had been replaced by a devoted personal assistant and a stalwart bodyguard. The Comanche helicopter, which had temporarily withdrawn to allow filming at Northwood to proceed undisturbed, rejoined the motorcade and provided cover from overhead. Immediately behind the APV and ahead of the police motorcyclists, the remainder of the Prime Minister's support team travelled in the newly commissioned, scarlet tour bus. On each flank, the bus sported a reproduction of Kireina's Lennon-inspired image of Henderton and the slogan 'Our Victory is Nigh'.

About a mile from the school, the motorcade halted, allowing the Prime Minister plus his PA and his personal bodyguard to transfer from the APV to the bus. Some two minutes later, Henderton was the first to emerge and wave to the admiring crowd.

Having captured his arrival plus multiple shots of telegenic schoolchildren enthusiastically waving Union Jacks and triangular NUP banners, the cameras tracked the Prime Minister into the school hall, where he took the seat reserved for him at the centre of the front row.

Mr Polzeath, the Headteacher, waited for the pupils, teachers and parents to settle and for the NBC director to give him the nod to address his audience.

'Our school is a community,' he began, 'and community is the bedrock upon which Saint Benedict's educates and nurtures its young minds. Our teachers and parents work as one to recognise skills, develop potential and care for each child throughout his or her time with us. As a diverse, multicultural community we encourage our boys and girls to value the best in every pupil's contribution.'

The Prime Minister leaned towards his PA. 'Always good to have a few watermelon smiles in front of the cameras,' he whispered.

'All aspects of our teaching programme,' continued the Headteacher, 'are designed to develop self-confidence and inner belief. We know that these qualities give our pupils the ability to seize opportunity when it arises, make intelligent decisions and drive themselves onwards to greater success. And who else could embody such qualities more completely than our honoured guest? Ladies and Gentlemen, boys and girls, it gives me enormous pleasure to be able to welcome to our school the Prime Minister, The Right Honourable Gilbert Lathum Henderton.'

The Prime Minister turned and accepted the heartfelt applause with a magnanimous smile. Once the hall was finally quiet, the Headteacher continued his address.

'However, before we have the honour of hearing from the Prime Minister himself, we have an offering from some of our brightest stars. In our short presentation on Britannia, you will hear from our Year 6 students, Soozie Greenwood, Rafiq Kumar, Chidi Damijo and Carina Li. Britannia will be portrayed by Soozie's mother, Ms Natalia Greenwood.'

Mr Polzeath initiated a second round of applause, during which the four eleven-year-old pupils left their seats on the front row, ascended the short flight of wooden stairs to the stage and located their marks to the left and right. They were joined from the wings by Soozie's mother, who took her position at the centre.

Natalia Greenwood had made an impressive job of her costume. Her flowing, white robes, clasped at her shoulders and belted at her slender waist, had been created from two antique evening gowns. The circular shield strapped to her left arm had been repurposed from the lightweight, plywood top of a defunct self-assembly table and was now overlaid with a Union Jack, perfectly centred and attached around the perimeter with meticulously spaced drawing pins. The dangerous-looking trident and the crimson-plumed Spartan helmet, which completed the costume to such powerful effect, were movie props spirited away from Pinewood Studios by Natalia Greenwood's ex some eight years previously. Soozie's mother raised the visor on her helmet, stood three quarters to the audience and looked purposefully into the middle distance. She had pale skin, blue eyes and was perhaps wearing a touch of lipstick. From beneath her helmet, tresses of blonde hair caressed her right shoulder. The Prime Minister was enthralled.

Soozie Greenwood was the first to speak. The eleven-year-old, who had spent several days practising and memorising her lines, enunciated clearly and confidently and was not afraid to make eye contact with her fascinated audience.

'The word "Britannia",' she began, 'has been used in several different senses throughout its history. To the Roman invaders, Britannia was the primitive land north of Gaul and south of Caledonia, but we are more likely to think of Britannia as the personification of our island home. As early as the first century AD, Britannia was depicted as a goddess, the female symbol of Britain, and her image began to appear on Roman coins.'

'A goddess indeed,' thought Henderton. Impressive as the young speaker was, the Prime Minister was considerably more impressed by her mother.

The presentation was continued by Rafiq Kumar, who was equally self-assured in his delivery.

'Early portraits show Britannia as a beautiful young woman wearing the helmet of a Roman centurion, wrapped in a white garment with her right breast exposed.'

'Oh, yes please,' mused Henderton to himself. 'Although perhaps a bit too much to serve up in a Primary School.'

'Britannia,' Rafiq continued, 'is usually shown seated on a rock, holding a spear and with a spiked shield propped beside her. On a later range of Roman coinage, she is seated on a globe above waves and represents Britain at the edge of the known world. In 1672, under Charles the Second, Britannia made her first appearance on English coins.'

The Prime Minister noted that Soozie's mother was not wearing a wedding ring.

Chidi Damijo and Carina Li were as eloquent as their classmates. When Carina thanked the audience for their attention, the cameras captured the resounding applause. The Prime Minister stood and invited the goddess Britannia herself to join him, as he was to make an important statement, not only to the teachers, parents and pupils seated there in the hall, but to the entire nation.

The focus of the school's presentation had been designated by Henderton's team during initial negotiations and provided the perfect lead-in to the Prime Minister's big announcement.

'Wonderful,' enthused Henderton. 'A first rate presentation in all respects. I see a bright future for the pupils of this school, a very bright future indeed. So, I extend my warmest congratulations to the pupils, the teachers and the parents of Saint Benedict's School. And now, I have something to announce. You will no doubt be pleased to hear, and you are indeed the first people in the country to hear this officially, that as soon as we have defeated the enemy, as defeat him we shall, this great nation will undertake to construct, as a symbol of our victory, a statue of Britannia, taller than the *Statue of Liberty*, on a site beside the Thames. And there will be a competition, open to every school pupil in the country, to design the statue itself. And who knows, with the head start the pupils here at Saint Benedict's have, perhaps one of you here today will be the winner.'

Mr Polzeath stood and led the effusive applause. The cameras closed in on Henderton and Britannia and when the director asked them to stand closer together, the PM was only too happy to oblige. As they smiled for the nation, Natalia Greenwood felt the Prime Minister gently place his hand on the small of her back.

Henderton had long harboured the idea of constructing a monumental statue of Britannia on the banks of the Thames and in recent weeks had been refining his designs. He intended a 120-metre steel figure, a resolute, windswept Britannia standing barefoot upon tide-threatened rocks. His vision was in essence the image to be found on the fine silver Britannia coins he regularly discovered in his Christmas stocking as a child and today made flesh by Soozie Greenwood's mother. Henderton had identified his preferred riverside location for the statue and now only needed the RAF to destroy the incumbent structure and level the site. The competition that he had announced, and that he was certain would enthuse the nation, was to take place in the post-Christmas grey of January. The winner would be the school pupil whose design most closely resembled his own.

Once Natalia Greenwood had thanked the Prime Minister wholeheartedly for hauling the UK out of the mire and rebuilding a country in which it was once more safe for children to go to school, she apologised that she must change and demurely took her leave.

Henderton watched her closely as she walked away and then spoke quietly to his PA. 'Find out if she's single.'

After a short break to allow the director to brief the crew for the next part of the shoot, Soozie, Rafiq and their entire class assembled on the stage for the Oath of Allegiance. With their right hand held open-palmed before them, they collectively declaimed their well-rehearsed lines.

'I swear, I will be obedient to my teachers, respect the law of this land and be faithful to the Prime Minister and Lord Protector of the United Kingdom, so help me God.'

The applause from their parents was as proud as it was spontaneous.

After a late but satisfying lunch, the Prime Minister was to be filmed taking part in a five-a-side football match on the school field. He removed his Savile Row jacket and silk tie, rolled up his sleeves and put on a pair of ageing trainers. Immediately, he adopted a defensive position in front of his team's goal. When Carina Li, who was playing for the opposition, ran on to a pass, Henderton sprinted forward and tackled the eleven-year-old, upending her robustly and leaving her sprawling on the grass. With characteristic energy, he dribbled past the three remaining outfield players, lined up a shot and hammered the ball past Chidi Damijo's forlorn dive and into the bulging net. The Prime Minister turned, punched his fist into the air and celebrated as though he had scored the winning goal in the dying seconds of the FA Cup final. With Carina Li still lying spreadeagled on the turf and completely winded, Henderton's assistant astutely decided that they were running short of time and wrapped up his involvement in the match. As the exhilarated Prime Minister left the field of play, surrounded by his PA, his bodyguard and his stylist, he wondered whether Natalia Greenwood had perhaps been watching.

46 UNCOMPLICATED
AS IT WAS

RAF Lakenheath, 17th July

An unexpected lull had descended upon RAF Lakenheath, at least as far as the pilots were concerned. Wing Commander Wakeman had announced that the station's fourteen F-95s were to be overhauled and that piloted operations would therefore be suspended for an interim period. Maintenance work continued on the MQ-25s, but it was not clear to Dibaba and her comrades whether the nocturnal flights were test runs or actual missions.

Since allowing herself to be unsettled by Xu's joke about Warszawski being on a date with Lieutenant Commander York, Dibaba had given some thought to the whole question of the regular 'cute couple' banter and had decided not to let it get under her skin. As far as she was concerned, the others could think whatever they wanted. There was nothing wrong with liking someone.

Most of the pilots spent increasing amounts of their unexpected downtime in the High School Sports Hall or the Upper East Side Fitness Center, but the afternoon found Dibaba and Warszawski alone in the bar, save, almost inevitably, for their dozing canine companion. The Labrador, however, was in for a rude awakening. Dibaba was about to give Warszawski a guitar lesson on the Gibson SG Special.

'We're going to start with a D chord,' she began, 'because it's only three fingers and it's sort of D-shaped, so it's easy to remember.'

'OK,' said Warszawski. In spite of any impression to the contrary that might have been created by his occasional air guitar antics, he had never studied music and had never touched a real guitar in his life. He already felt lost.

Dibaba strapped on the white Gibson, plugged it into the amp and showed Warszawski how to shape his fingers on the lowest three strings of the fretboard. She strummed the chord a couple of times so that he knew how it sounded and immediately ruined the dog's blissful afternoon doze. She then handed Warszawski the guitar, draped the timeworn leather strap around his shoulders and directed him to place each finger in sequence on the correct string and the correct fret to build up the chord. Dibaba had made it look incredibly easy, as though her fingers simply knew what to do without needing to be told, but when Warszawski tried, his third finger repeatedly rebelled and interfered with the half-decent job being done by the other two. Dibaba took the guitar back and showed Warszawski the pattern of the D chord a second time.

'The thing is,' he said, 'when you do it, your fingers are the other way round. It's confusing.'

Determined that she would get her tutee to play at least one chord by the end of the afternoon, Dibaba returned the guitar to him and, taking up position behind Warszawski and slightly to his side, demonstrated the structuring of the chord as though her left hand were his.

She knew that they had wandered into the 'cute couple' zone again and she wondered if he too felt conflicted. If she was intruding into Warszawski's personal space, he certainly didn't seem to mind.

As it was, he didn't mind in the slightest, but he was wondering why she had chosen to stand so close to him. Was she thinking of making a move? And would that necessarily be a bad thing? There was no question that he found Freebird attractive. He always had done. And during the hours of daylight they defaulted to each other's company whenever the opportunity arose. Maybe they would be good together. What would he do, if she were to place her right hand softly on his shoulder? Would he want to risk an enduring and important friendship for a relationship that might not last? Was now even the right time to be thinking like this?

'Hey. Ground Control to Major Gone,' said Dibaba. 'Are you paying attention?'

She ran through the construction of the chord a second time, before removing her hand from the fretboard and encouraging him to try. With repetition, Warszawski gained enough control of his reluctant finger to play the chord cleanly.

'I think I know the answer to this,' he said, 'but, how many songs can I play with a D chord?'

'With just a D, not a whole lot, but once you've learned G and C, you'll be ready to play "Sweet Child O' Mine" and "The Joker" and if we're going to play "Stairway to Heaven" at some point, those three chords are in there too.'

'Hell, Freebird, you should have led with that.'

Dibaba flashed him a smile. 'Led? There's a joke in there somewhere. OK. Let's give this a try. I'm going to sing the first three lines of "Stairway To Heaven" and when I get to the word "gold", play that D chord.'

Dibaba sang and at the end of the second line Warszawski hit the strings as requested and could hear that the chord underpinned her voice beautifully.

'Shit,' he said, thrilled with the result. 'That was amazing.'

'Just wait till you can play the whole thing.'

Warszawski could not contain himself. 'OK, Freebird, this is what's gonna happen. You're going to teach me a chord a week until I can play "Stairway To Heaven" from start to finish.'

'OK,' she said, swept along by his boyish enthusiasm. 'Game on. I'll have you busking it by your birthday.'

They repeated their single-chord version of the first two lines. Uncomplicated as it was, it brought a smile to their faces each time they did it.

47 OPPORTUNITY
IN ADVERSITY

London, 20th July

Although Martina had no idea where she was and was uncertain of the passage of time, she had spent the past thirty-six hours in what had once been designated the relaxation area of a vacated foreign embassy building in Belgravia, Central London. Martina was handcuffed to a steel ring which was bolted securely to the wall. The retaining ring had been installed at such a height that it allowed the prisoner to sit temporarily if she was prepared to stretch her arms painfully above her head, but precluded all thought of lying down.

The walls, floor and ceiling of the elongated room were completely white. At one end, the glass door to the Finnish spruce sauna permitted a glimpse of a stack of white plastic loungers and a pile of large, oatmeal cushions. On the tiled wall outside the sauna, a slatted wooden bucket with a pull-chain hung above the less traditional, gleaming chrome shower fittings. The small circular plunge pool appeared not to be filled.

There was no natural source of light, but the soft white lighting around the edges of the ceiling and the floor had remained on since Martina's arrival. She had no i-comm and no idea of the time or even whether it was day or night. Her attempts to sleep had been thwarted not only by the awkwardness of her posture and the absence of darkness, but by the relentless intrusion of sound. Constant white noise, punctuated by recordings of human screaming, emanated ceaselessly from the high quality speakers which had once treated the building's diplomats to a relaxing soundtrack of the rainforest or waves breaking on a deserted shore. About three metres from where Martina had been restrained, a solid, white therapy table would have made a more than acceptable bed for the exhausted and hungry prisoner.

Suddenly, the white noise was extinguished and the room was plunged into darkness. A door opened and two figures with torchlights on their foreheads entered. They covered Martina's head with a hood, unshackled her from the wall and bundled her onto the table. With purposeful aggression, Martina's captors forced her onto her back and immobilised her head with a medical restraining cradle. Having zip-tied her wrists firmly to steel rings fitted to the underside of the table, the guards tightened webbing straps across her ankles, knees, waist and shoulders. Martina could neither see her captors nor move her body and her sense of vulnerability was absolute. There was a period of intimidating, blacked-out silence before the cold water began pouring onto her hooded face. Within seconds, it penetrated her nostrils and mouth and she was forced to try to snort forcefully and then hold her breath. When Martina finally had no option but to inhale, she sucked cold water into her airway, triggering her gag reflex and convincing her that she was about to drown. After several excruciating minutes, the procedure suddenly stopped and her tormentors left the room.

Martina was left alone in the silence and the dark. She was

cold, shivering and utterly terrified. After an indeterminate but probably short period of time which served only to heighten Martina's shuddering fear of what might happen next, the door opened, her torturers returned and the waterboarding began again.

As Martina struggled once more not to drown and her inescapable terror destroyed all sense beyond the nightmarish moment, the door was pushed open, the lights were turned on and the Modsec officers were confronted by a Royal Navy Lieutenant.

'Stand down,' Batista shouted. 'That's an order.'

The Modsec officer turned the hosepipe away from Martina's face.

'I have orders to prepare the prisoner for interrogation, sir.'

'And I have orders to interrogate her and I am telling you to turn the water off.'

The water continued to flow from the hosepipe and splatter the white-tiled floor.

'You are no doubt intelligent enough to know from the braid on my arm that I outrank you,' bristled Lieutenant Batista. 'So, turn the water off and stand down.'

The Modsec officer reluctantly cut the water supply to the hose. 'I have my orders, sir,' he repeated.

His colleague said nothing, but she was clearly no less unhappy to be disrupted from her duties.

'For crying out loud,' fumed Batista. 'When did we become the Gestapo? Didn't we fight a war against this sort of thing?'

Batista instructed the Modsec officers to remove the hood, the straps and the zip ties and to find some towels and some clean, dry clothing for the disorientated prisoner.

Batista took off his jacket and placed it round Martina's wet and trembling shoulders. 'I'm sorry,' he said. 'This is not how human beings should treat other human beings.'

Still in a state of bewildered terror, Martina did not even hear his apology. All she knew at that moment was that her torment had stopped and for that, she was relieved beyond measure.

The Modsec officers returned some ten minutes later with a selection of clean towels, a dry towelling robe and some turquoise flip-flops. Batista then directed them to identify a secure room with a bed and decent sanitary facilities, where Martina could be provided with something to eat and allowed to sleep. He expressly forbade any further form of harassment, mistreatment or torture, informed the Modsec officers that MacDermott was to be given a minimum of forty-eight hours to recover and assured them that he would be checking at intervals on the prisoner's welfare. Manifestly disgruntled, the pair nonetheless acquiesced and left the room. Batista apologised to Martina once more and suggested she use the sauna to get out of her wet things, dry herself down and change into the towelling robe.

Within an hour, the abused and shaken detainee, still wearing the robe and the flip-flops, had been accommodated in an apartment on the top floor of the building. Martina lay on the bed, her heart rate and breathing closer to normal but feeling simultaneously exhausted and incapable of sleep. The waterboarding might have stopped, but Martina's fearful confusion persisted. She had absolutely no frame of reference that would help her predict what else might lie ahead.

After spending perhaps an hour staring open-mouthed at the ceiling tiles, some modicum of lucidity began to emerge, allowing Martina to get up from the bed and slowly look around the apartment. As well as a genuinely comfortable mattress, she had a small bedside table with a lamp, an unlabelled bottle of water and a plate bearing what looked like two cheese sandwiches. In spite of her hunger, she was still too adrenalised to eat them quickly, but she ate them nonetheless. Beneath the window were a desk and a couple of chairs. The apartment also had an en-suite bathroom and a small kitchen area with a toaster and a bread board sprinkled with long-hardened crumbs. She could almost have been in a mid-priced self-catering hotel room, were it not for the paramilitary guard on the door and the searing memory of her abuse. There was no clock in the room, but the sunlight streaming through the window at a lowish angle suggested that it was a good few hours before, or possibly after, midday.

The view from the window suggested to Martina that she was somewhere in London. If the building harbouring her apartment was anything like those opposite, she was on the fifth, or possibly the sixth, floor of a Georgian, Portland Stone building in a once expensive part of the capital. It was without doubt a considerable drop to the street below, but there might, she thought, be some way of escape via the roof. When she tried to open the windows, however, she found that they were locked. Any attempt to break the glass, she suspected, would simply attract the attention of the guard and might conceivably result in further mistreatment.

The guard, for his part, was completely aware that the windows throughout this former embassy building were fitted with bullet-proof panes and he was supremely unconcerned that the prisoner might attempt to shatter the glass and access the roof or call for help. As long as he ensured that the door to the apartment was always locked from the outside, she would not be going anywhere.

In Room 501 at the MOD Main Building in Whitehall, Major Security Officer Legend and the newly promoted Intelligence Officer Chandra were consuming a cup of lukewarm ersatz coffee as they discussed the question of Batista's potential vulnerability to a honeytrap operation.

'It might be trickier than we thought to prise Batista and York apart,' said Chandra. 'Based on the lovey-dovey lines of poetry they exchange, they seem pretty invested in one another.'

'Not necessarily a bad thing,' said Legend. 'That emotional investment might generate powerful and easily manipulated feelings of guilt if Batista can be inveigled into a compromising and easily filmed situation with a woman other than York.'

Legend was of the opinion that Chandra herself would be ideal for the part. Chandra, on the other hand, had not the slightest intention of prostituting herself for Modsec and asserted, perhaps rashly, that the service must comfortably have the funds to procure someone who would.

No sooner had the thought crossed Legend's mind that Martina MacDermott might ultimately be persuaded to buy her freedom by acting as a honeytrap for an idealistic and unwitting Navy Lieutenant, than she received an i-comm message informing her of Batista's high-handed disruption of Martina's preparation for questioning.

'Shit,' said Legend. 'Something's come up. Batista's just stopped MacDermott's waterboarding, ordered her some food and set her up in a cosy apartment on the top floor.'

'Why?' asked Chandra. 'Why would he do that? Is he trying to play good cop, bad cop or something?'

'God knows. I've never placed much faith in friend and foe routines,' said Legend, 'but following the Lieutenant's interference in established procedure, a good cop, bad cop scenario is, to all intents and purposes, exactly what we've got. Shit. What the hell was he thinking?'

'Maybe he wasn't thinking.'

'Well, obviously. Bloody hell. Can't the shit-for-brains Navy get anything right? Do their so-called ships even float anymore?' Legend tapped her fingers on the table as she calmed herself, considered her options and finally came to a decision. 'OK. This is what we're going to do. It pays to seek opportunity in adversity, so I suggest we let this thing run its course for a day or two. You never know. It might yield results. If it doesn't bear fruit, we'll revert to Plan A. So, arrange to have a listening device placed in MacDermott's room and we'll see what our captive cyberpunk has to say to her wannabe knight in shining armour. In the meantime, I'll make it crystal clear to our personnel in the Finnish Embassy that the stripes on Batista's arm have no validity and should be seen as no more than a fashion accessory.'

Having climbed the six flights of stairs to the top floor of the Embassy building, a second guard entered the room with a tray of food and a small alarm clock for Martina to plug in beside her bed.

'It's five o'clock,' said the guard. 'You can set the time yourself.'

Martina adjusted the read-out on the clock, wolfed down

the pasta and Bolognese sauce and ate the apples down to the core. Finally overcome by exhaustion, she placed the plate on the desk beside the bed, lay down and sank almost immediately into a deep but agitated sleep from which she would not fully surface for over thirteen hours.

48 THE SUBTLEST
OF BREEZES

Liverpool, 21st July

While most of the city still slept, Thomas was checking his vegetables in the back garden of the house in Menlove Close. Like Aston, he was extremely concerned about the whereabouts of their young friend and believed Freya's idea of a mystery boyfriend to be naive at best.

It was undeniably a beautiful morning in South Liverpool. Thomas's fears for Martina had caused him to wake with the rising sun and he was trying to displace his anxieties by spending the hour after dawn quietly tending to the garden. The sky was a uniform blue. The sun was cresting the rooftops of the surrounding houses and cast long shadows across the small patch of lawn. The grass between the vegetable beds was damp beneath Thomas's bare feet and traffic noise only intermittently competed with his almost whispered attempts to sing 'Superstition'. As he inspected the vegetables, Thomas was pleased to find four decent-sized courgettes and maybe half a kilo of purple and green runner beans to harvest. The tomatoes, on the other hand, were still too small and the squash threatened to overrun the patch of leeks. Although the air felt still, the subtlest of breezes caused the upper branches of the birch tree in the corner of the garden to sway gently. Here and there, worker bees and other pollinators already fussed from flower to flower and wood pigeons flirted noisily in the foliage of a nearby sycamore. Lost in a flight of fantasy, Thomas was moments away from imagining Adam and Eve appearing at the fence and introducing themselves as his new neighbours.

He was distracted from his daydream by the vibration of his muted i-comm. It would, he assumed, be a message from Aston telling him they needed to get ready for work. The communication was not, however, from his partner.

The message politely reminded Thomas of the Prime Minister's invitation to register his interest in the forthcoming Congress of All The Talents, an event of historic significance to be held at the North Greenwich Arena from the seventh to the ninth of August. It enthused about the unique opportunity the conference offered to take part in shaping the future of post-war Britain and regretted that only a few places remained available. Convinced, as before, that the invitation was of questionable provenance, Thomas simply deleted it and returned to his vegetables.

Occasionally, when the rays of the early morning sunshine caught Thomas's face, their sudden warmth distracted him from his plants and he was ambushed by thoughts of his missing friend and the fate that might have befallen her.

When the former Professor of Semiotics and Symbology brought the box of courgettes and beans into the house, he found Freya in the kitchen, rummaging in the fridge for some jam. She had not received any unexpected invitations from the Prime Minister and suspected that Thomas's message could be, as she put it, 'a bit dodge'. Convinced that Aston would embrace the communiqués as evidence that a return to democracy was on the horizon and might conceivably overreact to Thomas's cynicism, they agreed not to speak of it again.

Thomas raised the subject of Martina's absence and Freya confirmed that she had heard nothing from her friend since they had last seen her four days ago.

'That's not good,' said Thomas. 'It's really not good.'

Freya was, however, determined to stay positive and Thomas looked like he could do with a hug.

'It'll be OK,' she said, as she gathered him in her arms. 'You know you're one of life's worriers. She's got herself a man. I just know it. It's been going on for weeks.'

'Maybe,' said Thomas, still unconvinced.

Freya steadfastly refused to fret.

'I'm telling you, Thomas. Our Martina is somewhere probably not very far away, curled up in bed with the man of her dreams.'

'That's a beautiful thought,' said Thomas, unwilling to burst her bubble of positivity. 'You have sunshine in your soul, Freya Daniels. You truly have sunshine in your soul.'

49 THE GOOD COP

London, 21st July

When Martina opened her eyes, it was seven thirty-eight and her breakfast was on a tray on the desk beside her bed. Next to the food, a pile of neatly folded black clothing suggested to her that she might be bound for a work brigade. Given the mistreatment that she had suffered so far, she would probably accept forced labour as a win. When she examined the clothes more closely, she found that she had been provided with a pair of boots and socks, some Utility underwear, plus a black shirt with flap pockets on the chest and sleeves and a pair of black combat pants. It was a Modsec uniform. Presumably, someone in the building thought this was funny.

The paramilitary fatigues served to reinforce the idea that she was to be installed in a penal work brigade, but curiously now offered her a small crumb of hope. If she could somehow extricate herself from the room, she reflected, she might be able to bluff her way out of the building. It was, after all, what Kevin would do. The hard part was obviously how to get out of the room, but she would think about it, and think about it the way that Kevin would.

Spreading jam on her toast, Martina studied the moderately serrated edge on the knife blade and wondered how easy it would be to saw a hole in the insulation tiles which made up the suspended ceiling. The knife, she decided, did not represent her passport to freedom as there was no way that the guards would leave her in possession of any form of cutlery when they came to remove her breakfast tray. The toast finished, Martina left the knife on the plate, lay down on the bed and looked once again at the ceiling tiles. They didn't look that substantial. Not at all. Bit by bit, she teased out a plan.

At around nine, Lieutenant Batista skirted the southern side of Saint James's Park and made his way along Birdcage Walk en route to the Finnish Embassy. Where the sun penetrated the foliage of the London Planes, he momentarily enjoyed its warmth on the back of his neck. Batista was confident that he could, without too much difficulty, achieve a successful resolution to the hacker case and buy himself a ticket back to Brize Norton.

As far as the Royal Navy liaison officer was concerned, Martina MacDermott's five-second pirate broadcasts did not, under any conceivable circumstances, constitute a justification for torture. He felt the young hacker had already been punished more than enough and was ashamed to be even remotely associated with the authors of that punishment. Were it within his power, Batista would simply have freed Martina from custody and sent her back to Liverpool with a food parcel and a warning against further disruptions to the airwaves. Although his willingness to liberate her was rooted in a fundamental desire to treat Martina with humanity, he was also aware that the accounts of her mistreatment by Modsec might immediately persuade her accomplices to cease and desist from their illegal activities. Batista was equally certain, however, that the NBC meteorologists would forecast a snowy day in hell before Major Security Officer Legend gave her blessing to the idea of simply letting the prisoner go.

Whilst Batista had been surprised not to have been contacted by his Modsec overseer regarding his actions the previous day, the Lieutenant was in no doubt whatsoever that she would be fully aware of his intervention, would be monitoring the situation and would have issued clear instructions to the Modsec personnel throughout the building to oppose any further attempts on his part to take matters into his own hands. Batista would rapidly need to secure an outcome that would placate Legend and obviate further abuse of the prisoner.

Sometime after nine twenty, the Lieutenant ascended the stairs to the sixth floor of the erstwhile Finnish Embassy and asked the guard to unlock the door to the apartment. He entered, closed the door behind him and was surprised to see the captive dressed in black Modsec fatigues.

He enquired if Martina had slept well.

'Oh, I get it,' said the young prisoner. 'You're the good cop.'

'Let me assure you,' said Batista. 'I'm not a cop of any description.'

He noted that Martina had eaten breakfast and the snarky vitality of her response suggested that she had probably slept relatively well for someone in her unenviable situation. The Modsec fatigues created an unsettling impression and Martina's hair was still dishevelled, but she looked infinitely better than the first time that he had seen her. The apartment was airless and warm and the air conditioning vents appeared to have little more than decorative value.

'My name is Lieutenant Batista,' he said. 'I'm a liaison officer in the Royal Navy.'

'Are you here to interrogate me?'

'No, that's not why I'm here.'

'Can I leave, then?'

'No. At least, not yet. It's a little early to discuss your departure, I would say, but we be may be able to do that sooner than you probably imagine.'

'So what do you want?'

'Well, firstly, I want to reassure myself that you are well, but more importantly, I want to apologise for your treatment yesterday. Modsec can be heavy-handed, to say the least.'

'Shit, this is so obviously a good cop, bad cop thing,' said Martina, averting her eyes and shaking her head dubiously.

'You can call it what you like,' said Batista, 'but there will be no recurrence of yesterday. I promise.'

Batista was in no position whatsoever to issue any such guarantee, but gambled that he could negotiate a compromise with Martina that would end the hacking once and for all and put the prisoner's unquestionable talents to positive use. He was confident, if not entirely certain, that Legend would not have lost sight of the primary objective of their investigation and would view the agreement with Martina as an acceptable outcome for all concerned.

'From now on you will only be dealing with me,' said Batista. 'To be honest, I don't really know why you've been brought to London. This could all have been sorted out in Liverpool.'

'Do I get a lawyer?' asked Martina, knowing full well that she would get no such thing.

'Really, this has all got out of hand,' said the Lieutenant, side-stepping her question. 'The messages you plant in the NBC's newsfeed are, to be honest, no more likely to change the world than slogans sprayed on a subway wall.'

'Then why am I here?'

'The real issue, Martina, is not why you're here, but how we can secure your release. So, hear me out. I'm going to make you an offer. We're going to drive you to Liverpool. You are going to take me to your studio and we are going to remove your equipment and disconnect your power supply. Then you, plus any accomplices you may have, will agree to join the Royal Navy on five-year contracts and train as cyberwarfare technicians. You and your comrades will get a meaningful role in the Navy and the NBC will get its airwaves back. It's a win-win.'

'If you say so.'

Given what she had already experienced, Batista did not wish to pressurise Martina. Nevertheless, he had little doubt of the fate that awaited her should he fail to get a result, so he put his offer into sharper context.

'If you do not want to accept my proposal,' he said with an air of reluctance, 'the alternative is the Isle of Man.'

Martina weighed up the options. It was a rock versus a hard place.

'Douglas is not somewhere you get to come home from,' she said.

'Its reputation is founded substantially on rumour,' said Batista. 'It's a secure facility for sure, but it's not a concentration camp. And even if you choose to go down that route, my offer will remain open. You'll be at liberty to change your decision at any point, join the Royal Navy and leave the Isle of Man.'

The only option Martina wanted to hear about was the one where Batista admitted it had all been a terrible mix-up and sent her home on the train. Fantasies aside, she wondered if there could be room for negotiation. Maybe she could offer to sign up to the Navy without having to implicate her friends.

'How do I know I can trust you?' she asked.

Batista reflected for a moment. Appearing to do no more than let his eyes wander casually around the room, he satisfied himself that there were no obvious locations for covert cameras and reached into his pocket. He produced an antique smartphone which Martina could only assume was her own.

'Peace offering,' he said, as he threw it onto the bed. 'Anyway, I'll leave you to mull things over. Try to make yourself as comfortable as possible. We'll talk again this evening. If, in the meantime, you want to speak to me about anything at all, just alert the guard.'

Left alone once more, Martina was unable to make up her mind about the liaison officer and was uncertain whether she should even touch the phone still lying on the bed. From the recognisable pattern of scratches, it certainly seemed to be her device. Allowing her curiosity to get the better of her, Martina pressed her fingers to the screen, but the smartphone did not respond. Presumably it had run out of charge. Batista, she concluded, had clearly not been giving her the ability to make contact with someone. Then why leave the phone with her at all? She took the smartphone into the bathroom, lifted the lid off the cistern and dropped the handset into the water. Had the liaison officer just enabled her to destroy a piece of evidence? Or was it all part of his 'good cop' charade? She still had no idea if she could trust a word that Batista was saying.

In the all too familiar half-light of the Modsec Technical Operations and Surveillance Room, Chandra tapped Data Analyst Liam Hurst on the shoulder and gestured to him to remove his headphones.

'What have you got?' she enquired.

Hurst showed her the transcript. Every word of Batista's conversation with MacDermott had been captured by the listening device in Martina's clock. It was immediately apparent to Chandra that Batista's offer to the prisoner both overstepped the parameters of his assignment and undermined Modsec's authority. And what had he meant by the words 'peace offering'? Chandra decided that she would need to speak to Legend.

50 NOT HERE TO SEE IT

Martina's continued absence had spooked her accomplices in Troutbeck Park Gardens. Although Kevin and Kireina knew from personal experience that people sometimes simply upped and left without giving notice, there was no apparent reason for Martina to have done so. They could of course have tried messaging her, but the hackers had rigorously avoided communicating via i-comm and knew that now was not the time to begin.

Whilst it would have been downright foolish to make enquiries about Martina at the local police Station, Kevin suggested he could put his professional talents to use once more and present himself as a Modsec security officer wishing to inspect their systems and procedures. He was completely confident that the police would be no less susceptible to penetration than any other organisation and that he could, with little difficulty, gain access to their internal network and establish whether Martina had in some way fallen foul of the Law. It would also be useful to confirm that they had not in any way been connected to the recent theft of the NBC outside broadcast vehicle.

Although no-one doubted Kevin's abilities, Talira, Ricky and particularly Kireina were uneasy about the idea and suggested waiting at least a couple of days before embarking on a potentially precarious course of action. Kevin, still adamant that the risk was minimal, was outvoted and the group agreed to sit tight. Martina might, after all, have accepted a lucrative offer of work in Southport or Chester and walk through the back door any moment with a beaming smile and a much better pair of night-vision goggles. She might be hard at work rebuilding an antique air conditioning unit for their ops room or maybe even creating one from scratch. She could conceivably be ill, in which case she would recover and in due course reappear. There were any number of possibilities.

The four media-hackers also agreed that they should, in the meantime, definitely press pause on their disruptions to the NBC, dump their defunct assault rifle in the Mersey and prepare to relocate to a different house, if necessary at short notice. The idea that they might need to abandon the outside broadcast van that they had gone to such lengths to acquire did nothing to lighten their mood.

'Three days,' said Kevin, ill-disposed to waiting, 'and then I'm paying a visit to PC Plod.'

'Hell,' said Kireina. 'This is just too depressing. Come on. We can do better than this. Even if we don't broadcast anything for a bit, it doesn't mean we can't get stuff ready. And you know what? If we have to abandon the van, we have to abandon the van. We can always get another one. It really wasn't that hard in the end. Look, we got that van for a reason. Let's at least get our shit together and prepare something to broadcast.'

'Such as?' said Ricky.

'Wait there,' said Kireina, now with a mischievous glint in her eye. 'I think you're gonna like this.'

She sprinted upstairs and reappeared with Martina's battered laptop. As soon as the Maxxbook was powered up, she opened an app called *Animeita Pro 2*. As a first step, Kireina imported the video footage of Martina's family energetically performing 'Won't Get Fooled Again'. Next, she inserted four full-length cartoon figures which she had drawn in the style of the John Lennon self-portrait at the Airport. Finally, she linked each caricature to its corresponding figure in the source video and activated *play*. Immediately, the software transformed Martina and her family into engaging, long-haired and bespectacled avatars belting out the Who's eight minute classic with unrestrained gusto. Ricky, Talira and Kevin were enthralled.

'There's more,' said Kireina. 'Watch this.'

Whilst the initial rendering endowed the cartoon avatars with the exact movements and facial expressions of their three-dimensional counterparts, Kireina demonstrated how she could exaggerate the movements of selected figures to anticipate and emphasise the beat of the powerful song. It was magical.

'It's just a shame Martina's not here to see it,' said Talira, somewhat wistfully.

'She'll be back,' said Kireina, determined to keep everyone buoyant. 'And when she sees it, she's gonna ...' and here Kireina launched into song, over-emoting a line from the iconoclastic lyrics, 'smile and grin at the change all around.'

'She'll certainly smile,' said Talira. 'Especially if you sing like that.'

51 NOT YOUR CONCERN

London, 21st July

Some nine hours after making his offer to Martina, Lieutenant Batista reprised the twenty-minute walk from Admiralty House to the Finnish Embassy. He was hopeful, if not exactly confident, that the young activist would have concluded that it was better to deal with a rational Royal Navy liaison officer than a group of Modsec thugs. If common sense prevailed, Martina would accept his deal, the intrusions into the NBC's news tickers would stop and the idealistic cyber-hacker and her accomplices, assuming she had any, would make amends for their transgressions by utilising their skills in the service of the Royal Navy. With any luck, he would be back at Brize Norton by the end of the week.

Lieutenant Batista arrived at the impressive Georgian structure which, in strictly legal terms, was still the inviolable preserve of the Republic of Finland. He presented his security pass to the armed paramilitaries on the door and entered the building. As he began to cross the marble-floored hallway towards the staircase, he could see that his path was blocked by Major Security Officer Legend and two paramilitary guards.

'There will be no need for you to pursue any further conversations with the prisoner,' said Legend with a supercilious air.

'Where's MacDermott?' demanded Batista. 'Is she still in the building?'

'The location of the prisoner is not your concern,' said Legend disdainfully.

'This is my case and she is my prisoner,' he insisted.

'Well, I'm sorry to have to disabuse you of that impression, Lieutenant, but this is, and always has been, an MOD case.'

Batista looked Legend straight in the eye. 'What have you done with her?'

'Again,' said Legend in peremptory fashion. 'None of your concern. But what I will tell you, Lieutenant Batista, is that the prisoner was brought here to answer questions, not to be offered cosy little sweetheart deals.'

'Well, we all know how Modsec treats its prisoners,' said Batista, still glaring at Legend. 'Who gave you the authority to waterboard her?'

The Modsec officer remained supremely unruffled by Batista's bellicose stance and, reluctant to use the phrase 'none of your concern' for a third time, simply rolled her eyes and shook her head in mild irritation.

'I demand to speak to your commanding officer,' said Batista.

'Do you?' she said, almost wearily. 'Demand? I think you are failing to understand, Lieutenant, the extent to which the Navy has had its pompous little wings clipped.'

She allowed Batista a moment to reflect on this before nodding to the guards on the main door. Expecting the signal, they left their post and immediately took up position behind him, clearly blocking his exit. The Lieutenant was unarmed and manifestly outnumbered.

'Do it,' said Legend to the guards.

Instantly, the first of the paramilitaries hooded Batista from behind whilst the others wrestled him to the floor, pulled his arms behind his back and handcuffed him.

'Remove his i-comm,' she said. 'Take him back to Admiralty House and make absolutely sure he can't go anywhere. The prisoner can stay where she is. I'll deal with her in the morning.'

An hour later and six floors above, a guard entered the secure apartment to check on the detainee. He had brought no food and Martina deduced that the good cop phase was over.

'I'm feeling ill,' Martina lied. 'What if I'm sick in the night?'

'Don't be,' said the guard curtly, before removing himself and locking the door once more.

Abrupt as the guard's response had been, it had more or less told the prisoner what she was hoping to hear. Whilst she would be locked in, there would not necessarily be a presence at her door throughout the night.

Martina waited until the display on the clock read ten thirty and it was dark outside, then put her game plan into action. She switched off her bedside lamp and looked towards the doorway. No light penetrated the gap beneath her door, so she could safely assume that no-one was stationed on the landing outside. As she switched the lamp back on, a troubling thought suddenly entered Martina's mind. If they were no longer bringing her food, why had they left her with the clock? In fact, why had they even given her a clock in the first place? To be on the safe side, she unplugged the suspect device, took it to the bathroom and gently lowered it into the cistern to join her smartphone.

Certain that she could not be overheard, Martina devoted herself once more to her exit strategy. First, she took one of the two chairs in the room, walked to the door and wedged it firmly beneath the handle so that it could no longer be pushed down. She then opened the door to the wardrobe, removed the coat hangers from the chrome-plated steel pole and placed them on the floor of the compartment. Having eased the metal clothes rail from its brackets, she crossed the room and laid the metre-long pole on the desk by the window.

The easiest part of her plan complete, she took one step onto the wooden chair and a second onto the table, then bent down and picked up the shiny steel tube. It required no more than a single, tentative prod to dislodge the first of the insulating ceiling tiles from the matrix of aluminium support rails and within three minutes, Martina had removed a square of nine tiles and organised them in a tidy pile by the door. Above the desk, she could make out the three-hundred-year-old rafters and the modern waterproof membrane, which was all that now separated her from the roof tiles themselves. The young captive made a conscious effort to breathe deeply and not to rush. Time was on her side and she could definitely get out of the room if she kept her head and maintained focus.

Martina's next step was to lift the second of the chairs from the floor and place it carefully onto the table. She then stepped onto the bed, onto the desktop and onto the chair itself. With her head and shoulders in the roof void, Martina was able to use the pole from the wardrobe to push at the lowermost part of the roof. Whilst she could at this point lift the bottom of the heavy tile perhaps a couple of centimetres, she had spent enough time working on roofs to know that the waterproof membrane would be stapled to the rafters and would impede any further movement.

Undeterred, Martina climbed down from the table and moved to the small kitchen area. The crumbs on the breadboard had been her first clue that there might still be utensils in the drawers and a cursory check that afternoon had revealed a treasure trove of cutlery and metal kitchen implements. She removed both the corkscrew and the breadknife and returned to the gap that she had created in the suspended ceiling.

With repeated strokes of the tip of the corkscrew, Martina was able to scratch a big enough gash in the blue membrane to allow her to insert the blade of the breadknife and saw away at the fabric. Not wanting for determination, she eventually succeeded in removing enough of the waterproofing to access a square of four of the lowermost roof tiles.

Using the steel pole once more, Martina pushed at the lower edge of a tile in the upper of the two rows. It was heavy but by no means impossible to lever maybe fifteen centimetres upwards. As the tile rose free of the one immediately below, Martina wedged it in position by planting the lower end of the pole on one of the wooden beams that spanned the entire building and supported the rafters above. Breathing harder, the would-be escapee used her hands to push one of the two lower tiles upwards and, after perhaps two minutes of struggle, succeeded in disengaging it from its neighbour to the side. This was not an entirely silent process but Martina gambled that any personnel still present in the building would be dozing in a guardroom some six floors below.

With the first roof tile dislodged, she allowed herself a few moments to inhale the night air and take in the sight of the stars. Cautiously, and feeling less than secure on the precariously situated chair, she then manipulated the tile through ninety degrees and lowered her head and upper torso back though the ceiling. Martina allowed the chair to take the weight of the tile as she deftly placed first one foot, then the other back on the desktop. She then positioned the liberated roof tile flat on the seat of the chair, stepped from the side of the table onto the bed and breathed a massive sigh of relief.

Having granted herself a minute or so to relax and let her heart rate settle, Martina took the tile from the chair and placed it carefully at the foot of the bed, before climbing back into the roof void and systematically removing three more of the heavy terracotta tiles. Finally, she retrieved the breadknife and sawed through the thin wooden laths that had held the lower tiles in position.

Martina now had a gap large enough for someone of her size to climb through with relative ease.

52 ON THE ROOF

London, 22nd July

The two guards who arrived at seven o'clock to check on the prisoner were at first baffled by their inability to depress the door handle, but rapidly realised that MacDermott was either making some kind of protest or staging an escape attempt. When their efforts to speak to their detainee were met with stone-cold silence, they made several futile and frankly comic efforts to shoulder the door down like hard-boiled Hollywood cops.

Growing increasingly concerned, they hurried down the stairs and returned somewhat breathlessly with two fully loaded assault rifles. Having shouted a final warning to the prisoner, they emptied their magazines at the woodwork around the door handle until eventually the entire lock mechanism fell away. Once they had pushed the shattered door and splintered bedroom chair aside and had finally gained entry to the room, they were taken aback by the ceiling tiles and strips of pale blue roofing membrane which littered the carpet. Four terracotta roof tiles lay on the bed and a chair stood on the bullet-scarred desk by the window. The guards penetrated further into the room and were astonished to see a substantial hole in the ceiling and the blue of the summer sky.

'Shit,' said the first of the guards. 'She's fucking escaped.'

The pair turned on their heels, barrelled down the stairs

a second time and within sixty seconds, an alarm had been sounded.

Martina emerged from the en-suite bathroom, walked out of the door and hurried down the stairs as though she too were responding to the alarm.

When two Modsec paramilitaries appeared from a room off the landing to the third floor, Martina yelled 'The prisoner's escaped! Everyone downstairs!'

On the landing to the first floor she joined the back of a line of Modsec personnel queuing for Kevlar body armour and handguns. Once out of the building, Martina ran closely behind a group of black-uniformed guards heading in the direction of what looked like a small park. They stopped at the corner of the block.

'She's on the roof!' shouted Martina suddenly, gesturing upwards with her pistol. 'She's still up there!'

With the attention of the guards singularly focussed on the rooftops, the brazen-faced escapee slipped behind them, walked quietly across the road, jumped the low gates to the enclosed public garden and disappeared out of sight. With the pistol concealed inside her ballistic vest, Martina made her way quickly to the far side of the surprisingly well-manicured lawn, exited via the opposite gate and ran across the road, ducking into the first side street that she saw. The fugitive had no real understanding of where she was heading, but within about five minutes, she found herself at the tree-lined edge of a much larger green space, perhaps a mile across. Not far into the park, Martina's attention was drawn to a narrow, curving lake. Once she was certain that she was not being observed, she bent to her knees as though tying her bootlace, took the pistol from the inside of her Kevlar vest and slipped it quietly into the water. It had only been for show and was, in all likelihood, more trouble than it was worth.

Eager to put as much distance as possible between her and her captors, Martina pressed on. With the sun coming over her right shoulder, she calculated she was probably heading something like north. Still looking to all intents and purposes like a Modsec paramilitary with a serious job to do, the escapee was afforded a wide berth as she made her way purposefully across the park. With pavement beneath her feet once more and avoiding the busier streets for the moment, she tried to keep heading in roughly the same direction and within an hour, she was standing outside Swiss Cottage tube station. Thirty minutes after that, she arrived at another area of parkland, which the fading sign informed her was Hampstead Heath. She was hungry and thirsty and close to exhausted, but whatever her situation, she told herself, it beat the alternatives that were on offer yesterday and it sure as hell beat the treatment that Modsec had meted out.

In a quiet side street to the north of the heath, Martina chose to investigate a house, barely visible behind tall, bolted wooden gates and high brick walls but with foliage covering a corner of the roof. She removed her body armour, threw it over the gates and withdrew to a safe distance. She heard no immediate reaction and waited perhaps five minutes before dragging a faded green wheelie bin from the drive of the house across the road and clambering over the wall. Wearing her Kevlar vest once more, she scouted the outside of the property. The gardens were a mess and the front door was overgrown with Virginia creeper, but at the back of the house, Martina found a door that was closed but unlocked. She opened it slowly and shouted to see if there was anybody home, but received no reply and heard no sound.

Treading carefully, the fugitive went from room to dusty room checking for signs of life. The house revealed itself to be completely empty and, perhaps because of the high walls, appeared to have escaped the attention of squatters or other intruders. The property had running water, working solar panels on the roof and wardrobes full of clothes, some of which would undoubtedly fit her. The kitchen cupboards were surprisingly well-stocked and contained a certain amount of food that might still be edible. Whilst the sealed jars of strawberry jam looked like they might be viable, the multipacks of baked beans, squirrelled away at the back of the cupboard, constituted the real find.

Martina had no i-comm and no way of communicating with those she loved. She had no Credits and, at least for the moment, nothing useful to trade. On the other hand, she had food, water and somewhere to lie low for the night. She had found soap, toothpaste, a change of clothes and a useful, designer-branded leather rucksack. Perhaps more importantly, if Martina had gleaned anything of value from her recent experiences, it was the understanding that she also possessed unshakeable determination. Tomorrow she would begin the long walk to Liverpool. Kevin had managed it and she saw no reason whatsoever why she shouldn't manage it too.

53 START WITH AN EARTHQUAKE

London, 22nd July

At the age of eleven, Soozie Greenwood was too young to have any detailed recollection of the world before the Dark Age. She also had no clear memory of her father and all that her mother had to say about him was that he was dead and that she didn't miss him. Natalia Greenwood often reminded her daughter that when Soozie was a toddler, there were no schools, no shops and no police. There was only the daily challenge of surviving on what you could find whilst trying to evade those who carried weapons. Gilbert Henderton had changed all that and was now undoubtedly making a better world for both of them.

When two days previously, Natalia had informed Soozie of the Prime Minister's invitation for her mother to become the 'face of Britannia', the eleven-year-old had never felt more proud. The role, Natalia had explained, would involve a photo shoot, during which she would be modelling a professionally restyled version of her original Britannia costume. With all expenses covered by the Government, mother and daughter were to spend a weekend at Chequers in the capable hands of a world-class media director and his experienced production team. In due course, Natalia's image would become familiar to every household in the country and would play a vital role in inspiring British schoolchildren to dream up designs for the towering Britannia monument to be constructed on a site beside the Thames. Natalia Greenwood was not just honoured to have been offered this opportunity, she was in truth no less exhilarated than her wide-eyed daughter.

On the day of the shoot, Natalia, her daughter, plus Elsa and Berezirah, two friends invited by Soozie at the suggestion of the PM, excitedly embarked upon their first-ever flight in a helicopter. From the surviving helipad at Northwood, they covered the thirty nautical miles or so to the Prime Minister's country retreat in a matter of minutes. Henderton took the trouble to welcome them personally to the historic Elizabethan mansion, had their bags collected by his staff, and escorted them to their rooms on the first floor. After allowing the three girls a few minutes to explore the features of the luxurious room they would be sharing, the PM invited his guests for coffee in the Wellington Room where they were introduced to Garcia Stipe, the director of the shoot. Natalia Greenwood, still thrilled with her helicopter ride, found the Prime Minster unexpectedly affable and relaxed. Like the coffee, he was palatable, if not entirely genuine.

Before Stipe had finished his cup of ersatz, he checked the time and reminded the Prime Minister respectfully that they had a tight schedule. He must, he regretted, prise the lovely Ms Greenwood from his company, but made it clear that the PM was of course welcome to drop in on proceedings at any time.

Whilst Natalia was being dressed and made up, one of Stipe's assistants gave the excited girls a tour of the set, explained the purpose of the equipment and the green screen and patiently answered their forgivably ingenuous questions.

Natalia Greenwood had no experience of modelling and little idea of what to expect of a professional shoot. When, accompanied by her dresser and make-up artist, she was ushered from her improvised personal changing room into the oak-panelled Marlborough Room, she was amazed at the sheer number of people, the size of the green screen and the quantity of lighting equipment already in place.

The three young girls were enthralled when Soozie's mother appeared. Although the costume was clearly based on Natalia's original homespun design, it had been professionally restyled, meticulously fabricated, and hung beautifully on Natalia's slender frame. The make-up was virtually undetectable, but worked well under the lights to display her natural features to their best advantage.

Before the shoot began, the girls were swept up by Lovelle, their guide and carer for the day, who exuberantly promised them, amongst other things, a ghost walk, an interview with the Prime Minister and a close-up look at a missile launcher. Soozie waved enthusiastically to her mother and was gone.

Now confident of his model's undivided attention, Stipe called Natalia to one side, opened his Maxxbook 3D and revealed with unabashed delight his mood board for the Britannia shoot. It was, he enthused, a high-definition stream of consciousness portraying all the elements, qualities and nuances he wanted to capture. At its centre were two images of Britannia. The first was a twentieth century poster, in which a resolute and monumental goddess, with silhouettes of battleships on the horizon and uniformed recruits at her feet, proclaimed 'England expects' and advocated National Service in the war against fascism. The second was a photo of the commemorative silver sovereign coin, which featured a more defiant and sensuous Britannia, her hair caught by the wind and her diaphanous robes pressed close to her body by the buffeting storm. Linked to these central images were myriad depictions of sunny skies, storm clouds, the gods Poseidon and Aphrodite, Spartan warriors and unassailable rocky shores.

Unused in recent years to posing for anything other than i-drone selfies with her daughter, Natalia required considerable guidance and repeated correction from the director, which over time generated more than a degree of exasperation on both sides. Stipe was of course aware that Natalia Greenwood was the personal choice of the Prime Minister and as such could not be replaced. He therefore had to find a way to put his fledgling model at her ease and help her understand that what she was doing was so much more than smiling for holiday snaps. After another tricky hour with little to show for it, he called a break. They would take thirty minutes for lunch.

'Do you remember when you were a child,' said Stipe, searching for a parallel that might make sense to his charge, 'and you used to play games with your friends, where you would pretend to be a doctor maybe, or, I don't know, an elephant or a ghost?'

'Yeah,' said Natalia tentatively, wondering where Stipe was going with his allusion.

'Well, when you were a child, no-one told you how to act the part of the doctor. You just became the doctor. And then you were the doctor. Well it's kind of like that, Natalia darling. Imagine you're six years old again and you're playing a game and you want to be the goddess Britannia, the one with the helmet and the trident and all the power. Now imagine that all your friends are the waves and they will kneel before you and obey your every command, because you are the ruler of the waves.'

To Stipe's relief, his evocation of the childhood world of

make-believe resonated strongly with her and in the following session, Natalia was transformed, if not into a professional model then at least into something he could work with.

After two hours of what turned out to be surprisingly tiring work posing as the proud, defiant Britannia for the schools' campaign, Natalia was taken aback by Stipe's request for her to bare her left breast for the reference photos. When she queried whether that was entirely necessary, he called up a copy of her contract on his Maxxbook and quoted the clause permitting 'the finessing and adjustment of the original hand-made costume in line with classical images of Britannia and the taking of all appropriate photographs, including reference shots to inform and support the design process'. The director then referred to his mood board once more, enlarged the image of the silver sovereign coin and drew Natalia's attention to the subtly but irrefutably bare-breasted Britannia proudly defying the waves which lapped in subservience at her feet. He reassured Natalia that 'the more classical shots' would not feature in the schools' campaign, but were nonetheless essential for design and construction.

'And of course,' he said, 'it will be completely tasteful, little more than décolleté. And don't forget, Natalia my darling, your name will go down in history as the face of Britannia. And who knows how many doors will open for you in the meantime? Audiobook deals, media appearances, sponsorship. You name it. And just think how proud young Soozie will be of her celebrated mother.'

Natalia requested a few moments to herself in the changing area, ostensibly to study the picture of the coin and adjust her robes herself. After several self-conscious minutes experimenting with her wardrobe and pondering her options, the call of immortality proved too strong and she decided that, providing the shots were purely for the architects' reference and for that purpose only, she was prepared to proceed.

The Prime Minister interrupted the drafting and redrafting of his keynote speech for the Congress of All The Talents and wandered, somewhat aggravated by his lack of progress, down to the Marlborough Room to drink in the sight of Natalia Greenwood reprising her role as Britannia. Throughout the morning, Henderton had been scratching around for quotes from Churchill that he had not yet used to inform his own flights of oratory and had been repeatedly coming up short. His words to the assembled conference would have to give the delegates belief that divergent views were not only permitted but expected. He would have to convince the attendees that, with the war almost won, democracy was waiting tantalisingly on the horizon. Above all, he would have to inspire the fifteen thousand participants to return for Day Two of a conference that would, through a vibrant exchange of ideas, create a roadmap to the future. Henderton would not, however, give the conference the slightest inkling that the second day of discussion and debate coincided intentionally with the date he had set for Operation Ironstone. Neither would he reveal that the sprawling site currently occupied by the North Greenwich Arena had been earmarked as the location for his colossal statue of the goddess Britannia.

At the end of a fun-packed and obliquely educational day, Soozie, Elsa and Berezirah were buzzing to relate their experiences to Soozie's mother who had completed the shoot and was once again wearing the more demure clothes that she had arrived in. She was amazed to learn that the three girls would be sleeping in a bedroom once used by Admiral Lord Nelson and flabbergasted to discover that they had spent part of the late afternoon using a laptop to propel a caterpillar-tracked bomb disposal robot around a triangular course marked out for them in the grounds.

After dinner, Natalia readily accepted Lovelle's offer to help the overstimulated girls write up a short account of their day, to tell them a slow but engrossing South American folk tale and to settle them down for bed. She would message Ms Greenwood when they were quiet and ready to be wished goodnight.

With Soozie Greenwood and her friends now out of the way, the Prime Minister was delighted to have Natalia to himself and did not refrain from letting her know as much. After some discussion of the uncommonly exciting day the girls appeared to have had, Henderton enquired disingenuously about Soozie's father and quietly confirmed the intel from his PA that Natalia Greenwood was single and not currently involved with anyone. The conversation inevitably shifted to the topic of the photo shoot, which he hoped she had not found too arduous. Feeling surprisingly tired from the exertions of the day, Natalia Greenwood was only too happy to concede that modelling was harder than it looked. Without further enquiry, Henderton talked in detail about his vision for the Britannia monument. It would, he enthused, outshine the *Statue of Liberty* and be an enduring testament to national self-belief.

'My parents, God rest their souls,' he said, 'lived through an era of self-recrimination and spinelessness, when bleeding-heart liberals insisted we cringe with embarrassment about our history, about our traditions and about our culture.'

'Sad times,' said Natalia, somewhat dispassionately. Whilst she appreciated Henderton's leadership and was entertained by his bravado, she had no real desire to talk politics.

'Did you know,' he continued, 'that there was a time when the ideologues that controlled the BBC banned "Rule Britannia" from the airwaves? Can you believe that? Completely banned it. I tell you, those are the kinds of historical events we should be ashamed of.'

'Did you enjoy what you saw of the shoot?' asked Natalia, keen to redirect the conversation.

'Oh, very much so. I have to say, you look stunning in the new robes. The nation will be entranced.'

'Thank you,' she replied, not feeling that the flattery was entirely undeserved. 'Soozie is going to write a report about her visit to Chequers. And she's going to offer to do a presentation about her visit when she starts her new school.'

'That's wonderful,' said the Prime Minister. 'Based on my extensive experience of public speaking, I would suggest it is often better to start with an earthquake and build up to a climax.'

She raised an eyebrow.

The Prime Minister smiled. 'That doesn't just apply to my public speaking, by the way.'

What Britannia's make-up artist had told her that morning about Henderton's approach to the opposite sex would appear to have been completely on the money. He considered himself to be charming, but was as subtle as a wrecking ball.

When Natalia received Lovelle's i-comm message that the girls were ready to go to sleep, she thanked the Prime Minister for everything, regretted that she was tired and told him that she would go to bed after saying goodnight to her daughter and her friends. Before she could stand up, Henderton placed his hand intimately on her forearm and said how inspirational it was to have her at Chequers. He let her know that if she wished to continue their conversation after seeing the girls, his apartment was directly opposite hers and that she could simply let herself in.

'Every Caesar,' he said invitingly, 'needs a Cleopatra.'

For the second time in what had been a ridiculously hectic day, Natalia Greenwood had to consider her options. This decision, she felt, would not take up too much of her time. Henderton could make do with the photos.

54 SLOW START TO THE DAY

London, 23rd July

When Martina MacDermott awoke on a king-size double bed in an undisturbed executive house in North London, she at first struggled to work out exactly where she was, but she did know that she was safe and at that moment that was all she needed to know. She had no way of telling the time, but from the warmth of the air and the height of the sun she could see it was clearly not early morning. In spite of having slept for so long, the fugitive still felt tired, but all things considered, that was hardly surprising. It would be a slow start to the day and she wondered how many miles she would be able to cover on the first leg of her long walk home. Martina took the decision to have a shower, enjoy a decent breakfast and rummage around the house a bit more before she left. Who knows what she might uncover? She might find some high-value tradeables. There might even be a usable watch somewhere, or perhaps an i-comm. She would certainly take the canned food and the jars of jam.

After a breakfast of Seville orange marmalade, stale biscuits and baked beans, Martina undertook a more detailed examination of the contents of the beautiful but dusty house. In the drawer of a dressing table, she was delighted to discover an upmarket, solar-powered watch. Deprived of light for several years, the timepiece had stopped, so Martina placed it on a window sill, confident that it would readily re-energise. In a biscuit tin in the kitchen, she found the electronic key to a Land Rover and a small remote control which she assumed could only be for the garage and the gates. There was also a small blister pack with spare batteries for both. Suddenly, a heartwarming idea presented itself. Maybe she wouldn't be needing to walk.

Having replaced the batteries in the car key and the remote control, Martina opened the garage to reveal a black Land Rover EV with four flat tyres. Undismayed, she plugged the vehicle into the charging point on the interior wall, then located an electric pump and inflated the tyres one by one. If the tyres did not deflate and the lithium-ion batteries charged to full or nearly full capacity, she would have the ability to reach Liverpool in a matter of hours. Nevertheless, she would need to leave the Land Rover on charge for a substantial part of the day, so she postponed her departure until the following morning.

Martina had initially intended to travel wearing the clothes she had liberated from the wardrobe in the front bedroom. She would, she had thought, rough her Modsec fatigues up a bit, pack them in the leather rucksack and at the end of each day, would employ Kevin and Kireina's subterfuge of scamming a free meal and a bed for the night in any work brigade residences she could find en route. The discovery of the vehicle in the garage, however, presented the escapee with an entirely different set of options. Whilst she had no form of ID, a uniformed Modsec officer with a supercilious attitude and body armour on the passenger seat of her black Land Rover would probably not, she figured, be asked for any. She also wondered if there might be a wig or perhaps some hair dye to be found, but her search turned up nothing of use. Determined to change her appearance in some way, Martina removed the scissors from the cutlery drawer in the kitchen, took herself to the master bathroom and carefully trimmed her flowing locks into a tousled gamine look which, she decided, kind of suited her.

When evening came, Martina checked the Swiss watch on the window sill and was pleased to find that it was, exactly as she had expected, working perfectly. She went round to the garage and checked the tyres on the car. They looked fine, so she climbed into the Land Rover and pressed the *start* button. The vehicle's control and management systems booted up without fuss and in due course informed her that the batteries were fully charged and she had a range of 395 miles. That was more than enough.

Satisfied with her day, Martina returned to the house, showered at length and went to bed. She would, she was certain, sleep particularly well that night.

55 PROCESS OF VERIFICATION

Liverpool, 24th July

Beneath the partial shade of the sycamore which overhung the back garden, Kevin and Kireina devoted themselves to the task of camouflaging the NBC outside broadcast van with daubs of black, brown and olive-green paint. It was uncomfortably hot and in the forty minutes that they had so far dedicated to disguising the van, Kevin had already referred to Kireina three times as 'Sweaty Betty'. On each occasion, she had exacted retribution by flicking a dollop of paint onto the back of his no less sweaty neck. Conscious that time was of the essence, Kevin repeatedly resisted the temptation to engage in a full-blown paint fight, but warned that his revenge would come swiftly and when she was least expecting it. The affectionate mischief was a playful but ultimately fruitless attempt to provide some minor relief from the burgeoning tension. There had been no contact with Martina for over a week and the four media-hackers were growing more unsettled by the day.

They had, in the meantime, packed their bags ready for a swift exit, should the CCTV camera at the end of Troutbeck Park Gardens alert them to the arrival of police vehicles. Their escape plan was to abscond via the back garden to a parallel road where they had parked a re-plated and fully charged EV on the drive of an unoccupied house. They were camouflaging the outside broadcast van in the hope of keeping it from prying eyes and maybe returning to it once the dust had settled.

Although poised to leave at short notice, the group had not been inactive. Kireina continued to finesse the video of the Fatberg Four and generated increasing hilarity each time she demonstrated the latest rendition of her impudent work.

Kevin had finished the job of counterfeiting a range of useful identity badges for each of them, including a revamped Modsec ID designed to facilitate his planned penetration of the Central Police Station.

Eager to dispose of the AK-47 assault rifle still languishing in their panic room, Talira and Ricky had taken a short but nonetheless anxious walk to the garage of the house over the road and had hidden the antique weapon in an old golf bag. Avoiding the heat of the afternoon as Kevin and Kireina worked outside, the couple were now ensconced in the kitchen and were ploughing through the *Oxford Dictionary of Quotations* in search of suitable material to broadcast once they felt it was safe to resume.

Later, as the four activists watched the evening news, footage of the Prime Minister inspecting damage to Bristol University and to the surviving tower of the Clifton Suspension Bridge was rotated with clips of Henderton congratulating Civil Defence gunners and visiting some of the more telegenic casualties in the Bristol Royal Infirmary. At the bottom of the display, the news ticker shared its updates.

'Death toll rises after Bristol raid. City turns out en masse to applaud PM. Henderton: Enemy on verge of defeat. British victory will be a triumph of the will.'

'I see Josef Goebbels is still on the books,' said Talira dryly. Thinking once again about Martina and what might have become of her, Kevin was reminded of the flight-tracking software and decided to review the previous week's recordings. To his astonishment, the app had registered and tracked a number of flights over several nights. They had to be air raids.

'Hey guys, take a look at this,' said Kevin excitedly. 'We've got something. This is last night.'

Their curiosity aroused, Talira and Ricky joined Kireina and Kevin at the computer but struggled to interpret what they were seeing.

A map of the UK filled the screen. Three fast moving aircraft could be identified. One, labelled '161-MQ25-A', was heading north up the Lincolnshire coast; another, identified as '161-MQ25-D', was flying west along the M4 corridor; and the third, designated '161-MQ25-E', was overflying Birmingham and proceeding northwest.

'Whose planes are they?' asked Kireina. 'Are they ours?'

'That, my beauty,' said Kevin, 'is the mother of all questions. Let's see where they go.'

Kevin fast-forwarded the recording. The three aircraft reached Leeds, Bristol and Wolverhampton respectively, then turned and flew back exactly the way they had come. They all converged on, and apparently landed at, the same location, a military air base which the outdated Flight Tracker had labelled as 'RAF Lakenheath (USAF 48FW)'.

'Shitting shit,' said Kireina. 'It's the Americans.'

'It can't be,' said Talira. 'They're not even there anymore.'

'Maybe it's the RAF hunting down the intruders,' suggested Ricky. 'It said "RAF" as well as "USAF".'

'But it's an American base,' Kireina pointed out. 'I grew up near it.'

371

'Was,' said Ricky. 'Past tense. It was an American base.'

'Where are the enemy bombers?' said Talira. 'Why can't we see the bombers?'

Ricky cocked his head slightly and shot her a questioning look.

'Oh yeah,' said Talira, as it suddenly dawned on her that the enemy intruders would not be advertising their location. 'Got it. Stealth bombers. Makes sense now.'

'You know what,' said Ricky. 'You know how we've been thrashing around trying to agree what kind of video content to transmit. Could we do something with this? I mean, just put it out there?'

'Oh, now who's not making sense?' said Talira to Ricky. 'Look. Now is obviously not the time, but even if it were, we don't even know what we're looking at.'

'Oh, God,' said Ricky. 'You're going to quote Professor Underberg, aren't you? The one about the essence of ethical journalism. I can feel it coming.'

'The essence of ethical journalism,' said Talira in a Swedish accent that she knew to be patently worse than Ricky's, 'is a discipline of verification.'

Ricky had heard this so many times before, but smiled nonetheless. She was right.

'If those are the RAF interceptors,' said Kevin, now completely consumed with curiosity, 'why do you think they just turn around after reaching a certain point? Why doesn't it look like there's been some kind of pursuit? You know, some kind of engagement or interaction with an enemy aircraft?'

'Maybe they reach a certain point, fire their missiles and then get the hell out of it,' suggested Talira.

'If I didn't know any better,' said Kevin, 'I'd be tempted to say those flightpaths look no different to what you'd expect from a bomber.'

'Yeah, right,' said Kireina sarcastically. 'We're being bombed from Suffolk.'

'I see you found a use for the flight tracker, then,' said a familiar voice behind them. Martina had pulled her usual trick of sneaking in round the back.

Although the four immediately recognised her voice, they were massively confused by her looks. She had cut her hair short, was wearing intimidating, black fatigues and was carrying a small leather rucksack. The cocktail of sudden reappearance and bizarre make-over provoked a second of slack-jawed silence which was broken only by Kireina.

'Shit, Martina. Where the hell have you been?'

'How long have you got? First though,' she said, her voice now quivering, 'I could really do with a hug.'

As the tears began to roll down Martina's cheeks, Kireina enfolded her friend in her arms and let her sob it out. The others watched in concerned silence and waited for their friend's weeping eventually to subside. At some point, one of them withdrew briefly to the kitchen to put the kettle on. Feeling secure in Kireina's embrace, Martina eventually regained some scant degree of composure, took a chair and began slowly to recount her harrowing story as completely as she could. As she shared the details of her arrest and subsequent transfer to London, the four hung on her every syllable. Her traumatic account of the cruelty meted out by Modsec was received with looks of unbridled astonishment and horrified, unbroken silence. Ricky was the first to shed a tear, but he was not alone in his reaction.

'So you might want to consider whether the stingers are really worth the risk,' said Martina quietly, that part of her story now told.

'And we might want to consider,' said Talira, both aghast and incensed, 'how we can shine a light on the fact that our security services do not baulk at the idea of torture.'

'Before we decide to do anything,' said Kevin, 'I'll pay a little visit to the Central Police Station and see if the investigation is still active.'

This time, his suggestion was unopposed.

Martina's story was not yet complete.

'But how the hell did you get away from Modsec?' asked Kireina, at a loss to imagine how an escape might even be possible.

'By taking a leaf out of your boyfriend's book,' said Martina, the most tentative of smiles now adorning her face.

Kevin raised an eyebrow.

As Martina related in meticulous detail how she had duped the Modsec guards, brazened her way out through the main door and had driven to Liverpool dressed in the uniform of her captors, her friends were enthralled and amazed in equal measure. Kevin was particularly impressed.

'So that's pretty much it,' said Martina, clearly relieved to be back amongst friends. 'Here I am. I can't tell you how good it is to see you all again.'

It was the cue for a sustained and heartfelt group hug.

'Are you hungry?' asked Talira, as the five finally relaxed their collective embrace.

'You know what?' said Martina. 'That sounds great. But I'm going to go home now. It's so good to see you all and I really wanted to let you know I'm OK, but I so need to see my family.'

Martina changed out of the Modsec fatigues and into some of the more casual clothes that she had liberated from the house in North London. As she drove the short distance round to Menlove Close and her thoughts turned towards Freya, Aston and Thomas, she felt her emotions rising to the surface once more and wondered if she had the strength to articulate her story for a second time.

Still shaken by Martina's agonising account of her mistreatment, Talira and Ricky relocated themselves to their ops room and rapidly composed a stinger to go out on the NBC.

'Do it,' said Kireina, eager to dish out some kind of payback.

'Do it,' echoed Kevin, his initial caution now swept aside.

Ten seconds later, their message invaded every news crawl on every screen and every i-comm in the country.

'NBC uncovers evidence of torture conducted by MOD security services. Prime Minister promises full investigation.'

With luck, the stinger would begin to foment mistrust at the highest levels of government and pollute the well of power. At the very least, Talira thought, it would generate a merry-go-round of unnecessary speculation, enquiry and denial within the NBC and waste an awful lot of people's time.

When Freya answered the door to the already sobbing Martina, she immediately assumed that her sister had been dumped by her mystery boyfriend. Freya swept her up into her arms, hauled her into the house and hugged her as tightly as she could. Martina's body trembled as it released a second wave of emotion and her tears moistened Freya's shoulder. Drawn to the commotion, Aston and Thomas were relieved to see Martina, but immensely troubled to see her in such an appalling state. They too imagined that they were perhaps witnessing the sorry outcome to an unfortunate affair of the heart, but postponed their curiosity and discretely withdrew to make a pot of tea.

Once Martina finally regained sufficient control of her faculties to begin to explain where she had been, Aston and Thomas ushered her to the lounge, sat her down on the sofa and pushed a mug of freshly brewed rosemary tea into her hand. The raw emotion that was unleashed, as Martina recounted every last detail of her recent experiences, triggered tears, anger and expressions of love.

Martina was still in pain, but she was home.

56 HYPOTHESES AND EVIDENCE

Liverpool, 25th July

Kevin's infiltration of the police internal network was effected without fuss and yielded speedy and reassuring results. Tasked with giving the Modsec security officer a tour of the station, Detective Inspector Smith expressed complete confidence in the robustness of the police threat management system before introducing his guest to the offices, interview rooms and evidence rooms and more importantly, to the colleagues working in them. In the absence of a spare work station, the DI readily offered the high-powered visitor the use of his own modestly proportioned office for the remainder of the morning.

Within ten minutes of sitting down at DI Smith's desk, Kevin had accessed Martina's case files and could find no reference to Troutbeck Park Gardens or to any name other than Martina's. A file on the theft of the NBC outside broadcast van revealed the police to be woefully short of both hypotheses and evidence. The NBC crew had been oblivious to the theft; the Hilton had not a single functioning CCTV camera; and the investigation team had found nothing in the Auto-Drive truck abandoned in the hotel car park. As far as Kevin could ascertain, there was no cause for alarm.

When Smith returned an hour later to see whether the

Modsec visitor needed anything, the DI was not at all surprised to be informed that the police threat management system was as robust as anything the security officer had ever encountered. The Detective Inspector was pleased with this provisional assessment and looked forward to seeing the promised final report.

Following the removal of Martina MacDermott by Modsec, DI Smith had, in all honesty, given little thought to what might have become of the young prisoner. Had the DI been inclined to look for the files relating to her case, or the files relating to the incident at the airport for that matter, he would have found himself at a complete loss to find them. Kevin had located and expunged every last one. Furthermore, had the DI needed to use his spare i-comm for any reason, he would have struggled to ascertain its whereabouts. It was certainly not in the drawer of his desk.

57 THE FUME OF SIGHS

RAF Lakenheath, 26th July

As far as the pilots of 161 Squadron were concerned, the NBC film crew that had installed itself in Block F was a complete pain in the backside. Although there remained almost a week until the Prime Minister's scheduled visit to 'the air station that thwarted a coup', a number of producers, directors and technicians had already been on site for several days, storyboarding and filming scenes which would ultimately help document the history of the war.

Each morning, the pilots on Quick Reaction Alert duty, under close direction from the NBC production team, were filmed waiting in the Aircrew Ready Room before leaping to their feet in response to a non-existent alarm and rushing helter-skelter to their aircraft. The NBC cameras recorded them climbing hurriedly into the cockpit of their F-95s and lowering the canopy as though preparing to take off. The whole process was repeated several times until Kristian Conrad, the fastidious NBC package producer, felt he had captured the perfect mix of readiness and reaction and called it a wrap. At irregular intervals, the cameras recorded unscripted footage of the Squadron kicking back in the Mess, relaxed but implicitly ready to scramble, should the enemy interrupt their fragile bonhomie. In due course, Conrad planned to capture extensive footage of the QRA pilots taking off and streaking skywards before re-emerging from the clouds and landing safely, apparently having dealt with any incursions.

At night, offensive missions against ground targets throughout Britain continued to be flown, but only by the unpiloted drones.

For the best part of a fortnight, Chief Technician MacDermott had been fully engaged in programming the MQ-25s for their deadly sorties and the process had not been easy on his soul. In spite of Wakeman's assurances that civilian casualties on the nocturnal operations were both accidental and minimal, the 'ACD' code, ascribed in advance to each target, told an entirely different story. Substantial numbers of civilian deaths were repeatedly being written off in advance as acceptable collateral damage. The construct that MacDermott had no choice but to follow orders provided him with no measure of solace and with each murderous raid, his brooding guilt laid greater claim to his waking thoughts and subverted his attempts to sleep. Not once in MacDermott's life had he felt so utterly robbed of agency and for days he had been unable to see any way out of his bind that did not involve absconding from the base or somehow taking his own life. Whilst the Chief Technician felt that death might well represent the just desserts for his breaches of the Mortality Protocol, he knew that neither desertion nor suicide would do anything to put a stop to the raids.

The only choice he had, his conscience finally dictated, was to resist his instinct for flight and face the need for decisive action. His duty, he knew, lay in attempting to stop, or at least undermine, the programme of bombings. The Chief Technician therefore resolved that, in parallel to his inescapable work on targeting, he would devote every available minute to devising code which would cause the MQ-25s to interpret their take-off command from Wakeman as an instruction to run their engines down. None of MacDermott's early attempts, however, made the slightest dent in the AAVs' superbly configured threat management systems.

When not involved in filming for the NBC documentary, the pilots of 161 Squadron passed the days in predictable fashion. Frenetic games of five-a-side football were organised. Bosko led extended karaoke sessions. Above average quantities of Whoopty Whoop wheat beer and Tennessee bourbon were consumed. Gunatillaka and her Royal Navy friend often put in an appearance, but Itoje and Becker sloped off so frequently that it ceased to be a source of amusement or provide any further basis for a sweepstake.

When Gunatillaka and York appeared in the bar a couple of hours before the start of the Ops Manager's evening shift, the room was as deserted as it was dishevelled.

'You did warn me,' said York, taking in the mess.

The two officers straightened the place up a bit and helped themselves to a drink from one of the X-Change store crates. Although York was as happy as ever to chew the fat with Gunatillaka, she was also sorry that none of the others were there. In spite of being required to subject everyone on station to a security interview, the Lieutenant Commander had made these conversations as cursory and as humane as possible. With Gunatillaka as her wingman, she had gradually been accepted into the culture of the Mess and had already delivered several off-key renditions of Rod Stewart's 'I am sailing', much to the amusement of all concerned.

Gunatillaka caught York checking her i-comm.

'Any reply?' she asked.

'No,' said York. 'Not yet.'

Batista's responses to York's recent messages had become sporadic and unpredictable. The Lieutenant Commander could only assume that he was still somewhere in London, up to his neck in time-consuming and pointless work for the MOD.

'Should I message him again?' York asked.

'Only if you want to come across as needy. And nobody likes high-maintenance. Like you say, he's probably not getting a moment's peace.'

'Yeah, you're right. You're right. Hell, Gunnie, just listen to me. Have I turned into some kind of lovesick schoolgirl?'

'Not for me to judge,' said Gunatillaka, 'but I've got your back either way.'

'I can remember one more quote from *A Midsummer Night's Dream*,' said York. 'Then you're going to have to help me find words of my own.'

'I hear you've achieved cult status with the Regiment,' said Gunatillaka, smiling as she steered her friend onto a different topic of conversation.

Slightly embarrassed, York fiddled momentarily with the cuff of her jacket. 'I wouldn't call it that.'

The Lieutenant Commander did not go out of her way to bring up her sporting past, but had nevertheless been recognised by a lance corporal in the RAF Regiment as the inspirational young captain of the GB hockey team at the Mumbai Olympics. Word had rapidly spread and, always happy to answer their questions, particularly about the epic fightback against the Netherlands in the semi-final, York had indeed become something of a folk hero amongst the soldiers. When she was out of earshot, the Lieutenant Commander was now almost universally referred to as 'Blondie'.

As the pace of her initial interviews relented, York had attempted to cover her back by reporting to Benjamin that she was gaining the trust of the personnel on the base and suggesting that this might well pay dividends. Benjamin, obsessively committed to micromanaging Wakeman, keeping MacDermott's nose to the grindstone and briefing the Prime Minister on preparations for Operation Ironstone, could not have cared less, as long as York stayed out of her way.

In the relative comfort of her new office at Modsec Central in Battersea Park, Intelligence Officer Chandra was anxious to rescue something from the ashes of the Martina MacDermott case. Whilst the prisoner had led them a merry dance in Belgravia before disappearing without a trace, Chandra felt she might yet be able to make something of the situation with the two Royal Navy liaison officers, one of whom was currently under lock and key in a secure hospital, waiting for his broken metatarsals to mend. Batista's captors had been more than diligent in carrying out Legend's orders to make sure that he could not go anywhere.

Scrolling back and forth through the exchanges on Batista's i-comm, Chandra pondered how best to reply to the latest message he had received from York. Like many of their more recent communications, it looked like a quote from Shakespeare and Chandra decided that it would be expedient, for the time being, to respond in a similar vein. In due course, she might inveigle the lovelorn Lieutenant Commander into compromising herself in some way. Chandra had tasked her field officer with tracking down and requisitioning a compendium of Shakespearian quotes, but after two days of searching the licensed bookshops of Central London, he had been able to produce nothing more than a dog-eared copy of *Romeo and Juliet* clearly no longer boasting its full complement of pages. It would at least, Chandra consoled herself, be replete with references to love. Reluctant to read the entire play, the intelligence officer was relieved to discover what seemed to be a suitable line towards the end of Act One, Scene One.

The message 'Love is a smoke raised with the fume of sighs' arrived whilst York was conducting an interview with Flight Lieutenant Itoje and her fleeting glimpse of the poetic quote initially warmed her heart. Her interview with Itoje rapidly wound up, the Lieutenant Commander looked once more at her i-comm, but on closer inspection the message did not easily concede its meaning and left her more than a little confused. Nevertheless, she was delighted simply to have received a reply.

After more than a fortnight without flying a single mission, the pilots of 161 Squadron received a memo from Wing Commander Wakeman apologising for the enforced lay-off and explaining that those F-95s not required for Quick Reaction Alert were still receiving essential maintenance in preparation for Operation Ironstone. The mission, he revealed, was to be a major undertaking and would require the participation of every aircraft and every pilot on station. He thanked them for their forbearance and expressed his confidence in their professionalism.

If Wakeman's statement had been intended to cast enough light on their situation to put the Squadron's pilots at their ease, it had failed. His circumspection served only to provoke a slew of increasingly uncomfortable questions amongst the underemployed and unsettled aircrew. What kind of a mission could possibly require such a collective effort and such formidable firepower? Did Wakeman's reference to every aircraft on station include the MQ-25s as well as the F-95s? Could they rule out the possibility of civilian casualties on such a massive operation? Had the Government now revoked the legal status of the Mortality Protocol? The speculation could no more easily be contained than a bushfire.

58 GREEN AND
INCREASINGLY PLEASANT

London, 26th July

The Prime Minister had conceived Operation Ironstone as a spectacular re-run of the Blitz and the harbinger of his ultimate triumph. To endow the war with the kind of blood-and-thunder finale the PM demanded, Wing Commander Wakeman and his Modsec overseer planned to stage the action over Central London as an intense daylight battle between unidentified 'intruder' bombers on the one side and RAF interceptors on the other.

In fact, both the piloted F-95 intruders and the unpiloted MQ-25 interceptors would carry air-to-surface missiles and both would attack the North Greenwich Arena, but for the benefit of the NBC cameras they would do so in significantly different ways. At a height of 15,000 feet and at a range of 10 nautical miles from the target, the MQ-25 drones were to launch their weapons covertly and inflict the initial shock of destruction on the Congress of All The Talents. Thirty seconds later, and in full view of the waiting TV cameras, the 'enemy' F-95s would conduct a second but overtly close-range and low-level missile strike against the Arena before circling and eventually appearing to be intercepted and driven off by the pursuing RAF MQ-25s. Civil Defence Units would be on standby throughout and, once all twenty aircraft of 161 Squadron had cleared the target zone, the anti-aircraft gunners would contribute to the spectacle in traditional fashion by raking an empty sky with sustained and raucous 35mm cannon fire. Having completed their mission over the capital, both the F-95s and the MQ-25s would return to Lakenheath, where they would refuel and re-arm before launching devastating strikes against further targets the length and breadth of the country.

The many thousands of casualties on the ground would be an inherent feature of the day's events, but the onslaught would represent the last desperate action of an exhausted enemy who would subsequently capitulate, withdraw its forces and allow the Prime Minister to announce that he had fulfilled his promise of victory.

Behind a solid desk in an oak-panelled study now adorned with large colour prints of the trident-wielding Natalia Greenwood, the Prime Minister was using the video conference he had scheduled with Major Security Officer Benjamin to dish out a drubbing regarding the coverage of the recent raid on Wolverhampton.

'I don't give a rat's ass how many casualties there were,' he fumed. 'The point is, if they're buried under mounds of rubble, there's absolutely nothing for the NBC to film and we've as good as wasted our time.'

'Point taken, Prime Minister,' replied Benjamin, surprisingly contrite, 'but we are addressing the situation as we speak. It's simply a case of fine-tuning the targeting to make the collateral damage a little more... well, collateral.'

'See to it,' said the PM. 'Get it right. Now, Benjamin, listen hard and make sure you're recording this. There are a number of additional targets to be included in Operation Ironstone. Obviously, the North Greenwich Arena and the Scottish and Welsh Parliament buildings are non-negotiables. However, after a certain amount of reflection, I have decided that we should take the opportunity to expunge the Birmingham Bull Ring, that brutalist excuse for a cathedral in Coventry, plus those godawful skyscrapers in Liverpool from the face of our green and increasingly pleasant land. Add them to the list. If there are any mental hospitals in the vicinity of these targets, then so much the better. So, Major Security Officer Benjamin, do you understand my instructions?'

'Yes, Prime Minister.'

'Have you made a recording of this?'

'Yes, Prime Minister.'

'And do you foresee any reason whatsoever, why Operation Ironstone cannot be executed in accordance with my exact wishes?'

'No, Prime Minister.'

'Good. Three for three. And make sure the NBC has something to make the nation get its hankies out for. Thank you, Benjamin. That will be all.'

'Sir.'

The Prime Minister ended the video conference without valediction, leaned back in his executive chair and spread his shoulders. Drumming his fingers on the arms of the chair in jaunty self-congratulation, he considered the multiple pictures of Natalia Greenwood that adorned his office. He was sure that she too could be bent to his will.

59 HEAVY AND
UNEXPECTED BLOWS

RAF Lakenheath, 30th July

First to walk down the ramp of the A-600 onto the runway at RAF Lakenheath were two platoons of Modsec paramilitaries, assault weapons slung loosely over their shoulders. One by one, they clambered aboard the four waiting trucks and were transported forthwith to the various points around the base where additional numbers were required. The first platoon was deployed to reinforce security on the gates and at a number of perceived weak spots around the perimeter. The second created a cordon around the Command Block where the initial filming of the Prime Minister was due to take place.

The security of the base confirmed, the loadmasters discharged the Gurkha armoured patrol vehicle and gave the signal for the PM and his constantly growing entourage to emerge.

With the hulking A-600 transport plane forming a dramatic backdrop, NBC camera drones preceded the Gurkha, capturing its steady progress along the runway. Above the Prime Minister's seat, the hatch had been opened, allowing him to stand with his head and torso proud of the vehicle in the authoritative manner of a World War Two tank commander. With the breeze in his ears and the summer sun in his eyes, Henderton had little to do other than maintain his imperious posture for the cameras.

On the concrete pan outside the Command Block, an empty lectern draped in a Union Jack stood on a low, carpeted podium. Bolt upright on the tiered stand immediately behind the rostrum, a platoon of RAF Regiment troops, in fatigues and blue-grey berets, anticipated the arrival of their recently self-appointed Commander-in-Chief.

The APV pulled up, Henderton emerged and Wing Commander Wakeman and Major Security Officer Benjamin warmly welcomed the Prime Minister to RAF Lakenheath, 'the station that thwarted a coup'. Kristian Conrad, the NBC package producer, promptly fitted the PM with a microphone and a translucent earbud and ushered him directly to the lectern.

As the PM's lengthy and characteristically derivative address was relayed around the base, York and Gunatillaka were tucked away in the Ops Room with a large pot of Utility tea and a packet of digestive biscuits. As they listened closely to Henderton's words, the pair engaged in an extended round of bullshit bingo which, perhaps unsurprisingly, York won by a country mile.

With the Prime Minister's arrival, welcome and opening speech all in the can, the producer called for a ten-minute break, during which he disappeared smartly to the outside broadcast truck. Having taken advantage of the hiatus to enjoy a clandestine snifter of Utility gin, Conrad returned, apparently suitably refreshed. With the TV crew called once again to action, the Prime Minister extolled Wing Commander Wakeman's prowess in saving the UK from the threat of insurgency, before formally presenting him with the Distinguished Flying Cross and announcing his thoroughly well-deserved promotion to the rank of Group Captain.

After lunch, Wakeman escorted the Prime Minister to the Tech Room, where the stony-faced and tight-lipped MacDermott was required to fit the leader of the nation with a flight suit and helmet. In the Aircrew Ready Room, the seemingly indefatigable NBC producer captured a sequence of action shots of the PM leaping up in response to a putative threat, running at full tilt out of the building and climbing into an F-95 Lightning. The images were gold dust and could easily be spliced into the previous week's footage of F-95s taking off and returning to base. The sight of the Prime Minister taking the controls of an operational combat jet would unquestionably invite widespread admiration.

Following the exertions of the shoot in the Aircrew Ready Room, Henderton was ferried back to the A-600, where he spent an hour in his private quarters ostensibly dealing with pressing affairs of state. He devoted the greater part of his time to scrutinising his architect's initial sketches for the Britannia monument and was pleased to have no trouble recognising Natalia Greenwood's sylphlike figure and attractive features in the designs. Checking his personal updates, the Prime Minister also gained considerable satisfaction from the news of a healthy and constantly growing demand for tickets to the Congress of All The Talents. Finally, he responded quickly and concisely to a knotty financial query from his sister Bella who was still finding her feet as Secretary of State for Employment.

His business concluded, the PM returned to the Command Block for a carefully staged visit to the Officers' Mess, during which he would once again be performing for the cameras. At Wakeman's insistence, and in the interests of the smooth running of the shoot, the bar had been cleared of its usual incumbents. Dressed once more in the borrowed flight suit, Henderton scrutinised the Mess and was singularly disappointed with most of what he saw. He feared that the bottle-cluttered bar, the dog-eared vinyl albums strewn across the armchairs and Bosko's discarded hoodie with the call sign 'Joker' indelibly scrawled on the back did not reflect the vision of Britain he wished to project. Conrad was immediately summoned from his conversation with a sound engineer, torn off a strip and bluntly instructed to 'sort this effing shit-hole out'. The NBC package producer, in spite of his own feeling that the bar conveyed an air of admirable insouciance, acknowledged the Prime Minister's concern and promptly instructed his assistant to clear the empty Whoopty Whoop bottles and sandwich crusts from the countertop. He assured the PM, still manifestly unimpressed with his surroundings, that neither the album covers on the armchairs nor the flippant definition of the word 'ejection', still legible above the bar, would be visible to the viewers. Only marginally placated, Henderton thanked God for the small mercy that the creeping smell from behind the counter could not be registered on video and directed Conrad to keep the shoot-time to the bare minimum.

Having furnished the Prime Minister with a half-empty beer glass, the producer required no more than five minutes to film Henderton standing at the bar, smiling and chatting jovially to Group Captain Wakeman. In the outside broadcast truck, Conrad would later bookend the footage with pre-recorded shots of Bosko, Xu and Lopez relaxing in the Mess and would foster the illusion that the Prime Minister of Great Britain, having flown an F-95 to the defence of the nation, was now winding down in the breezy company of his RAF comrades.

Released from his final media commitment of the day, the PM called an urgent meeting with both Wakeman and Benjamin in order to run through a number of supplementary but nonetheless important matters relating to Operation Ironstone.

Still somewhat unsettled by his unfavourable impressions of the absent pilots, Henderton was not in the easiest of moods.

'The Officers' Mess looks like a bloody youth club,' he complained. 'Call themselves professionals? How do they hit their targets when they can't even put a bloody sandwich in the bin?'

'It's a question I have often asked myself,' said Wakeman, 'but rest assured, Prime Minister. They do hit their targets.'

'I'll have to take your word for it, Jonnie. How you tolerate it is beyond me. Of course, we'll have no further need for these jokers after Ironstone.'

'By which you mean what exactly?' queried Wakeman.

'By which I mean that your slapdash pilots here will know too much for their own damn good and as such, they may constitute something of a loose end.'

'My thoughts, entirely, Prime Minister,' affirmed Benjamin, only too willing to ingratiate herself. 'It wouldn't be the worst thing if the Squadron were not to survive the operation. It is, after all, easier to bury a body bag than an inconvenient truth. As you say, Prime Minister, no loose ends.'

'See to it,' said the PM. 'Don't bother me with the details. Brief me when you've finalised the plan.'

Following Martina's heart-to-heart about her involvement with the authors of the stingers and the revelations about her traumatic experiences at the hands of Modsec, Aston's enthusiasm for Gilbert Lathum Henderton and the NUP had withered and would never recover. As he and Thomas, after another arduous day in the sewers, followed the *Evening News* on the NBC, their usual differences about the Prime Minister were conspicuous by their absence. The pair welcomed the PM's assertion that the RAF had both the will and the means to strike heavy and unexpected blows against the enemy, but their appreciation extended no further. The footage of Henderton climbing into an F-95 and taking off to intercept an enemy threat was, Aston flatly declared, 'a load of tosh'. A week ago, he might have been impressed to see the Prime Minister piloting a combat plane in defence of his country, but the scales had fallen from his eyes and he no longer felt able to take the NBC's reports at face value. Remarkably, he was now looking forward to seeing the next unauthorised contribution to the NBC news crawl by Martina and her shadowy friends.

'No way can Henderton fly a jet,' said Aston, as the bulletin ended. 'No way can that be true.'

'It must be true,' said Thomas, not without a hint of irony. 'We saw it on the state-controlled news.'

60 ALL UNDER CONTROL

RAF Lakenheath, 31st July

In Block J, Group Captain Wakeman and Major Security Officer Benjamin convened in her office to review the deployment of the Squadron's aircraft for the forthcoming Operation Ironstone. Given the growing number of targets specified by the Prime Minister and his requirement that the Squadron's potentially loose-tongued pilots should not survive the mission, they needed to make a number of significant adjustments to their original plan.

Whilst it was highly improbable that the two NUP members would ever decide that they liked each other, they were both long-standing and loyal servants of the National Unity Party and agreed unreservedly on a number of key principles. They concurred in the first instance that the Government of Britain must be, and must remain, a bulwark against anarchy, strong enough to ensure there could be no backsliding and decisive enough to ensure progress. They were equally united in the view that democracy was inherently inefficient, at best a foot on the brake of dynamic government, at worst a mutinous sickness leading to complete political paralysis.

In light of their first two points of agreement, they concluded that so much firepower must be brought to bear on the Congress of All The Talents that none of the fifteen thousand delegates would have even the remotest chance of survival.

It still made sense, therefore, to deploy both the piloted and the unpiloted aircraft to secure the devastation of the North Greenwich Arena.

Their conversation then turned to the trickier matter of tidying up what the Prime Minister had referred to as 'loose ends'. Group Captain Wakeman proposed that the best way forward would be for each of the autonomous MQ-25s to shadow one of the piloted aircraft. As originally planned, the unpiloted drones would launch their missiles first and from distance, but once the F-95s had conducted their high-profile follow-up strikes on the Arena, the MQ-25s would simply eliminate the superfluous and untrusted pilots with radar-guided air-to-air missiles. The drones could then return to Lakenheath, be rearmed and subsequently deal with the Prime Minister's personal list of architectural eyesores in what would now need to be two subsequent waves of bombing. The Group Captain estimated that Chief Technician MacDermott would need to devote perhaps a week to the programming and pointed out that additional pylons would need to be found and fitted to the MQ-25s. He was completely confident, however, that all twenty aircraft would be ready for the eighth of August, the second day of the conference.

'See to it,' said Benjamin. 'I don't know about you, Group Captain, but personally, I'm excited. We're bringing an end not just to the second Battle of Britain but to the war itself, maybe to all war. Think of that. We're talking about a date that will go down in history. Do afternoons get any better than this?'

'Maybe not,' said Wakeman somewhat tentatively.

Benjamin rolled her eyes. 'For God's sake, Wakeman, it was a rhetorical question. Anyway, business concluded, I think.

You may leave. Give MacDermott his brief and set him to task. I think I might pay a visit to our Chief Technician this evening. Just to make sure he doesn't need any help with his decision-making.'

Some six hours later, Major Security Agent Benjamin quietly entered the Tech Room. She was immediately unimpressed with its scrapyard vibe and with the presence of an antique arcade games console not far from MacDermott's work station. The Chief Technician, entirely focussed on his efforts to code a default engine cut-out for the MQ-25s, was completely unaware that she was standing behind him.

'I trust you do not waste time playing on that thing,' she said sharply.

MacDermott's fingers leapt away from the keyboard and his entire frame stiffened. Recognising the voice, he turned around. He would not give her the satisfaction of looking intimidated.

'Can I help you, ma'am?' he said, knowing he was not going to like what he heard.

'I don't think so,' said Benjamin calmly. 'I just wanted to check that Group Captain Wakeman has briefed you and that you have sufficient time to complete your assignment.'

'It's all under control, ma'am. It's a large number of aircraft but in essence it's straightforward programming, at least for the second and third waves. The London part of the operation will require careful co-ordination but it's all doable within the time frame you've set.'

'Good,' said Benjamin. 'And if any issues arise, do not hesitate to ask for support.'

Benjamin smiled blithely and MacDermott, without knowing why, reciprocated.

'You're a lucky man, Chief Technician,' said the Modsec officer. 'I hope you realise that.'

Sickened at the prospect of programming the deaths of tens of thousands of innocent people, MacDermott did not feel in the slightest bit lucky. He was lost for a response, but had no doubt that Benjamin would elaborate on her assertion.

'You are not just a witness to history,' she continued, 'you are one of its ghostwriters. You have been given the honour, as well as the responsibility, of preparing 161 Squadron for a battle that will win the war and secure peace in our time. Victory will bring with it stability and prosperity for future generations, and Ironstone, the operation you have the privilege to be a part of, will be acknowledged as the counter-strike that broke the enemy's back and forced him to grovel for terms. I'm telling you, Operation Ironstone will be as famous as the Battle of Hastings.'

'I understand,' said MacDermott. He resisted the urge to point out that at the Battle Of Hastings, it was the invader who had prevailed.

'I have no doubt that you will devote your considerable abilities to the completion of your task, Chief Technician. However, should you have any doubts about your orders or deliver anything less than your best, let's not forget that I have the power, at a moment's notice, to reward disloyalty with a lifelong posting to some shit-shovelling penal work brigade in a flat-vowelled backwater of Britain, probably somewhere well to the north of Leeds.'

'I think you have laid out my options with perfect clarity,' said MacDermott. 'I have no desire to let you down.'

'Nobody ever does,' said Benjamin. 'Anyway. Good to talk.

I won't disturb you any further.'

Benjamin turned, cast a final disapproving eye over the *Space Invaders* console and departed. It had been an entirely satisfying day.

61 PROPORTIONATE
AND NECESSARY

RAF Lakenheath, 31st July

Dibaba and Warszawski were lying shoulder to shoulder in the bunker where she had recently spent the entire night. Nearby, the dog lay panting on the sand, staring intently at a squirrel and ready for the chase, should the bushy-tailed rodent make the foolhardy decision to descend from the tree.

They had gone round in circles trying to figure out what kind of operation Wakeman might be planning and had settled into silence as they looked through the canopy of overhanging branches towards the azure flecks of an almost cloudless sky. She liked feeling the warmth of his shoulder next to hers and wondered if Warszawski was ever tempted by the idea of taking her hand, of making a move and being more than inseparable, dog-walking comrades. She was beginning to picture how she might react if he were to kiss her, when suddenly the logical and strangely risk-averse part of her consciousness interrupted her reverie. Her thoughts, she decided, were a recipe for complication and, given the situation they found themselves in, her timing could not have been worse. In any case, the RAF, as Wakeman had made so disparagingly clear when they arrived on station, did not exist to help pilots find romantic partners. Dibaba sat up, deliberately breaking their slight but clearly significant physical connection. Had she been bold enough to open up to Warszawski, she would have discovered that he had been making himself apply the Wakeman Protocol to their relationship for as long as she had.

Dibaba sought to distract herself by treating Warszawski yet again to her hypothesis that humans had evolved from light.

Unconvinced, Warszawski flashed her a smile. 'OK, Flight Lieutenant Einstein, assuming the word "evolution" can apply to a non-biological process, just exactly how does light evolve into matter?'

Before Dibaba could answer, her i-comm pinged.

'You told me to tell you straight next time,' read the message. 'I need to talk to you.'

'Shit,' said Dibaba. 'We need to go.'

The brisk walk to the Tech Room allowed Dibaba ample time to brief Warszawski on her request for greater clarity from MacDermott, were he ever required to program civilian targets into one of her missions. It also saved her from having to attempt a definitive answer to Warszawski's question about light evolving into matter.

When a highly agitated MacDermott revealed the parameters for Operation Ironstone, Dibaba was as close to dumbstruck as she had been in her life. For Warszawski, the idea that the Prime Minister might order the extermination of perhaps twenty thousand civilians and the subsequent liquidation of 161 Squadron was so utterly inconceivable that he initially processed what he had heard into something he had the capacity to imagine, namely a large-scale but otherwise routine raid against a variety of unoccupied targets. MacDermott was forced to display Wakeman's detailed mission brief on a large 2D wall-screen before it finally sank in that Operation Ironstone was not a standard demolition job but an exercise in mass murder. Warszawski asked MacDermott to copy the list of operational objectives to his i-comm. He was certain he wouldn't be the only one who would need to see cast-iron evidence of Wakeman's intentions.

In response to Dibaba's proposal that the Chief Technician should try to sabotage the drones, MacDermott detailed his failed attempts to program the MQ-25s to run their engines down when they received a launch command. Their threat management system, he conceded, was a work of genius and he was by no means confident that he could breach it. If launched, the autonomous aircraft would do exactly as commanded, come what may.

Dibaba and Warszawski encouraged MacDermott to continue his work on subverting the MQ-25s, thanked him for his integrity and headed directly for the Mess.

The other members of the Squadron were installed in the bar, engaged in the habitual pastimes of listening to guitar-driven music and consuming sufficient quantities of wheat beer to induce a modicum of relaxation. Flight Lieutenant Bosko had looked for something suitably loud and brash amongst the collection of vinyl albums and had been attracted to an LP by a woman called Alice Cooper. Bosko did not know the record, but the artwork on the cover featured the fork-tongued head of a snake and scrawled handwriting on a garish, blood-red background and seemed to promise that Alice Cooper and her music would be anything but dull.

The aviators had been joined by Gunatillaka and York who, still in their running kit, were flaked out on the sofa after completing two laps of Lakenheath's perimeter path. Anticipating her time at Lakenheath to be completely task-orientated and possibly short, York had not brought any sports kit with her, but with the help of her running partner had successfully liberated a pair of decent-quality trainers, some navy blue shorts and a grey T-shirt from the unsupervised X-Change superstore. In the course of their visit, Gunatillaka had also tracked down a broad-tipped marker pen and had written 'Blondie' in block capitals above the silver-winged USAF symbol on York's T-shirt.

Dibaba and Warszawski, with the Labrador in tow, arrived from their meeting in the Tech Room still aghast at MacDermott's revelations. Quickly, Dibaba counted round the room to establish if everyone was present. Satisfied, and slightly surprised, that the entire Squadron was in attendance, Warszawski walked straight to the turntable and to Bosko's obvious annoyance, lifted the playing arm off the record in the middle of a belligerent guitar solo. Curiously, York and Gunatillaka both woke up the second the music was interrupted.

'Listen up,' said Dibaba. 'The shit is about to hit the fan.'

The pilot recounted what she had discovered from the Chief Technician and incited a blizzard of incredulous questions and outraged expletives. When Warszawski distributed Wakeman's detailed mission brief via i-comm, he managed to dispel the disbelief on the part of some, but served only to provoke an incensed desire in Flight Lieutenant Xu to go to Wakeman's quarters in the dead of night and strangle him in his sleep. Once the ensuing hubbub subsided, Dibaba called the Squadron to order.

'Given that carrying out Wakeman's orders is one hundred percent out of the question,' she said, 'and none of us really want to murder him in his bed, we seriously need to work out just what the hell we are going to do.'

Bosko suggested that they should follow Freebird's example and, if their scanners confirmed multiple heat signatures from the target, they should simply deactivate their weapons, fly back to base and confront Wakeman. Her proposal fell at the first hurdle, however, when Callaghan pointed out that it did not deal with the question of the MQ-25s. The autonomous drones would still be in position to launch their own missiles at the North Greenwich Arena and would proceed to pursue and attack the F-95s once they had done so. At this juncture, Dibaba detailed the Chief Technician's unsuccessful attempts to hack into the operating system that governed the MQ-25s and his lack of confidence in the prospect of sabotaging them.

Suggestions such as collectively refusing to fly or deserting en masse removed the pilots from the crosshairs, but would expose them to a court martial and more importantly, would still leave upwards of twenty thousand unsuspecting civilians in a range of high-profile targets who would stand little or no chance of survival. Without the participation of the piloted F-95s, the drones might possibly lack the firepower to kill everyone in the North Greenwich Arena in one fell swoop, but even that could not be guaranteed.

The Squadron agreed that if they were to obviate an act of mass murder, they would have to use their F-95s to neutralise the AAVs on the ground or, failing that, destroy them in the air. Furthermore, a return to Lakenheath, with the prospect of a court martial, would be out of the question and an exit strategy would have to be devised. Ideally, they would identify redundant airstrips where it would be safe to land and abandon a combat jet. In extremis they could resort to the altogether more risky approach of pointing their aircraft in the direction of the North Sea and ejecting somewhere before the coast. Either way, they would still need some kind of plan to evade eventual capture.

The majority of the aviators were inclined to agree with Callaghan when he asserted that they now had clear objectives and should begin to analyse the practicalities. The drift towards a consensus was halted by Flight Lieutenant Lopez.

'The elimination of the AAVs would definitely save the lives of the conference delegates and the civilians at the other targets,' he said calmly, 'but only for now, only until Henderton comes up with some other batshit plan to silence unwanted voices for good. Think about it. His Night Of The Long Knives would really just be on hold.'

The discussion stopped dead in its tracks. The implications of what Dibaba knew she was about to say ran contrary to her most basic instincts and made her blood run cold.

'If we want to stop the murder,' said Dibaba nonetheless, 'we have to stop the murderer.'

The silence was now palpable.

'To be clear,' said Xu. 'You're proposing we kill the Prime Minister.'

'That's exactly what she's proposing,' said Lopez.

'No,' said Dibaba. 'No it's not. At least, I don't think so. Fuck, I don't really know what I'm proposing, to be honest. But Pinball is right. We have to see the bigger picture. Henderton won't stop unless somebody stops him.'

'One of the first things they taught us at Cranwell,' said Bosko, 'is that war is inherently unethical. Always has been, always will be. So if we're looking for an ethical military intervention, we can forget it. We ain't gonna find one. The only real choice we have is to do something or to do nothing. And if we're gonna do something, the nearest we get to ethical is to make sure that what we do is, quote, "discriminate, proportionate and necessary". Sorry. I totally swallowed the textbook at college. Anyway, that's it. Here endeth the lesson.'

'If it is up to us to stop him,' said Itoje, 'we have a squadron of F-95s that are completely up to the job.'

'But we also have a duty not to harm civilians,' countered Dibaba. 'The PM may be an arsehole, but he's a civilian arsehole, a civilian arsehole with civilian rights. The Mortality Protocol protects him as much as the delegates at the conference.'

'Although,' said Warszawski, 'didn't the PM make himself Commander-in-Chief of British Armed Forces? I would say that makes him probably the least civilian person in the entire country.'

His point was anything but moot and Dibaba knew it.

'Fuck, you're right,' she said. 'He's the Commander-in-Chief. He pissed his civilian status down the toilet when he made himself C-in-C.'

'Also,' added Warszawski, 'I don't think MacDermott needs to waste any more time trying to hack the MQ-25s' operating system. I think there's a much simpler solution.'

62 PRO PATRIA

Liverpool, 6th August

It was a big day for the Liverpool South work brigade. At ten seventeen precisely, after nigh on six weeks of hacking away at the seventy-metre-long plug of rancid, congealed fat and human detritus which had been blocking the Central Sewer, Thomas and Aston punched a hole through the final curtain of saponified waste, removed their respirators and inhaled the salty air drawn in from the Mersey.

'It was a shit job,' said Thomas, 'but somebody had to do it.'

'We came, we saw, we kicked its greasy ass,' said Aston, beaming as he fist-bumped his partner with his disgusting gloves.

Once the final blocks of putrid, fatty waste had been removed for processing, the sluices had been opened and the sewer had begun to flow freely for the first time in fifteen years, Aston and Thomas were invited to finish their shift early. Commander Duke, the brigade leader, presented them with what appeared to be an authentic bottle of Bio-Blitz laundry liquid as a token of her appreciation and told them to take the rest of the day off.

The two liberated brigade workers breathed in the untainted air as they walked slowly home. They were proud of the job they had done, were relieved to be finished and were reluctant to give the slightest thought to what they might be ordered to do next. Once back in the house, they put their foul-smelling clothing directly into the washing machine for the first of several washes, then made excitedly for the bathroom, where they used copious quantities of laundry liquid as shower gel.

The following day, Commander Duke assembled the brigade in military rows and expressed her genuine appreciation for the sustained toil conducted over six arduous weeks in the most challenging of circumstances by the hard-working brigaders of Liverpool South. Her single visit to the face of the fatberg, she conceded, had been enough to last her a lifetime. The brigade commander then led a prayer for the souls of the colleagues who had lost their lives during the excavation and revealed that a plaque commemorating their service was to be commissioned and ultimately displayed on a prominent building in the city centre, in all likelihood somewhere directly above the sewer. She congratulated the brigade for completing their task a full two weeks ahead of schedule and announced, to general relief, that the fatberg currently blocking the sewer beneath Crosby would be the preserve of the Liverpool North brigade.

Commander Duke then called each brigade member forward by name and presented them with a National Hero of Labour medal. The polished, circular medal was cast in an aluminium-silicon alloy and featured an idealised image of inspired and indefatigable work brigaders armed with picks and shovels and collectively gazing beyond the space they inhabited to the future they were so proudly working to construct. The image was augmented by the inscription *pro patria*, which Thomas translated for Aston as 'for my country'. The perhaps more accurate translation of 'for the fatherland', he decided, had an unfortunate ring to it.

Whilst Commander Duke was at pains to emphasise that she was not at liberty to grant leave, she had decided nonetheless that it was medically prudent that those workers involved in the clearance of the fatberg should self-isolate for five working days, shower vigorously during the lay-off and ensure that they had not incubated any contagious diseases. She was confident that her managers would approve her decision, especially considering the early completion of the project.

In their week of officially sanctioned quarantine, Aston and Thomas smelled sweeter by the day.

63 A THOUSAND YEARS OF PEACE

London, 7th August

Outside the impressive dome which sheltered the North Greenwich Arena, banners proclaiming 'The Congress of All The Talents' and 'No Repeat of Yesterday' offered only occasional shade to the patient queues of delegates. The best part of fifteen thousand attendees stood in long, chattering lines, waiting for those ahead of them to clear security and to permit another couple of steps towards the main entrance. Once bags and credentials had been carefully examined by the Royal Marines on security detail, delegates had to negotiate the gently curving concourse of the shopping and entertainment complex which surrounded the arena itself. The retail units, which had been vacant for years, were to serve throughout the three-day conference as office spaces for invited organisations, as catering outlets and as breakout venues for meetings, presentations and discussions.

The huge arena at the heart of the domed complex had the capacity to host all fifteen thousand delegates for the Prime Minister's keynote address which was due to open the event at eleven o'clock that morning. The early arrivals noted the cathedral-like quality to the voluminous space, an effect created in part by the vertical, almost solid-looking columns of blue light emanating from the overhead projection systems and in part by the efficiency of the air conditioning. Outside the architectural shafts of light, the seats and the walkways were bathed in a softer, more calming shade of Baltic blue. At the far end of the arena, a circular ash-floored podium stood on polished tubular steel legs and could be accessed by either of the two short flights of steps to left and right. Already, camera drones hovered around the perspex lectern as the NBC director, fully committed to capturing the conference for posterity, rehearsed close-ups on the technicians still checking the audio links.

Behind the stage, a bank of five ultra-high-definition screens bridged the arena in a gentle arc. The huge, central widescreen display would present the images in such detail that the delegates in the most distant seats would discern not just the emotion but the faintest beads of sweat on the faces of the speakers. The black-garbed technician, at that moment removing wax from his right ear with the fingernail of his index finger, had clearly not been warned. The four auxiliary screens were smaller and would display graphs, photos and video content. When the Prime Minister addressed the assembled conference, the smaller screens would simply present images of a Union Jack swaying gently on a summer breeze as the words 'Reconnect', 'Reconstruct' and 'Reunite' crawled quietly from right to left.

The ninety-six VIP suites, sandwiched between the upper and lower stands and providing private catering and viewing for two thousand delegates, had been distributed amongst the most prominent representatives of the decommissioned universities, redundant political parties and disbanded media bodies. The supporters, advocates or former employees of these organisations would be shepherded into coherent blocks above and below the ring of well-appointed suites or onto the floor directly facing the stage at the western end of the arena.

The huge conference space filled almost imperceptibly. As Richard Moon, the recently redeployed Secretary of State for Justice, took to the stage to introduce himself as Master of Ceremonies for the next three days and to declare the Congress of All The Talents officially open, the last of the delegates were still clearing security.

Moon ran efficiently through the house rules. He advised the delegates that washrooms were located on all levels and in the concourse outside the arena. He pointed out that the NBC would be filming the entire event and politely reminded the attendees that the use of personal recording devices was not permitted. He also reassured them that no fire drills were planned and that, in the unlikely event of an alarm, they should leave via the emergency exits indicated. Moon then welcomed the distinguished guests to an event which, he was certain, was of historical significance. He particularly thanked those delegates who had rearranged prior commitments to find time to contribute to the imagineering of the future.

Moon was especially thankful, he affirmed, to the Prime Minister who, amid his heavy burdens, duties and responsibilities, had joined the delegates in Greenwich to dignify and magnify the work of the conference. He then enthusiastically invited the attendees to extend the warmest of welcomes to the Prime Minister himself, the Right Honourable Gilbert Lathum Henderton.

Immediately, the blue columns of light began to flash to the pulse of the almost deafening music pounding from the heavy-duty sound system. Moon dissolved from the scene as the Prime Minister ascended the short flight of steps to the stage and took his position behind the lectern. When the music abruptly stopped, the flutter of applause, though audible, was no more than polite. It was by far the least enthusiastic welcome that Henderton had received since his foundation of the NUP and it unsettled him. No matter, he told himself. They were not really his people anyway.

The Prime Minister had wisely opted not to deliver modified chunks of Churchill to an audience perhaps better equipped than most to recognise them and the speech had laid considerable claims to his time. If his words were to achieve anything today, it would be to ensure that the arena was completely full the following morning when the aircraft of 161 Squadron were due to take to the skies.

Henderton began by reminding the conference of the horrors of anarchy and of how far the nation had come under the leadership of the NUP. During the Dark Age, a conference such as this, he contended, would have been literally unthinkable. He echoed Moon's affirmation of the historical significance of today's gathering. He declared that, with victory in the war both certain and imminent, it was time to look to the future and to lay the socio-political foundations for a thousand years of peace. He enthusiastically invited the delegates to be free in their thinking and to respect each other's views. Perhaps surprisingly, he encouraged the conference not to hold back from airing their criticisms of the NUP and the Government, as long as those criticisms were neither hateful nor destructive. There had been enough hate and destruction, he affirmed, throughout the years of anarchy and war. As Henderton delivered his speech, his rhetorical pauses failed to trigger the usual rapt responses and on two occasions were met with an uncomfortable silence. When the Prime Minister concluded by thanking the conference for their attendance and wishing them luck in their exciting and historic endeavour, the applause was again no more than cursory. All the more reason, he thought, to view the delegates as a problem rather than a solution.

64 FORGIVE THE INTRUSION

RAF Lakenheath, 8th August

It was 0800 hours and Major Security Officer Benjamin intended today to be the last morning she would spend on this windswept and dreary base. She had not set foot outside RAF Lakenheath in the two months since her arrival and had not at any point enjoyed the slightest form of social activity. With every pilot in 161 Squadron waiting in the Aircrew Ready Room and every aircraft on station being fuelled or loaded with ordnance, the Modsec officer knew that the successful execution of Operation Ironstone would permit her to return to the people she cared about and re-engage with metropolitan life. The destruction of the North Greenwich Arena would be her signal to leave.

Benjamin was also eager for an opportunity to confirm in person to the Prime Minister that she had torched the viper's nest in Greenwich and left absolutely no loose ends at Lakenheath. Whilst her priority was, as it had always been, to advance the agenda of the Party and execute the decisions of its leader, she congratulated herself that her career could only benefit from her success.

Group Captain Wakeman was equally aware of the pivotal nature of today's operation. He was looking forward to the clarity that Operation Ironstone would bring to British politics. He was looking forward to the declaration of victory and the national celebration that would erupt in its wake. Above all, he was looking forward to the prosperity and cohesion that the National Unity Party would inevitably deliver. The Prime Minister's assurance that Wakeman would, in due course, be assigned a post more befitting his new rank, only served to enhance his confidence that today was going to be a day to remember.

If the Wing Commander had experienced any compunction about the imminent demise of the aircrew, he had successfully come to terms with their loss. In the grand scheme of things, their collective sacrifice would benefit the entire nation and was therefore, in the final analysis, a price worth paying. Furthermore, the risk of death was part of life in the armed forces and the pilots all knew what they had signed up for. And in any case, given the inherent instability of GMSV, they were living on borrowed time as it was. The thought had crossed his mind, however, that the task-orientated and highly diligent Major Security Officer Benjamin might consider the Group Captain himself to be something of a loose end once Operation Ironstone was concluded. For that reason, he would be wearing his Glock 17 service pistol throughout the day.

In the Ops Room Gunatillaka was caught unawares by the request from the pilot of the approaching RAF helicopter for permission to land at Lakenheath. Permission granted, the Comanche put down and the pilot informed Gunatillaka that his orders from Modsec were to refuel and to remain on the helipad pending further instructions. The Ops Manager rapidly inferred from this that the helicopter was Benjamin's taxi home. If so, she could think of a much better use for it and immediately messaged York.

Under normal circumstances, Major Security Officer Benjamin would have been extremely unhappy for York to intrude into her office and lay claim to her attention. Today she was incensed.

'I don't know what you think you are doing here,' she snapped, 'but I gave you explicit orders to stay out of my way, Lieutenant Commander. Those orders have not changed. You may leave.'

'Forgive the intrusion, ma'am,' said York politely. 'I understand from the Ops Room that you are due to helicopter back to the MOD this evening. As I report to you, ma'am, I'm slightly confused as to my continued status. Am I to travel with you, to remain here, or to return to Brize Norton?'

'Well, you'll certainly not be travelling with me, if that's what you're thinking,' said Benjamin with obvious contempt. 'As for the other options, frankly, Tinkerbell, I don't give a toss either way. But if I did not make this clear to you already, I've got more important things to do than listen to a loved-up teenager wondering if she'll get to see her pretty little boyfriend any time soon. Dismissed.'

'Sorry for the intrusion, ma'am,' said York, almost obsequiously. She turned, left Benjamin's office and walked down the stairs to the exit from Block J. Once outside the building, she messaged Gunatillaka.

'You were right about the Comanche, Gunnie. Game on.'

65 ASSAULT ON THE EARDRUMS

Liverpool, 8th August

In Menlove Close, Aston and Thomas were making the most of their break from the work brigade by spending the greater part of every morning on the sofa. As they discussed what to cook that evening, they glanced occasionally at the TV which was currently broadcasting a clip show of Gilbert Henderton's most significant achievements. Martina, now completely open with her family about her political activism, was spending the morning with her hacker friends but had encouraged the two men to keep an eye on the NBC news as, she insisted, something unusual might be about to happen.

Thomas was aware that the Congress of All The Talents, to which he had been repeatedly invited, should in theory have begun the previous day, but the NBC had made absolutely no mention of it. The quarantined work brigader could only assume therefore that the conference, as he had suspected, was not a real event and that he had been right to treat the regular reminders with caution.

As the delegates to the conference slowly trickled into the North Greenwich Arena to reclaim their seats for the second day of discussion and debate, the same NBC bulletin was being presented on the five screens above the stage. The delegates were aware that the PM would not be attending in person for a second day and the compilation of Henderton's most engaging moments was presumably his chosen way of reminding them of his unquestionable importance and his enduring popularity.

Suddenly, and without any form of continuity announcement, the footage of the Prime Minister was supplanted by a music video featuring a collective of line-drawn, computer-animated rock musicians. A single power chord from the guitar anchored by an insistent staccato figure on the keyboard grabbed the attention of the delegates. When the entire band kicked into an impassioned rendition of 'Won't get fooled again', it was patently clear to everyone in the arena that this assault on their eardrums did not constitute a part of the official programme. The NBC had been hacked.

'We'll be fighting in the streets / With our children at our feet / And the morals that they worship will be gone,' emoted the long-haired, bespectacled singer from the massive central screen.

In the OB truck outside the arena, Stella Paterson's frantic efforts to pause the broadcast, reduce the volume, or overwrite an apology all came to nought and her attempts to communicate by radio with the technicians in the arena were thwarted by the sheer volume of the music. As a last resort, she abandoned the truck and frustratedly tried to push her way through the lines of participants in the forlorn hope of finding someone who could kill the electricity supply to the entire North Greenwich site.

Aston was initially so agog to see this enthralling, computer-assisted animation of the Fatberg Four hammering out their recording, that several seconds elapsed before his awareness translated to action and he yelled to Freya 'We're on the telly!'

Freya was no less flabbergasted than Aston and Thomas and they all watched open-mouthed until their final crashing power chord closed the iconoclastic song. It had sounded amazing.

'Bloody hell,' said Freya, still almost paralysed with astonishment. 'She kept that quiet.'

'She certainly did,' said Thomas, wide-eyed with wonder and wholeheartedly impressed.

'Although, that's the loudest quiet I've heard in a long time,' said Aston. 'But you go, Martina. You stick it to them. Take that and shove it up your fucking jacksie, you shit-brained torturers.'

66 NO LOOSE ENDS

RAF Lakenheath, 8th August

Operation Ironstone began officially at 1100 hours, the exact time that former Secretary of State Richard Moon was welcoming the delegates to the second day of the Congress of All The Talents and was apologising for the technical difficulties they had experienced. In the Operations Room at Lakenheath, Group Captain Wakeman and Major Security Officer Benjamin were fastidiously overseeing the endeavours of Flying Officer Gunatillaka and Chief Technician MacDermott.

The Ops Manager was sitting quietly at her usual station facing Wakeman from across the large 3D virtual map which occupied the centre of the room. Although outwardly calm, Gunatillaka was massively concerned that MacDermott might not have the temerity to brazen things out until the launch of the drones. Once in the air, the MQ-25s could not be turned around and would complete their mission exactly as programmed. It would only be a matter of time before it dawned on Wakeman and Benjamin that the Chief Technician had created a mission program which was significantly at variance with the parameters they had set. Wary of the reaction of Benjamin and Wakeman once they realised that Operation Ironstone was not proceeding as anticipated, Gunatillaka had procured a service pistol from the armoury and stashed it in the top drawer of her desk.

MacDermott was installed at a work station two rows behind Gunatillaka and slightly to her right and spoke not a word. He was seeking only one thing from Operation Ironstone. Redemption.

By 1110 hours, the ten pilots of RAF 161 Squadron had taxied their line of heavily-armed F-95s to the threshold of runway 24 and were awaiting individual clearance for take-off. Responding to the specific commands from their Ops Manager, each pilot in turn eased their fearsome aircraft onto the runway, allowed the turbofan engine to run up to a roar, and accelerated into the air. Once all ten pilots were airborne, Gunatillaka organised the Squadron into two flights of three and one of four, which then smartly circled the base at well-separated altitudes. Closely studying the holographic map which was the focus of the Ops Room, Wakeman could identify the F-95s by shape and colour and the individual pilots by their accompanying code. Everything looked exactly as it should.

Responding to the electronic command from Wakeman's work station, the ten fully-armed drones, which were to shadow and ultimately eliminate the F-95s, taxied in an immaculate line to the main runway. As Operation Ironstone was a daylight raid and the NBC cameras in Central London would be on standby to capture the action, the unpiloted MQ-25s had been painted with red and blue RAF roundels on their squat fuselage and slender wings. Having reviewed the metrics of each of the autonomous aircraft and satisfied himself that there were no technical problems, Wakeman transmitted the order for the MQ-25s to launch and carry out their mission. There would be no turning back.

The Group Captain then focussed his attention once more on

the 3D map at the centre of the Ops Room. After launch, each MQ-25 would rapidly link up with a piloted F-95 Lightning and track it doggedly to the target. The first of the autonomous aircraft completed its take-off without incident, but instead of shadowing its intended quarry, the MQ-25 deviated from the expected course, climbed to five thousand feet and headed directly north. The second and then the third followed suit.

'Is there a fault?' asked Benjamin, a look of considerable concern now occupying her face.

'No, ma'am,' said Wakeman, anxiously casting his eyes back and forth over the metrics on his displays. 'I'm not seeing any fault alerts.'

The Group Captain watched a fourth MQ-25 take off and, exactly as the others had done, head unerringly in the direction of the Arctic Sea. Finally, the penny dropped. If there were no faults showing, the AAVs could only be doing what they'd been programmed to do. They could only be doing what MacDermott had programmed them to do. Wakeman stood up suddenly and glared at the Chief Technician.

'What the hell's happening, MacDermott? What did you do?'

'Sir, I am struggling to understand what is happening,' he lied. 'I'm just looking for fault reports.'

'Turn them around,' ordered Benjamin.

'We can't,' said Wakeman. 'They're now completely autonomous. Flying 360 degrees at Mach One or above, they'll eventually run out of fuel and crash into the sea.'

'Somewhere north-east of Iceland, by my calculations,' said MacDermott, unable, or perhaps unwilling, to maintain the pretence any longer.

'Shit, MacDermott you pathetic little worm, this is treason.'

'Well, that's one way of looking at it, Sir. But at least we won't be butchering civilians anymore.'

'You shit. You'll be court-martialled for this. You know the penalty for treason.'

MacDermott calmly rose from his seat and perhaps for the first time since his arrival at Lakenheath, looked Wakeman straight in the eye and held his gaze.

'It is forbidden to kill, therefore all murderers are punished, unless they kill in large numbers and to the sound of trumpets. *Vive le* Mortality Protocol. Sir.'

'There's something else,' said Benjamin, looking anxiously at the F-95s on the central map. One of the three flights appeared to be heading 225 degrees, which meant they were not aiming for London.

'MacDermott, you arsehole,' barked Wakeman. 'What the hell have you done?'

'Sir, the F-95s are all heading towards their programmed targets.'

The microsecond of initial reassurance was superseded by the realisation that MacDermott had also programmed alternative targets for the F-95s. The Group Captain was apoplectic.

'You arsehole,' he snarled. 'You fucking excuse for a human being.'

At this point, Wakeman managed to regain sufficient self-control to interrupt his stream of invective. Regardless of the rage he felt at MacDermott's insubordination, he knew he had to try to curb his anger and abort whatever mission the Chief Technician had programmed. He would deal with his treachery later and deal with it severely. Wakeman summoned as much composure as he could muster and opened his comms to the Squadron. Unusually, the pilots had maintained complete radio silence since take-off.

'Break, break,' he announced, as clearly as he could. '161 Squadron, all aircraft. Abort Ironstone immediately. Repeat. Abort Ironstone immediately. Acknowledge.'

Dibaba was first in.

'Lakenheath Ground, this is Freebird. Could you verify the status of the MQ-25s? They appear to be heading 360 degrees. Is everything going to plan?'

'Mission abort,' repeated Wakeman. 'That's an order.'

'Lakenheath Ground, this is Stairway,' said Warszawski. 'I have visual on a bandit. May be some kind of zeppelin.'

Warszawski instructed his i-comm to play track one of Led Zeppelin's third album and the pulsating opening bars of 'Immigrant Song' overwhelmed the comms in the Ops Room. Wakeman and Benjamin were treated to a screeching Viking war-cry of a song that urged its Norse protagonists onwards to the fray whilst warning Valhalla to prepare a place for the fallen. The Squadron were clearly following their own agenda and were irretrievably beyond his control. Wakeman contemptuously muted the hammering audio feed and glowered at MacDermott.

'Step away from your station,' he ordered.

Without any hint of a warning, Benjamin took out her service pistol, aimed it at MacDermott and fired. The bullet ripped through his right arm and shattered the visual display unit behind. The Chief Technician felt like he'd been hit with a base-ball bat, was flung off balance and fell to the floor. Gunatillaka instantly took cover beneath her desk, but Benjamin fired off a round at her vacated work station to impress on the Ops Manager that she was by no means exempt from injury. The shot penetrated the table top and severed an electrical cable, causing several of the monitors to cut out. A second shot in Gunatillaka's direction embedded itself in the wall.

'For Christ's sake put the gun down,' said Wakeman. 'She's not going anywhere.'

'No loose ends,' said Benjamin. She turned and fired off three shots in rapid succession at the centre of Wakeman's chest. The Group Captain collapsed heavily to the floor without uttering even a moan.

Across the room, Gunatillaka was franticly fumbling at the drawer to her desk, desperate to retrieve the means to defend herself but terrified of presenting her hand as a target.

Although Benjamin had no precise understanding of the Squadron's new objectives, she knew that the F-95s needed to be stopped and her only hope was to use Gunatillaka, whose voice the pilots might possibly trust.

'So, Flying Officer Gunnie-whatever-your-name-is, unless you want to join your friend in a two-person race to bleed to death, you will speak to the Squadron, you will tell them that Wakeman and Benjamin have been eliminated and you will tell them to abort Operation Ironstone and to return to base.'

'I'm hurt,' groaned Gunatillaka from below the desk. 'I'm going to try to stand up.'

The Operations Manager was not hurt and was simply playing for time. As she finally managed to place her hand on the grip of her pistol, Gunatillaka was startled by the deafening clatter of sustained automatic gunfire. During the intense seconds that followed, all she could hear was the ringing in her ears and the sound of her own agitated breathing.

'It's OK, Gunnie,' said York. 'You can get up.'

The Lieutenant Commander had been accompanied by the two guards on the door to the Command Block. Having thanked the first of the soldiers for his help, York returned the automatic rifle to its rightful owner and surveyed the scene in the Ops Room. Wakeman and Benjamin were both dead. Three metres from Gunatillaka, MacDermott was lying on his back pressing hard on his arm with his left hand. The Ops Manager immediately activated her comm and called for an ambulance to take him to the med bay. She despatched the guards to locate a medical kit, then with York's help, improvised a tourniquet for MacDermott's arm with her own jacket. Within what seemed like seconds, the two guards reappeared with a substantial first aid box, dug out some dressings and compressed both the entry and the exit wounds to stop the flow of blood. MacDermott was clearly in considerable pain but still had colour in his cheeks and was talking coherently.

'I've got this,' said a grateful Gunatillaka to York. 'He's gonna be fine. You go.'

'Thanks, Gunnie,' said York. 'I'll be in touch.'

They exchanged a glance and the Lieutenant Commander was gone. Outside the Ops Room, she grabbed the hurriedly packed bag that she had dumped at the door, started up a Land Rover and headed directly to the Comanche still waiting on the helipad. Briefed by Gunatillaka, the pilot had already begun running up the turboshaft engines and was standing by to fly York to Navy Command HQ in Portsmouth. At a cruising speed of 275 knots she would be there in less than half an hour. In the meantime she would use the Comanche's radio to rally the support that she was certain must still be there.

67 V-DAY

London, 8th August

Under the pretext of wishing to review the latest security arrangements in his sprawling residence, the Prime Minister steadily climbed the narrow staircase to the top of the Italianate tower overlooking the complex, grey roofscape of Whitehall Palace. The hatch which permitted access onto the gently pitched, lead-dressed platform was closed but unlocked. It had been well over a century since the London Blitz and Henderton was keen to ensure himself the best possible view of the forthcoming spectacle. It was a bright if somewhat airless day and even at a distance of several miles, he was certain he would have little difficulty witnessing the dramatic aerial battle that was about to take place.

The PM chatted briefly to the pair of snipers on duty atop the tower and allowed them to elicit a wave from the other members of their team who were stationed at various points on the roof of the Grade 1 listed building. Pleasantries exchanged and the potential for meaningful conversation exhausted, the Prime Minister relieved the first guard of his binoculars before instructing the two paramilitaries to vacate their post and wait for him at the bottom of the staircase. He had no fear of heights and would, he assured them, be perfectly safe behind the balustrade.

Looking up at the red, white and blue of the Union Jack

hanging listlessly on the flagpole above him, his thoughts drifted to Britannia and he decided that once today's business was concluded, he would contact Natalia Greenwood and invite her for a second photo-shoot at Chequers, perhaps without the distraction of her daughter on this occasion.

He checked the time on his i-comm and, using the Shard as a rough indicator of direction, looked eastwards towards Greenwich. He was unsure if he would be able to make out the flashes from the missile strikes but he would at least hear the satisfying explosions as the North Greenwich Arena was razed to the ground. He was absolutely certain, however, that he would not miss the subsequent excitement of aerial combat as the drones set upon the piloted aircraft of 161 Squadron with lethal prejudice.

At two in the afternoon, he would solemnly address the nation from the steps of the Durbar Court, the ostentatious internal courtyard within his newly acquired official residence, and proclaim that the war had at last been won. He would also declare the following day to be a public holiday and a day of celebration for all. In due course, he had decided, the ninth of August would become an official bank holiday and would be known officially as 'V-Day'. Before the first anniversary of victory, construction of the 120-metre Britannia monument would begin on the vacated site beside the Thames, but there would, as a matter of national security, be no record of the Congress of All The Talents in any document, report or historical account.

Still peering towards the eastern horizon, the Prime Minister did not hear the approach of the F-95s piloted by Flight Lieutenants Itoje, Becker and Lopez or see their Partisan missiles streak across the summer sky. When he registered a sequence of surprisingly thunderous explosions, the blast did not, as he was expecting, come from the direction in which he was looking but somehow from behind him. Instinctively wheeling round towards the source of the detonations he was dumbstruck by the sight of The Blade, the fifty-six storey glass tower in the middle of Battersea Park, falling almost vertically down on itself, generating a sustained tremor and finally an improbably huge, rolling plume of dust and smoke. Although only the atrium and lowermost twenty floors in the building were occupied, the landmark skyscraper had for the past five years been the central office of Modsec and its sudden obliteration annihilated at a stroke the Prime Minister's conviction that he was the master of his own destiny. With the inconceivable taking place in front of him, he had no plan and no instinct for what to do next other than to barrel down the stairs as fast as his feet would carry him.

Time was not on his side. With Red Flight clear of Central London, Warszawski, Bosko, Dibaba and Callaghan, unleashed their own weapons. The sixteen missiles, which had been programmed by MacDermott to pinpoint each wing of Whitehall Palace in turn, bore down at twice the speed of sound and reduced the imposing building with its impressive, classical facades, rich decoration and grand carvings to smoking rubble whilst the disorientated Prime Minister was still racing down the staircase.

The massive eruptions which destroyed the Prime Minister's Palace inevitably caused extensive damage to surrounding buildings in the Westminster Security Zone and incurred a large number of casualties, some of whom were lying strewn amongst the debris in the street. The buildings in Downing Street had all been completely demolished, as had all but the northern end of the National Unity Party Central Office. Across the road from the NUP, almost every window on the Whitehall side of the MOD Main Building had been blown in. Inside the damaged structure itself, the power had failed, all communication systems were down and a state of almost total confusion prevailed. Some Modsec personnel attempted to help the injured, whilst others tried somehow to make sense of what was happening and engaged in frustrated efforts to communicate with decision-makers. Many simply had no idea what to do.

In the commandeered Comanche, Lieutenant Commander York was rapidly approaching Navy HQ on Whale Island, having succeeded in making contact with Commodore Sir David Novotny, the most senior Royal Navy commander still in office. As keen to be free of his NUP shackles as the top brass in both the Army and the RAF, Novotny had secured support from the Armoured Household Cavalry Regiment in Combomere, some twenty-five miles from Central London, and from the less heavily armed Grenadier Guards stationed at Wellington Barracks on Birdcage Walk. It took the Guards no more than twenty minutes to arm themselves and deploy to the Security Zone, where they blocked the main entrances to the MOD and responded in kind to sporadic gunfire from Modsec paramilitaries within the heavily damaged building.

Now established in an ops room in Navy Command HQ, York devoted her considerable energies to maintaining and co-ordinating the lines of communication between the three branches of the Armed Forces. Within an hour she had galvanised several units from the Army and Royal Marines to deploy to MOD buildings around the country, where they confronted and contained the incumbent paramilitaries who were now disorganised and bereft of orders from London. Whenever the opportunity arose, the Lieutenant Commander snatched a moment to check the personal messages folder on her i-comm. There was still no response from Batista.

Some two hours after the devastating raid on Whitehall, the leaderless Modsec troops threw in the towel once half a dozen Household Cavalry tanks arrived to support the two platoons of Grenadier Guards. With the firefight over, it was deemed safe for the paramedics who had massed at the entrances to the Security Zone to enter the scene of devastation and begin their urgent and sometimes gruesome task of dealing with the injured and the dead. They were followed by teams of fire fighters who doused flames, staunched billowing smoke and attempted to pull disorientated survivors from the rubble, exactly as they had done at Northwood.

68 ON OUR HANDS
EITHER WAY

Chequers Court, Buckinghamshire, 8th August

At Chequers, the Modsec troops operating the surface-to-air missile platform in the grounds of the estate were alerted to the approach of three fast-moving aircraft by their radar, but, in the absence of any intel about a possible attack, unwisely assumed the aircraft would simply pass overhead. Within ten seconds of the guards' costly error of judgement, the Elizabethan mansion that for a century and a half had been the official country residence of the Prime Minister of Britain was a redbrick ruin.

Having circled Chequers to confirm the extent of the damage, Merton, Xu and Finnan planned to fly west and attempt a landing at Cotswold Airport, once an RAF base but for years simply an unused runway flanked by scores of rusting commercial airliners. The shaken Modsec guards, still tracking the escaping F-95s on radar, threw caution to the wind, illuminated their targets and launched all four of their Firespike missiles. SAM-alerts sounded immediately in the cockpits of the three F-95s and the pilots instantly deployed multiple radar-reflective decoy drones to attract the missiles towards expendable targets. The electronic countermeasures bamboozled three of the surface-to-air missiles, but the fourth relentlessly closed in on Xu's aircraft and within seconds, the

Firespike's proximity fuse detonated its fragmentation warhead, battering the F-95's left wing with shrapnel.

Although none of the steel shards penetrated the aircraft's graphene composite skin, enough disruption was caused to the avionics and to the flaps to rob Xu of control. The pilot immediately informed the others that she had sustained catastrophic damage and had no option but to eject. She throttled back the engines, let the aircraft descend to four thousand feet and pulled the levers on either side of her seat. If she escaped injury, and this was by no means certain, she would find a safe location and wait until Finnan and Merton could acquire a vehicle and track the signal from her beacon.

To the east, Itoje, Becker and Lopez landed successfully at Norwich airport, commercially unused for over eight years and also a storage facility for superfluous transatlantic passenger planes. At over forty miles to their agreed rendezvous, they would comfortably need two days to cover the ground on foot, but were confident that they could locate an unoccupied house with working solar panels and a usable electric vehicle. There might even be a suitable EV abandoned somewhere on the airport site.

Dibaba, Warszawski, Bosko and Callaghan had agreed to pilot their aircraft to Wattisham Airfield, a former Army Air Corps base in Suffolk, which, like Norwich Airport, had seen no purposeful activity since before the Dark Age. Although the four had resolved to maintain radio silence until they needed to determine a landing sequence, Dibaba had not the slightest desire to play 'Free Bird'. She was in no mood whatsoever for celebration.

Dibaba, Warszawski and Callaghan landed their aircraft without incident, but Bosko snagged one of the discarded braking parachutes in her right main landing gear, locking the wheels and causing her to veer off the runway and onto the overgrown grass. The rougher terrain caused the forward gear to collapse, ploughing the nose of the jet into the earth and shredding the fibre-glass radar dome. Bosko was shaken but otherwise unhurt and when she raised the canopy, she was suddenly hit by the heat of the afternoon. Looking around, the pilot was relieved to detect neither smoke nor flame. Satisfied that she had done no more than render the F-95 completely unserviceable, Bosko removed the survival kit from the ejection system and threw it to the ground. The orange bag was swiftly followed by a much smaller rucksack containing a few items of casual clothing, recently liberated from the X-Change Store at Lakenheath, and a small, blue and white wash bag that had also taken her fancy. Having successfully descended the two built-in steps in the F-95's tilting fuselage, the pilot discovered that the stowed boarding ladder would not deploy, presumably as a consequence of her less than textbook landing, and she was forced to make a two-metre jump backwards onto the grass.

'Beats the crap out of ejecting,' said Warszawski, as he helped her to her feet.

Without further ado, the four pilots carried their bags the five hundred metres to the semi-derelict control tower. In the relative cool of the deserted building, Callaghan was able to make contact via i-comm with the other members of the Squadron, including the injured but otherwise cheerful Xu. She had sustained substantial bruising and a six-centimetre gash to her leg during ejection, but, using the medical tools in her survival kit and the stubbornness she had inherited from her father, had managed to clean the wound on her right thigh, stitch the cut and apply a sterile dressing. Xu was currently lying, she was happy to report, in a more than comfortable bunk on the upper deck of a dusty tour bus which had once belonged to a tribute band called 'The Tumbling Dice' and was parked, for no reason she could fathom, on a forgotten farm in the hushed Oxfordshire countryside. The pain-killers in the med kit, she added, were stupendous.

Callaghan also connected with Gunatillaka who recounted the chaotic sequence of events at Lakenheath and reassured the pilots that the RAF Regiment troops had secured the base and that the Modsec draftees were relieved to be rid of their black baseball caps. She expressed her confidence that MacDermott would recover from his injuries, but was certain that he would need to remain in the med bay at least for the time being. He would therefore not accompany her to their agreed rendez-vous point, the thatched cottage in Great Finborough where Gunatillaka had lived for several years.

'Make yourself at home,' she added. 'I'll find a spare Land Rover and bring supplies. And the dog. And *Classic Rock Classics*. With luck, my knackered old turntable will still be there.'

'Get beers from the X-Change store,' said Callaghan. 'The door's open.'

In a long-abandoned ground-floor office within the control tower building at Wattisham Airfield, Bosko, Dibaba, Warszawski and Callaghan emptied their survival bags of everything except the water, the stainless steel cup, the food rations, the flashlight, the multipurpose knife and the compass.

It was no more than five miles to Great Finborough as the crow flies and they were unlikely to need anything else. The four carefully stashed their flight suits in a rusting filing cabinet and changed into their recent X-Change Store acquisitions. The collection of liberated T-shirts, shorts and combat pants sported upmarket designer names and logos, but were in a carefully selected range of hopefully inconspicuous autumn colours.

In spite of the relatively short distance to Great Finborough and the limited chance of encountering anyone whose curiosity might be aroused, the pilots nonetheless agreed that it would be wise to split into two groups.

Bosko looked at Callaghan, certain that the virtually inseparable Dibaba and Warszawski would want to stick together.

'OK, Watchtower,' she said brightly. 'Let's go. *Vamanos.*'

There was little in the way of woodland and Great Finborough was almost directly north of the southern tip of the airfield, so navigation would be a relatively uncomplicated affair. Callaghan and Bosko set off first, opting to follow farm tracks and field boundaries. Warszawski and Dibaba allowed them a ten minute start before striking out along minor roads and overgrown footpaths. Keeping an eye on the time of day, the position of the sun and the compass, they zig-zagged their way through farms and across fields in the general direction of the village. After some discussion of the events at Lakenheath, Dibaba fell silent and walked noticeably more slowly, weighed down by the burden of what they had done.

'You OK?' asked Warszawski.

'We killed a lot of people today,' she said heavily.

'We did. But we also saved twenty thousand innocent lives, maybe more. It was the lesser of two evils.'

'Yeah, well. Let's not try to delude ourselves. The lesser evil is still evil. We still have blood on our hands.'

'I know. It was never going to be pretty. But like Joker said, the only real choice was to do something or do nothing.'

For several seconds neither spoke.

'Thirteen years ago,' continued Warszawski, 'United Nations peacekeeping troops in the Caucasus stood by and watched as ethnic cleansing was taking place in front of them. They could have intervened, but they didn't.'

'This is not the same,' said Dibaba. 'Anyway, I'm not disputing the logic of what we've done. We all agreed to it. I'm just saying it doesn't feel good. How many of the people who lost their lives today were actually Party members? How do we know the Palace wasn't just full of work brigade conscripts or regular cleaners just doing their job?'

'We can't know,' said Warszawski, 'but the alternative was even worse.'

'Blood on our hands either way,' said Dibaba.

Warszawski could not fault her reasoning. 'Yeah,' he conceded. 'Blood on our hands either way.'

They walked on.

Once more it was Warszawski who eventually broke the silence. 'What was it again your dad used to say about hindsight?'

Dibaba shook her head and offered a reluctant smile. 'Oh, no. No, no. Don't try to pretend you've forgotten. I know exactly what you're doing.'

He caught her eye. 'Tell me anyway.'

Dibaba allowed herself a moment. 'He used to say that hindsight is the least merciful form of wisdom.'

'Well. There you go. Your dad nailed it.'

'He did. Of course he did. And I get it it. I absolutely get it. It still doesn't make me feel any better, though.'

'Hell, Freebird. Coulda, shoulda, woulda.'

'Yeah, I know. Coulda, shoulda, woulda. Copy that.'

He put his arm around her shoulder, gave her a comforting hug, then left her to her thoughts. They walked on in silent reflection, punctuated only by occasional and perfunctory conversations regarding distance and direction. Dibaba struggled to make peace with her soul and Warszawski could think of no other strategy that might have saved the lives of the conference delegates and could have arrested the drift towards dictatorship.

Cocooned in their own thoughts, the pair had scant awareness of the passage of time, but suddenly realised that they could be no more than a mile from Great Finborough. At this point Dibaba did something she had never done before. Without a word, she took Warszawski's hand. In response, he simply gave her fingers a squeeze and gently caressed her knuckles with his thumb. When inevitably their eyes met, they exchanged cautious smiles, perhaps acknowledging the contradiction that this unexpected moment also felt long overdue. They walked on, taking comfort from the intimacy.

Warszawski was the first to speak. 'So, Freebird, we're holding hands.'

'Yep. That pretty much sums it up.'

'Are we on a date?' he asked, now beyond curious to know exactly what was happening to their friendship.

'Some date. The thing is, Stairway, I've got no idea how this shitstorm will pan out and I've got no idea what I want to do when it's over, but I know I want to do it with you.'

Warszawski gave her hand gentle squeeze. 'Are we sure about this? They say you should never take a big decision on a rough day.'

'I'm really not sure about anything,' said Dibaba. 'But I think we've both been in denial for long enough.'

'Can't argue with that. Definitely in denial. With the crocodiles.'

'Exactly,' she said, smirking at the reassuring jocularity of his response. 'With the crocodiles.'

She lifted her arm and kissed the back of his hand. It felt as natural as everything else they did together and when Warszawski reciprocated, Dibaba shot him the warmest of smiles.

Protruding above the treescape and caught in the rays of the afternoon sun, Dibaba and Warszawski could now make out the steeple of a church in what had to be Great Finborough. The pair pressed on, still with no visual on their precise destination, but at ease with their general direction.

69 THE FINAL CONVULSION

London, 8th August

The nine p.m. TV announcement by Royal Navy Commodore Novotny proclaimed to the nation that the air attack on Britain's seat of government, though it had claimed the lives of the Prime Minister and many others, could be taken as the final convulsion of a desperate enemy teetering on the brink of defeat. In spite of the damage to Westminster and the high level of casualties, a squadron of RAF interceptors had succeeded in destroying the entire wing of enemy aircraft conducting the assault. Furthermore, in an operation off the coast of Portugal, a squadron of Royal Air Force fighter-bombers in consort with Royal Navy submarines had sunk the four colossal aircraft carriers from which, throughout the conflict, the waves of hostile raids had been launched. Though the enemy remained to be identified, the war was, the Commodore declared, finally over. Tomorrow would be a day of national celebration.

70 MOTHERHOOD, TRUTH AND JUSTICE

London, 9th August

The morning after the momentous events in Whitehall, the collective expression of joy at the outbreak of peace was tempered by an outpouring of grief for the charismatic leader who had dragged the nation out of the Dark Age, had organised the systematic and steely fightback against a clandestine foe and had lost his life in the final act of resistance.

At the southern end of Whitehall, Natalia Greenwood and her daughter joined the long and sombre queue to enter the Security Zone, walk to the site of the Prime Minister's palace and add Soozie's small posy of garden flowers to the thousands already there.

'Will they still build the statue of you?' Soozie asked.

'I can't really be sure,' replied her mother. 'It was the Prime Minister's idea, so maybe not.'

Privately, Natalia Greenwood surmised that the plan to construct the Britannia statue in her image would, without any shadow of a doubt, have died with its author. She consoled herself, however, that she might well have ended up having to fend off Henderton's advances on a regular basis as the price of her footnote in the history books.

Outside the devastation of the Security Zone, the grief of the mourners was counterpointed by the swelling public mood of celebration. A joyful crowd of cheering, flag-waving revellers surrounded the Victoria Memorial and filled the street outside the gates to Buckingham Palace. To gain a better view of the King, many people shinned up street lamps, signposts or flag poles. At the bottom of the steps to the memorial, overjoyed citizens stood atop the massive bronze lions or hung on to the human figures personifying *Manufacture* and *Agriculture*. The boldest, or perhaps the least sober, members of the throng clambered onto the marble plinth of the memorial itself and clung to the statues of *Motherhood*, *Truth* and *Justice*.

A huge roar erupted as the ageing monarch, in his uniform of Commander-in-Chief of the Armed Forces, was wheeled onto the balcony to observe the commotion. At the behest of his nurses, the King mustered a wave for his jubilant subjects and wondered as they cheered if perhaps it was his birthday. Similar scenes of celebration unfolded in cities, towns and villages the length and breadth of the country. Before the monumental neoclassical columns which graced the eastern facade of Saint George's Hall in Liverpool, Martina, Freya, Aston and Thomas mingled amongst the partying multitude. Aston had brought a pair of drumsticks and at every opportunity rattled out the solos from 'Wipe Out' on lamp posts, road signs and metal bins. Martina and Freya clasped hands and intermittently belted out the lyrics to 'Won't Get Fooled Again'. For his part, Thomas happily wafted the huge, red and white chequered flag that was presented to him by a smiling, and undoubtedly inebriated, stranger.

71 A QUESTION OF IDEOLOGY

London, 16th August

A week after the victory celebrations and the hangovers, the reconstituted Joint Forces Command, under the interim leadership of Commodore Novotny, invited Richard Moon, the former Secretary of State for Justice, to act as chair of a multi-party steering committee which was to consider the recommendations from the extended Congress of All The Talents and prepare a plan for elections and the resurrection of Parliament.

Lieutenant Commander York was designated as Moon's liaison officer. At York's request, she would eventually be supported by Lieutenant Batista once he had recovered from the injuries inflicted during his incarceration. In her first meeting with Moon, York recounted in detail both Henderton's orchestration of the raid on Northwood and his plan to eliminate every delegate to the conference in the North Greenwich Arena, including of course, Moon himself.

'Be in absolutely no doubt,' said York. 'Neither Modsec nor the NUP has any viable future in this country.'

'I understand,' said Moon, staring at the table and still trying to come to terms with the revelations.

'As chair of the steering committee,' said York, 'your brief will be to act as an independent moderator of debate, basically in the mould of the Speaker of the House of Commons but without all the histrionics. You will be democratic, non-partisan and efficient and you will aim to schedule elections for the first anniversary of the outbreak of peace. Are we absolutely clear on this?'

Moon looked up and caught York's gaze. 'I'm completely happy with that. To be perfectly frank with you, Lieutenant Commander, my membership of the NUP was never really a question of ideology.'

On the *Six O'Clock News*, an unfamiliar presenter announced that the NBC now had a new Director General and a more familiar name. Under the leadership of Amy Sweetman-Kirk, the former Director of News and Current Affairs ousted by the NUP, the Corporation was to revert to its traditional title of the British Broadcasting Corporation and would no longer be the mouthpiece of the Government. The BBC would now be independent in all matters concerning the fulfilment of its mission and would provide accurate and impartial news to help citizens engage with the world around them and participate in the democratic process. The Corporation would also, as a matter of course, face competition from independent broad-casters who would be bound by a similar requirement to act in the public interest.

In Liverpool, the five media-hackers were overjoyed at the rein-statement of independent news broadcasting and resolved to suspend their intrusions into the nation's airwaves. Nevertheless, they determined to keep the stolen outside broadcast van in full working order in case the promises of freedom of speech and parliamentary democracy were not fulfilled.

Talira in particular could not contain her excitement at the news about the BBC and felt certain that she would be able to return to her old job in Salford Quays. Furthermore, both she and Ricky were now working on a story that they considered to be very much in the public interest. Intrigued by Kevin's observations about the flightpaths of the aircraft based at Lakenheath, they had left the flight tracker software running night after night. Although prepared for the unexpected, their recent review of aircraft movements on the day of the Whitehall Palace raid had left them wide-eyed with disbelief. The trajectories of the ten F-95s that took off from RAF Lakenheath aligned with Kevin's previous observations that the flightpaths seemed to betray no evidence of engagement with enemy aircraft. Whilst one of the RAF interceptors had seemingly crashed in Oxfordshire, the subsequent landing of nine of the F-95s at a number of disused provincial airfields continued to baffle the couple. Furthermore, the apparently one-way flights directly north by the ten MQ-25s made no sense whatsoever. If the movements of the MQ-25s were not puzzling enough, the tracking software had failed to record any evidence of the squadron of RAF fighter-bombers which had ostensibly destroyed the enemy's fleet of aircraft carriers off the Portuguese coast. Somehow, it didn't amount to a coherent narrative. Had the enemy carriers conceivably been located somewhere in the Arctic Sea and had the MQ-25s perhaps failed to sink them all and been brought down? Or had it been some kind of suicide mission? Had the truth been somehow sanitised or possibly even censored? If so, to what end?

Confused as they were, the tenacious pair were nonetheless confident that the resurrected BBC would be only too keen to sink its teeth into some real journalism and would want to support their investigation into the baffling data. They resolved to schedule a meeting, ideally with Amy Sweetman-Kirk herself, at the earliest opportunity.

Kevin and Kireina were forging audacious plans of their own. Kireina, with Kevin in tow as her PA and all-round fixer, had conceived a tour of the biggest art galleries in the country, where she intended to adorn their pristine walls with arresting images and thought-provoking epigrams. Kevin was more than ready for the role Kireina had conceived for him and was excited by the challenge of ghosting the anarchic artist past security staff and into galleries that would increasingly be on their guard for her visits. In the meantime, the pair would revisit Kireina's portrait of Henderton at John Lennon Airport and change the slogan once more, this time to 'Nothing to kill or die for'.

Kevin, Kireina and Martina planned to use the Land Rover for a brief trip to London, where they would spend a couple of days in the house near Hampstead Heath that Martina had used during her escape from Modsec. Whilst Kireina introduced Martina to her acerbic artwork still on display in the Tate Modern, Kevin would pay a visit to the Ministry of Employment, amend all but one of the key details in Martina's records and generate an ID card to match her new profile. Whilst she would still have the same first name as the young electrician who had been arrested in Liverpool a month previously, the similarity would extend no further.

In the meantime, Martina was working on the i-comm Kevin had liberated from the Central Police Station. She had already risen to the challenge of wiping the device clean and restoring it to factory settings. As soon as she had her new ID, she would consider whether it was perhaps safe to contact her brother through the more conventional channels. If not, she could always get another smartphone, although probably not from PJ.

Martina had also promised to teach Freya some basic electronics and in return, Freya was teaching Martina how to read music and play the bass guitar. Inspired by their successful rendition of 'Won't Get Fooled Again', the family in Menlove Close had resolved to keep rehearsing and recording, but were engaged in an ongoing debate about what to play, whether they should try to write their own songs and where they would want to perform. So far, they had made only one major decision about the band: it was not going to be called The Fatberg Four.

72 RIDE HOME

Great Finborough, Suffolk, 16th August

As the daylight faded, the reddening sun began to be all that Flight Lieutenant Merton could see in the rear-view mirrors of the Tumbling Dice tour bus. The fuel, siphoned in the dead of night from ageing farm vehicles, had lasted well and would unquestionably get them to their destination. With the first stars visible in the darkening sky, Merton stopped the bus on the Finborough Road no more than fifty metres away from Gunatillaka's quaint but undeniably tatty Suffolk cottage. Neither the throaty rattle of the poorly maintained hybrid engine nor the noisy hydraulic brakes mustered sufficient volume to distract those inside the house from Lopez's particularly uninhibited performance of 'Pinball Wizard'. Obeying the brief but characteristically precise instructions in Gunatillaka's i-comm message, the three aviators easily located the narrow lane which passed the front door to the cottage. Xu, still wearing her torn and blood-soiled flight suit, pushed at the unlocked door, made a theatrical entrance and shouted 'Does anyone need a ride home?'

Her sudden appearance was met with an all-round roar of delight which triggered an immediate fit of excited barking on the part of the dog. Merton and Finnan followed the limping Xu into the cool, low-ceilinged room and the new arrivals were engulfed in relieved embraces and enthusiastic back-slapping.

The three recounted the events surrounding the raid on Chequers and their only partially successful attempt to evade the surface-to-air missiles. Xu talked vividly about her ejection from the F-95 and spared no-one the details of the gruesome and painful repair job she had conducted on her own leg. Their tales of liberating diesel for the tour bus from rusting tractors were followed by an unfettered celebration of comradeship which lasted almost until dawn.

As they had done for the past seven mornings, Dibaba and Warszawski woke up in bed together and greeted each other with a bleary-eyed smile, a tender kiss, or a gentle stroke of each other's hair. Although the raid on Whitehall still weighed heavily on their souls, neither had the slightest regret regarding the change in their relationship status. The couple had certainly not shied away from intimacy, but as neither had foreseen the need for contraception when planning their escape strategy, they had enjoyed their nights together in ways that did not run the risk of pregnancy. As he thought about making a pot of rosemary tea, Warszawski had a sudden idea and whispered in Dibaba's ear.

'Worth a try,' she said sleepily and kissed him.

He pulled on some clothes, opened the bedroom door and almost tripped over the still nameless Labrador who knew that they were awake and was patently expecting a walk. Followed by the dog, Warszawski crept past Xu and Finnan, who were sound asleep on sofa cushions on the floor of the lounge and were still fully clothed. The front door had been left slightly ajar, so Warszawski slipped quietly out into the morning air, leaving the door on the latch behind him. As he climbed the steps to the interior of the tour bus, he was surprised to encounter Itoje, who had spent the night on board with Becker.

'If you're looking for condoms,' he said, 'don't bother. I've checked.'

When Warszawski returned to their room, he gave Dibaba the thumbs down.

'Shame,' she said softly. 'Especially after that five-star review you got from Watchtower's sister.'

Shortly after Gunatillaka awoke, she received an i-comm message from York. The Lieutenant Commander informed her comrade that she had spoken personally with Commodore Novotny, who had confirmed that there was not the slightest question of 161 Squadron facing a court martial or in fact any form of disciplinary action. They should therefore report to Wing Commander Flowers, the new Station Commander, at their earliest opportunity, as he was particularly eager to retrieve the F-95s from the various provincial airfields where they currently stood. York added that she had seen Batista briefly and that he was making progress in his recovery, but that it would be months before his fractured metatarsals would fully heal. She thanked Gunnie for her friendship and looked forward to a time, hopefully soon, when they could see each other again, go for a run and maybe share a bottle of Whoopty Whoop beer in the Mess.

Once dressed, Gunatillaka used the radio in the Land Rover to contact Lakenheath. She confirmed to Wing Commander Flowers that she had recovered the entire Squadron and that the pilots would make their way back to base later that day. There would be no need to send a truck as they had commandeered transport of their own. She regretted that the Land Rover she borrowed had a punctured tyre and no spare, but informed him that she would return with the pilots. The conversation concluded, Gunatillaka removed the spare tyre from the Land Rover, took it to the shed and left it there. She returned with a screwdriver, stabbed the sidewall of the vehicle's nearest tyre and watched it slowly deflate. She knew that the celebrations would inevitably kick off again on the bus and the Ops Manager had not the slightest intention of trailing behind in the Land Rover.

After a breakfast of porridge and strawberry jam, the Squadron loaded their few possessions onto the tour bus and began the slow journey north to Lakenheath. Bosko wasted no time in proposing that they use the impressive music system to play the songs that had initially inspired their call signs. Having run the gamut of classics from 'Free Bird' to 'All Along the Watchtower', Bosko pointed out that Gunnie, their beloved Ops Manager and hitherto sworn enemy of call signs, did not have a song of her own, but in all honesty, totally deserved one. She scrolled through the music collection on her i-comm and enthusiastically proposed a track called 'Strange Kind Of Woman'.

'Seems about right,' said Gunatillaka with an appreciative nod. 'Just let me tune up my air guitar.'

73 A FUNERAL NONETHELESS

London, 17th August

At roughly the same time as the raucous Tumbling Dice tour bus finally presented itself to the bemused guards at the main entrance to RAF Lakenheath, Lieutenant Commander York, Commodore Novotny and Steering Committee Chairman Richard Moon were inspecting the remedial work being carried out in Whitehall. As they made their way along the famous street, they avoided the fractured beams and boulders of brickwork or Portland Stone and picked their way carefully across the carpet of broken glass. Here and there, a vague smell of charred oak still hung in the air. In the MOD Main Building, many of the broken windows had been boarded up, but there were few signs of activity. The three visitors passed the entrance to Downing Street, where contractors had begun the unenviable task of sifting through the many tonnes of rubble for human remains before transferring the debris, in the first instance, to Saint James's Park.

'It was a beautiful building, the old Foreign Office,' said Novotny, casting an eye further down the street.

'Perhaps it can be rebuilt,' suggested Moon.

'Perhaps,' said the Commodore, before changing the direction of the conversation. 'Maybe our first priority should be to resurrect the Foreign Office itself, not just reconstruct the building. Once a democratic government has been elected, the

Joint Forces Command will present it with a proposal to organise humanitarian expeditions to France, Belgium and Ireland. Whilst all the evidence speaks to the contrary, we may yet find there are survivors who would welcome our help.'

'I would support that,' said Moon.

'Assuming you are elected,' said York.

'Indeed,' replied the Chairman of the Constitutional Steering Committee, suitably chastened.

At the southern end of Whitehall, reverent citizens still queued patiently for the chance to be allowed briefly into the Security Zone, lay flowers near the ruins of Whitehall Palace and pay their respects to the late Prime Minister.

'Henderton was an orator for sure,' said Commodore Novotny, 'but hardly a team player. Still, he served a purpose. Up to a point.'

'If, sir,' said York, 'by "hardly a team player" you mean "narcissistic sociopath", I might be inclined to agree with you.'

'It's unlikely we'll ever discover his remains,' said the Commodore, 'but the nation will expect a funeral nonetheless.'

'And do we bury a devil or a redeemer?' ventured York.

'Well,' said Novotny, looking pointedly at the countless floral tributes which festooned the security fence and littered the Whitehall rubble, 'I think we all know the answer to that one.'

THE END

ACKNOWLEDGEMENTS

For help, encouragement and advice: to my wife, Suzanne. Also to Celia Almeida, David Coombes, Sue Colclough, Tony Cox, Chris Freudenthal, Glyn Jones, Ashley Nixon, Lynne Preece, David Ripley, Jo Ripley, Dawn Sayers, Dave Twine, Vidar Utne, Tima Utne-Iyer, Paul Watkin. And to James Essinger and Zoe Verner of The Conrad Press and Charlotte Mouncey of Bookstyle, without whose insights, skills and professionalism, this book would not have found its way to you.

ACKNOWLEDGMENTS